BLUE EYES IN BLACK WONDERLAND

BLUE EYES IN BLACK WONDERLAND

ERIN L. MCCORMACK

LONGTALE PRESS
BEDFORD, MA

This book is dedicated to the following people:

GW—Beautiful, bold, and bigger than life—everything I aspired to be; a woman destined to touch many lives, including mine.

BT—Our time was brief, but it meant a lot to me; a true friend when I needed one.

Elwood—Because every girl needs a little Starlight.

My sister, Maura—Who fed me and sheltered me, and put up with me and my antics at a certain time of life; and a friend and supporter all of my life.

My Aunt Tesha, Irene Patricia McCormack, who encouraged me in writing, theater and the arts.

Acknowledgments

A lot of people go into the making of a book. Many thanks to those who've helped me on my way:

Foremost, Katie Sherman, editor and collaborator in this endeavor. She provided the energy, insight, revisions and "patches" that made the story flow, fixed the language, made all the copyedits, large and small; and most importantly, gave me the support and enthusiasm to get this work done in the best way we knew how.

My writing group members, talented writers, all: Beverly Breton Carroll, Robin Grace, Denise Waldron, and Peggy Yalman, for sticking with me through the long, long process.

The folks at Serenity Yoga, for providing a place and time for my body to catch up with my mind, and to allow me to continue my writing without all the back and neck pain.

Maisah Robinson, for helping me find the story in a meandering narrative.

Claudia Fox Tree, for including me in fun celebrations, singing at the drum, and her knowledge and perspectives on racial awareness, and how things can be better.

Henry Louis Gates, Jr. and *Finding Your Roots*, for helping to show the deep and tangled roots of so many Americans, and the many surprising connections between us.

My three men, Donald, Dylan, and Derek Koundakjian, who have lived with me through the creation of this book, and all that goes with it; for accepting that writing is a part of me, and something worthwhile.

ERIN L. MCCORMACK

BLUE EYES IN BLACK WONDERLAND

Prologue

Santa Cruz, California, early 1980s

Celia wrestled with the door lock, her heart thumping from the hurried walk and the bad news.

"Argh!"

Her face, already tight with sunburn, was hot with emotion: frustrated by the key, eager to get out of the late summer heat into the cool of the apartment, and frantic to make that phone call home. But dreading it too.

It couldn't be true, what they said at the Registrar's office—that there was no money and she could not enroll in classes. Not even one. No auditions, either.

She put down her school bag and the folder of papers to jiggle the key and push open the door. Inside she stopped, listening. No sounds; nobody home. Just her own smiling face on the poster in the hallway for a production of *Alice in Wonderland,* just closed, at the Santa Cruz Summer Theater, herself in the leading role. The photo certainly flattered her: the girlish figure in a pinafore, with blue eyes and long blond hair as if she came right from the cover of the book.

"Argh." She dropped the folder and bag onto the kitchen counter. The reviews had not been as complimentary: "A dreamy, frothy Alice, seemingly oblivious at times to the wonders around her."

Somehow, things were not going as well as expected for an aspiring actress starting her sophomore year at college, with good grades, a handsome and talented boyfriend, and plenty of friends in the theater department.

She went first to the sink for a glass of water to quench a desperate thirst. She picked up the phone, extending the cord to its end, and sat in the least wobbly chair at the table. As she dialed the number to Orange Grove, she pictured the modest ranch with three bedrooms and a bath, not a lot of room for five people: her mother; step-father, Gordon; their seven-year-old, Shane; and Gordon's other kids on weekends and a month in the summer.

"Hello?" her mother answered, almost breathless, like she was expecting and fearing the call.

"Mom, it's Celia."

"Oh, Celia. Hi, sweetie. Sorry, I thought it was the doctor. We're waiting for test results. Another case of hurry up and wait."

Celia blew out a breath. "Do you want to call me back, after you talk to the doctor?"

"Well, yes, maybe that would be a good idea. Or," she seemed to reconsider. "No, we have to talk, and it's important. I've been trying to reach you, but no one ever answers the phone. I left a message on the machine. Did you get it?"

No. So often her roommates played the messages, and then forgot to leave a note.

"No. What is it?"

"Honey, we're having some problems here, and you'd better come home. You know, take a break from school."

Celia felt her lungs squeeze in her chest. There it was, real. Still, she made herself speak evenly, breathing, as she was trained, from the diaphragm. "Do you mean Shane, or is it money?"

"It's both, really. Here's the thing. It's a bit of an emergency, temporarily. Gordon's contract was cancelled, so there's no money coming in—cash flow, I mean. And we were denied coverage for Shane's current treatment, so everything is coming out of pocket—the last of our savings, really. It just all happened at once, and, well, it's a mess."

She stopped there, and Celia could hear her sniffle. She pictured her mom, petite, dark, and delicate like her sister, Grace, but without Grace's backbone and determination. More like Celia, in that way—sensitive, artistic.

"So, what you're saying . . ."

"Honey, what I'm saying is that we can't pay for school right now, and nothing toward rent, either. You're going to have to come home, and see what you can find around here until we get back on our feet. I'm sorry, really sorry. . . ." Then, of course, she broke down crying, and there was nothing Celia could say that wouldn't make things worse.

After a moment, her mother said, "I really have to go, in case they're trying to get through. You have money in your account, right, for bus fare? Just let me know when you're coming. We can talk when you get here. We'll figure something out."

"Sure, Mom," Celia said, trying not to upset her mother further. "Wow, that's tough. Don't worry about me. Just take care of Shane and . . . well, everything." She sounded fairly upbeat—a pretty good actress after all.

She put down the phone, not seeing the room around her.

Wow. It was true. They were right on campus: there was no money in the account. No money, period. Celia could barely think what that was supposed to mean, what she was supposed to do. Then, slowly, the fog began to clear. No apartment share. No classes and papers and scenes to practice. No Carlos or his music or his kisses. No theater gossip with her best friend, Janelle. No first-night nerves and last-night parties.

That was a lot, all gone at the same time.

She crossed the kitchen, opening the slider to the small balcony that connected to the fire escape. Two floors below, the courtyard was in deep shade. Celia placed her elbows on the railing, gazing into the secluded space, where a Romeo might serenade his Juliet in moonlight. There, Carlos might strum on his guitar and sing to her. Or, maybe not. For the first time, a real doubt surfaced, gripping her gut. If the problem with money was real, so might Carlos's absence from college. Why had he not returned from his summer job in Southern California? Why hadn't she heard from him in weeks? A small bird rose from the patio to a tree branch, regarding her with a bright eye.

"And a nightingale sang," Celia quoted, sadly.

But it was only a chickadee, and after a moment it flew away. That was the message, Celia decided, stepping back into the living room. She was leaving this place and this life, for now.

But she was not going home, not to that place in Orange Grove. She loved her mother, and Shane, maybe even Gordon in a way. But not that place. And, in truth, they had little room for her there.

She picked up the phone again and dialed long distance. The answering machine came on. Damn. Grace wasn't home yet.

"Hi, Grace. It's me. Celia. Can you call me, please? I need to talk to you. It's, well, Mom said . . ."

"Hold on," Grace's voice came on the line. "I just got in. Give me a sec." There was the sound of a door closing, and her keys clattering on the table. Celia could picture her in her nurse's uniform, probably still crisp and spotless even after a busy shift.

"OK," Grace said, catching her breath. "I'm here."

"Grace, what is going on?" The words just blurted out. "I don't understand. What's happening to us, to our family?" She could hear a note of panic in her voice, hysteria, almost. But she couldn't help it. "Mom said, Mom said . . ." and then her throat closed up, so she couldn't get the words out.

"I know, Celia. I know," Grace's voice came across the miles, calm and even. Five years older, at twenty-four, she was Celia's "Little Mother," even though the baby sister was now two inches taller. Who helped Celia get her first bra? Who taught her to drive on summer vacation? Who sent Celia to the student health clinic for birth control when her first real romance got serious? Not Mom. And not Carlos, even after five months together, and Celia attending his every performance. Carlos was so many good things: handsome, talented, passionate, and very sweet. But he was not that good at dealing with things like sex. Or feelings. Or problems. But Grace was.

"There's a problem," Grace said, "and they really are stuck, for the time being. There's no money for college, and you're going to have to deal with it."

"But how? How could they let it happen?"

"Celia," Grace said. "It's been bad for a while; you just didn't know. They didn't want to tell you. Mom thought she could come up with the money. She tried everything, but she just couldn't. And then Shane's seizures were getting worse, and that had to come first."

Celia forced herself to speak. "I can't. Grace, I really can't go back there. . . ."

"You can come here," Grace said, "to Sutton, with me."

"Are you sure?"

"Of course. You know that. We've been through bad times before, with Dad, and then Granny. You'll be fine. We'll get through this."

"Thank you, thank you, thank you, Grace," Celia heard herself babbling. "I'll get a job right away. And I won't spend a dime, except to help out, of course."

"OK, OK," Grace said. She let go a long breath. "But, listen to me, Celia, carefully. You have to understand that the Eastern Shore of Maryland is far different from where you've lived—New York or California. There are no gay rights marches here or feminist bookstores or holistic medicine types. It's like fifty years ago in some ways, just starting to change."

"Um, I see." But Celia was unable to picture it, really. "Well, then," she said, "it's only for a little while, and I'll have you there, and I'll be busy working and making lots of money."

"Hm . . ." There was silence over the phone line. "Just watch yourself and pay attention to how things are done around here."

"Like what, do you mean?"

"Shave your legs and wear a bra, to start with. It's great to be a free spirit, but I don't want to see you hurt or in trouble. It's a small town and I can't afford to lose my job if you end up ruffling feathers or offending someone—even if you don't mean to."

Celia had to laugh, finally. "Me? Oh, come on, Grace. I'm very friendly and outgoing. Everybody likes me."

"Don't count on it. That could change too." Grace sounded so dire. Then she cleared her throat. "Well, we'll cross that bridge when we get there. Meanwhile, we've got a plan, right?"

"Right."

They went on to discuss the details of moving. Rent was paid through September, but Celia was eager to go, now that the decision was made. Anything to avoid thinking about the sudden black hole in her life. Tonight she would pack and call Janelle to break the news. They'd find a time to meet to give Janelle the new phone and address, and to ask her to look out for Carlos. And to say good bye, of course, for now. Tomorrow, a trip to campus for costume returns and a few farewells, then a stop at the bank to close her account and withdraw the money for a flight to Baltimore, the nearest airport to where Grace lived.

Celia hung up, excited and relieved. Grace understood; she knew how things were. Grace would help make things right. It's just temporary, she told herself. An adventure. Or, you might say, just another role to play.

Chapter 1

Sutton, Maryland, a few days later

Monday, Celia woke to bright sunshine flooding the living room where she'd spent the night on the sofa. Her new "bedroom" had no blinds yet. Grace's apartment was not large, a one-bedroom on the second floor of the complex behind the hospital where she worked. Grace had made the curtains herself, and pillows in matching print. On the mantel and end tables were pictures from home: a black and white of their parent's wedding, one of Celia in a ballet costume, and the two of them as girls. Celia recognized the braided rug and antique hutch from Granny's house; she'd died just before Grace left for college. Everything else Grace must have picked up over the years, paycheck by paycheck, in her practical way.

In the short time Celia had been in Sutton, she'd seen little besides the view out the apartment window. Her flight to Baltimore had arrived in the dark, an hour late due to thunderstorms. After the reunion with Grace and getting the luggage, she couldn't see much on the car ride to the Eastern Shore in the dense mist—a few small towns with worn brick houses, closely packed together. After that she must have dozed and remembered only crossing a long bridge over a featureless body of water. A couple times the wind shook Grace's little Chevette, and past the bridge, a storm came up from behind. Jolted awake by thunder, Celia peered out the window to seeming emptiness. Grace had slowed down, following the highway to the right, heading south. Flashes of lightning illuminated the landscape, field after field, mostly dead corn stalks and an occasional stand of tall trees. And everything flat, flat, flat.

Then they'd arrived at the apartment, and Celia had slept all of Sunday. But now, on a clear and dry Monday morning, she was up and ready to take action, whatever it might be.

Grace was already gone, leaving a check for Celia, a set of keys, directions to the center of town, and the daily newspaper on the kitchen table. Celia had her toast and coffee looking through the help-wanted ads: home health aid, parking attendant, filing clerk, receptionist at an insurance company, and a couple of waitress jobs. Wetting her finger, Celia turned the page. Nothing further, and nothing she could see herself doing. Unless she had to. But she had to do one of these jobs, or something like them. She had no real skills. Just potential and charm, things that didn't pay by themselves.

Celia showered, shaved, and dressed, then returned to the kitchen to leaf through the newspaper for the ad that had stuck in her mind: wait staff at the Grand Marsh Inn. Why not? She had waited tables at a family-style restaurant one summer. Granted, there were a few mix-ups: poached eggs, shirred, over-easy—they all looked the same to her. Food was not really her thing. However, the tips were not bad in spite of the mistakes. A little stage presence didn't hurt.

She could do this.

Experience required; must be quick, neat, professional, up to European standards of service, in historic town center; apply at Grand Marsh Inn, 14 Chester Street, Mon. through Fri. 10 to 11 am. Excellent tips; benefits after six months.

European standards caught her eye, and *excellent tips.* She had been to Europe, junior year in high school with the French Club. At one point, her mother had taught them how to set the table for fine dining. There might be interesting customers to talk to. Historic: she liked quaint, old things. All good. She folded along the crease and tore out the ad, putting it in her purse along with the check. Rummaging in Grace's closet, Celia found a black skirt and blue blouse. She pulled her hair into a ponytail and then wound it into a large bun. Putting on some of Grace's lipstick and squeezing her feet into Grace's shoes, Celia's outfit was complete. It was just after ten o'clock. Grace said it was an easy walk to the center of town, maybe twenty-five minutes. Out the door she went, ready to apply for new, albeit temporary employment. Maybe, just maybe, she could make this work, a way out of this stupid dilemma.

The Grand Marsh Inn was a stately, four-story, brick building with arched doorways. The place was large, almost a block long. At the front entrance, she was met by an older black man in a crisp uniform with shiny buttons, a golden chain peeking out from his vest pocket. His hair, under the uniform cap, was all white, but his skin was surprisingly smooth and unlined. He smiled before he spoke.

"Good morning, miss. Can I help you?" His voice was slow and full of music, from somewhere deeper in the South.

Delighted, Celia returned the smile. "Good morning," she said. "I'm here to apply for a waitressing job. Where should I go?"

The man looked momentarily confused, as if he had mistaken her for someone else, a guest perhaps. "The entrance to the dining room is around the corner. You best go there and ask for the manager."

Celia gazed down the block. What a grand place it was, with lots of rooms and lots of people, hopefully with a spot for her. "Thank you," she said. And then, responding to something in his face, added, "Do you think I have a chance?"

"Why, of course, miss." Leaning closer, he added, "They're right busy in there."

"Oh, good!" She took a quick a breath. "I hope I'm not too late."

He laughed, pulling a watch from his pocket, attached to its chain, and showed it to her. "No, miss, right on time. You, go on, then."

She read his name tag. "Well, thank you again, Mr. James."

His eyes crinkled. "Just James."

"And I'm Celia." She turned to leave, making a wry face. "Well, here goes."

"Best of luck, Miss Celia."

Miss Celia! No one called her that since her grandmother, in fun or in trouble.

When she opened the door to the dining room, she was blinded coming in from full sunlight to a darkened space. It took a moment to make out the high-ceilinged room in shades of green, gold, and burgundy with velvet upholstery on the chairs and dimly lit chandeliers. The tables, maybe twenty or twenty-five, were set with white cloths, and napkins folded into the shape of birds. The full-length drapes were pulled shut, presumably to keep out the heat and prevent fading. And on the walls were more birds and views of endless marsh in paintings with gilt frames and small lights. Hushed and expectant, the room was like a church almost, or a theater.

From out of the shadows, a tall figure appeared, taking long, slow strides in her direction. He was very dark-skinned and could have been any age, twenty to fifty. His mouth opened to reveal a missing front tooth.

"Can I help you?" The man had a surprisingly deep voice, true bass. Celia couldn't help staring at his jack-o-lantern smile. Had he just lost the tooth, and come into work anyway? Or else, had he lost the tooth some time ago and not understood about basic dental care? He, too, was in uniform, the shirt cuffs a little short for his bony wrists, and the same bow-tie as the doorman. Despite his somber appearance, he looked her over in an interested way.

"Yes, please. I'm looking for the manager, to apply for a job."

"Come with me." He turned and she followed. As they crossed the room, Celia caught a movement in a corner alcove, the flash of a white apron behind a long dark counter and the sparkle of glass—a bar, and a bartender, setting up for the day.

"Are you a waiter?" she asked the tall man. He slowed for her to catch up, but didn't stop.

"Nah," he said with another ghastly smile. "I bus the tables, that's all. The man in charge of the trays."

"Oh, I see." It wasn't until they reached the door that she realized he had been joking.

They went through a pair of swinging doors, entering into a large, brightly lit kitchen with four work stations. Several people were already at work behind the counters prepping food or cleaning, quiet, except a radio playing at low volume. Smells of coffee and bacon lingered in the air, and Celia realized that the Inn must also serve breakfast. She could feel a slight ripple through the room, but no one looked up at their passing. Her escort led her down a short hallway off the back of the kitchen and stopped at a closed door marked "Manager."

"That's Mr. Becker. And his wife, too, Miz Becker." From inside came a light buzz of voices, male and female. Celia called out a quick "thanks" as the busboy left in the direction of the kitchen. She knocked.

"One moment, please," said a man, and then, "You may come in now." A slight accent. German, maybe?

She stepped inside a bright, wood-paneled room. "Good morning. I'd like to apply for a job."

A middle-aged man and woman were seated at desks, neat and uncluttered in spite of the piles of paper, files, and office equipment. In front of them stood a pale, slim woman in a dark suit and nametag, clipboard in hand. All three had turned at Celia's entrance. The man, red in the face with a receding hairline, motioned her inside.

"We'll finish later, Pauline," he said to the young woman, who didn't look much older than Celia despite the suit and careful make-up. Her fingernails against the clipboard were impressively red and sharp. She gave Celia a haughty look, almost disdainful, as she brushed by, leaving a draft of strong scent.

"So," the man began. "I am Becker; this is Mrs. Becker. We are the managers here, both the Inn and the dining facilities."

Celia nodded.

"I must tell you, our reservations and front desk are fully staffed for the season."

"Oh, no," Celia said, shaking her head vigorously. "I meant a waitressing job. That's what I'm here for."

His mouth opened and even Mrs. Becker's eyes seemed to widen with surprise. "Ah. You saw the ad, then?"

"Yes," Celia said. "I thought it sounded very . . . interesting, and, and stimulating." The wife, stern-faced and stout, pursed her lips so little frown lines appeared. *Maybe stimulating was not the right word. Rewarding?* Mr. Becker pushed his chair back, placing his elbows on the desk.

"Yes, this establishment is one of the finest in the area. You have experience?"

"Some experience, yes."

"You are eighteen . . . ?"

"Oh, yes. Nineteen in January."

His eyes narrowed. "You are not from here, I think?"

"No," she said quickly. "But I live with my sister now in Sutton; she works at the hospital."

There was a moment's pause while Mr. Becker stared at the ceiling and then at his wife, who did not look back. His gaze returned to Celia. "The job is demanding," he said. "It requires strength and stamina."

Celia pushed back her shoulders. "Oh, I'm stronger than I look. And my balance is very good, from all the dance classes I've taken."

A small smile crossed his lips. "I see. Our menu is quite extensive, and it is important to remember every detail."

Celia's hand crept into the air. "That is not a problem. My memory is excellent. I have had to remember hundreds of lines in a play, sometimes."

Now Mr. Becker was nodding, relaxing. Mrs. Becker, however, remained stone-faced.

"Many important guests stay with us," Mr. Becker said. "Business executives. Government officials." Then he stopped, without further explanation. That meant it was Celia's turn.

"From Washington, D.C.?" she offered, hopefully.

He tipped his head in acknowledgment. "Of course. And Baltimore and Annapolis. In addition, we hold weddings and banquets. These people expect the best service."

It was, Celia realized, a test of some kind. Not so much her abilities, but her attitude, perhaps. She was sure she could do the job, and do it well. And yet, somehow, they were not convinced.

She took a quick breath. "I think it would be a wonderful place to work," she said. "This is such a beautiful building—and historic." That last bit because it sounded good. "I enjoy meeting new people and talking with them. A little, I mean, while I'm serving, of course. That has to come first."

Their faces were starting to brighten, to come around; she could just tell. In a burst of enthusiasm, she quoted: "In every job that must be done, there is an element of fun."

17

Mrs. Becker apparently did not appreciate Mary Poppins's words of wisdom. Her face tightened and at last she spoke. "Not fun," she said. "This is not a place of fun, but work. We do not want to hear laughter and foolish chatter from the staff."

Immediately, Celia realized her mistake. "Of course not!" she said, projecting her voice. "I didn't mean that. Really, I am very serious. And dedicated and hardworking. And a quick learner and . . . serious. I understand about being professional and giving proper service." And then, in complete sincerity, "I will be the best waitress I can be."

Her words hung in the air for some time before there was a response. Finally, Mr. Becker looked at Mrs. Becker, who gave the slightest shrug of her shoulder. They seemed to reach an agreement. "I will finish with her," Mrs. Becker said to her husband, and then, dismissing him, "Virgil needs a signature."

After he left, Mrs. Becker handed Celia a pen and paper. "You must fill out the application completely. You may sit here." She indicated a chair next to a small round table. At the doorway, she turned back. "I will speak to you again when you have finished." And then she left, leaving the door slightly ajar.

Celia filled out the application as truthfully as she could, while still being helpful to her cause. She worked on careful penmanship and good spelling. When she finished she looked around the room and, hearing no footsteps, walked over to the sideboard where she picked up a foil-wrapped chocolate from a bowl. *Swiss!* But of course she didn't take one. And good thing she didn't, as Mrs. Becker soon reappeared at the doorway, silent on her approach.

Celia sat silent while Mrs. Becker looked over the completed application. At one point, she frowned, looking up. "From California you came here?"

Celia cleared her throat. "I went to college in California, but there was a problem. . . ." She tried to speak calmly, not too fast. "That's why I'm staying with my sister for a while and looking for a job, to—"

"If you work here," Mrs. Becker interrupted, "you must commit to stay through hunting season and the holidays. Those are our busiest times. We need reliable people who will work hard, and of course, be welcoming and pleasant to our guests."

"Oh, I can do that, I'm sure," Celia said, sitting upright. To herself, she said, *Hunting season?*

Mrs. Becker looked up. "Then you have a job. We will need you at lunchtime to start. You will train with one of our experienced waitresses. You are available on Wednesday morning at ten?"

Celia nodded, and an unexpected smile of excitement came to her face. "Thank you so much," she said, standing up to leave, but Mrs. Becker raised a finger. "One minute, please."

She got up from the desk and went over to a cupboard at the back of the room. From inside, she took out what was clearly a waitress uniform, neatly folded in a clear plastic bag, and then looking at Celia, pulled out another.

"You must try them on and choose the best fit," she said. Celia thought she meant for her to take them home, but she walked with her to the door, and indicated a ladies' room down the hall.

"You will show me, please."

Celia entered the bathroom and tried the first uniform, which was too large, and then the second, which fit much better. It was a short-sleeved, black dress in a polyester material, with a hemline well above her knees.

"Not very practical," she muttered. Reaching behind to pull the long back zipper, Celia felt the hemline rise to the top of her thighs. When she put on the flouncy white apron, she looked like a maid in a French farce.

"Call me Mimi," she said in a French accent to the mirror.

Mrs. Becker nodded approvingly at Celia's silhouette in the doorway. "Yes, that is good. You must take care to pin your hair properly." And then, contemplating the fullness of Celia's bun with a few escaped strands, "Or perhaps a haircut."

She turned and went back to her desk, making a mark on Celia's application. "The tips will be very good, I assure you, if you attend to the details and behave always appropriately. We will see you on Wednesday then, yes?"

Celia nodded and repeated, "Wednesday." Mrs. Becker took a seat, returning to her paperwork, and Celia walked out of the office, a little skip in her step. She had a job! They had their doubts, she could tell, but she'd won them over, thank God.

"European standards, *la-di-da*," she murmured as she finished changing in the ladies' room. As she put her new uniform in the bag, she realized she should return the other one to the managers' office. She grabbed the second uniform, heading out the door and down the hall. Just as she was about to turn into the open doorway, a man stepped out in front of her, on course for collision. A black man, dressed all in white, with something like a shower-cap on his head and a slip of paper in his hand. He put out the other hand to keep from plowing into her. When he let go, there was a light imprint of flour on her sleeve. He was a cook, she realized.

"Oh!" she said.

19

"Watch out where you going," he said, scowling. She was so surprised, she couldn't form a sentence.

"Oh," she said again, and then added, "sorry."

"You OK?" he asked, stepping away. He was young, she could see, and good looking, in spite of the ridiculous hair cover.

"Mrs. Becker," she got out. "I have to return this." She held out the extra uniform in its bag.

"She ain't there," the young man informed her. "Just leave it on the desk." Then he gave her the once over, his eyes running up and down her figure in the slightly too small skirt and blouse, lingering a moment on her hair. Then he turned to leave toward the kitchen.

Oh, boy, Celia thought, shaking her head, a little giddy. What am I getting myself into? The crazy uniform and the fussy European managers. Hunting season. Missing teeth and angry chefs. Then, propelling herself into motion, she chanted under her breath, "The tips! The tips! The tips!" She envisioned the white apron loaded with coins and bills, almost too heavy to carry. Smiling, she left through a back entrance, the uniform tucked under her arm. Wait 'til Grace hears I got a job! Turning the corner and crossing the street, she gave a wave to James the doorman as she passed.

Chapter 2

Celia returned home along the same route, and flopped onto the sofa, kicking her shoes to the floor—Grace's shoes, a little scuffed now, and dusty. Her toes were pinched and she had a blister. There must be a short-cut, she mused, if she had to walk to work every day. And she needed some shoes of her own, other than sandals and Chinese ballet slippers. Black working shoes to go with her new uniform.

After changing, she unpacked her clothes into the drawers and closet space that Grace had cleared, recalling with an occasional giggle her interview at the Inn. She was a bit giddy, perhaps, with all that she wanted to tell Grace: the elegance of the place, somehow getting the job, all those crazy characters. She moved slowly, lingering over favorite outfits and admiring Grace's sleek new suits, until she stepped back, blinking with light-headedness. Somehow, after the morning's excitement, she'd forgotten lunch. In the kitchen, she fixed a peanut butter sandwich, standing at the counter. Brushing crumbs into the sink, a sudden inspiration came to her. She began poking through the refrigerator and cupboards looking for something tasty for supper, a nice surprise for Grace when she returned after a long day. In a few moments, she had a meal plan: macaroni and cheese, ham steak, and peas. Satisfied, Celia thought next about doing a load of laundry. Instead, overcome by yawns, she sat back down on the sofa, cradling a pillow in her lap. All around her, Grace's clean, orderly, cozy space; everything so different from Santa Cruz. Funny the twists and turns of life, Celia reflected; how she had just landed here, so unexpectedly. She really had to be an asset to Grace, and not a liability. She was thinking these things as she stretched out, pulling down the blanket and stuffing the pillow under her head as she let her eyes shut. The next thing she heard was a key in the lock.

Hurriedly, she sat up, replacing the pillow and blanket and finger-combing her hair.

"Surprise!" she said as Grace opened the door. "I've got news."

"Oh?" Grace came into the room, putting her purse down on an end table.

"I got a job, the very first one I applied for." Celia snapped her fingers. "Just like that, starting Wednesday. Can you believe it?"

Grace looked dubious, and then, strangely, a little disappointed. "Well, all right then," she said, nodding and running a hand through her own short, dark hair. "So, tell me."

"Waitress—at the finest establishment in town, the Grand Marsh Inn. They had an ad in the paper." Celia paused. "Have you been there? It's really nice."

Now Grace's lips curved in a wry smile. "Not yet," she said. "But it looks *tres elegant.* And you want to work there, because . . ."

"The money, of course! At a place like that, the tips are bound to be great. All those big spenders, right?"

"Hm . . ." Grace took the cushioned rocker, moving a pillow out of the way—cross-stitched, most likely by Grace herself. From all those times back home that Grace sat across from Granny Jones in that very rocker, head bent over that careful stitching, while Celia played dress up with Granny's long, silk dresses and pearls.

"What?" Celia said. "What's wrong with that?"

"Nothing is wrong," Grace said, "and you're probably right about the money. But . . . here's the but. I found something at the hospital that might be really good too."

Celia was stumped. What could it be? Plumping pillows? Delivering cards?

"Medical records. There's an opening right now. I talked to the woman in charge and told her about you. They provide training and health insurance. Plus," and this appeared to be her ace card, "they will pay for a couple classes a semester, in anything related, business or health care. It's pretty wide open."

"Oh," said Celia, trying not to laugh, it seemed so unlikely. "Not bad. What's the pay?"

"Five dollars an hour to start. Plus the benefits. You could probably move ahead quickly—you're a quick learner."

Celia made a face. "Not as good as waitressing!"

"No, not right away. But will you get insurance at the Inn?"

"Well, no; maybe later." Who knew about stuff like that? Who cared?

"Then you better not end up in the hospital."

Medical records? It sounded so boring, not to mention lonely. The picture that came to Celia's mind was a basement room with metal shelves, no windows, and artificial lights. And there she was, reaching up and an entire avalanche of files falling on her head.

"Hey," Grace said, "the job is yours if you want it. You should give it some serious thought."

Celia sat up straighter on the sofa. "Oh, I will, Grace. I will."

22

A door slammed nearby, and shortly afterwards a car motor started up, leaving the parking lot. Most likely the unsmiling, gray-haired lady who lived below. It was so quiet at the apartment complex, you always noticed someone coming or going. Celia turned back to Grace, prepared for another try.

"I understand what you're saying. But I really want to try this waitressing job. It seems like such an interesting place, all very high class. Businessmen and government officials come there." And then she remembered, "Especially for hunting season." She paused. "What is that, anyway? Do you know?"

"Ah, hunting season," Grace said, rolling her eyes. "It's like a holiday almost. Ducks and geese—waterfowl. They're crazy about it down here. I don't know the details, but the hunters come in the fall and set up in these little huts and then shoot the birds and eat them. Last year, one of the doctors did rounds in his hunting gear—you know, camouflage." She shrugged. "So, that's what you want to be a part of?"

"Oh, I don't know. But people like that, they have money, right? So, that will trickle down to me. See!"

Grace didn't look convinced. "I realize medical records sounds pretty dull to someone like you. But it's a good way to learn about the hospital and the health field. I could see you in patient services or even a social worker some day." Grace smiled encouragingly. "You could still do your theater on the side. Maybe you need to think about developing marketable skills, something to fall back on."

"OK, OK, I hear you." Celia got up to set the table and start her planned dinner. "But I can't think about anything when I'm this hungry."

After dinner, Celia took an early bath to let her hair dry before bed. Grace had put out fluffy towels that matched the red and yellow shower curtain and left a container of bath beads on the rim of the tub—the same kind Granny Jones used to use. As the tub filled, Celia sat on the toilet lid trying to come up with a way to convince Grace that the Grand Marsh Inn was better, and how to avoid going to the hospital at all. How could she explain that sometimes an idea was good, but it just didn't fit, didn't feel right? In this case, Mom would understand better. Maybe she could talk to Grace. Mom had always supported her acting dream—taken her to rehearsals, bought all the costumes and stage makeup. When she was a young woman, Mom had wanted to be a pianist; that was her dream. But she had given it up for Dad, and Grace and Celia, Grandma and Grandpa, and Granny Jones.

Celia looked for a face cloth in the cabinet under the sink and came across a brown leather shaving kit, taking it out in shocked surprise. She couldn't imagine that Grace had a regular male visitor that she had never heard about. She unzipped the top, fingering the worn surfaces of the brush and comb inside. And then she knew, in an instant, that it was Dad's kit, which she had not seen in years and years. Funny how Grace would have it here, with her. And then, stroking the leather, Celia remembered there were all those years that Grace had with Dad before Celia came along. A kind of mythical time in her mind, golden, but sad, too, with the miscarriages, the longed-for babies who didn't make it into the world. She put the kit back, turning off the bath water, and stripping off her clothes to get into the water.

Celia was in the tub when the phone rang. With the door ajar, she caught bits of conversation on Grace's end: ". . . sounds like an improvement . . . such terrible side effects." Talking to Mom, or listening, rather. Then she heard her own name: "settling in . . . yes, waitress, I know . . . she'll have to tell you. . . . I'm not really sure . . . yeah, pretty upset." That was enough. She submerged beneath the bubbly water, her hair fanning to each side. If only she could breathe underwater. She wanted to tell Grace how much she felt at home in water, like she'd been a sea creature in another life. Or a mermaid. Only that would sound silly, and not like she was taking things seriously. Of course, with a whoosh, she had to come up for air. She rinsed with a plastic bowl, all that heavy, wet hair. Out of the tub, she wrapped the towel around her head and pulled on a night gown. In the living room, Grace was off the phone.

"Well," Celia said. "What's the report? I know it was Mom." She plopped down on the sofa, her elbow displacing a couple of framed photos Celia had set up on the end table: Carlos with his guitar and one of Celia and Janelle in Greek robes for *The Trojan Women.* The only vestiges of her life in Santa Cruz.

"Not good," Grace said, kneading a pillow in her lap. "It's the same old mess. They're facing bankruptcy, and they may end up in Mexico to get medical services for Shane. Gordon is a wreck, and Mom is worried about his mental health." Grace shook her head. "And of course, now she's worried about you, and me."

Her tone was so somber, not like the old, can-do Grace.

"Come on, Grace," Celia coaxed. "Things will work out, eventually. We've been down before, after Dad died, and then things got better."

Grace looked away, toward the calendar on the wall—mallards on a marsh. "Mom called me last week too," she said, finally. "She asked if I could pay your tuition."

Celia gave a start. "No!"

"But I paid cash for my car, and that's it for savings. Had I known, I might have financed it."

"Don't say that, Grace. That's not right. She shouldn't have asked you."

"She also said that she regretted she had no skills to make money outside the home. And that, maybe she wouldn't have married Gordon if she hadn't felt the need for support after Dad died." Her eyes widened. "Here's the bottom line: we're on our own; there is nothing else."

Celia sat back in her chair, chastened. The room was silent until a siren sounded down the street; of course, they lived so close to the hospital.

"All right, then," Celia said quietly. "I'll go to the hospital tomorrow."

Their eyes met again, sober.

Then, unexpectedly, Grace smiled, her whole face transformed. "You know what?" she said. "I think you may be right. Go for the Grand Marsh Inn, at least for now. It's probably a better fit and better money. We'll see what happens after that." Then she actually laughed. "I'm sure you'll have some great stories to tell. God knows, we need something to laugh about."

Tuesday Celia woke early, the sun weak but promising a warm, hazy day. She remembered the phone call and the conversation of the previous night—and remembered, too, with a spark of excitement about her new job. She sat up, swinging her legs off the sofa bed, already charged up with determination to do her best, meet her challenges, and not be a burden on Grace. She took a step on the carpet, wincing. Then she remembered the walk and the blisters on her foot. In the bathroom, that other question came back in her head.

"Hey, Grace," she called. She rinsed her mouth and spit.

Grace was in the living room with her coffee. "Yes?"

"Is there a shortcut to the Inn from here—I mean, walking?"

Grace didn't answer right away. Instead, Celia heard her get up and open a drawer. "Come in here when you're done," she said. Celia dried her hands and put the towel back.

In the living room, Grace was seated on the sofa, the coffee cup on the end table and a map spread across her lap. When she saw Celia, she patted the cushion next to her. Bent over the map, Celia oriented herself to Sutton and the surrounding area. She was surprised to see they were so close to the Chesapeake Bay.

"Sutton's not very big, is it?" she said.

"No, but it's sort of a regional center—the hospital, the courthouse, a department store. There used to be a lot of wealth in the area." Grace's fingers swept along the river that fed into the Chesapeake. "I guess there still is. There are some big homes along the river—mansions, really. You can't even see them from the road."

"Oh, that's nice," Celia said absently. She was focused on the center of town, the distance from the short dead-end street where they lived to the intersection where the Grand Marsh Inn was located, taking the diagonal, rather than going along Main Street. "I could just cut through here," she said.

Grace shook her head. "That neighborhood is pretty rough. Robbery, breaking and entering, and late night fights, according to *The Sutton Chronicle.*" She pursed her lips. "It's considered a black neighborhood and this is kind of a dividing line." She drew her finger along a street. "When I moved to Sutton, they told me at the hospital to avoid those blocks."

Celia snorted. "You're kidding, right?"

"I know. That's not the way we were raised, but that's what I was told—being young, single, female, new to town."

"They were just trying to scare you," Celia said, digging a toe into the braided rug.

But Grace didn't back down. "I think they were trying to be helpful." She shrugged. "Don't ask me how or why, but that's the way it is."

"But it's ridiculous," Celia said. "Who says there's a line?" She looked at the map again. "I can't believe anyone obeys some imaginary rule about an imaginary line. Maybe it used to be like that, but it can't be now." The mantel clock chimed, as if to call attention to the passing of time, then and now.

Grace sighed, folding the map and getting to her feet. "Don't forget, they had plantations here, and slavery. There's kind of a Southern feeling about this place, both the good and the bad." At the hutch, she put the map away, turning back. "I'm just saying, 'different rules.' Use your head, OK? I don't want to hear about you getting robbed of all your hard-earned money—or worse."

"Rape, do you mean?"

"Well, no, that's not likely to happen. Well, against white women, anyway." Grace shook her head. "The guy would never get away with it, like they say, 'hunted down like an animal.' One of the old-timers at the hospital told me there was a lynching here as late as the 1930s. See what I mean?"

Celia nodded dumbly, not quite believing.

"More like robbery, or some kind of assault, that could happen." Grace's lips were pressed together, bemused, as she rose to her feet. "One more thing. Get up. I want to show you something."

Celia followed her sister to the back of the kitchen, where Grace pulled back a blue-checkered curtain. Behind the apartment complex was a large, marshy area, and beyond that a row of small, rickety houses, partially obscured by trees and fences.

"That place there," Grace said, pointing. "The white building with the big covered deck. Do you see it?"

Celia nodded.

"The Starlight Lounge," Grace said, mock-glamorous, "the most dangerous place in town." She was smiling, but serious. "Maybe half a mile from here, would you say? Not even. You can hear the music sometimes. It's not a place you want to drop in for a drink. Seriously, I've heard gunshots. Whenever there's a lot of drinking, there's bound to be trouble. Right?"

Celia nodded, not saying anything. *Wow,* she was thinking, *what kind of place is this?* The apartment complex was well-maintained, nicely landscaped, and close to the hospital. It all seemed so cozy, and safe. Celia pictured herself on the deck of her apartment in Santa Cruz, sipping wine with Carlos and their friends, watching the surfers ride home on their bikes, a low-rider cruising by, somebody in another building, chanting *Om.* People thought California was strange, but there were some odd things about this quaint little town: hunting season and forbidden streets and the Starlight Lounge.

Grace went back for her coffee cup, dumping the grounds in the kitchen sink.

"That's it for me," she said. Her bag and keys were ready on the table. "Got to go. And you?"

Celia turned from the window. "Me?"

"What's your plan for the day? All ready for tomorrow?"

"Definitely," Celia said, and then, narrowing her eyes, "I think. Oh, yeah—shoes. I need some good work shoes. Right, at the shop you told me on Main Street."

"And?"

Celia blinked. There must have been more; yes, there was. "Oh, and a hair cut—well, a trim."

Still Grace hadn't moved.

It came to Celia. The shoes; the blisters. "And pantyhose."

Grace smiled, but Celia frowned. She hated pantyhose.

Now Grace was ready to leave. "Have a good day," she waved, as Celia followed her to the doorway.

"You, too."

The downstairs door banged shut behind Grace. Celia stood immobile, feeling somehow abandoned, alone and unsure.

"No big deal, you silly," she scolded. She pictured herself in costume—that is, the uniform-—under the chandelier lights of the dining room at the Inn, speaking her lines smoothly and confidently. Charming, as always. Then came the memory of uplifted faces and a wave of applause—her audience at the last performance of *Alice.* They loved her; well, they were very enthusiastic. Too bad about what that stupid reporter said, "lightweight". What did he know? It's just that…well, it would have been nice for Carlos to be there and see it, or Grace, or Mom. But, it wasn't to be. Carlos wasn't due back until the very end of summer. And, as she explained to Grace, it was hard for him to communicate, being out on a boat so much of the time. Still, there was kind of a blank, a void where some proud, familiar face should have been.

She shook her head, catching her pretty reflection in the mirror on the wall next to the door.

Grace, of course, would be back at the end of the day. And tomorrow was the start of her new adventure, a new opportunity to make an impression, improve her skills, and make some money! Being paid for her talents, she liked the sound of that.

Chapter 3

On her first day of work, Celia was nervous and excited, like the jitters before going on stage. Her uniform was neat and proper, and her newly trimmed hair was tamed with plenty of bobby pins. Pantyhose and new work shoes and just a touch of make-up, since she wasn't under the spotlights. At the last minute, she added a little blue dolphin pin to her collar, for a boost of color and confidence.

Grace had wished her luck before leaving for work. "They won't know what hit them," she predicted.

"Oh, come on," Celia said. "I'm very serious." But then she laughed.

At the front entrance to the Grand Marsh Inn, James greeted her as she passed on her way to the kitchen door.

"Good morning, miss," he said, standing to attention and giving a quick salute. "Reporting for duty?"

Of course, he could tell from her uniform.

"Yes, sir," she came back, returning the salute and then breaking into a smile. "I hope I don't blow it."

"No, Miss Celia, everything looks ship-shape." And then he added, "With that smile, you're going to do just fine."

Inside, Celia walked up a hallway past a row of lockers and the time clock and through the wide-open kitchen area, nodding at anyone she passed. So far, she didn't recognize anyone, and she hoped the Beckers were expecting her. She stopped at the swinging doors into the dining room, peeking over her shoulder at the stations lining the kitchen walls, already buzzing with quiet activity. Not a soul looked back, as if they hadn't even seen her pass through.

On the other side of the small window of the swinging door, a lady with cat-eye glasses sat at one of the tables, legs crossed, flicking a restless foot. Celia stepped through the doors into the plush, quiet room.

The woman wore the same uniform as Celia, her iron gray hair permed with a curl of short bangs. She gave Celia the once-over, green eyes shrewd behind her glasses.

"You're the new girl," she said, no-nonsense, her voice flavored with the local accent.

"Yes, I'm Celia. Pleased to meet you. I was worried—"

"I'm Faye. I'll be taking you around for the training."

"Oh," said Celia. "That's so kind of you. It's been a while since . . . well .
. . where I worked before was quite different, not nearly as nice." She let out a
nervous giggle. "Kind of a zoo, really."

A doubtful expression crossed the woman's face. "Well, come on," she
said. She picked up a menu from the table, and gestured for Celia to sit, side
by side. "Let's go over this."

"Do I need a pad and pencil?"

"No orders today. Not until you know what you're doing. There's a lot to
learn in this place."

There *was* a lot to learn. First, all the items on the menu—and that was
only lunch. Then the proper set-up for each table. The wait stations and all the
items that were stocked there. The bar and all the fixings; Celia hadn't even
thought about *those* kind of drinks. The grill and all the stations in the kitchen.
Pick-up station, drop-off station, where and how to stack the trays.

After an hour's time, she was thirsty, tired of smiling, and a little
overwhelmed. And the customers hadn't even arrived. Other wait staff
appeared, mostly women. They wore nametags, but Faye didn't bother to
introduce her. Did she maybe have a few doubts?

By one o'clock, the dining room was about half full, not a busy day.
Leading Celia to an unoccupied corner table, Faye gave Celia tips about filling
out the order pad, shorthand and neatness. And then she announced she was
going home.

"You are?" said Celia, a bit taken aback.

"Yes, I am. I'm just covering for Anita." Her head tilted in the direction of
the Beckers' office. "They asked me to. I'm retired. My legs aren't what they
used to be. And I can't take the nonsense anymore." She gave Celia a frank
appraisal. "You seem like a nice girl, so here's some free advice. If you want
to keep your job, you've got to act like you're happy to serve the customers,
even if they're rude and arrogant, and even if you're tired and having a bad
day."

Celia could imagine a table full of successful, well-groomed men and
women, rich probably, thinking they're better than everyone else. But
meanwhile, she stayed cool and courteous, knowing it meant nothing. As to a
bad day, she generally didn't have too many of those; sad sometimes, but not
mad or pouty.

"Oh," said Celia, "I can do that. I'm really good at it—acting, you know.
That's my field."

Faye, finally, broke into a smile. "Oh, is that right? Well, I'm sorry I
won't be here to see it. But some of the staff here, the young ones, they don't

seem to care about service; just the tips. Twenty years ago, we were all pros—not these, well, other types." Whatever that meant.

"Well," said Celia, carefully, "I don't know about them. But I'll try my best. I really will. My teachers always used to say on my report card: *eager to please.*"

"Not too eager," Faye said, but she was chuckling. "Especially with the men that invite you upstairs, pretty girl like you. You have any problems, go to Anita. She'll straighten things out." She pushed her chair back, standing upright with some effort.

Celia scrambled to her feet. "Oh, well then, thank you, Faye, for the training."

"You're welcome, dear. Good-bye and good luck."

"So, I won't see you after this?"

"I may be in a few hours during hunting season. Hard to say no to that money." Faye nodded meaningfully. "You'll see, if you stay on."

"Am I done too?"

"Oh, no, sweetheart. You're going to shadow Wanda for a while, see what she does."

"Wanda?"

"The black girl with the glasses." She gestured across the room to a waitress just delivering a tray of drinks. "Not a lot of personality, but she's good, smart. Better than some of those others." She made a face. "I'll tell her to come get you when she has a moment. You can wait here, and observe."

She padded away, leaving Celia to wonder if the Grand Marsh Inn was the right place for her after all. She hadn't seen the Beckers since she'd come in, and not the tall fellow with the missing tooth. Not the snooty girl with the red claws, either. Celia thought she saw the chef she'd bumped into that day and said a friendly hello before realizing it wasn't him, but another black man in a white uniform.

In another moment, Wanda appeared, beckoning. She was a big-framed girl in her early twenties with thick glasses and a round face. Her short, straightened hair was parted on the side. Celia stood up, eager to start.

"Got two tables," Wanda said. "I'll do first one; then you do the other, just like I do."

"What?" Celia was confused. "But Faye said, not until I'm ready."

Wanda puffed out her cheeks. "This is how you get ready. Come on."

Celia's heart beat quickly. *Was she ready?*

The dining room was almost empty, the tail end of a slow day. They approached the first table together, three ladies in their forties who each wanted lobster bisque and a Caesar salad, with iced teas. Pretty simple.

At the second table, Wanda put the order pad into Celia's hands and said to the elderly couple, "This is Celia. She's new, and she's going to take your order."

Like twins, they turned to her with bright, kind eyes behind matching glasses. Two turtle soups, one with the pork chop dinner, the other roasted turkey. Plus two gin and tonics.

Celia followed Wanda to place the orders in the kitchen, pick up the drinks in the bar, and return to the tables. Next came the soups, then the entrees. Easy! The older couple wanted coffees and to split a piece of pecan pie. But no rush, dear.

"That wasn't bad," Celia said to Wanda afterwards, as they cleared the tables and finished the side work.

"Here's your money," Wanda said, giving Celia the ten-dollar tip from a fifty-dollar bill.

"Oh, my!" said Celia, eyes wide. "Are you sure?"

"That money's yours."

"Thanks, Wanda!"

"OK, OK. So, what's for lunch? Lamb chops, maybe, roast beef. How about you?"

Celia's eyes widened. "From the menu?"

"What they got left, sure." A glimmer of a smile came to Wanda's face. "Come on, then. Let's see what looks good."

For the rest of the week, Celia worked mainly with Wanda while taking on more tables of her own. Each day, the hour before noon was focused on prep work: stocking the wait stations and filling sugar bowls and condiment servers. Celia sat and folded napkins into bird shapes with some of the other staff: Brenda, a red-headed mother of three; Pam, the youthful bride-to-be; and pale, moody Evelyn. She, too, had recently left college, and Celia gathered her dad was some mucky-muck in town. When asked, Celia told them she'd moved from California and was staying with her sister.

"California?" Brenda said. "Why on earth would you come here?"

"Well," Celia said, resting the half-folded napkin on the table. "There was a family issue, and I had to leave college for a while, but I plan to go back as soon as I can. I was studying theater, music, dance." She warmed to her subject, plucking out the wings of her napkin swan or goose, whatever it was. "I know it's not the most practical, but that's my real love, and I think I have some potential. I've got to at least try, right?"

There was little response, except raised eyebrows. Only Wanda looked up at Celia with interest.

"My sister wants to go to New York to see a musical," said Pam, her flock of napkin birds complete. "You couldn't pay me to go. I can't stand the city."

"Oh, well, Broadway," Celia said, off-handedly. "That's the big time." She had to shake out and refold her last napkin. "It's too bad there's so little theater around here. Or much of anything like that, as far as I can tell." She gave a sigh, meant to be humorous. "I guess I just have to bide my time and make as much money as I can, until I can leave."

No one laughed. Pam and Brenda exchanged a look across the table. Maybe Celia's comment hadn't come out quite right. With a blush, she gathered her cloth creations onto a tray to distribute among the tables.

Over the next few days, Celia met most of the staff and started to get more familiar with "life at the Inn." Brenda and Pam were tied at the hip, always meeting to whisper urgent messages. Evelyn continued sullen, without an extra word for anyone. Wanda worked every weekday lunch shift, reserved but helpful in unobtrusive ways. There were two guys: Roland and Tony, one black, one white; both brisk, professional, and clearly very close.

And then there was Anita: quick and experienced, she seemed to make more money than the rest of them. She had large, expressive eyes, warm brown skin, and a throaty laugh. With her carefully relaxed curls and a touch of lipstick, she reminded Celia of one of those black actresses, Lena Horne or Dianne Carroll, glamorous in her own way. Mid-thirties, maybe? She was well-spoken and had gone to college and worked in Philadelphia before returning to the Eastern Shore. There was a teenaged daughter, although no mention of a husband. And a small gold cross that twinkled at her neck. All she had to say was, "On my way" in her clear, ringing voice to get her orders lined up and ready to go, no matter the rush in the dining room.

Celia's first week at the Grand Marsh Inn flew by without incident, although at night she dreamed of guests calling "Miss! Miss! Miss!" She enjoyed the walk down Main Street, the late-summer flowers in manicured gardens, and the shop windows full of pretty scarves and all kinds of waterfowl decor. On arrival at the Inn, she got a friendly "Good morning, Miss Celia" from James, the doorman, so gentlemanly in his sharp uniform and Virginia accent. If she had a few minutes, she stopped for his report on the weather or special events at the Inn: weddings, conferences, all kinds of meetings. But he was always careful to check the time on his pocket watch for Celia so she wouldn't be late.

During the second week, Mrs. Becker asked Celia to get coffee supplies from the downstairs kitchen. She made her way for the first time to the basement level, where most of the prep work was done, including baking, salads, and desserts. Light bounced off the stainless steel storage shelves and large, industrial refrigerators. Everyone worked intently, like at a factory. No one looked at her as she loaded her tray with cans of coffee and sugars and sweeteners. Out of maybe twenty or twenty-five people, she was the only white person in the room.

On her way back upstairs, she paused in the stairwell. From the landing, she could see through the windows of the lower kitchen doors, all the figures focused on their tasks. It was like watching a silent movie from some other time and place, almost like another country, where they spoke a different language. A couple times, when she passed some of the kitchen staff on the stairs or in the break room, she could hardly understand their speech—the regional dialect, with unfamiliar words and strange grammar.

Growing up outside Rochester, New York, Celia had only one black schoolmate, Myra, a shy, sickly girl with taped glasses and clothes that smelled of wood smoke. But she was a good speller and liked to read the same books that Celia did. Celia didn't mind being Myra's library buddy, unlike some of the other kids. At the beginning of middle school, Myra and her family moved away, but nobody knew where or why.

Driving by run-down sections of Rochester, their mother often clucked her tongue, shaking her head. "What a disgrace people have to live like that." Through the window, Celia could see faceless walls of brick buildings, broken windows, and tiny yards of dirt where the grass and trees barely survived.

"Why do they live there?" Celia asked.

"Not because they want to, honey," her mom said, glancing at the back seat. "They wouldn't if they had a choice. Black people have gotten a bad deal in this country. That's what I'm trying to say."

Even after they moved to California, there were few black faces at her suburban high school, and three black students, total, in the Theater Arts Department at college. Here in Sutton was something new. Grace had said that things were different here, that there were lots of black people living in the small town and neighboring countryside. But somehow that hadn't registered with Celia, didn't really mean much, until she started working at the Inn. Not that she was fearful in any way. What harm could come to her under the watchful eyes of the Beckers? But she had never expected to find herself in a situation like this, sometimes the only white person in view, surrounded by so many black people.

Back in the upstairs kitchen, the lunch chefs were setting up at their stations. The head cook, Virgil, was a black man, middle-aged, angular and bony, with glasses and a prominent mole on the side of his face. He didn't smile much, but he didn't raise his voice much either, and he was generous in the portions of food he put on the plates. Next to Virgil, with the same white apron but a shorter hat, was Warren, who was relaxed and good-natured with the most infectious laugh. The assistant chefs, those who manned the grill or plated the entrees, were all men. Almost everyone who actually touched the food, cutting, measuring, cooking, baking, or arranging on the plate, was black. It was just Celia and some of the wait staff and bartenders who were white, and not many at that.

On Friday, after the lunch rush died down, one of the younger chefs, Jeremy, stopped Celia at the serving station. He was about twenty, short and well built, always talking or singing, constantly in motion. It was clear he liked the role of joker and was known for his come-on lines to the girls. Jeremy had given her the nickname "Dolphin Girl" for the pin she wore on her collar.

Most of the wait staff was already gone, either checked out or in the break room. She put an empty water pitcher on the bussing cart. Four of the guys were talking behind the pick-up station, cleaning and shutting down the grill. When she approached, all conversation stopped.

"Hey, Dolphin Girl," said Jeremy. "I got something for you."

"What is it?" Celia looked up, surprised.

"You got to come back here so I can show you," he said, his voice light and teasing.

"I can't," Celia said. "You know, because of safety and, uh, health reasons." That's what Mrs. Becker had told her, but even as it came out of her mouth, it sounded kind of ridiculous.

"Come on," he cajoled. "What's the matter? Afraid of these boys back here?" Jeremy's eyes were twinkling. The other guys grinned and looked down at their hands. "Just come here to the side, then."

Celia wiped her hands on her apron and went to the side entrance of the station while Jeremy walked over to his side of the half-door. He pulled out a fishing lure from his pocket, shaped like a fly, shiny, black with yellow and iridescent blue, with a hooked point at the end. "How you like to wear this on your collar? We call you Fly Girl."

Celia could feel the eyes of the other boys on her. Was it a joke? A flirtation? Or just a friendly gesture?

She took it from him, looking at it closely. "It's pretty, Jeremy, but I don't see how I can wear it. It's too sharp and heavy." She tried to give it back, but he wouldn't take it, so she put it down on the stainless steel counter. "You should keep it and use it, you know, for fishing."

He left it there, opening the half-door and coming through to stand next to her. "You're a good dancer, huh, Celia?"

Celia hesitated. "Well, I like to dance," she said.

"They say you trained at dancing. Probably queen of the disco."

"Not that kind of dancing," she said. "Modern and, you know, ballet."

There was no response, none. All four of them looked stumped.

"Swan Lake?" she prompted, lifting her arms over her head in a graceful circle. Still nothing, so she bent in a *plie,* rose to her toes and turned, and then took a small leap, her back leg lifted in *jette.* Landing, she bowed her head with a smile.

Her audience was rapt, and then Jeremy started to clap and they applauded.

"Girl can dance," said Cuffie, the boy with the golden tooth. "Do some more."

"Look like a butterfly," said one of the others.

But Celia's demonstration didn't get her off the hook.

"Put up the music, Tilghman," Jeremy directed one of the younger boys, pointing to a radio on the shelf. The music came on, at least the thump, thump of a song, funk or soul, the melody lost in the large, open room.

"Celia gonna dance with me, right Celia?"

"Not here," Celia said, looking from face to face with an uncertain smile.

"Oh, yeah, where we gonna dance, then?" Jeremy said, moving his shoulders in rhythm to the music. He reached out a hand to her. "Come on, come on."

"No." Celia shook her head and stepped back, almost bumping into the tray rack. "Not now."

"So, tell me, when we going dancing?" Jeremy was dancing now, smooth on his feet.

Celia pictured the clubs in Santa Cruz where she had gone with Carlos and their college friends, the noise and smoke, flashing lights, and young people intoxicated with drink and the music.

"Maybe we could go to a dance club sometime," she said. "Everybody, the whole group, we could go after work."

The guys started laughing.

"Yeah, take her to the 328 Club," someone said. Phil A. was it? The short-necked one with small eyes and a powerful build. "She glow like a light bulb in there."

"How about the Starlight?" the boy with a chinstrap beard said, and they broke up over that. Celia frowned. Grace warned her to stay away from that place beyond the marshes behind the apartment.

"How 'bout you just take my hand, and we take a quick turn?" Jeremy said with a broad, charming smile.

Celia stood dumbly, her arms crossed at her waist. Footsteps sounded in the hallway, and they all turned to look. Jay, one of the cooks during the dinner shift, came into the kitchen, sizing up the situation with a glance. He stopped in a bay along the wall, where he buttoned up his white jacket and fitted the cap over his hair. Celia recognized him from their near collision outside Mr. Becker's office. She didn't know Jay as well as the others, but he seemed more serious than most of the other young men. She looked toward him hopefully; maybe he had some business with Jeremy and the other guys. He met her gaze, and then headed to a side station, bending to pull out pots and pans from the lower shelves.

Then Anita entered from the dining room, banging through the swing doors with an empty tray and bulging pockets. She came to a dramatic halt in front of the station, glaring first at the assembled group and then the fish lure on the counter.

"What is going on here?" she demanded. She turned to Jeremy. "Is this your nonsense?" Her voice dropped lower, quieter. "What did I tell you?" Then she addressed the rest of the group. "Don't you have work to finish, or do you want to be here all day?"

She placed the empty tray on the rack and took Celia by the elbow. "Come on, let's have some lunch." Celia caught Jeremy's eyes, shrugging her shoulders: *No use resisting that commanding tone.* Not that she had really needed someone to come in and rescue her. Jeremy pulled a long face, but returned behind the counter without a word.

Phil A. served up two plates of pork chops with mashed potatoes and green beans, rolls on the side. Celia carried the food to the break room, while Anita brought their drinks.

Everyone else had eaten and left. They took seats at the long, narrow table in the windowless room, all white walls without a spot of color.

"Don't let them play with you," Anita scolded as she poured cream into her coffee, stirring vigorously. "You can't even see it, can you? You're the new girl, new thing in town. It's like cat and mouse, a little game they like to play, especially Jeremy. But Becker won't like it, if he sees that going on."

She paused with a meaningful expression. "You understand what I'm saying, right?" Then she smiled, pushing one of her rolls over to Celia. "Eat up, you boney thing. You need more hip and more elbow if you're going to get ahead."

Bowing her head, Anita thanked the Lord for the chops and potatoes, ending with, "May He preserve us from all manner of fools and patience-tryers." She looked up expectantly until Celia contributed a hasty "Amen."

Chapter 4

After a few weeks, Celia was assigned a full-time schedule, lunches and a couple of dinner shifts. Most days she worked with Wanda. No matter what time Celia arrived, Wanda was there earlier, in the exact same chair in the break room, pouring over the newspaper. Her heavy, clear plastic glasses were perched on the end of her small, flat nose; it was a wonder they never slid off. Wanda didn't volunteer much personal information. The most Celia could get out of her was that she lived with her mother, who had a disease called lupus, and two younger brothers; she had graduated from Sutton High; and she didn't have a boyfriend. Celia could never find much to talk about with the other wait staff who were busy with their families, after-school sports, and getting a good bargain. Or, of course, Pam and all her wedding plans. Or Evelyn, who glowered at everyone, except guests, of course.

Without question, the most fun and lively waiters were Roland and Tony, who loved to tease but were helpful in their way, giving Celia the low-down on some of the regular customers. Once, after all the guests had gone, Roland burst into a song from *Oklahoma* in a fine tenor—a mutual fan of Broadway musicals! Celia joined in until Mrs. Becker appeared out of nowhere: "Quiet, this minute! There will be no singing." She barely glanced at Roland, but shot Celia a look of unmistakable warning. What was the harm? Celia realized it was not professional, and that Mrs. Becker ran a very organized dining room. But she began to suspect, too, that Mrs. Becker had her doubts about her. Mrs. Becker continued to watch, narrow-eyed, as everyone fell in line back to work.

Unbidden, a smile came to Celia's lips as she resumed her side work. "Off with their heads! Off with their heads!" she cried, silently. With that shrill voice and imperious manner, Mrs. Becker reminded her of Janelle as the Queen of Hearts in the summer production of *Alice in Wonderland.* She wanted to tell someone, but then thought better of it. Still, for the rest of shift she couldn't quite shake the notion, how there was something about the Inn that was a little topsy-turvy and surreal, like the Alice story, with its own rather unusual cast of characters. Better to tell Grace after work; Grace would appreciate it.

When Celia worked her first evening, a Tuesday, Anita took her through the dinner menu, pointing out the differences. Then, during the following shifts, she would appear at Celia's table, giving instructions in a quiet voice. Surprisingly, it was Mr. Becker who demonstrated the elaborate specialties at the dessert station: cherries jubilee or Baked Alaska.

Celia was to assemble all the elements onto a cart and roll it to the side of the guests' table where Mr. Becker would appear with a lighter and put on the finishing touches with a true showman's flourish. Three times he helped Celia prepare the desserts, assisting her at the table while Mrs. Becker watched from across the room, unsmiling.

Mr. Becker was in and out of the dining room, as his other duties allowed. But one day he parked himself near the doors to the kitchen, with no other intention, it seemed, than to observe Celia. That was the time she sloshed gravy onto a woman's sleeve and had to apologize a hundred times while they dabbed it off with a wet napkin. It made her nervous, Mr. Becker watching her like that.

"Argh," she said as she cleared dishes to a cart alongside Eldridge, the bus boy, tall and slim—he of the missing front tooth.

"What's the matter, Missy?"

"Mr. Becker, why is he just standing there?" Celia said. "He was looking right at me when I spilled the gravy."

Eldridge smiled. "He like how you look, pretty thing. That's all."

"Oh, no," she groaned. "I hope that's not it."

"You got nothing to worry about," Eldridge advised, flicking open a balled up napkin, adding it to his pile. "He won't try nothing with Miz Becker around. He like a cat got no claws. He think it good for business, have nice looking girls around. Miz Becker think the pretty ones nothing but trouble—too distractin'." He nodded sagely. "Probably right too. She the one you got to look out for."

When she looked back across the room, Mr. Becker was no longer in sight. No Mrs. Becker, either, for the minute. And the last of the lunchers were getting up to leave. Celia relaxed, hands on hips, watching Eldridge stack the dirty plates and saucers by size, not just dumping them in willy-nilly, like some of the others.

"Yeah, you're probably right," she said. "It's just so frustrating. I think I'm doing fine, and something stupid like this happens."

"We all got trials, honey-chile," Eldridge said, not looking up. "That girl, Josie, she on my last nerve. Everything I do, she undo. She stupid, but she stubborn, and she have to have her own way."

"Sorry to hear that," Celia said. She had to agree the chubby bus girl with the off-focus eye and garbled speech was not very helpful, often scolding Celia for no apparent reason. Eldridge continued about his business in a calm, methodical way, bending from the middle like one of those slow-moving, long-legged birds—a crane was it, or heron? When he spoke, there was a bit of a lisp and a certain way he expressed himself, a shake of the head, a pursing of lips. Could he be . . . was he gay? Celia knew gay men from her time in theater arts, but none quite like this. Or was it just the lisp from the missing tooth that threw her off? He certainly wasn't shy. And not as old as she'd thought. Twenty-four, Wanda told Celia when she'd asked. The same age as Grace—imagine.

Celia prodded herself back to work, bunching soiled napkins and putting silverware into the plastic bin. "Why does she even work here—Josie?"

"Her mother head of Housekeeping. They can't get rid of her, no way. Where she gonna go, ugly like that and soft in the head? 'Sides, she love it here. Never miss a day, and strong as a bull."

"Really?" Celia wanted to know more. But Mrs. Becker strode into the room, and Celia and Eldridge pushed the cart into the kitchen. Celia forgot about the conversation until she saw Josie later on, seated on a stool in the kitchen, scraping an empty bowl of cream and licking her fingers. The buttons of her shirt strained over her generous middle, and one was missing, which surprised Celia. Plus, the bobby pins stuck in her hair right and left, did little to keep down errant tufts. No doubt Eldridge was right: special status.

Celia soon discovered that Mrs. Becker didn't miss a thing, and that mistakes in the dining room could be expensive. Once, Celia mixed up orders, serving a dish to the wrong diner, who began eating before the mistake was discovered. There was quite a fuss. Mrs. Becker came with Celia to the table to apologize. The dish would be corrected, of course, and there would be no charge. That sounded very generous to Celia, until she realized there was a charge—to her earnings. Another time, she forgot to add in the price of dessert and coffee. That, too, was taken from her pay. And not every guest was patient and understanding as she learned the new items, especially some of the alcoholic drinks that she was not familiar with. She brought a glass of whiskey to a woman, already slurring her words, who said, "Are you an idiot? I said whiskey sour."

Some of the other waitresses were not so crazy about Celia either; strangely enough, it was mostly the other white women. Initially, they were pleasant enough, if not exactly friendly. A nod and a smile, or a helpful suggestion. But clearly they were reserving judgment until they saw more.

"Miss Mary Sunshine," someone called her one day, and she overheard a rather unflattering imitation of her nervous giggle.

Plus, after an older gentleman took Celia's hand to slip her a twenty-dollar bill, she saw Evelyn pucker up and bat her eyes as if she'd been an outrageous flirt, which she was not.

The turning point, though, came on the day that Celia entered the break room with her lunch tray. Clumped at the near end of the long table, Pam, Brenda, and another girl sat together sharing a meal, while at the other end, Wanda sat alone, looking at a newspaper. After a moment's hesitation, Celia walked to the chair next to Wanda and sat down. Not that Wanda was so welcoming or anything. But Celia's eye had caught the headline of the article she was reading, "Mystery disease killing dozens in U.S.," which interested her. And it just seemed unkind to ignore Wanda and join ranks with the others, when they'd never gone out of their way for her. Rude, and maybe even racist.

"Why so many men?" she asked Wanda about the article, who looked up, surprised. After a moment she answered, "Gays."

The other women were preoccupied with their food, it seemed. Only Brenda looked at Celia and Wanda with a spark of distaste or disapproval. And then she turned, shutting her face, and it was like they were in separate rooms. Celia raised her eyebrows at Wanda, who looked wary. They were stuck with each other now, like it or not, lunch pals and news buddies.

On a Friday, Mrs. Becker sat a group of doctors' wives in Wanda's section. They came every week for lunch and drinks, five middle-aged ladies with their hair expertly styled, wearing dress suits with scarves or broaches. Normally, Anita handled them with kid gloves, but she had taken a day off. At the wait station, Celia saw storm clouds gathering on Wanda's face and leaned over to whisper.

"You should see yourself," Celia said. "I know they're fussy, but you can handle them."

"They don't like me," Wanda said, "and I don't like them, either. I had them once, and that was enough." Her eyes narrowed as she added, "Ten percent tip; that's nothing."

At the hostess stand, Mrs. Becker gave the girls a warning look.

"Mrs. Fenton, she's the worst," Wanda muttered, flipping the page of her order pad. "Miz Bossy Boss. Why does she have to repeat everything I say? Make me look like a fool."

The problem was that when Wanda set her face a certain way, she did look sort of grouchy and indifferent. But Celia couldn't very well tell her that.

"Let me take them," she said. "You can have that table of six when they come in." She pointed at a table reserved for a group of engineers.

Wanda's mouth opened, but no words came out.

"Doesn't that sound better?"

Wanda shrugged, "I guess."

"Just let Mrs. Becker know. I'm sure she won't mind, coming from you." Spinning around, Celia presented herself at the side of the circular table. The doctors' wives—four regulars and a newcomer—were so busy chatting that they didn't see her at first. She sang out a cheerful, "Good afternoon, ladies."

Five heads turned in her direction, first in confusion—she was not Anita—and then with polite smiles—she was there to take their orders.

"Well, hello there, young lady." The woman to Celia's right looked over her bifocals. "Where's Anita today?" Mrs. Fenton, no doubt, with that commanding voice. "It just makes my week to see her."

"I know," Celia said sympathetically. "It's too bad she's out today. She always says she gets such a kick out of you ladies."

That brought little smiles to their faces.

"I'm Celia, and I'm new here." She let her shoulders drop. "I know there's nobody quite like Anita, but I'll do my best."

That was all she had to say, and they were perfectly happy with their substitute waitress. She knew enough to put in the drink order right away.

When Celia returned with the drinks, they still hadn't looked at the menus.

"Absolutely no salad," said the bleached blonde in purple. "Just appetizers. I could make a meal of them." She sighed. "It's so unfair. Oh, how did I get so fat? I used to look just like Celia here. That uniform is so cute—maybe I should take up waitressing."

Each time Celia stopped by to take their order, they sent her away. "No hurry, no hurry."

After the second round of drinks, the youngest of the women, dark-haired and bright-eyed—Debra-something—took Celia's arm. "You look so familiar. Have I seen you somewhere?"

Celia shrugged, shaking her head, as the woman furrowed her brow.

"Maybe at the hospital?" the woman said. She sounded like a northerner, New York or New Jersey. Somewhere away, and probably livelier than the Eastern Shore. "My husband is Jim Levine, head of orthopedics, and I work in the accounting office. We're new here too."

"My sister," Celia guessed. She tucked the empty tray under an arm. "Grace Lennon. She's a nurse."

"A little shorter, dark hair?"

"That's her," Celia said.

Debra turned to the bleached blonde. "Roselyn, did you know that? Celia's sister works at the hospital. Grace Lennon, the nurse on the medical surgery floor."

Roselyn blinked once, then twice, focusing. "Yes, I see the resemblance." A slow smile spread across her pink face. "But the coloring is different—like, like Rose Red and Snow White, don't you think?" The ladies twittered.

Mrs. Fenton spoke up. "I coordinate the volunteers, and Grace sometimes comes by the office. She's so quick and capable."

"But not as outgoing as Celia here," said Roselyn. "Or bubbly."

"Don't embarrass her," Mrs. Fenton clucked.

"But she's adorable!" Then turning back to Celia, Roselyn continued, "So, what's your field? I mean, what's your real interest, outside of here . . ." She gestured dismissively at the elegant dining room and beyond.

"I'm . . . well, I want to be . . . an actress."

A wave of excitement went around the table. "An actress in our midst!"

"Tell us some of your favorite roles," Debra prompted.

"Oh, I would love to," Celia gushed, and then lowered her voice. "But I'd better not, in the middle of . . ." She looked around. Mrs. Becker was out of the room. All of her other tables were occupied with their food or lingering over coffee. The engineers were just settling the bill with a calculator.

"Oh, stay," Roselyn implored. "Nobody needs you right this minute."

"All right, then," Celia said, taking in their hopeful, expectant expressions. "Hermia, from *Midsummer Night's Dream,* that scene where she's fighting with Helena over that boy, Lysander." They nodded encouragingly. She cleared her throat, closing her eyes. And then, suddenly, she blinked as if into stage lights, her cheeks caked with makeup, and the swish of polyester satin as she half-turned. She tipped her head up and spat venom:

And are you grown so high in his esteem;
Because I am so dwarfish and so low?
How low am I, thou painted maypole? speak;
How low am I? I am not yet so low
But that my nails can reach unto thine eyes.

For a moment the women sat wide-eyed in their chairs. Then they applauded, as a few heads turned curiously in their direction.

"Wonderful! Marvelous!"

"Oh, thank you, thank you," Celia said with a little bow. A touch of heat came to her cheeks, the pleasure of performing and having an audience. It's true, she had loved that part, but even she wasn't sure where that bitchy little scene had been called up from. She looked hurriedly around, but the dining room had returned to its normal state.

"That was quite a transformation," Mrs. Fenton said, with a sharp, critical look. "You're very good."

Embarrassed, Celia made a funny face. "I better go get your food." From across the room, she felt Wanda's eyes on her as she headed to the kitchen.

At three o'clock, the ladies got up to leave. Mrs. Fenton took charge of the bill. A few drinks, some good food, a command performance—the ladies left a very generous tip. Watching the doctors' wives head out the door, Celia fingered the tip money in her pocket. Over a hundred dollars for a four-hour shift. *Holy cow!*

"Hope to see you again," she said brightly as they departed.

"Oh, we'll be here," Roselyn said, but her tone was not as bright. "Where else would we go?"

As soon as they disappeared, Wanda was at Celia's side.

"They tip you good?" she asked.

"Yes," Celia said. "And they were very sweet."

"Yeah, they probably like your type," Wanda muttered.

Celia cocked her head. "What do you mean by that?"

"You could be the daughter, or the little sister."

Celia laughed. "Come on, Wanda. You know that's not it. They love Anita."

"Yeah, well . . ." Wanda didn't complete that thought.

"Hey," Celia said. "How did you do with the engineers?"

Wanda nodded, a little bashful. "That worked out good."

"You have to admit, we did pretty well for two girls on the lunch shift." Celia jostled her own fat pockets. Then she poked Wanda's pocket, holding her gaze until she saw a smile appear at the corners of her mouth, which turned into a full-fledged grin.

"Now let's get out of here," she said. The cashier was not available to exchange her coins for larger bills, so she went through the kitchen, punching out and grabbing her sweater. Wanda waited and they walked out together. Celia heard Jeremy call out, "Ain't one of you girls gonna marry me? I'm looking for a rich wife."

Outside the Inn, the two women parted ways. The air was cool, brisk, streaks of sunshine breaking through the dark clouds. Standing on the corner, Celia took in the brick walks and mature chestnut trees, an older couple stopped in front of an antiques store. Sutton was such a pretty place with lots of nice people, some of them quite wealthy and quite generous. She just wished there was someone to tell about her good fortune. Grace wouldn't be home tonight until almost ten, after the class she was teaching at the community college. Passing the front entrance, Celia looked for James in the lobby, but he wasn't in sight.

She crossed the street, headed down the block toward Main Street. She stopped again, pivoting on one foot. The short-cut. Why not? It took at least ten minutes off her walk home. She'd taken it half a dozen times already, and nothing whatsoever had happened, either good or bad. Few people were out during the day. A couple dogs had barked at her, especially the times she was singing to herself, bouncing along, but they were either fenced or on a chain. Mid-afternoon, after the lunch shift, she'd seen small groups of students returning home with their backpacks. All black, as Grace had said. The first time, they had stopped, five or six kids, watching her from across the street. Otherwise, they kept to themselves.

Celia set off, familiar with the route, no danger of getting lost. Some of the houses were a little shabby, a few with falling roof tiles or broken window panes. But the yards were raked and trash bins put to the curb. A woman's face appeared at a window as she passed, not smiling. When Celia waved, she waved back, belatedly. A gray cat watched from the middle of the driveway, its tail flicking back and forth.

The wind picked up, shaking the leaves. Her sweater flapped, but her pockets hung heavy, stuffed with coins and bills. A couple of raindrops hit the top of her head, so she quickened her pace to a slow jog, her pockets banging at her sides. From half a block behind, she heard a shout. Something hard and sharp hit her calf, making her jump like a startled rabbit. A bee sting, she thought first. But then suddenly dozens of small, hard objects pricked her back and legs from behind, and she realized she was under attack. She ran, stumbling blindly down the street.

Oh, my God, someone's shooting at me! Celia crouched low, trying to protect her head and face. Bills and coins dropped out of her pockets, but she couldn't stop or look around. Another prick on her forearm, and one on her calf. She bent over, running as fast as she could, looking for cover. Someone was trying to kill her, or at least, trying to harm her or chase her away. Just like Grace had said; they wanted her out of this neighborhood. She should never have come here.

But then, nothing. No shouts, no bullets, no motion, no sound at all. *How could it be so quiet? Did the guns have silencers?* Or, then, she thought, if not bullets, then what? She looked up: hail? Could hail sting like that? She didn't know. The sky was gray and windy, but only a few scattered raindrops fell harmlessly. Then a small brown ball flew by, and she saw where it bounced and landed: *an acorn.*

Several voices shouted: "Go on! Get out of here! Scat! This our place. Go back where you belong!"

Celia twisted to see who it was, and an acorn hit her cheek, narrowly missing an eye. Her hands went up protectively as more acorns flew past. And then a rain of acorns, most of them aimed at her feet, making her skip awkwardly. A small rock bounced off the pavement in front of her, and she wasn't sure if it was thrown or she had kicked it up. That wasn't funny at all; dangerous. And who were they to cast stones at her?

"Stop it! Just stop it!" Celia screamed. Tears had started to run down her cheeks.

She ran for a large oak tree, crunching the dropped acorns underfoot. At the tree, she looked down the street but saw no one. They had probably hidden in the overgrown bushes. Under the canopy of the tree, the raindrops did not reach her, but she felt a wetness on her chin. When she wiped it, her fingers came away red—blood.

She found she was shaking, and made herself take a few calming breaths. Then she stepped back out into the street, looking for her assailants. A flash of white sneakers rustled the bushes, belonging to a blue jacket and a backpack. Only one figure remained in sight, a boy with wide-set eyes wearing a red baseball cap and a sweatshirt with a large "B" across the front. Then he, too, disappeared. The high school kids, the ones who had watched her taking the short cut through their neighborhood. They must have been keeping an eye out, thinking she would eventually return.

Stupid kids, she said to herself, *dirty, rotten, disrespectful kids,* although in fact they were not much younger than she was. She closed her eyes, summoning the fury of one of those women from the Greek plays, handing down curses. If these kids were watching, let her be haughty, scornful.

"I know who you are," she shouted down the street, "and I'll tell them at the high school." An idle threat, maybe. But at least she had spoken up to them, hiding on her like a bunch of cowards. She turned on her heel, striding away. Her heart was still beating fast, and nausea rose in her gut. But she would not allow herself to run or look back. She rounded the corner to her street, praying that no one had followed. At the outside door, the key jammed in the lock.

Argh! A surge welled up in her chest, both anger and sorrow. It was not right. She should be putting the key into the apartment door in Santa Cruz, not here. Or meeting Janelle at the coffee shop to talk about auditions. Or hearing Carlos's voice on the answering machine: "I'm here and I can't wait to see you. Our ship was lost at sea, but I made it to shore." Something like that. All of her, every molecule, was geared up for that life, the college student, always preparing for the next show or recovering from the last one. Focused on her role, being a part of it all. Not like this, starting over in some new place, an unwelcome stranger, attacked on her way home from work. So what, it was acorns? So what, it was ridiculous, and they were laughing at her somewhere nearby?

She gave up, leaning against the door, until she noticed a movement at the window of the downstairs apartment. Instantly, her game face reappeared. Putting down her purse, she tried the key again, withdrawing it slightly and turning again. The door clicked opened. Celia mounted the stairs to the apartment. Without emptying her pockets, she went into the bathroom; her hair had come loose from the bobby pins, and mascara was smeared under her eyes. The small red dot inside a pink circle would fade by the time Grace got home: her battle scar. She washed up, combing out her hair. Finished, she gazed at her reflection, moist and pink. A nice face that people liked. But not those kids. They did not like her or her face.

Chapter 5

She didn't tell Grace what happened on the shortcut home, and she didn't tell anyone at work, either. It was a passing, unpleasant incident, that's all. But she no longer took the shortcut home in the afternoon. Of course, she kept to well-lit Main Street after the dinner shift, which could be as late as eleven. But she continued to cut through in the mornings, especially if she was running behind. Every time she passed the site of the assault, she stuck out her tongue, kicking at the fallen leaves and acorns. *Stupid kids.*

Besides this one ugly occurrence, things were working out rather well in her new work situation. The money, evidenced by the full tip jar on the counter at home, was very good. Even Grace had to agree. In spite of that silliness with Jeremy and his boys, Celia felt more at home in the kitchen and enjoyed the fast pace, the give and take, and the friendly banter. She spent pretty much every shift with Wanda, although she could still be hard to read. She was a good waitress all right, capable and efficient. During breaks, Wanda liked to talk about things beyond the Eastern Shore, politics or news, whatever she read in the paper that day.

The male waiters, Roland and Tony, were a lot of fun, too: quick-witted and so dramatic. When the coast was clear, they did imitations of customers, staff, and even the Beckers. It didn't take long to figure out they were gay, and a couple. Celia had a few gay friends from the theater, so she was not perturbed by the two of them together or their behavior, although once in a while their candid remarks made her blush. They were not from the Eastern Shore, and Roland, at least, had a college degree, as well as a beautiful tenor singing voice. The kitchen girls sighed over Roland, who was dashing, handsome, and black . . . "What a waste." And well-to-do, too, apparently. Roland's father had some high government position, in accounting or the post office. No one knew much about Tony's background, Louisiana, maybe. . . .

When they were both home at night, Celia updated her sister about happenings at the Inn. One night, they sat at the table over a dinner of cod and baked potatoes, salad on the side. Like at the Inn, Grace used cloth napkins, but hers had cheerful yellow and blue stripes.

"James is my pipeline for information," Celia said, pouring lemonade from the pitcher.

"James?"

"The door man. He knows everything that's going on—weddings, banquets, conventions, etc." She took a long drink before going on. "Plus, he brings me treats—you know, pastries and some of those fancy Swiss chocolates." She smacked her lips. "So good."

Grace was not smiling. "I thought they were from the bakery on your way home."

"Nope. James." Celia summoned the kitchen vernacular. "He's my main man."

"Smuggling food? That can't be right, Celia."

Celia blew a raspberry. "Oh, come on, Grace. You know me better than that. It's leftovers from the buffet table in the banquet room. Otherwise, they have to throw it away. So, he saves me a few, wraps them up in a napkin, and gives them to me when I come in the morning. I just put them in my purse for later."

"You've got to be kidding me."

Celia had tucked into her food as Grace stared. "No, really. It's fine. He's so sweet."

"Is he after you?"

Celia sputtered, her food close to spraying the table. "No way! He's old, like sixty at least." She closed one eye. "Maybe seventy. It's hard to tell." She opened her eye again. "And a gentleman. He's just a really nice man and he likes me."

Grace put her hand to her face, but she was chuckling. "You are too much, Celia. Just too much." She started in on her dinner, chewing thoughtfully.

Celia was on a roll. "Everyone is *so* excited about hunting season. You should hear the talk: 'Like money raining down from the sky,'" she imitated, sprinkling with her fingers. "The hotel goes all out for these guys. They bring their guns and keep their dogs with them in the room. If they get anything, like a duck or a goose or . . ." she waved the knife vaguely in the air, "whatever, the chef will prepare it for dinner. Breakfast starts at four. I'm not signing up for that shift, no way. I need my beauty sleep."

"Sounds very….lively."

"And then, there's that business with the nicknames. Everyone gets a nickname, whether they like it or not. They call me Dolphin Girl, because of that pin I wear, you know." She tapped where her collar would be.

Grace nodded.

"It's not bad," Celia said, "compared to some of them. Jonezie for Josie, that girl who's kind of. . . retarded? Warren's name is SJ for Slim Jim, on account of his long, lean physique. Tony is Tiny. And there's Phil A."—Celia spelled out the name on her napkin—"or Filet, like a piece of meat. Get it?"

Grace laughed, shaking her head. Celia liked to make her sister laugh—she could be too serious, sometimes.

"For the longest time," Celia went on, chewing thoughtfully, "I thought there must be another Phil: Phil B. or Phil W., but there isn't. His real name is Philemon, sounds just like *filet mignon*." Celia paused to swallow. "I'm not sure what it's all about, the nicknames. Some kind of power thing, about who makes them up . . ."

Grace was on her feet, taking her plate to the sink. Then she opened her purse on the counter, searching inside. "Nothing so exciting at the hospital, I'm afraid—except, of course, people dying on occasion. And babies being born."

"You'll never guess what Wanda's nickname is."

Grace wagged her keys at Celia, and then headed toward the hall closet. "Sorry, Celia, I have to run. Tell me later, OK?"

Celia had forgotten Grace had a meeting, which would probably run late. She was out a lot. Sometimes they barely saw each other during the day.

"Sure," said Celia. She heard Grace at the door, and then her footsteps returning to the kitchen, where she stood in her fall coat, a scarf around her neck. Celia was sitting chin in hand.

"Wanda the Wonder?" Grace said. "Is that it?"

Celia looked up with a half-smile. "No." Then she caught her sister's eye, waiting. "Chips or Chipper like a chipmunk. She has these round cheeks and a little chin and, you know, she's brown with brown hair and a few freckles. But it's funny because she's not really very cheerful at all."

"That's a good one," Grace said. Her lips twitched, between a smile and something else. "Celia, I know you're here by yourself a lot. Haven't you met anyone you can do things with? Someone your age or your kind of interests?"

Celia met her sister's gaze. "Don't you have to go?"

"They always start late; I don't need to be the first one there."

Celia exhaled. "There are lots of nice people. Anita, but she's like thirty-something, and a mother. Wanda's my age, but she's so private about everything and she doesn't have a car, either." She put down her fork. "Not really."

Grace hiked her tote bag to her shoulder. "You know, some of the nurses and physical therapists go to a club in Weston, country and blue grass music, some rock. Roxanne says it's a lot of fun." That was one of Grace's friends from the hospital, a fellow nurse. "Maybe we could go out with them sometime."

"Sure," Celia said. But, really, she was thinking *awkward.* They were all so much older, with serious jobs, and worked in the hospital. There would be talk about blood and tube feedings and rehab, all that unpleasant stuff.

"That would be great." And then, "You'd better go, Grace. You know how you hate to be late."

Toward the end of lunch on Friday, Celia spotted a new customer at one of her tables. A single man, and not a hunter. He was approaching thirty, with a few gray hairs and a healthy tan, nicely put together in a dark suit. She could tell his eyes were following her as she finished up at a table of slow-pokes and assumed he was looking for quick service. Celia approached his table with an apologetic smile and friendly hello. As she leaned in to take his order, she could make out the scent of cologne, pleasant, subtle, and probably expensive.

He returned her greeting with a smile, and a tip of his head, checking her out certainly, but in a relaxed, discrete way.

"Good afternoon, Celia." He was looking at her name tag. "I am so looking forward to a nice lunch. It's my first time here, but several of my colleagues have recommended it. Is it as good as they say?"

Off the top of her head, Celia replied, "Everything I've tried has been good, and I can honestly say there are few complaints about the food."

"And the service?" he asked.

"I try my best," Celia said, blushing. She wasn't sure what he was up to, but hoped he would just let her take the order. *Come on,* she thought. *You're a little old for me, mister.*

"I'm sure you do," the man nodded. "In fact, I know you do. A good friend of mine, Mike Casey, told me about a charming young lady with bright blue eyes and beautiful blond hair who waited on him last week. That must be you."

Now Celia was totally embarrassed, but the way he held her eyes, she couldn't look away. She did her best to think of something smart to say. It wouldn't come.

"It could have been anyone," she said, holding out the order pad in front of her as a sort of shield, hoping her pen at the ready would remind the man of food and drink.

"No," he disagreed. "Mike said how you were so friendly and fun to talk to."

Me and my big mouth, Celia thought, now recalling this Mike who had been promoting her to his friends. She scanned the room to see whether her other tables might be looking for service. But no, her other tables were empty, except the two couples she had just been to. She did see Roland passing through the dining room, looking with interest. Also, Eldridge and Josie were on duty at their stations, making no attempt to pretend they were not watching.

"I'm still new here, and believe me, I get mixed up plenty of times," she said, looking back into light, expectant eyes. "Now you've said that, I'll probably do something stupid."

"Oh, no," the man said. "It doesn't matter about the food. Bring me a bowl of soup, and I'll be satisfied." He paused. "I'm sorry to put you on the spot like this. I've been on a dull, dull business trip, on my own for the last week, and I was just trying to make conversation. I hope you don't mind."

Celia relaxed her stance. "No, of course not. I enjoy talking to customers, and it's not busy. You know my name is Celia. What's yours?"

"Davis," he said. "Davis Barnes," and he shifted in his seat to pull out his wallet, which he opened to withdraw a small white business card: *Davis Barnes, of Annapolis, Maryland, Consultant in Delivery and Distribution Systems.*

"It's nice to meet you, Davis," Celia said, sliding the card into her pocket. "But I'm sure you must be hungry. Why don't you let me take your order."

"All right, as long as you promise to stop by later."

"Sure," Celia said, having overcome her initial surprise.

The lunch shift remained quiet, due perhaps to the reluctance of the retirees to fight the pouring rain. After delivering his scotch and soda, Celia stood a few minutes chatting with Davis, noting his long, shadowed cheeks and strong chin. He filled out his business suit well and had an easy-going charm. It wasn't hard to fall into a conversation about Annapolis, the Eastern Shore, and his upbringing in the mountainous western part of the state. It was nice to hear word of the outside world. Just as she was describing her first impression of the California redwoods, she detected movement and muffled voices behind her, and she had the distinct sensation they were being observed. She hurriedly finished her comment.

"Is there anything else I can get for you?"

"Just one last refill." He held out his coffee cup. "I'm supposed to get to Annapolis by four o'clock, but I have absolutely no desire to get back on the road."

Celia just smiled, and blushed again, hearing another wave of whispering in the background. As she entered the kitchen, the buzz of conversation came to a halt, and she felt twenty pairs of eyes on her. She stood in front of the pick-up area, although there were no food orders for her. With a sigh of exasperation, she turned on her heel and headed back to the dining room without a word, stopping by the coffee stand to pick up a pot for Davis.

"Thanks so much, Celia," Davis said. "That will be all, just the check, if you don't mind." Looking around the quiet dining room, he added, "Any chance you could join me for a cup? My treat."

"Thanks, but I really can't," she said, the words coming out fast. "The managers are European, and very old-fashioned about things like that. But I appreciate the offer."

She picked up the pot, ready to leave, when he placed his hand over her hand. She looked up, confused.

"Go out with me sometime?" he asked.

"I . . . I . . ." Celia stammered. She couldn't very well say he was too old. And he was very nice and attractive, for an older guy.

"I'm enchanted," he said. "You are the real thing, charming and genuine, and beautiful."

Now Celia was staring in dismay. The room was strangely silent; she knew that ears were listening.

"I can't. I just can't," she said quickly. "I'm so flattered, but I have a boyfriend back in California. He's planning to come out for the holidays, hopefully," she improvised. "He's my college sweetheart, and it's really serious, so I'm trying to stay loyal to him. I really am."

This time there were snorts and chuckles in the background, that even Davis could hear, but it didn't seem to bother him.

"That's all right, then," he replied, not in the least offended. His voice, if anything, was louder and carried across the room, reaching the few customers finishing their meals, who looked over curiously.

"How lucky he is to have a nice girlfriend like you. I hope he does come back soon and find you, and sweep you off your feet away from here." He waved his hand, and his gesture seemed to take in the dining room, downtown Sutton, and maybe the whole Eastern Shore.

Celia was dying of self-consciousness, amazed at how the whole room had become their audience. The older couple next to them smiled indulgently, while Pam whispered to Brenda, rolling her eyes.

"I'll be back this way," Davis continued, "sometime in the next few months. I'll stop by, and see how things have turned out for you. Maybe I'll be in luck. And meanwhile, if you want someone to talk to, you've got my card. Give me a call."

How pleasant he was being about this, considering he had just been rejected, publically.

"That's so kind of you," she murmured, and let him squeeze her hand. There was nothing left to do but make out the bill and collect her tip.

Oh, no! she thought, *the tip! I hope it's not too extravagant.*

He left her ten dollars on an eighteen dollar bill. What would it have been if she'd said yes?

The kitchen was alive with voices when she entered; one of the bus boys dropped his voice to imitate Davis, in front of the guys at the grill. The waitresses were huddled by the coffee and hot water machines. They looked up when she passed, and Brenda murmured, "Our very own Cinderella."

Well, all right, it was kind of funny, but not that funny. Why were they making such a big deal about it?

"Hey, Dolphin Girl, how come you won't go out with that white dude?" asked Jeremy, never one to mince words. All the guys behind the grill stood at attention.

"That is none of your business," she said, wheeling away.

At the drink station, she poured herself a cold milk, overhearing snatches of her words and then what Davis had said, summing up her role, and then his. Downing the last of her drink, she couldn't take it anymore, and went into the break room, where she found Roland and Tony finishing up their lunches.

"Here's Celia," said Roland, dabbing his lips, rising and pushing in his chair. "I hear you've got an admirer. What's the problem? Too old? Too slick? He wasn't bad at all, that I could tell. Picky. Picky."

Tony pointed at Roland's empty chair, and Celia sat down. "Roland, give me a couple minutes, OK?"

Roland nodded and was gone.

"That was embarrassing," she admitted to Tony.

"I didn't see it, except at the end," he said. "I was worried he might get down on a knee."

"Come on, Tony," Celia said. "Not you, too. Why is everyone making such a fuss? It's my business."

"Not around here, it's not." Tony said, turning to face her. "Listen, Celia, this is how it is. People here don't know what to make of you, and some of them are jealous of the attention and the tips. They thought you made up that story about your boyfriend because you didn't want any of these guys asking you out."

"Why would they think that about me?"

"Who knows? You're an unknown quantity. There's no evidence of a real boyfriend, and besides, out of sight, out of mind. I'm sorry to say that's how it works with a lot of people."

Celia frowned, drumming her fingers on the table. "Is that supposed to make me feel better?"

Tony considered. "No, I guess not. But now, at least, they don't think it's just a line to keep the homeboys away. Obviously, you used it on that prime gentleman out there. So, now they just think you're foolish and deluded, about some boy back in California who is past history. Right? You haven't seen him since when?"

Celia calculated. "Three months, almost four."

Was it true how they saw her? Was it true that's how the world works?

Tony, surprisingly, put his arm around her. "I know how it is. Believe me, I've been there. But, you know what?"

"What?"

"I believe you," he said simply. "I believe in true love. So too bad for the rest of them. Let them think what they will. Just shake it off, Celia. Grab a quick lunch, and come to Peebles with Roland and me. We're doing some early Christmas shopping."

"No, thanks, Tony," she smiled at the petite young man, who rose and straightened his bow tie. "But I feel better. Thank you."

"Listen . . ." Tony added. "We're going to have a little party, and you've got to come. Some friends down from D.C., old college pals." He batted his eyes. "A few theater folks and musicians. People a little better suited to your taste and culture."

Celia's eyes widened. "That sounds great! I am so dying to dress up and have some fun."

"I'll fill you in later." He turned to leave, carrying his tray with leftovers. Celia realized how hungry she was, peckish and perhaps over-sensitive. It was sustenance she needed, and calories. She returned to the kitchen, standing in front of the food counter.

"Pork roast and butternut squash," she requested, followed by a less than gracious "Please." She ignored the grins, until she found Warren standing at attention by her side.

"You don't know, none of you. I bet a guy would wait for Celia," Warren declared in front of anybody listening.

She turned her head, blushing. He had come to her defense. Now the guys behind the grill, Jeremy, Phil A., Cuffie, even Jay, looked skeptically at the two of them, but no one said another thing.

"Have lunch with me, Warren," Celia said. "I saved a seat for you," she added, hoping it would throw a little of that business back in their faces. "And help me decide how I should spend all that money I made today." She decided to round up Wanda, who, like Switzerland, had declared her neutrality in the battle over Celia's affairs. Well, she never showed any interest in romance, so why start now? Anyway, the shift was over. Enough silliness for one day.

They ate quickly and then got their jackets, preparing to leave in the pelting rain. There was one more obstacle to get past: Josie, hanging at the doorway, watching for Celia. Not to be outdone style-wise, Josie had taken to wearing barrettes with flowers and butterflies, suitable for children, which annoyed Celia to no end.

"Hey," Josie said. Her good eye was trained on Celia. "Why you turn that man down?"

"Josie, would you move, please?" Celia said. "You're blocking the door."

"You some kind of fool," Josie said, wrinkling her nose. "He look just like the man on the wedding cake. And he rich, you can smell it."

Josie took one step sideways, and Celia walked by, unable to keep a scowl off her face. It was almost too much—called a fool by someone not right in the head. But Josie had got the last word.

On the way toward the town center, Wanda had nothing to say, and yet, Celia had the impression that she was somehow pleased with the outcome of the afternoon, like Celia had come out ahead.

As they parted ways, Wanda lifted her head enough to flash Celia a shy smile. Celia had to laugh to herself, *what a pair*: she in her purple raincoat and Wanda with a rubber slicker and overstretched wool cap pulled down almost to her chunky glasses. Then, walking blindly along the sidewalk, she began to replay the whole affair from Wanda's eyes, seeing Celia and Davis from across the room. Of course, it was a compliment to be asked out by a well-groomed, apparently successful and well-mannered gentleman like Davis. And, whatever Wanda might think her motives were, she had said no to that man, who had been, or could be, a ticket to something, or somewhere, better than waiting tables at the Grand Marsh Inn. So what, that she got that invitation by virtue of her youth, her looks, and her hair, not to mention her skin color. But Celia had decided to stay as she was—just another waitress making her own way, still a part of Wanda's world.

When Celia arrived at the apartment building doorway, she had to shake off the rain from her fingers to open her purse for the keys, but she had a smile on her face. In spite of the heckling at the Inn, she had come out all right; in fact, thanks to Davis Barnes, she had done pretty well for herself.

Chapter 6

After another long, busy shift, Celia stood in the back hall with her pockets full of money, no place to go and nothing to do. It had remained a gray, overcast day, but not raining. Shopping? There was really nothing she wanted, and she was trying to save money. A walk? The library? Boring, boring. What was lacking, she decided, was fun, and company. Someone to pal around with, and gossip a little, like back at college.

The kitchen had emptied out pretty quickly. The other waitresses tended to make a bee-line out after lunch to get home for kids, laundry, soap operas. Only Wanda remained, carefully putting away her earnings in her bag, slowly buttoning her brown, shapeless sweater. Too bad she didn't pull herself together more. She had a mind like a calculator and could total up orders in a flash. Wanda reminded Celia of one of her step-brothers—smart, all right, but not much in the way of social skills. She was kind of a nerd, a black, girl nerd, but not in a bad way. Not everyone could have Celia's easy manners.

Wanda pulled on her knit cap, heading out, probably on the way to the bank or something. Unless Celia stopped her. Quickly, Celia crossed the room, blocking Wanda's exit.

"Hey, how about a beer and a slice at the Pizza Palace?" Celia said. Neither of them had finished the "hunter's stew" lunch special.

Wanda's face screwed up, ready to decline, as soon as she could think of a decent reason.

"I know you like to play those video games," Celia coaxed. "I've heard the guys talk about you. Pretty good, apparently."

A slow smile came to Wanda's lips, then her eyes.

"True?"

"Pretty much."

"Just for an hour. Something to do; won't kill you." Really, Celia didn't want to say that she just didn't want to go back to the quiet apartment. "I know you have money coming out your ears. Just like me."

Wanda was wavering.

"Oh, come on, Wanda," Celia said. Wanda shrugged, giving in.

The Pizza Palace was already crowded, and very warm inside, almost steamy. Celia's hair floated up around her shoulders. They took a back booth and ordered a large pizza. After their beers arrived, they sat in silence. Celia glanced at the video games on the back wall.

"All right," she said, pointing at Pac Man. "I guess I'll try. Even though I know you're going to beat me."

They moved over to the stools by the video machines, where Wanda put quarters in to start the game. Celia stood behind, sipping her beer, barely able to follow the game play. The buzzes and beeps were annoying and the blinking lights were bothering her eyes. Wanda played with a silent intensity, clearly master of the game. Then Celia took her turn, playing wildly with spirit, but within a few minutes, she was dead and out of it, conceding victory.

"I'm next," a deep voice behind Celia announced. She turned to see a slight, dark-haired man with a thin face. He had a five o'clock shadow over pale skin and hairy forearms where his sleeves were rolled up. Although his suit was conservative, he sported a loud, red-striped tie.

"Larry," Wanda said, sucking in her plump cheeks and jutting out her jaw.

"Wanda, you are good, you are good," the man said. He barely seemed to notice Celia. "More ability in your little pinky than any of these jokers— except me. I've beat you a couple times."

"Not in a while," Wanda said, with the slightest trace of a smile. Celia smirked. She couldn't help it. Wanda was being almost flirtatious, for her. Larry had to pass behind Wanda to take the vacant stool, and Celia noticed that his hand rested briefly on her shoulder as he squeezed by.

Wanda won. After the game with Larry, they returned to their table, the pizza set on a stand on the table with a stack of paper plates and napkins. Celia wondered if Larry would join them, but he put on his jacket and left. At the booth, they slid in to the benches. Celia took a knife to divide and serve the pizza.

"Interesting guy," she said, holding a slice in front of Wanda, "that Larry. Does he come here a lot?"

She got nothing from Wanda but a shrug, then prolonged silence as the pizza hovered over Wanda's plate. Celia gave up, giving Wanda a slice and then serving herself. Just as she was replacing the knife, a familiar voice boomed behind her, male and merry.

"Look at the two of you," said Warren, his eyes alight with happy surprise. "That pizza looks good. And beer!"

There was nothing to do but invite him to join them. He carried a glass of beer back to the table and slid in next to Wanda, helping himself to a slice.

"Isn't that something, you girls out for a good time," Warren said.

Hardly, thought Celia, but she was glad to see Warren. Wanda was not exactly a party girl.

"More like drowning our sorrows in beer," she teased. "After putting up with all those demanding customers—or even you tough guys at the grill."

"Not me," Warren said, a little foam mustache over his lip. "I'm just a little ray of sunshine." That was kind of true. Warren was such a happy-go-lucky guy, never in a bad mood. Bright, well-spoken, unfailingly cheerful.

"Mr. Sunshine," Celia agreed.

"And you, you . . . you're like that little thing that slides down the rainbow."

Celia was stumped. "A leprechaun?"

"Yeah, yeah," Warren said, his head pumping. "Something like that. Little Miss Lucky Charms, always ends up with the pot of gold."

Celia burst out laughing, not sure if he was playing her or not, if it was some kind of flirtation or not.

"Oh, right, that's me, for sure. What about Wanda, here? She's making plenty of money too."

"Yeah," Warren agreed. "But she's all up to her secret plans; more like the mad genius type. Nobody knows what goes on up here." He tapped the side of his head.

"Warren!" Celia was a bit shocked, but Wanda didn't blink an eye. In fact, she finally looked relaxed, for her.

"That's all right," Warren said. "Me and Wanda, we go way back. Some kind of cousins, right?" He poked Wanda with his elbow. "Oh, we're all cousins around here."

"Really?"

"For sure. Cuffie, Phil A., Josie, all of us are related someway or another. Family everywhere; can't get away from it."

"Except me," Celia said, a bit ruefully. "Well, except for my sister, of course."

Warren gave her a look. "You never know," he said, a crooked smile appearing. "Might be our long-lost white cousins, come home at last. Could happen."

"Ha!" said Celia, with a giggle. "I doubt it."

Around them, every table was full, including families and young professionals. Some black and some white, one of the mixing places in town. Wasn't it something how something like pizza brought people together? Warren and Wanda were on to some gossip at the Inn, somebody Celia didn't know, but she sat back, nibbling at her slice. The complaints, the comments, the teasing even, not so different from being out with her friends in Santa Cruz. Celia finished another glass of beer, along with the pizza. As hot as it was, she took off her sweater, feeling full and relaxed. Wanda was smiling, enjoying herself. Warren, of course, could have a good time anywhere. Her new comrades, she said to herself, her friends and amigos. The banter, the argument—it was just like college, almost. Only none of them were actually enrolled.

And then, like a scene from a bad movie, Warren's face dropped and he twisted in his seat, ready to duck under the table or flee. He had caught sight of something beyond Celia's shoulder that apparently had spooked him badly.

Celia turned to look. No police. No bad guys. A young black woman, their age, had entered the front doorway, stepping up to the counter. She was a full-figured girl in tight-fitting clothes and a pouty mouth. Pretty, though, with the long nails.

"Pick-up, please," the girl said.

"Got to go," said Warren scrambling to his feet. Lines of worry, or maybe terror, had crossed his face.

"No! Wait! What's the matter?" said Celia. Wanda was looking, too, at the young woman, causing the corner of her lips to curl up. No guns or violence, anyway, Celia decided, surprised at her own jumpiness.

"Boy's room," Warren got out, sprinting toward the back of the restaurant, bumping into the chair of an old-timer.

"Hey, boy!" he shouted, but Warren had turned the corner, disappearing from sight.

Celia turned to Wanda. "What the heck? Is he hiding from that girl, or what?"

"Might say that," Wanda agreed, but she wouldn't be pressed for more details. Celia watched the girl another moment, drumming her keys on the counter. When the teenage boy brought out the pizza box, she opened it, letting the steam out.

"You call that pepperoni pizza?" she said, loud enough for most of the room to hear. "There's hardly anything on here."

The boy shrugged.

"Put some more on, and pop it back in the oven."

"Can't," the boy said. "Oven's full."

The young woman puffed out her cheeks. "Oh, fine. Just get me the pepperoni, and I'll do it myself at home."

The boy retreated into the kitchen, returning with a small paper plate of pepperoni, which the girl took from him, placing it inside the box and handing over the money. Wanda and Celia watched, eyebrows arched and grinning, until the girl left.

"Whoa," said Celia.

In a moment, Warren reappeared, looking furtively right to left as he made his way back to the booth and sat down.

"Sly dog," Wanda said into her beer glass. "I guess Celia doesn't know about your baby's mama?"

"Baby!" Celia cried, practically jumping out of her seat. Oh, my God, what another surprise, all these crazy people. "Seriously? You—a father?"

He nodded.

"Oh, my goodness. That's incredible." Another image of Warren in his kitchen whites came to her, this time with a little baby over his shoulder spitting up on a napkin.

Warren looked away, down at the table. "Baby boy, named Troy. That girl, Cheryl, we went out in high school and she got pregnant. Everyone said I had to help out."

Celia slapped the table. "Well, of course. There's no question about that."

"But we're not together anymore." His jaw began working, even without food. "I can't stand her. I wish I never had to see her again. She told me she was taking birth control. She showed me the pills, but she didn't use them. She wanted a baby. She didn't have anything else, no job, no plans, so she got this baby on me. I had my sights on college; I did pretty well at school. Instead, I ended up full-time at the Inn. After the baby was born, last summer, she was living at her mom's and I've been giving her money every month." A dark expression crossed his face. "That's my life, too, she was fooling with. I didn't want to be a father, not yet. Now she's got what she wanted, her own apartment, the federal aid, you know—welfare. That was her whole plan."

Celia sat back, open-mouthed. "I can't believe that someone would do that deliberately."

Warren gestured helplessly, looking to Wanda.

"That's what she did," Wanda confirmed. "She used to talk about it at school. She not the only one, either, lots of other girls too. Black and white. That's how they get out from home, start their own life."

"But there's a baby to take care of!"

"That's right," Wanda said. "Give them something to do. They're not going to school, anyway. No money; nobody encouraging them. And what kind a job they going to get? Might as well be a mother, have your own place."

Suddenly, Warren looked so glum and forlorn, Celia felt bad. She might have come down a little hard, a little righteous even, without meaning to. But it had come as a bit of a shock, this other side of Warren's life she had no idea about. Really quite serious and a lot for him to deal with. And what about his dreams, dashed like her own?

"Warren . . ."

ERIN L. MCCORMACK

The waitress appeared with the bill. It was nothing at all, really, compared to what they charged at the Inn. Celia pulled her wallet out of her purse, as the others put money on the table.

"Wait a second," she said, not moving from the table. "Warren, why don't you think about going to college now? They're OK for the moment, right, the baby and, uh, his mother? You could take some classes; work part-time. I don't see why not."

"You really think they'll take me?"

"Oh, definitely," Celia said. "Once they see how smart you are, serious, hardworking." Maybe it was the beer, but she was getting worked up. "At least put in an application, and see what happens. You can do it, Warren."

"Aw," he said, his face falling. "I don't know if I can face that application. So many pages, and you have to write a little story about yourself."

Celia pondered this a moment. "The essay," she declared, finally. "Don't worry. I'll help you. We'll make it look really good." She swallowed a burp. "We have to believe in ourselves, first, if we want other people to believe in us."

Warren appeared awestruck at her impromptu speech, while Wanda was more like dumbstruck.

Celia raised her empty glass. "So, how about a toast, to Warren and his future?"

His smile was flickering back, but Wanda was frowning. "What about me? Don't I have a future, too?"

"To all of us, then, and our great futures." They clinked glasses, and Warren's face lit up to his eyebrows.

"May we meet again in thirty years, rich and famous," he said. "Or at least fat and happy." He let out that patented, irresistible laugh, his good humor restored. Celia was glad to see his spirits lifted, and a flush of warmth and good will radiated through her body. They got up from the booth, ready to pay the tab and head out from the sauna to the cool gray twilight.

Celia stepped outside the door, watching as the street lights started to blink on. It wasn't late, but she wasn't eager to return to the apartment, unlikely to see anyone else for the rest of the day. They stood clumped on the sidewalk, sated with pizza and beer.

"Want to come over to my place?" she asked, suddenly.

"Nah," said Wanda.

"Sure," said Warren. "Where is it?"

"Not far. Maybe ten minutes."

"Ain't got time," Wanda said.

"We can walk Celia home, anyhow," Warren said, shaking his head at Wanda.

"I suppose."

Celia couldn't help smiling. Warren, of course, was being friendly and polite. Wanda acted like she was going to have a tooth pulled. They set off while she explained about Grace and the hospital, and how she'd come to Sutton. And then they were at the modest doorway of her modest apartment building, and Celia fumbled for her keys at the bottom of her purse.

They heard a car door shut behind them, followed by footsteps on the sidewalk. Automatically, as if a signal was given, Warren and Wanda started turning away.

"Wait. It might be Grace," Celia said. "You can meet her."

She got the door open and flicked on the front light with Warren and Wanda next to her. It wasn't Grace's face that appeared up the walkway, but the nursing supervisor, home late from work or shopping, glowering at the three of them.

"Oh, hello!" Celia called out. "I thought it was Grace."

"Well, it's not," the woman said, taking in the two faces behind Celia. She said nothing, walking around them into the entrance hall, and shutting the door behind her with a bang.

Celia, Warren, and Wanda giggled.

"Oops," Celia said. "Wrong person. You can meet Grace another time. If you come again, we can watch TV or put on some music. I'll make cookies!"

"You sure you want us back?" Warren asked, only half-teasing.

"Of course."

"I don't think she does," Wanda pointed with her chin.

"No, maybe not. She doesn't like me, either, for some reason. I really don't know why. It's a mystery, I tell you."

She waved them off. "Until next time."

Wanda shrugged.

"There will be a next time," Celia declared. "There's no reason we can't hang out here between shifts. And," she rattled on, inspired, "we'll invite some other people from the Inn, too. Lacey or Phil A. That tall girl, Vanessa. We can play cards or you can teach me some cool black dance moves." It sounded great to her. Warren was beaming and Wanda began to crack a smile.

"Bye, Celia," was all she said with a flip of her hand.

"See you guys later."

A few days later, early in the morning, Celia found out the reason Nurse Harrison was so unhappy with her. She was lying on the sofa and heard Grace's steps going down the stairs, the sound of female voices, and then Grace coming back up the stairs. When she opened the door, Celia had pushed herself upright on her elbow, rubbing her eyes.

"It's Francine Harrison," Grace said, making a face. "She wants to talk to you—to us. Just grab a sweater."

At the bottom of the stairs, in the joint front hallway, Francine Harrison, Nursing Supervisor, was dressed for work and not smiling. She held firm to the traditional cap, white dress and white shoes, while other nurses, like Grace, sometimes wore more work-like scrubs.

"It's this door," she said, as soon as Celia arrived, Grace behind her. "It's got to be locked, at all times. That is the rule."

Celia opened her mouth, and then shut it.

"Twice I've come home in the afternoon and found it unlocked. And now, this morning, I checked and it was not locked. I believe you, young lady, were the last one in. We never had this problem until you came."

"Oh, I . . ." Celia started. Her feet were cold in the unheated stairway. "I must have forgotten."

"That is no excuse," Nurse Harrison said. "Do you realize if someone wanted to rob us, we have practically invited them in? The insurance company would never take a claim seriously. Nor should they." She paused for effect. "Or worse. We could be attacked at night in our own homes. Once someone gets through the front door, they could get to either of us."

What Celia felt like saying was, "I didn't realize it was such a high crime neighborhood." And then, "Who's going to attack you, you old prune?" But she didn't.

"I promise," she said, "I'll make sure the door is locked—every time."

As she headed back upstairs, Celia wondered if it was because of her friends that Nurse Harrison was so worked up, not that they made much noise. It was such a small, quiet town. And they had so little to rob. But she had gotten the message; she was not to forget to lock the door. Ever. Or else . . . or else something bad, for Celia and for her sister.

Chapter 7

Warm, mellow October and hunting season was in full force at the Grand Marsh Inn. In the late afternoon, Celia had to step around the bird carcasses on the floor, waiting to be cleaned, stuffed, and roasted. The orders were non-stop, no real breaks, just time for a quick bite and trip to the ladies' room. The dining room was hot, noisy, and crowded with hunters celebrating their success. Celia found herself struggling to keep up, especially with the drink orders, and a couple times Wanda and Anita stepped in to help. Once she almost dropped a bowl of soup, when a man's hand slid from her elbow to her backside, cupping her bum before she pulled away. Her bright-eyed cheer started wearing a little thin.

In the kitchen to pick up an order, she reminded herself, "Game face, game face."

Just then, Anita passed. "Ooh, that lemon must be sour."

Celia was focused on balancing her tray. Anita stepped closer, catching her eye. Her hand rose toward Celia's chin.

"How about I tickle you?"

Celia glowered, then Anita made like she was going toward her armpit.

"How about here?"

Gripping the tray, Celia had to laugh. "Ha, ha. Very funny. Want this tray on your head?"

"That way, girl, that way," Anita skipped away, pointing toward the dining room. Celia blew a raspberry at her and pushed her way through the double doors, but there was a smile on her face.

The very hardest service, in Celia's experience, was in the Grille, the room on the other side of the bar, open all day for light meals. During hunting season, if a group of fifteen or twenty hunters all arrived at the same time, they were served family style in the Grille. Two rows of long tables were lined up end to end, no table cloths. The advantage, of course, was being so close to the bar. The problem was that there was little room to maneuver between tables. Celia sometimes felt like she was running the gauntlet, all those protruding arms and legs and elbows. And the hands, the hands! Plus, the noise! Sometimes it was like lip-reading to get an order.

Some of the men, she had to admit, were real sweethearts, beaming with health, wealth, and satisfaction. Most of them were middle-aged, from out of town. But some of the local men joined them, old granddads and younger men. Some of them really cute, and probably rich, and always smiling at Celia. Celia couldn't deny that the Grille was a festive, rollicking place. More than one hunter wanted to show off their dog; and more than one wanted to have a picture taken with Celia. The older guys liked to slip her extra bills, hand to hand, even on top of the very generous tips. Who was she to say no?

The trouble was if a group came in at noon and spent the afternoon drinking, then things started to get sloppy, and fresh, including the language. Then Celia preferred the dining room with the couples and businessmen, and civic groups. It was quieter and less hazardous.

Celia was surprised when Mrs. Becker handed her a slip for *Delivery, Room 326*—Room Service—her first time. And even more surprised when Anita flew to her side and plucked it away.

"You don't want to do that," she said. "Not now, not those guys. Let me take it, and you can finish my six-top. It's just desserts and coffee. Come on, I'll set you up."

"Are you sure that's all right?" Celia asked, trailing after her. She was relieved, but a little disappointed not to finally see another part of the hotel— "the upper realms."

"I'll tell Mrs. Becker I'm going up." And then, as she studied the slip, under her breath, "I don't know what she's thinking," making Celia wonder if Anita thought she, Celia, couldn't handle room service. What, exactly, was going on up there? Gambling? Orgies? What?

Wanda had followed Celia and Anita into the kitchen, where they stood at the dessert station, assembling plates and bowls. "I told my table they got no more dark meat from those birds, and now they crying about it. Big babies."

"I certainly hope you didn't say it like that," Anita frowned, placing slices of pie and cake on the tray. Celia was in charge of scooping ice cream. "I know you finished high school. So why don't you help yourself and speak better English?"

"Stop picking on me," Wanda retorted. Then she continued, a syllable at a time: "I can talk like that if I need to." Then she switched back with a crank of her neck and a twist of her lips. "Why should I, if it's just us?"

Celia's mouth opened in surprise. Perhaps it was like formal and informal forms in French and other languages. She would have to ask Wanda about it— another time. At the moment she was tickled and rather pleased to be included in the "us." Across the way, they had an audience. Jay, the assistant grill chef, was watching the three ladies at the sweets station with a bemused look, almost a smile. Unlike Virgil, he was soft-spoken and even-tempered during the rush times. When Celia caught his eye, he didn't look away. But neither did he wink, thank God. She liked the smooth tone of his dark skin against the white uniform, and his very perfect teeth. Handsome, Celia thought, but not all that friendly. Too bad he didn't smile more.

Anita wouldn't be deterred. "How much did you get from that table of eight?"

"None of your business," Wanda said.

"I got sixty dollars from a two hundred dollar check, because they like me and they like my style. I know you didn't do that well. But you could. How about you, Celia, honey? You're looking a little flustery. Everything OK?"

"I guess so. I just can't keep up with them all, trying to talk to me at the same time."

"That's right," Anita nodded, spooning the whipped cream. "They want to be the one to get your attention. You've got to keep the ball up in the air, like you haven't made up your mind yet, who's the most desirable of all those sweaty, chubby he-men. That's how the tips come on. If they rub you on the bum, you give them a stern look and say, 'Buns are not on the menu.' Then you smile. They just can't wait to give that money away. You've got bills to pay. You're the one in charge. That money is yours."

Anita finished the last bowl. "All set, Celia. I'm going up." Anita waltzed out of the room. Gazing after her, Celia tilted her head to one side. Anita's attitude seemed a bit more commercial, or you might say cynical, than what you'd expect from someone so Christian.

In the dining room, passing out coffee and desserts to her group of rowdy hunters, Celia wondered if she could ever say the words that Anita had said. Not likely. Not her. She'd just have to get by with tepid smiles and stay away from roving hands.

During a brief lull between shifts, Tony sat down with Celia in the break room. His pale little mustache twitched. "You OK, Celia, dear?"

Celia put down her glass of milk, drained. "Barely. You know, last night I dreamt I was being attacked by ducks and geese, feathers all over the place."

Tony smiled sympathetically. "But you're doing great, really, for being thrown into it. Just remember the money. It will all be over soon, and won't we be sorry. Don't forget—next week is the party, Thursday night. No gifts, unless you want to bring a bottle of wine."

"Yeah, thanks, Tony. Just tell me how to get there. And your phone number."

On the back of her order pad, Celia jotted down directions to their house, a neighborhood just on the edge of town that she knew was a little older and a bit run down. The back of her mind was wondering what kind of party this was going to be. But she had so few invitations, she wasn't going to turn it down. And she was sure it would be interesting.

Roland appeared with his food, taking a seat next to Celia. "Ah, party plans."

"So, who else is invited, anyone from here?" Celia asked. And then, with sudden inspiration, "Eldridge?"

Roland and Tony laughed, rather too loudly.

"Just because he's gay?" Roland replied, stirring his soup. "You think we're one big support group? Sorry to shoot your balloon, but he's not on the guest list."

"Seriously, Celia." Tony was leaning on his elbows across the table. "He's a bit strange, a little creepy, like. . ."

"A spider?" Celia blurted out. "A caterpillar?" Things that Eldridge reminded her of sometimes.

"An undertaker," Tony said, with a roll of his eyes. "That deep voice, the long face. Put a long black coat on him—can't you see him greeting mourners at a funeral?"

"More like a corpse, I was thinking," Roland put in—just for effect, Celia knew. "No—a cadaver, I mean. That's the word I was thinking of. Don't tell me he doesn't look like death warmed over."

"You guys are terrible," Celia scolded, cleaning the crumbs around her plate. "How can you talk about the poor guy like that?"

"Oh, there's worse," Roland went on with a glint in his eye. "We suspect him of being a male prostitute. For the guys who come from out of town, looking for some anonymous action."

"No!" Celia said, both shocked and angry, although she didn't know for sure that it wasn't true.

"He has nobody regular in town that we know of, and he hangs out at the Starlight and talks to these old dudes, who come up to see him. What else do you think it is?"

"I'm not even listening to you," she said, primly. "Well, then, will there be anyone I know? How about Anita?"

"Oh, I don't think so," Roland said. "She's got a prayer meeting to attend, or something. You do realize, don't you, that she would be casting stones at all our petty foibles?"

Celia had noticed that relations between Roland and Anita were not the warmest. They worked well together and made a great team in the dining room, but didn't appear to socialize much. It was true; Anita was serious about her church stuff. Still, she could be a lot of fun.

Roland had just finished his soup when Mrs. Becker appeared at the doorway, her sleek head and sharp nose like a bird of prey.

"To your stations, please; another group has arrived."

Celia jumped to her feet, grabbing her dishes to drop on the bussing cart. Roland and Tony followed her through the kitchen.

"Whores, all of us," Roland sneered, when Mrs. Becker was out of hearing. "What we do for money."

"Fill me in later, about the party" Celia said, passing through the swinging doorways and catching view of her table of ten damp and hungry men. "Oh, my."

After the last of her tables departed, Celia popped into the ladies' room to wash the Crème Brule from her fingers. Catching herself in the mirror, she almost laughed. What a sight! Her face was shiny and pink from the heat and the exertion. The coins in her pockets pulled down her uniform, while the bills puffed out her thighs. Placing her hands on the counter, she inhaled deeply. Without counting, she knew it was the most money she'd ever made for a day's work. It was dizzying the way the money was adding up. Maybe she and Grace could plan a little getaway—a trip to New York City to see a show? Or, could there really be enough to think about returning to college for spring semester? No, that would be a miracle. More likely, she should wait it out until the fall. But perhaps a car, a used one. Oh, the possibilities.

"You silly," she told her reflection as she dried her hands. What did she need a car for, if she was just going to walk to work with nowhere else to go? She grabbed a paper towel to wipe a glob of gravy from her apron before returning to the dining room to finish up.

Done, finally. In the hallway, she clocked out and took her sweater off the hook. She couldn't even button it closed over all the money she was carrying. She should have stopped by the cashier, but she waited too late. Now she was weighed down by all that coinage and would jingle like a belled cat all the way home. Oh, how she wished she had a magic chariot to transport her. Or, a way to click her heels like Dorothy in Oz to get back home. She had looked into riding Grace's bike to the Inn, but there was no rack to lock it, and they wouldn't let her keep it inside. Now that was a picture, her pedaling away with all that money in her pockets; more like the witch than Dorothy.

"What you smiling at?" Jay came up next to her, jacket over his arm. "They's no one here."

"I know," she said, helpless with fatigue. "I mean, I don't know why, I just am."

He studied her a moment. "You like it here? Being a waitress?" he asked.

"It's pretty good," she nodded. "The money is great. But the work is hard, harder than I thought. It's good for now, I guess."

"You a college girl, right?"

Just for a second, she wondered if he was teasing her for sounding so simple.

"Yup, in California," she said.

"Maybe that's why you so sunny." Jay smiled at his own joke. But the look behind his eyes was serious, probing. "Always so polite and cheerful to everybody, even those punks behind the grill."

Celia's eyebrows shot up—Jeremy, did he mean? A flutter ran through her chest, to think he was watching her, noticing her so closely.

"I kind of have to be," she said. "Don't I? I depend on them to get my orders, and I might as well be on friendly terms. Does that seem strange to you?"

"Nah, that's cool."

"Why do you ask?" she said.

"No reason at all. Just making conversation." He was ready to move on. Celia looked at him briefly, his fine lips, his dark curly hair matted down with some kind of gel that made it glisten. He was surely handsome. But he wasn't much of a talker, and not much of a smiler, either.

Jay pressed his lips together, regarding her. "I guess I got to go now." He pulled on his jacket, pulling his car keys out of the pocket. Then he turned back. "See you tomorrow." Celia started smiling again. "Good night." Even after the door closed behind him she was still smiling, and shook her head, thinking how foolish she must look.

Chapter 8

After the Thursday lunch shift, Celia came home and showered, stopping to pick up a bottle of wine for Tony and Roland's party. It had been a long time since her last evening out: fun clothes, good food, and interesting conversation with colorful, creative types, like some of those memorable parties at college. She pictured the happy multi-cultural—multi-sexual, you could say—group gathered around the table, discussing Reagonomics, race relations perhaps, and the so-called death of Broadway. Roland could play the piano, she knew, so maybe they would gather around and sing a few songs. She wondered if they might play games like charades, which she liked, or strip poker, which she didn't. Dress up, perhaps? What if they were in drag? She applied eyeliner with a shaky hand, laughing at her crazy imagination. *Ready for anything!*

Just at the doorway, she ran into Grace, home late from the hospital.

"Whoa!" she said, viewing Celia's outfit. "Are you in a play or something?" She closed the door behind her with an expression somewhere between stressed and amused. Of course she was teasing.

"No, silly. I'm going out tonight, a little party across town. Remember, I told you?"

Grace frowned. "Party? I thought you were just going out for drinks and food with some friends."

"Well, they are friends, from the Inn, Tony and Roland. They're hosting a party at their house."

"Hold up a minute," Grace said, coming in and putting down her things. "You sure this is a good idea? How well do you really know them? And, you're going on your own?"

"First of all, they're gay, worry-wart. So no one's going to be after me, I'm sure. Do you *not* want me to take the car?"

Grace exhaled. "No, that's not it. I trust you'll keep your wits about you. It's just . . ."

"What?" Celia couldn't imagine.

"Oh, I don't know," Grace said, frowning. "For a quiet place, people get up to some crazy stuff. There are drugs here, too, pills and cocaine. That's not just the city. I know," she shook her head. "I work at the hospital."

"Nothing like that, I'm sure," she said. "They're into Broadway and antiques, and exotic dessert drinks. I'll be fine." She blew Grace a kiss as she took the car keys from the hook on the wall.

"OK," Grace said. "Have a good time—but, be careful."

It was a short ride to the party, down a quiet side road. Tony and Roland's house, a rental, was a small white cottage, a bit run down but homey with beautiful autumn flowers in the front garden.

Tony met her at the door. "Celia, dear, so nice to see you! Come on in. You look splendid." He gave her a peck on the cheek.

He was also dressed up for the occasion, with an old-fashioned plum-colored smoking jacket, his thin brown hair smoothed back with gel. Celia had the impression that he wore a touch of blush and maybe even shadow around his eyes.

"Hi, Tony. Where is everybody? Am I early?" she asked, stepping into the front hall and peering past him. Hers was the only other car in the driveway.

"Maybe just a teensy bit. We did say eight o'clock." He took the wine from her, murmuring. "How nice," and led her into the kitchen, offering a seat at the table. "Roland's still getting ready. He just got a phone call. You know, our company tends to run late, out of pure inconsideration, I suspect. Let's get you set up with a drink."

Roland appeared in the doorway, whiskery and half-dressed, and looking more than a little put out.

"My sister!" he exclaimed.

"Manners, Roland," Tony said primly, handing a wine glass to Celia. "Say hello to Celia."

Roland took a breath.

"Hello, Celia," he said, managing a smile. "Welcome to our home." He took a moment to assess Celia's outfit, which appeared to pass muster. Then he noticed one of his shirt cuffs was undone, and began to fiddle impatiently with it until Tony stepped in to push the cufflink through. Then they took seats at the table across from Celia, Roland helping himself to a crab cake on the tray of hors d'oeuvres.

"They're on their way," Roland said, after swallowing. "Simone and Paul, from D.C., should be here shortly."

"Your sister!" Celia exclaimed. "Great. I can meet her . . . them. Is she older or younger than you?"

"Twenty-four."

Celia clapped her hands. "Just like my sister! You know I live with her, right? You'll have to meet her, Grace. She's great, my biggest supporter. Maybe she could have come. . . ."

Roland shook his head. "They're not staying. Just stopping by on their way to a meeting in Salisbury. It won't be long, thank God."

Tony blinked rapidly, and his sparse mustache appeared to twitch. "If only Paul could come without her."

This all sounded a bit strange to Celia. "What's the problem?"

Roland and Tony looked at each other. They really did look like a married couple in their cozy kitchen with a cheerful red-checkered cloth on the table, a calendar on the wall, and Mickey Mouse magnets on the refrigerator—just like the ones at home, Celia's old home.

"Simone's a bitch," Roland said, finally. "Really, I'm not exaggerating. She's a social activist, and she's on everyone's case about black power, social justice, blah, blah, blah. All that change the world stuff, and she keeps trying to drag me into it."

"She doesn't think well of white people," Tony chimed in, "especially not me."

Celia almost laughed, it sounded so improbable. "Why are they coming at all?"

"Just to abuse us," Roland said with a flutter. "And . . ." Roland looked at Tony, and stopped.

"It's like this, sweetie," Tony said breathlessly. "Paul, well he's our connection, if you know what I mean. The guy with the goods." Surely he didn't mean stolen watches?

Celia must have looked confused, so Tony spelled it out. "The nose candy, the 'caine, a little after-dinner treat. It's something we enjoy once in a while, when we can get it."

"Tony thinks it adds a little excitement to life on the Eastern Shore," Roland added dryly.

"Oh, I see." Just as Grace had said. Oh, dear. Well, it was just part of life, here or California. Celia's previous experience of people waiting to snort their next line of cocaine was not very impressive. She looked longingly at the scallops wrapped in bacon and began to wonder if the party was a good idea after all.

"So," Tony continued, "we put up with them. Be prepared," he warned Celia, "and get ready to run for cover."

Celia had to laugh, incredulous.

Roland was looking at her, now serious. "Celia can deal with her, right, Celia? She's a lot of hot air, that's all. Simone, I mean."

Then Tony started singing the Elton John song, "The Bitch . . . the Bitch is Ba-ck," and Roland left to shave and finish dressing. Celia drank down her glass of wine, which Tony promptly refilled. In spite of the dreaded Simone, he seemed upbeat as he bustled about the kitchen. Was it the cocaine he was looking forward to? Celia couldn't help thinking back to the past summer in Santa Cruz, when their neighbor, Mark, had been dealing the fine white powder out of the apartment next to hers. Late night knocks on the door, occasional shouting. The people headed to and from Mark's apartment were not a cheerful, hearty sort of crowd. Counting out napkins as Celia nursed her drink, Tony stopped suddenly. "Did you hear a car?" He peered through a window where they could see car lights pulling into the driveway. "Company!" he called out, and Celia went with him to answer the door.

Simone was not a large woman, maybe an inch taller than Celia, and a little more filled out. Attractive, but not as good-looking as her brother, with the same wide-set eyes and high cheekbones. Not as dark as her brother, either, Celia noticed. Her hair was pulled back and set off with a wide, purple headband. She wore a full-length skirt, like Celia's, with a button-down white blouse, opened to show a braided gold necklace that matched her earrings. For a social activist, she didn't have any problem with nice jewelry.

"I'm Celia, just moved here," Celia offered, breaking the silence. Paul looked her over briefly with no interest. He was tall, slender, light-complexioned, with small, refined features and metal-framed glasses. He looked like an intellectual, but not the kind, unworldly type. He merely sniffed, then made his way down the hall to the bathroom.

"Oh, yes, new girl at the Inn," Simone said, stopping there, and then for some reason looked down at Celia's feet, where Chinese slippers peeked out from under her skirt.

"Right," Celia agreed. "That's me." And then, "Roland said you were an activist. That must be very interesting, and, you know, a good feeling that you're doing something important." She paused but didn't like the silence. "In college, back in California, I was in an activist group, for protecting baby seals."

Simone's head cocked and she blinked, once. "Seals?" But there was no interest in her question, only disdain. Celia blushed, not sure if Simone's cause was just so far above hers, or she couldn't imagine Celia as a serious activist. They were not kidding about Roland's sister; she was nothing at all like Grace.

Roland appeared. "Simone," he said, not warmly.

"Brother." Her voice was just as cool.

Paul reappeared at their side, and he and Tony disappeared into the living room, to take care of business, apparently. A put-upon looking Roland led

Simone and Celia back to the kitchen, where he handed Celia her glass and poured a drink for himself.

"A glass of wine, Simone?" he said, pleasantly enough.

"No. We're about business." She frowned at Celia, clearly wishing she was not there, and then took a flyer out of her purse, putting it on the table in front of Roland: RALLY FOR REPARATIONS it said. Whatever that was. "Why don't you come on Saturday? Sing for us. Lend your voice to the cause. Do something useful."

Celia felt like a fly on the wall, pretty much invisible, as long as she didn't stir. She didn't want to reveal her complete ignorance, but she didn't see how she might slip away, or to where.

Roland bunched his face. "Don't start, Simone. I said no. I don't know how many times I've said no. As far as I'm concerned, I'm bothering no one, and what you're doing is pointless."

"Not pointless," Simone returned sharply. "It's justice, long over-due, and it won't happen without every brother and sister working for it."

Celia was even less sure if Simone meant the two of them, brother and sister, or all black men and women. Roland caught her eye, and for a moment his face softened.

"Simone's talking about reparations," he explained, "the government paying money to blacks today in reparation for the harm done by slavery a hundred years ago." And then to Simone, "A pipe dream. Ain't going to happen."

Simone's face contorted with anger. "But at least we're trying, standing up for ourselves, instead of hiding out here playing house with that little man," she sneered. "Wasting your talents. Wasting your education. All those opportunities Dad and Mom worked so hard to give us."

"Right," Roland said, just as darkly. "And now Mom and Dad want me back in D.C. making a splash with my sweetheart. A couple of queers; I don't think so."

Simone rose to her feet, clenching her hands and growling in frustration, and Celia was momentarily frightened for the appetizers laid out so beautifully on silver trays. *No, not that!* But they heard voices and footsteps in the hall.

"Forget about him," Simone hissed. "He's weak; he's nothing."

Just then Paul pushed open the door to summon Simone. Quick business, indeed. Simone grabbed her purse, leaving the flyer.

"Ready?" Paul said. He had never even acknowledged Celia's presence. She didn't even register with him. Without a good-bye or shaking hands, they were gone; only Tony was smiling.

"Party time!" he called out. And then, looking from Roland to Celia, "What? Simone? Was she that bad?"

Celia couldn't deny it. "Pretty tough." Roland still looked a bit flustered.

"Come on, come on," Tony said. "They're gone, and the night is young. We've got our party favors. Let the good times roll." With a shrug, Roland left to finish dressing, and when he reappeared, he was clean shaven and debonair, with a top hat and cane to greet his guests.

Tire wheels crunched the gravel outside, and Celia saw a set of headlights in the driveway. Within a minute, two men appeared at the doorway, whiny and querulous. The taller man related how they had gotten lost and ended up almost in Delaware. Celia recognized him from the Inn; he was one of the bakers. His date was a guy who, Celia learned, worked at the florist shop in Sutton. It was evident to Celia that they were already somewhat drunk, or high, which probably contributed to their getting lost.

More guests arrived, including a carful from D.C.: an aspiring poet, two musicians who played in a jazz band, a large Hispanic woman with tousled hair who had the lead in *Evita,* and an earnest young female journalist for an alternative Washington newspaper. Two more men arrived together, but were not gay, and one of them was some rising star on the tennis circuit. He was cute and blond, but he talked of nothing but himself, tennis, and his opponents. There was even a chef from some famous restaurant in D.C., Dan Lee, who was apparently revolutionizing Asian cuisine in the capital. Within a short time, the appetizers had disappeared and the drink bottles stood empty. The smokers were herded to the back deck, and Celia only faintly caught the smell of weed, dissipated in a soft breeze.

But it was fun; Celia was having fun. They played a spirited game of charades and another holding a card to your forehead with some famous person's name, and you had to guess who. Someone cranked up the record player and they were dancing in the living room and on the back deck. At one point, Roland sang at the piano, accompanying himself to "Moon River" from *Breakfast at Tiffany's* to which he knew all the words. This led into a melody of songs from hit musicals, which Celia joined in, followed by a serenade to the moon out on the deck, accompanied by a neighbor's dog. And, at midnight, everyone gathered at the dining room table for a toast to Roland and Tony—their one year anniversary. Kisses and cake all around.

After the toast, Tony herded Celia back into the kitchen for a talk. "Everything OK?" he asked.

"Splendid," said Celia, a bit tipsy, taking a seat. "After Simone left. Boy, she's something else."

"Forget all about it, like she never was here. Just a bad, bad dream. You know, Celia, we invited a couple of straight guys just for you, but I'm sorry to say they're complete duds."

"Oh?" said Celia.

"The tennis player," Tony said. "So self-involved. And the poet, oh dear, what a bore. Sorry."

"No worries," Celia said. "Besides, you know . . ." She had to burp. "Excuse me. Carlos. He really does exist."

Tony patted her hand. "I don't doubt it, sweetie. Just from what you've told us before, I'm started to think he may have disappeared over the horizon."

"We didn't break up," Celia squirmed in the chair. "We didn't even fight. Things were going really well. He said he'd be back for fall semester. I'm sure he meant it."

"Yes," Tony said. "I'm sure he meant it when he said it. But you know how life is." His shoulders drooped. "No letters? No phone calls?"

"Well, he was away at sea, so he really couldn't, could he?"

"And when he returned, if he did return?"

Ah, that was the question. As far as Janelle had told her, Carlos had not been seen.

Roland popped into the kitchen, cocking an eyebrow at Celia. "Advice for the love-lorn?" Smirking, he turned to Tony, "After-dinner drinks, Tony? I thought you were . . ."

"Forgot."

"I'll help," Celia said, rising to her feet, hoping to dodge any more personal comments.

"You're so kind to offer," Tony answered smoothly. "Actually, Roland, would you mind?" He had a pleading look. "So I can get back to the living room, just for a sec? Celia, sure you don't want a toot?"

But she nodded no, and Tony scurried away. Assembling glasses on a tray, Roland muttered, "I only wish he wasn't so in love with that stuff." Maybe Celia's love life was forgotten after all.

After a few minutes, Tony returned to the kitchen, his eyes bright, with a light powder around his nostrils, wetting his lips and rubbing his forefinger quickly along his gums. Roland gave him a quick, critical glance and disappeared into the living room. Celia finished rinsing the assorted drinks glasses, placing them on another tray. Tony helped himself to a clean glass and a tall drink of water from the tap.

"Ah."

From the living room, they heard Roland resume his singing: " . . . *I'm going to wash that man right out of my hair*" . . . totally ridiculous, of course, but Celia got it. Unexpectedly, Celia found herself smiling. "He can really sing," she said to Tony.

"Yes, he can, and he does, whenever the spirit moves him." Tony handed her a bottle of amaretto and a bottle of Kahlúa and led the way. Everyone had gathered into the living room, crowding around while Celia handed out cups and glasses.

Another chorus began, loudly, "For They Are Jolly Gay Fellows, For They Are Jolly Gay Fellows."

That's why they didn't hear another car pull in the yard. It was only when a blue light beat across the dining room wall that they realized there was more company, only this time it was uninvited—police.

Roland was on his feet, but calm. "Tony," he said in a low voice. "Everything out of sight, out of reach, under the deck if you can."

Tony moved into action, taking a plain paper bag out the deck door with him. Celia, standing next to Roland, watched uneasily as the seated guests twittered among themselves, a bit nervous, a bit resentful. It was only a party with friends, after all. But what would the cops think about this somewhat unusual, artsy gathering, with a "mixed" crowd, including some rather exotic folks from out of town, undeniably high.

There was a loud rap on the door. From the living room doorway, Celia saw Tony return, sliding the deck door behind him, remaining in a dark corner, mostly hidden behind a wide lamp shade. Roland headed to the front hall, a hand on Celia's elbow, pulling her after him. His other hand was buttoning up his white shirt which had been undone practically to his waist in the heat and revelry.

"With me," he said, under his breath, and Celia almost gasped as she realized she had become an official accomplice. And if . . . and if they somehow found out about the drugs, there'd be trouble, big trouble. A story in the paper for everyone to read. And maybe even her picture, along with Roland, both a little worse for wear. Grace would not be happy, not one bit. Celia took a deep breath.

Roland opened the door, where a uniformed officer stood under the front porch light.

"Good evening," Roland said, in his educated voice, but not too refined. "I'm sorry, is there a problem?"

"You live here?" the officer asked.

"Yes, I do," Roland answered, and then, stepping back practically onto Celia's toes. "Come in, officer, please." This was mild, neutral Roland; the sardonic jokester was not in sight. Nor, thankfully, was Tony with his velvet coat and smudged eyeliner.

The officer was in his mid-thirties, tanned and outdoorsy, a hunter probably. But he didn't look or sound alarmed, more or less business as usual. Until he scanned the living room, taking a closer look. Perhaps not quite what he expected.

"Noise report from a neighbor," the officer said, now standing in the hallway. "And some of these cars are parked illegally, too far out into the road."

"Sorry about that. We'll take care of it right away," Roland said.

"Lots of people here?" the officer inquired. Maybe he was starting to wonder about funny business. "I see some out-of-state license plates."

"A dozen or so," Roland said. That's when Celia realized a few partiers must have slipped out to the woods behind the house. "A few friends down from the city."

The officer eyed Celia, behind Roland's shoulder. She smiled at Officer Reid, according to his badge. His eyes lingered, although she didn't think it was in appreciation of her smile or her carefully put together outfit.

"No underage drinking?"

"No, sir."

"Young lady," the officer said to Celia. "How old are you?"

"Eighteen," she said. Legal age.

"Driver's license, please."

She got the license from her purse, and of course, it did say eighteen, and was registered in California. The officer looked it over and returned it to her, his lips sliding side to side, still not satisfied. Something wasn't adding up.

"From California?" he said, staring at Celia. "Long ways from here." She could feel Roland's eyes on the side of her face, and Tony's eyes on her back. With the slightest pucker of his lips, Roland was directing Celia to go on, distract, charm, as she did so well. She might have been a bit tipsy, but she was not drunk.

"I'm staying with my sister," Celia said, a bit chirpy. "She works at the Sutton Memorial Hospital. I work at the Grand Marsh Inn, at least for now, until I can get my real career underway." And then she turned, gesturing with an arm. "A lot of us do; we're just having some fun, it's been so busy, especially because of hunting season, you know?" She laughed, pretty fake. "I'm not complaining. The money is great, and the hunters are always a lot of fun and so generous."

Officer Reid nodded. The hospital, the Inn, the hunters. It was pretty much what it looked like, local folks having a party. Besides the wine and beer, what else could he see besides leftover veggies and dip or coffee drinks? Was there a whiff of marijuana? Possibly. Nothing too wild. Not the heavy, duty stuff— or its purchase and sale. Nothing that might lead to violence or accidents.

"So," he said to Celia, "nothing of interest here? Nothing for me to see if I were to step into the living room?"

"Oh, no," said Celia. "I can say personally that I haven't seen anything wrong this whole night. Just a fun time, singing and dancing. We were just having after-dinner drinks."

Peering into the room, all the officer could see was a quiet group of seated folks, a few with glasses on their knees. And a piano, with the keyboard open. And the sheet music to *Mary Poppins*.

Now the officer looked back to Roland, less unsure. Vocal Roland, now so calm and restrained. And then Officer Reid's gaze came back to Celia, and there was a smile on his face, the kind for pretty girls.

"All right, then," he said. "Just keep the noise down, and get those cars off the road. It's a hazard."

"Right away," Roland said, "Officer Reid." There may have been a note of old Roland in his voice, but Officer Reid was already on his way back to the patrol car.

When the door was shut and the patrol car had backed away, before anyone had gotten up from their seats, Roland turned to Celia.

"Our little actress, so convincing."

"Oh," Celia said, turning to find Tony at her side. "It's was nothing. I mean, technically, it was true, right. I mean, I really didn't see. . . . anything."

"You were magnificent," Tony said, flushed and trembling a little, clearly in a state of awe. But Celia found herself looking down at her Chinese slippers, remembering Grace's words. It was all a little more than she had bargained for. And, good as it was, Celia knew it wasn't a performance she was especially proud of. And seeing it, briefly, through Grace's eyes, Celia knew that Roland had used her, maybe not intentionally. The consequences of getting caught in the house with drugs would have been bad enough; it would also be an embarrassment, made public. It was perhaps time to start thinking of heading out, before any more trouble came to pass. But not before Tony and Roland had her between them, placing a kiss on each cheek. There was a flash, and someone had taken a picture.

Chapter 9

Back at the Inn for the dinner shift on Friday, Tony and Roland greeted Celia with kisses and compliments. Apparently, they considered the *soiree* a huge success, and made her out to be some kind of heroine, saving the night and the party from Police Officer Reid. And for enduring a kind of trial by fire with the fire-breathing Simone.

"Isn't she love-ly?" Roland warbled, taking Celia's hand for a waltz spin. "Isn't she won-der-ful?" Anita caught Celia's eye in passing, and her look was not encouraging. Maybe she had some idea about the drugs and party scene, something Anita definitely did not approve of. Afterwards, on the way out of the kitchen, Tony pulled Celia aside to say they were already making plans for a get-together with Roland's high-school friend Leona, who was the Artistic Director at the college in Salisbury. Celia would love her. Leona was just back from New York, off-Broadway. That's why she wasn't at the party. There would be all kinds of theater talk. Maybe the four of them could drive to D.C. for a night on the town. Celia nodded, but avoided an answer. It was tempting but maybe the kind of temptation that could lead to more trouble. Last night's party was a bit of a close call.

Throughout the evening, Celia had to stifle some sneezes and cover a couple coughing fits—allergies or a cold? Plus, her energy level was lagging, unusual for her. The late nights, the hard work, maybe it was catching up. Finally, toward the end, she couldn't hold back one very loud sneeze, and it seemed the whole room said, "God Bless You," in chorus. *Yikes!*

As Celia turned in her coins and bills for the evening, Anita was at her side, talking about a business course she was taking. They walked together to clock out and then got their coats. At one point, Celia was overtaken by another sneeze. In a fur-trimmed wool coat and purse in gloved hands, Anita scanned her critically.

"You walking home?"

"Sure, I always do."

"All the way to the hospital?"

"It's not far. Maybe twenty-five minutes."

"Too far in this weather with a cold coming on." Anita looked put out. "Well, I can't help you. My car's in the shop and I'm getting a ride." She was frowning at Celia's purple raincoat. "Girl, don't you have something better than that? Something warm?"

"Not really," Celia said, with a huff. "I didn't need it in California."

"That's the first thing you need to get with all that money you're making."

At the top of the hallway, a tall figure came into view.

"Jay, you leaving now? Give this girl a ride home. It's two minutes from here, going your way."

Jay looked from Anita to Celia and then back to Anita. Did he not want to give her a ride? He wasn't the friendliest guy in the world, but she kind of thought he liked her, or at least, didn't dislike her. Guys tended to like her. Why wouldn't he like her?

"If you can give Cuffie and Phil a ride, you can give Celia a ride, too."

He hesitated. "I ain't leaving yet."

"She can wait."

Jay shrugged. He couldn't say no to Anita, either, like any of them.

He turned to Celia. "Sure, I give you a ride. Give me five minutes."

Celia felt like she didn't have much say in the matter, but it was cold and she was tired, and she wasn't going to argue with Anita. She nodded with an uncertain, grateful smile.

A few minutes later, at the door of Jay's VW bug, Celia looked around. "What about the other guys?" she asked.

"They're not here. Left early," Jay said, opening the driver's side door to get in.

"Oh," she said, still standing there.

"Go on," he said. "Get in."

Sliding into the passenger seat, Celia said, "I appreciate you giving me a ride home, Jay. Really. Anita is great, but sometimes she seems to think I'm a kid. Know what I mean?"

Jay nodded, looking straight ahead. "Where we goin'?"

What is up with this guy? Celia wondered. Wouldn't kill him to make a little small talk. Clearly, he wasn't going to dish on Anita. But, for heaven's sake, she wasn't looking for gossip, just a little polite conversation. Right? But inside his car, close to him, just the two of them, she felt her heart beating faster and her mouth going dry as she spoke.

"Down Main Street and then the second street on the right, Hopewell."

"You got an apartment there?"

"Well, my sister's."

"You got a sister here?" Jay seemed mildly surprised.

"Grace. She's five years older than me and she works at the hospital. She got a pretty good job right out of college, a nurse."

He glanced at her, doubtful. "All the way from California, she came here?"

"No, not like that. She never lived in California. She was, I mean, we were, living in New York, that's where we're from, originally. Then she went to college, and got a job, so she never moved there. She moved here." She gestured out the window. It didn't come out very clear, but he didn't ask further. Probably didn't really care.

Without traffic, it was less than five minutes to the apartment. Jay pulled into the parking lot. "Where you want I should drop you?"

She pointed. "There, on the other side of the lamppost."

Jay stopped at the curb. Celia picked up her pocketbook from the floor and a few coins spilled out. She was torn between picking them up or leaving them. She scooped up the quarters, leaving the smaller ones.

As she turned to say thank you, Jay was frowning at the apartment building.

"This where you stay?" He made no attempt to cover his disappointment.

"Well, yeah. Why?" Did he imagine something grand?

"Seem like you belong some place better than this," he said, waving at the squat brick apartment building framed by naked tree branches. He continued with the smallest curve of his lips, very nice lips. "Big house with a porch swing. Yeah, that's more like."

"Well, this is where we live, and it's fine." But he was right, Celia realized with a pang. That was the house she used to live in, quite a long time ago.

"I get a house sometime," Jay remarked, more to himself than her. "Saving my money instead of blowing every paycheck like some of those jokers. This car not fancy, but it's paid for."

"Oh, that's good," Celia said vaguely. She took her hand off the door handle, turning to him. "So, what about you and your family? It's only fair."

"Nothing to tell."

"Well, where do you live?"

"Outside of town. I live with my aunt and uncle, and one of my sisters. We got a big family, in different places."

"What about your parents?"

"They in Baltimore." After a pause, he continued. "My mom works in food, too, at the hospital kitchen." He smiled slowly, and Celia realized he was trying to be funny.

They sat in silence, just the hum of the engine between them. She glanced once more at his handsome profile but he had no more to say.

"Well, then," Celia said, pushing the door open. "I better say thank you and let you get home."

"Welcome. You working tomorrow?"

"I am."

"I see you then. Goodnight." He tipped his head in farewell. Celia got out, hurrying to the apartment door, key in hand. She mounted the stairs, equal parts exhausted, giddy, happy, and bewildered.

The next night, also blustery, Jay on his own offered Celia a ride home, along with Cuffie from the grill. When Cuffie pulled open the front passenger door, Jay told him to get in the back and "let the lady ride in front." Cuffie was mad about something that happened with one of the other cooks and complained the whole way to Celia's place, where she got out and said goodnight without having said another word.

The next evening shift that Celia worked was the following week. It was still cold, but not as cold. And, following Anita's advice, along with her sister's, she ditched the funky old raincoat and bought a blue winter coat. Her sister even volunteered to drive over her car in the early evening and leave it for Celia to drive home later. But Celia wouldn't let her. It wasn't far, plus she could probably get a ride if she needed.

Between the busy season and the change of weather, she had developed a sniffle and a raspy voice, but she didn't want to miss work. At the end of her shift, she stood at the door where she had met Jay before to catch a ride home. When he saw her, he walked over quickly. "I'm going out with the boys tonight. Can't give you a ride."

Unable to cover her surprise, Celia stared blankly a second. "Oh, sure. No problem."

He studied her a moment. "You OK? You look kind of white, I mean, even for a white girl."

Celia smiled weakly. "Just a little cold. I'm fine and I have this new winter coat. See?" She spun around, letting the coat flap open.

"You wait here. I tell those boys I come right back. I can drop you home quick."

"No, no. Don't be silly. I don't expect you to be my ride home every time we work the same shift."

"Come on, Dolphin Girl." Jay pulled on her elbow. The pressure alarmed her, and her own strong reaction to being so close that she could see the fine pores of his skin.

"No," Celia said, resisting. "I'll see you later. Have a good time." She walked away quickly, determined. After she crossed the street and bent into the shadows of the closed store fronts, she laughed at herself. *What are you thinking?*

At home, in bed, she was restless under the covers. What should she do after the upcoming holiday season was over? School? Another, different job— with benefits and all that? Working and going to school? Nothing came to mind, and she was so tired, she fell asleep. In the night, she had a dream about losing her new coat, but when she woke the next morning, she was feeling better.

Celia declined the offer to work an extra evening, and the next time she saw Jay was at the end of a lunch shift that he was also working. He was clearly in a good mood, joking and teasing Celia and all the girls.

"Look who went to charm school," Celia heard Roland remark to Tony about Jay's change of manner—after Jay left the kitchen, of course. The cleanup was almost done, and everyone was hanging around the grill for no particular reason. Jeremy was out sick, and Warren had taken a couple days off.

"Oh, he's all right, Jay," Tony said. "He just takes himself and this job too seriously. He's such an old man sometimes. He's got his plans—the wife, the house—just put a little gray in his hair."

"You tempted by that fine specimen, Princess?" Roland went on, putting an arm around her waist. "I am."

"You better not be," Tony warned.

Eldridge came up, inviting himself into the conversation. "Nah, he not for you, Roland, and he not for you, either, girl." He shook his finger at Celia. "Stay away from that pretty boy, you don't want to get tangled up with all that."

Celia wasn't sure what he was getting at. Jay's attitude? His playing around? He didn't seem much like a playboy, even his flirting when he was in a good mood was pretty mild and not directed at anyone in particular.

"He likes Celia," Tony came back. "Anyone can see that. He always has her order up, well, right after Anita's. I know," he whined, leaning against the side of the large grill. "I'm the one always waiting. I'm not saying it's your fault, Celia."

Roland was taken by another idea. "Who can we find for our Celia? She's got that mysterious missing boyfriend in California. Who knows if he'll show up again. Celia deserves better than that. Our princess needs a prince, but where is he?" Then, smiling and bowing low in Celia's direction, he added.

"Of course, she really deserves someone like me, but alas . . ." he held the pause a moment. "I'm already spoken for."

There was a moment of reflection.

"How about all those rich guys out there?" Cuffie stuck out his thumb in the direction of the dining room. "Remember that sweet-smelling Romeo? Next time, give somebody a chance, Dolphin Girl. Ain't there some guy can sweep you off your feet and take you away from here?"

She laughed. "Maybe I don't want to go away from here. Did you think of that? At least not yet, while the money's good. Plus, they're all married, or else old, and . . . they have bad breath or pot bellies," she finished, sounding foolish to herself.

She got a good razzing for that.

"Where are all the nice white boys around here?" Roland asked indignantly. "And I don't mean those chicken farmers or crab catchers."

"They mostly go away to college, and the city," Cuffie answered. "Maybe they come back later, after they got all the money. They don't hang around no no-life place like this, except they come hunting with they dads on the weekend. Hunt, hunt, shoot, shoot." He aimed an imaginary gun in the air, taking out an imaginary duck.

"Well, that's no good then," Roland said.

"Why they got to be white boys?" Tilghman asked. He was a sixteen-year-old high school kid, working part-time, with aspirations to be a chef. "Plenty nice black boys, too. They make good money at the frozen food plant in Derry."

"What, six dollars an hour?" Roland scoffed. "That's not much more than you boys make."

Celia shook her head. "I don't need a man to take care of me—thank you very much."

"Of course, Celia here has her dreams," Roland conceded. "She doesn't need a good man. She just needs a man, someone to fool around with. Well, here you go," he said, sweeping his arm across the cooking station. "Try them all, one at a time. See if they're as good as they say."

With that, there was a general smirking and cackle of laughter. Celia felt her face grow warm. The discussion was taking a bit of a wild turn. She didn't know how to answer, and wished she could find a quick way out.

"No, don't you do that, Celia," Eldridge put in unexpectedly, his deep voice serious. "They got to share the good news all around. Next morning, they be talkin' bout titties and ass over the fried eggs."

"Titties? Fried eggs?" Tony squeezed his eyes closed, and groaned. "Oh, Good Lord, that is bad."

Once the others got it, they laughed loudly and uncontrollably. They got on a roll, trying to outdo each other, and someone took a marker to draw an illustration on the whiteboard where they noted the items that had run out—*86'd* for the evening. Eldridge, who could outdo the rest of them with outrageous remarks, looked upset at his unintended joke. Celia realized he had been trying to defend her. She, too, was embarrassed and realized that she probably had been too indulgent. Then one of the bus boys pushed through the doors from the dining room, his eyes wide.

"Miz Becker coming this way," he said. But with the noise, not everyone heard, until Roland shouted. "Shut up, you idiots, Mrs. Becker's on her way."

That stifled the noise, while the picture, one breast or egg only, was quickly erased. When Mrs. Becker appeared, most of the cooks had found some way to look occupied, and Celia was flipping through her order pad, pen in hand. Mrs. Becker stood a moment, in the center of the room, glaring, but there was nothing evident to comment on.

"I should hear nothing from the kitchen. There must be attention to work," she barked, before crossing the floor to the hallway.

After she left, a muffled chatter broke out. Just then, Josie arrived from the dining room, followed by Anita in her overcoat, looking irritable and upset.

Josie said to her, "They having a party in here, like I tol' you."

"Hi, Anita," Celia said quickly, blushing slightly. "How come you're here today?"

"I wanted to change Thanksgiving for New Year's, but Becker won't let me," Anita said tersely. "What was all that commotion? This is supposed to be a workplace."

"No cause for alarm," Roland said, coolly. "We were just trying to find a boyfriend for Celia here, a noble cause, I think. Some of the candidates got a little overeager."

Anita scoffed. "You turn everything into a crude joke. What is wrong with you, anyhow? God gave you more intelligence and talent than you know what to do with. You could set an example for these boys, but all you do is waste time playing games like this with other people's lives."

Roland pressed his hands together, bowing his head. "Saint Anita, holier than all of us, here to remind us of our sins." He was back to his old mocking tone, a sneer at his lips. "I never asked to be poster boy for black men. I have enough trouble living in my own skin. How dare you judge me."

"I judge you, because I know what you're doing is wrong, and so do you."

"Enough," Roland said, turning his back on her and moving across the room to Tony and the break room.

To the rest of the staff, Anita said, "This is a workplace, not a playground or a dance club. Becker will catch you at it one of these days, and that will be the end of your jobs. Is that what you want?"

Without a peep, everyone went back to their own business.

Anita led Celia to the far side of the kitchen. "Celia, honey, you're not thinking. What if Mrs. Becker finds you in here like this? Didn't you tell me you need this job?" She pointed back at the grill station. These guys are stuck here, but you're not. You're going somewhere . . ." she gestured toward the door, "else. It's not worth the risk. Don't get caught up with their nonsense."

She stopped, and then went on more gently. "I can see it's hard for you. You're like a fish out of water. You don't know your way around here, and you want to be nice and get along with everybody. But I'm telling you it's not like California. People here are different, and they view things differently. Just watch yourself."

Celia felt that she was being reprimanded, again. "I don't see how I'm doing anything wrong," she said.

"I didn't say you were. But, even so, you're going to run yourself into trouble this way. And if you do," she said gravely, "hold your head up until the trouble passes, or you're not going to make it."

Without a farewell, Anita left, and Celia went back mechanically to the last of her duties, a little shaken. As she put away her order pad and punched her time card, she saw Jay had returned to the kitchen with his jacket. He wagged his head at her, holding up the car keys. She shook her head with a friendly wave and walked away, knowing not to accept the offer of a ride. Not tonight, anyway, until she figured this whole thing out.

On the way home, the cold air in her face, Celia could smile at what happened, as silly as it was. She wasn't some high school kid. She had a year of college behind her, practically nineteen years old. She could handle herself with men, at least young men. Another thought brought her to a stop. Anita was jealous! That must be it. Not so much about the boys, men, whatever. She was jealous of the attention, and maybe even the tips. She was used to being Queen Bee and now here was Celia surrounded by the drones, getting lots of honey—if that's what you called it.

Bitter gusts swirled around her ankles and knees, propelling her past the store fronts, many decorated for Thanksgiving, and even one with snowmen shopping for Christmas—too early! Well, she could handle Anita. Anita liked her, she knew, and in her own way sought out Celia's company, to talk to her—mostly about a business class she was taking, and some ideas for starting her own business—a copier franchise, maybe, or natural skin products. Celia knew nothing about business, but she was a good listener. The only thing she wasn't crazy about was how Anita kept on her about church and her soul. But in an odd, intuitive way, Celia knew that Anita needed her. And, jealous or not, wanted to preserve her from harm. Anita knew the area, and she didn't. It was probably wise to keep distance from Roland and Tony, as entertaining as they were. It was true, what Anita said, she wasn't long for this place, while they, apparently, were content to stay for the rest of their lives.

All too soon, the peak of hunting season had passed, but things remained lively at the Grand Marsh Inn. Tuesday was a good day on the lunch shift, with no trouble at all. Celia had finally learned to get the drink orders straight, and the kitchen crew was in a good humor, working at a steady pace, although the dining room was short of bussing help to clean tables. Nice customers, too, mainly older couples who were in no hurry and had time to chat; plus businessmen, always good tippers and not too demanding. Yes, there were also some lady shoppers, so indecisive, and picky about the food and service. They remained pleasant to Celia, though, no matter what small things she overlooked, as long as she kept smiling. But they were harder on Wanda, whose very posture conveyed resentment.

At dessert time, Celia poured coffee at a table of "ladies who lunch." One of them, a well-dressed woman in a red boiled-wool jacket, asked about the hunters. Explaining in some detail about the guns and the dogs, Celia missed the cup. Instead, the coffee dripped off the table onto the lady's purse on the floor by her feet.

"Oh, no!" Celia exclaimed, seeing her mistake. "I'm so sorry. Let me clean that for you." She became flushed and shook her head, grimacing. "Oh, dear. I'm such a klutz."

The lunch ladies assured her. "It's no problem. Nothing is ruined, just a little damp." They all laughed, and the lady in the red jacket joked: "Did my husband send you here to make me stop spending his money?"

In the end, she got a generous tip, probably more than she would have otherwise. She smiled to herself, thinking, *I'm never going to be much of a waitress, but a little small talk sure goes a long way.*

In the kitchen, someone had seen what happened, and spread the word about Celia's coffee spill.

"What they tip you?" asked Warren behind the grill, waving a spatula for her attention.

Celia had a whole audience waiting.

"Twenty dollars," she said, pulling out the bill to show them. The guys on the cooking line whooped and hollered, making a commotion, and Celia couldn't help giggling.

"I know, it's crazy," she said.

"You some piece of work," said Jay, who was working lunch and dinner shifts. "I think we call you Superwoman. You can't do no wrong."

Celia never knew what to make of Jay's comments, not so light and humorous as the others.

"Well, thanks, Jay, you can write my next job reference," she teased back, but he didn't laugh.

Show and tell was over, and Celia returned to the dining room. As she went to clear her empty tables, she saw there was a backup with the busing trays on the nearby rack. Stooping to pick up a napkin, she jumped at the loud, violent crash behind her. The full, dirty trays had been stacked so steeply, they slid to the ground leaving a mess.

Mrs. Becker came over, scowling, and summoned the staff, declaring in an angry whisper that whoever had used the stand should be docked for the broken glass and chinaware. Eldridge said he had nothing to do with it, even though Celia knew he had, when he bussed her table of six. Mr. Becker was drawn by the noise and went to his wife's side, speaking briefly. Mrs. Becker then announced they would dock all the staff if no one stepped forward. Just then, a crowd of local businessmen entered the room noisily, the Rotarians' annual recognition luncheon. With a dismissive gesture, Mrs. Becker sent everyone back to work, staying herself to supervise the pick-up. When things finally quieted, she ordered the entire staff to gather in the kitchen.

"Will anyone admit to stacking their trays in such a fashion?"

No one spoke.

"Eldridge?" Mrs. Becker asked. "You were there, I think?"

"Not me." Eldridge shook his head emphatically. "I didn't do it, and it's not fair you punish us all. Everyone put stuff everywhere. We need more people to move it, that all."

Mrs. Becker did not look happy with Eldridge's response but had to relent, with no more evidence to go on. No more was said about docking earnings. With a sigh, Celia headed to the drinks station for refills, with Eldridge close behind.

"You did too," she murmured. "I saw you. How can you lie straight-faced like that?"

"Expert, I guess. Lot a practice. Pretty good, huh?"

Celia filled two pitchers of iced tea, and took the plastic wrap off a bowl of lemon slices, as Eldridge placed glasses of ice on the tray. "Is that something you want to be good at?"

"Sure," Eldridge said. "It save a lot of trouble. Why I owe them the truf? That their problem to fix, not mine. They don't like me, they get rid of me if they can. You think I help them do that? No, little missy."

Celia was still disturbed. She could understand his reasoning, in a way. But still, it wasn't right. Was it?

"Wise up, honey. You like a baby here. You can do how you like, but I show you how it is." When she didn't respond, he added, "I be your big black mammy, take care of you, brush out that hair, make it so pretty." Celia couldn't help smiling. Warren, in his chef's hat, strolled over.

"What's up?" Warren cut in. "Are you guys in trouble? We heard the crash all the way in here."

Celia rolled her eyes. "No, we're safe for now, I guess. They can't fire us all."

"I get this," Eldridge said, taking the tray from Celia. "Don't let this boy waste your time, or there will be trouble." He turned to leave, giving her a wink.

Warren stepped closer, leaning in. His kitchen whites were fairly soiled, but his eyes were bright with purpose.

"So, Celia." He scanned the area, dropping his voice. "I'm working on my college application, the essay. You got time to look it over?"

"Sure," she answered as softly. "You got it with you?"

"Nah. I'll bring it tomorrow. Maybe we can find a few minutes."

Celia wrinkled her nose. Nothing here at the Inn was likely to be private. "How about you come by the apartment tomorrow after the lunch shift? We can take care of the essay, no one looking over our shoulders." And then she had another thought—maybe that'd be too private. "And Wanda, too. Or Lacey and those guys. We can take care of business then hang out for a while!"

His smile was radiant. "Thanks, Celia. You're the best." And then, a shadow of doubt, "You sure?"

She tossed her head side to side. "Sure, I'm sure."

Warren was summoned to the grill, leaving Celia standing there alone, done for the day. She had nowhere, really, to go. Wanda had already left without a word, and Celia wondered if she was miffed about something. She pulled on her jacket, heading slowly toward the exit, deliberating whether to stop at the corner pharmacy to pick up shampoo and deodorant. Outside the back door, she stopped abruptly. Jay was leaning against the hood of his blue

VW, arms crossed over his chest. He had already changed out of his cooking whites into jeans and a University of Maryland sweatshirt. He must have kept a change of clothes at the Inn, like some of the other staff.

"Hey," he said when he saw Celia. She walked over to him.

"Hi," she said.

"You goin' home?"

"I guess so. I've got to count up all my earnings, you know." A bit feeble, she admitted to herself.

"You making a fortune in there."

"Not bad." Celia smiled, embarrassed. "It's good money, especially right now."

"What you want to do with all that money?"

"I don't know," Celia said, her shoulders slumping. "It's not that much, after I pay my bills and put away something for savings." She wasn't prepared to discuss her plans to decamp for California and return to college as soon as she could.

"Don't you want nice clothes, like all the girls?" he asked. Celia wondered if that was a criticism of her wardrobe, and then realized that he rarely saw her out of uniform.

"Well, I'm not much of a shopper," she admitted. "But I love to look."

Jay uncrossed his arms, standing upright and tipping his head toward the car.

"You want to come to Weston with me, take a ride? They got lots of stores there."

"Weston?" Celia repeated. It was a bigger town, maybe half an hour or forty minutes away. "You mean, now?"

He shook the keys. "That's what I'm saying. I got some errands to run, and I thought you might like to look around."

Celia's mouth gaped until she closed it, telling herself to think before speaking. She wanted to go, badly. And with Jay. But should she? Her brain buzzed, all kinds of thoughts circling around. He wouldn't try anything; that she was sure of. But was this a date of some kind? For all the time they spent together at the Inn, almost three months now, five or six days a week, often double-shifts, Celia didn't know much about Jay. Mostly, they were just so busy. But he was also quiet and didn't engage much in the teasing and gossip. Private about personal stuff, like Wanda. Still, you could tell something about a person's character by how they acted, and Jay was steady, hardworking, efficient, and didn't lose his head yelling at people, like some of them. For a while, Celia had thought he was dating a girl on the downstairs kitchen staff because she saw them a few times, heads together, laughing. Turns out, they were cousins, according to Eldridge. Who knew?

But really she *knew*; she could tell Jay liked her, in a way.

Outside the Inn, Jay was waiting for an answer: Did she want to go to Weston with him, or not? He jangled the keys again. "Well?"

Well, Celia reflected, Anita was the one who told Jay to give Celia a ride before, so it must be all right to hang out.

"I would love to!" She couldn't contain herself.

"OK, then, let's do it." He smiled broadly, obviously pleased.

She had to smile back.

"Let me go home and change first," she said, the words rushing out. "I'll be back in half an hour. Is that OK?" She started at a trot, about to cut behind the dumpsters, headed for the short-cut.

"Wait up, girl," Jay said, waving her back. "I give you a ride."

Chapter 10

An hour and a half later, Celia and Jay left the bustling metropolis of Weston, heading back to Sutton and taking a left, where Jay said there was a small harbor opening up to the bay. He had finished his shopping quickly at the hardware store and then the auto parts store. A bit dull, but it was fun walking along the busy sidewalks, window shopping and people watching, just part of the crowd. Celia didn't buy anything except a palm tree deodorizer, unbeknownst to Jay, to hang from the mirror in his car. A little thank you. Just before leaving Weston, they went to the drive-through at Burger King and got some food, which Jay paid for. A date? Kind of, but not really.

At the harbor, they parked and watched boats swivel at their moorings, sunlight making pathways on the water. The glass of the car window was getting cooler, but it was cozy inside, smelling of French fries, burgers, and the warmth of their bodies.

"How far is it to the ocean from here?" Celia asked, wiping her chin with a napkin. "I miss the beach."

"Maybe a couple hours, the other way, to the Delaware beach."

"Do you like the ocean?"

"Only been once." Jay cocked his head. "It's all right. Kind of windy, and sand get in the food."

"Don't you like to swim?"

He grinned, boyish and cute. "I never learn how."

"No!" Celia was astonished. "I love to swim, just like a fish. Maybe I could teach you."

"I don't know about that." Jay folded up his food wrappers, and pushed them inside the hanging trash bag. He kept a neat and tidy car, just like his station at the Inn. He had just gotten brand new floor mats, and an old air freshener hung from the mirror, but the pine scent was gone.

"It's such a pleasure, Jay," Celia said, still working at her burger. "Swimming, I mean. You don't know what you're missing."

"That why you Dolphin Girl," Jay laughed at her. "What that thing, girl and fish? Mermaid. You some kind of mermaid, return to the water at night."

In the waning light, a couple girls strolled along the dock. Teens, one of them with her arms wrapped around, shivering from the breeze. Cute girls in tight jeans, maybe hoping to run into some guys. Celia watched Jay watching them. Of course he would. Why wouldn't he? But he tipped his head back, eyes downcast.

"Back in California, there some blond boy with a surfboard come out on the waves and kiss you?"

Celia smirked, hiding her fluster. "No . . . He has black hair and black eyes. His name is Carlos, and he's a sailor, not a surfer."

Jay whooped. "You making it up."

"I am not. He's part Mexican, part Italian, and I met him at college. He's studying sociology, and he plays the guitar. I have his picture at home. Handsome *and* intelligent."

Jay laughed good-humoredly. "That's wild. Pretty strange place, sound like." He sat back, his head against the headrest. "That's the boy you waiting on?"

Celia squirmed, her knee knocking the hanging trash bag. "I, well . . ." and then the words spilled out: "I don't know what's up with him, really." It sounded so pathetic. Why did she even say it? Then she had to rally, turning it back on Jay. "So, what about you and your girlfriend, or girlfriends? You must have a few."

Jay's eyes were almost closed, squinting against the low-angled sun. "Oh yeah, sure, dozens, like all the black dudes. At least the handsome ones."

"No, really. Do you have one?"

"I got a little book at home," Jay said. "A girl for every letter of the alphabet."

Celia went along. "What's under H, I wonder?"

"Henrietta."

"And X?"

"Xenia."

"O?"

"Or—landia," he got out quickly.

That made her giggle. "Oh, I doubt that very much."

"Maybe," Jay said with a straight face. "You want I should put your name under C?"

"No way," she said with some heat, realizing it was the first time he was really flirting with her. "I am not waiting in line for any man, especially not in alphabetical order." She laughed at her own comeback. "I still didn't get a straight answer out of you. Have you got a girlfriend?"

Jay paused a second. "Yes, I do. We off again, on again, all the time. Now we off."

"Oh," said Celia, a little disconcerted. Somehow, she really thought he didn't have one, or had many. Now she pictured some sexy, tough, black girl with a threatening look on her face.

"Really off, or just temporary?"

Jay shrugged. "Don't know. She pretty mad right now." When Celia didn't say anything, he continued. "She got ideas how things supposed to be, between us, I mean. She get upset if I don't go along."

"Then why do you still go out?"

Jay looked perplexed. "Well, she good in her heart, really," he said, and then, shaking his head. "She fine, really fine. She the best one around here. She just so hard in some things."

Celia sighed. She'd heard enough to know that this was likely the last car ride with Jay, or should be. Ah well, silly thoughts. But it had been a nice outing, a lovely afternoon. She finished her drink, opening the door to pour the slushy ice cubes on the ground.

"It's getting cool," she murmured, crumbling the cup into the hanging waste bag.

Jay turned to her. "Should we get back?"

"Oh, no," Celia said, sitting back. No matter what this was, she did not want to leave this comfortable bubble inside the car with Jay. Not yet. "It's just about sunset. Look at the colors in the sky." A large sailboat was pulling into the dock, and several birds took off, black against the gold and purple clouds. The sparkle off the water was almost blindingly bright, celestial.

Jay started the engine, turning on the heat. Then he leaned over behind Celia, reaching his arm to the back seat. He had to hoist himself between the seat backs, and Celia saw his jeans ride down from his waist, revealing his underwear and the muscles of his torso. Just for a second, she thought, *Is he going to make a move?* But she really didn't think so. After all this, it would have been quite a surprise. He handed her his jacket.

A few moments passed in silence, as they watched the boat come to rest and a man hop onto the dock to fasten a rope around a pier.

"It's so beautiful here," Celia said. "More beautiful even than all those pictures. I can see why people love it. There's a kind of peace about this place, don't you think?" She gestured toward the harbor. "Right now, see how the sky is glowing; everything looks like it's been touched with gold."

"Hm . . ." he said. And then, unexpectedly, he reached over, lifting a strand of Celia's hair, holding it in a shaft of light, which made it shine. "Yeah," he said, "just like gold." His smile was teasing, but his eyes crinkled warmly.

"You like it here, then?" he asked, returning his hands to the bottom of the steering wheel, fine hands, a chef's hands, clean and well kept. No calluses, just a small white knick or two against the dark skin.

"Oh, some things I like a lot," Celia said. "And some people." She didn't mean it to sound suggestive, just the simple truth.

"But you still in a hurry to get back to California, soon as you can."

"Not this very minute," Celia protested. It sounded like he expected her to leave tomorrow. "Not until I can afford to go back to college." She dropped her head and swallowed. "I can't stay with my mother and step-father. There's no place for me there, really."

Jay seemed to mull that over.

"Your daddy, where he at?"

"Oh," she said, straightening. "He's dead. He died from a heart attack when he was forty-four."

"You was a little girl?"

"Seven years old."

"Then your mom remarried?"

"After a while." She repeated the script she'd told many times over the years to people who'd asked about her family. "We lived with my grandparents, my mom's parents, in their house. About five years. Then she married Gordon and they had a son together, Shane. That's why we went to California, so Gordon could start a business—or at least try to."

Her finger traced a decal pasted on the dashboard: *Straight ahead, no detours* on a bold red arrow. A morale booster, maybe.

Jay glanced over from the wheel. "What's your daddy's job, your own daddy?"

"Well, he was a lawyer, a small-town lawyer."

Jay's lips tightened. "Now I know he make a lot of money, being a lawyer. And you had a big house, too, and maids."

So that's what he was getting at. "No, not really," she said, a little exasperated. "We had a nice house, and someone came once a week to help my mom with the cleaning."

"You rich, then."

"Is that what you think? I'm some rich girl just hanging out here for fun?"

"You talk rich."

"No I don't. How can you say that? I don't have a car or nice clothes or jewelry, or, or anything."

"I mean how you talk."

"Oh, that." She found herself laughing. "That's my training, you silly. I'm an actress, so I have to project my voice, and e-nun-ci-ate clearly. That's all."

"If you say so."

"Don't you believe me?"

He shrugged, but then his smile widened. "You for real, or you the best actress of them all."

"Why, thank you," she said, with a comic bow from the waist. "I'll take that as a compliment, either way." But was it?

The men had come off the boat, walking to their trucks; and the teen girls had long since gone, huddled into their hooded sweatshirts. Jay backed out of the parking lot and followed the road to the highway headed north. A quarter moon was rising in a blue-black sky, and they passed a few cars with their headlights on. Jay switched the radio on for the trip back, which seemed so quick.

They were coming into Sutton now, some commuter traffic, and Jay slowed down behind a car that was signaling left at the light. He gestured at the woman, who was timid about turning.

"Go on, Grandma," he said. "Get a move on." But he didn't blow the horn. Then the lady turned, and left them sitting at a red light.

A car came around the corner, passing them, and Celia recognized the driver, Roxanne, Grace's friend from the hospital who lived near their apartment.

Celia waved, but Roxanne didn't see or didn't realize it was Celia sitting in the blue VW with a handsome black man at the wheel. Celia's hand faltered, thinking maybe it was better that Roxanne didn't see her anyway, or not mention something to Grace.

The light turned, and soon they passed Sutton High School, and places familiar now to Celia. It seemed like they had reached the end, of the ride and conversation. She was disappointed to see the sign for her street. Suddenly they were in the parking lot, and Jay pulled into a spot close to her unit, turning off the radio. Celia shrugged off Jay's jacket, handing it to him. He put it in the back seat, brushing her shoulder with his arm. Celia's lips parted, but no words came out.

After a moment, Jay said, "You working tomorrow?"

"No, my day off." Celia paused. She had her hand on the handle, cracking open the door, warm air escaping. She wondered if, maybe . . . But Jay kept his hands on the wheel and his eyes looking forward.

"I guess I'll see you later, then." Celia got out of the car, walking toward the apartment doorway. After a few steps, she turned, flagging him.

"Wait!" She went to the driver's side, and Jay rolled down the window with a questioning look. Celia took the small, flat package out of her purse.

"This is for you," she said. He slid it out of the bag and dangled it from his fingers, the too-green palm tree and too-sweet smell of coconut.

"Yeah, thanks," he said, almost bashful.

"Thank you," she said, with a tip of her head. "For the ride, and, well, everything. It was nice; really, really nice."

Celia had trouble getting to sleep that night, for a change. It took her a while to settle down on the sofa bed, pushing her covers down to her feet and then pulling them back up. Jay. No question about it, she was in a state about Jay. Excited about their trip to Weston, replaying their conversations and seeing again the profile of his face while driving.

He liked her, she could tell. She started grinning to herself, with the pleasure of the thought.

And she liked him, too. At least, she thought so. If anything, he seemed even more handsome than when she first met him that day outside Mr. Becker's office. It can't be him changing, could it? Then it must be her, and how she saw him, maybe getting more used to him. Was it the attraction of his being black? Not really. Or maybe. She had not come looking for a black boyfriend or any boyfriend at all. Maybe it was more the fact he was so admired, valued by the people at the Inn, that little world.

But what about Jay himself? Was he her type, so to speak? Harder to tell. Generally quiet, hard-working, not the friendliest. Not the best sense of humor, that she could see. Neat, clean, maybe a little too well-pressed. He had some curiosity, about her anyhow, if not the greater world. Oh, who knows? And what did it matter? What was she even thinking? Whatever her feelings, it would probably be a bad idea to get involved with someone here. This was not California; that would not be good judgment. And there was still the question of Carlos, that crazy, unfinished business.

Still, she couldn't help her dreams. They were sitting in Jay's car. He touched her hair, her face, and then he kissed her.

The next morning, Celia showered then dressed leisurely in sweat pants and a t-shirt until it was time to get ready for her volunteer service at the hospital. She put out a clean blouse and dark pants on the bed and hung her pink volunteer jacket over the doorknob to the bathroom. The day was clear with pale sunlight and felt warmer than it had been.

The doorbell rang. That was a surprise. Celia went to the window, but it was too late to get a view of whoever was standing downstairs. She scanned the parking lot for a mail truck or maybe a service vehicle, and spotted Jay's car parked along the curb. Was it his, or someone else with that pale blue VW bug? The bell rang again. *Damn,* Celia thought, *I haven't even put on makeup.*

Through the peep-hole, she could see it was Jay, also in sweats, with a blue and white windbreaker and sneakers. Not on his way to work. Celia opened the door, totally dumbfounded. What would bring him by like this, so early?

"Hi!" she said, and stopped there, not knowing what to say next. Jay looked almost shy, but he said, "Hey." Celia could tell he was embarrassed, looking side to side around her. Then he looked up and smiled. She couldn't help smiling, too, and wondered could he tell he'd been in her thoughts? She was happy to see him, really happy, like it was the best thing that could have happened that morning.

"Take a ride with me? You say it your day off, and I don't start work 'til late. Anywhere you want. You want me take you to the ocean, we can go."

"I would love to, Jay!" Celia said, her forehead creasing. "More than anything, but I can't. I have to be at the hospital in about an hour, for some volunteer stuff." She waved her hand, wishing it would just go away.

"Just skip it," he said, frowning. "Place won't fall down without you."

"I know. You're right. But I can't, I just . . . my sister . . ."

He stood there, looking down, and finally replied. "OK, we won't go."

"I'm sorry. It was so nice of you to think of it, though. Maybe another time."

Jay's eyes were focused up the stairs behind her. "Your sister home?"

"No, of course not." Celia laughed. "She has a real job, full time, and sometimes at night." And then following his train of thought, "Do you want to come in?"

"You want me to?"

"Yes, sure, of course."

She could only meet his eyes a moment, before she broke his gaze. "Come in; we're upstairs." She followed him up, thinking, *Oh, my God. What now?*

Inside the apartment, they stood a moment looking around.

"Would you like something to drink?" Celia asked. *What was there?* Juice or milk. Coffee? She couldn't see him drinking tea. No wine, not even a beer. Well, it was too early for that . . .

"No, thank you."

Celia started toward the mantle. "Here, you can check out some pictures— my family, some plays I was in, friends in California, our old house in New York . . ."

"Never mind about the pictures," Jay said, his voice lower, fuller.

Celia turned back. "Don't tell me you're going to grill me again about my questionable background," she said with a nervous giggle.

He walked over to the sofa and sat down. "Come here."

Celia considered. As she remained standing, she thought rapidly. *Are we going to do this? Is it going to be OK? Do I want this?* She felt like she was hovering just off the floor, looking down at the scene. But her arms and legs were taking over for her, propelled by the rush of heat and emotion through her body. It was hopeless; she was giddy, and silly, and lonely. It had been a long time since she had been with Carlos, since she had kissed anybody, since anyone kissed her. She walked over to where he sat watching her.

She sat next to him, letting her bent leg rest against him, and almost instinctively he put his hand around her waist. Here we go, she thought, waiting like a diver to take a plunge. What would they taste like, feel like, his kisses? She offered her face to him, her lips. But, strangely, he hesitated, looking first at the floor and then to the ceiling. What was wrong?

"Last night," he said finally. "I couldn't get you offa my mind. Yeah, you was in my dream," he explained, nodding. He turned slightly, angling himself toward her.

"Really?" she said, surprised. And then, hopefully, "A good one?"

He didn't answer right away. "Kind of strange."

Not exactly the romantic lead up Celia was expecting, but she could see in his face that it was there, this dream, hanging over him, like a cloud. He ran his tongue over his lips.

"We were goin' at it, me and you," he said, which made Celia blush all over. "We makin' out and all, and then my mother come in the room and start yellin'. She mad, real mad. But the funny thing is that she not mad about you bein' there an all. She say you stole her dress—yellow dress she got for a weddin' one time."

Celia's eyebrows arched, none too pleased. This was not very romantic. But, clearly, he was uncomfortable. Superstitious, maybe?

"So you get up and start runnin', but she after you with a broom. You run out the door, and then it get so peculiar, I don't know what."

"Well, you've got to tell me now," Celia said. Romance would have to wait.

"Outside the house, you turn into a bird, like a chicken or somethin', but you still got the same face, and the same hair like you do. And you tryin' and tryin' to get up into the air, but you wings don't work, so you just hoppin' along. Then I come out the house tryin' to help you, but my mother take the broom to me, and she whackin' me good, like she used to. Then you gone, disappeared like that." He snapped his fingers. There was a crease in his brow; his brown eyes were perplexed. It was no joke.

Celia shrugged, helpless to understand any of it.

"Well, at least you tried to help me," she said, patting his hand. "That was nice. You know, I had a dream, too, last night. Not like yours. About riding in the car, like we were yesterday." A thought struck her. "Maybe it was that Burger King food we ate."

Jay sat gazing at her, and then a smile broke through and began to spread. It was *the* smile, the signal to proceed. He moved closer, pulling off his jacket. She could smell him, and see the imperfections of his skin where the slight whiskers poked through on his chin.

Wow, she thought. *We're really going to do this.* From his hair she looked back at his eyes, and then his beautiful mouth. *He's so . . . wow. Yes, I want him. I want this.*

She leaned toward him, and his arms went around her, gently.

"You OK with this?" he asked softly. She nodded, she couldn't wait for that first kiss. His lips were soft and warm. His eyes seemed to be smiling at her, from amusement or pleasure, who could tell? He was taller than Carlos, but not as heavy, smoothly muscled. They moved together, clasping and stroking. Now he seemed happy, eager, hungry for her, too. Maybe he had also been lonely for a while. Maybe he was ready to move past that old girlfriend. . . .

They took his shirt off, and then the t-shirt that she was wearing, no bra. Skin to skin, chest to chest, when she felt his heart beating as fast as her own, it was all she needed to be sure.

Here we go.

Afterwards, Celia pulled the afghan down from the top of the sofa bed over the two of them.

"So, now you know," Jay said with a bit of a smirk.

"Know what?"

"What it's like with a black man. That's what you wanted to know, right?"

"No!" Celia protested. "That's not why." Then she thought maybe it was, in part. "Maybe a little bit, I guess." She paused, at a loss. "I just . . . I . . . like you."

"Yeah, that's nice." He continued to hold her gaze.

"You were more gentle than I thought you'd be."

"You think I be rough?"

"You seem so stern sometimes. That's all. Sometimes you seem mad."

"Yeah?" he said, looking surprised.

"Yes."

"But not at you. I ain't mad at you." For the first time, Celia felt like he was relaxing, not testing, just being himself. He started pulling his fingers through her hair, combing the curls out straight and then patting them down against her head. He caught her glance. "You mind if I do that?"

Celia shrugged, not minding at all.

"I always wanted to see how it feel like," he said. "Soft, like you."

"Oh, really? Everyone tells me I'm too bony."

"Yeah, you that," he said with a smile. "But in your face and your self I mean. Real sweet. Sweeter than sweet."

"Well, thanks, Jay."

They were quiet, the refrigerator humming.

"I don't want to move," Jay said, yawning widely. "I could just stay like this, like two birds in a nest."

"Yeah, right," said Celia laughing. "And I'm the big yellow bird that can't fly." Then, checking the clock in the kitchen, she was startled to see the time so late. "But we can't. I mean, I can't. I have to get ready." She kissed him once more on his lips before sitting up and looking for her clothes.

What happens next? she thought vaguely, and then put her attention to the business of getting washed up and dressed. Just time for a quick rinse. Jay was dressed when she returned to the living room in a bathrobe.

She walked him to the door.

"See you at work, I guess," Celia said, trying to calculate when they'd next be together. "I'm not working this weekend. We're going to Wilmington tomorrow, my sister and I, for Thanksgiving. My next night is Monday." That seemed like such a long time away.

"You take care," was all Jay said, zipping his jacket and checking his pocket for keys.

"Jay!" Celia remembered suddenly, calling after him on the stairway. "I'm sorry we didn't get to the shore. I'd still like to go sometime."

Without turning around, he waved good-bye.

Chapter 11

As she packed for the trip to Wilmington on Thanksgiving morning, Celia kept going over the time she had spent with Jay, both happy and anxious. He never asked about birth control, although she was on the pill. How would he know that? Maybe he assumed that because she had a boyfriend, or because she went away to college, she knew how to take care of matters like that. Maybe he was trusting to chance. Or, maybe he didn't care.

Celia threw jeans, a fresh shirt, pajamas, and some underwear into the duffel bag. She'd need a dress as well. The sweat pants were too ratty-looking, the ones she wore when Jay came over. Was he planning to sleep with her when he arrived at the doorstep, or did it just happen, since his original plan of going to the Delaware beaches had fallen through? Or, maybe he thought after a day at the beach that something would come up between them. But where? And how?

And what about Carlos? The last she heard from Janelle was that he had not returned to school or the apartment with Eddie. No one in the music department knew where he was—somewhere not in Santa Cruz.

"Right." She pushed some socks through a gap in the zippered bag. What about Carlos? Would she ever see him again? And if she did, what would she tell him? What was this, between Jay and her, anyway? Then she remembered the dress, and opened up the bag again with a sigh. And a slip, if she could find one.

Grace drove to Wilmington and they found Roxanne's parents' house on a little side street with sweet cottage homes. Roxanne met them at the door in a sweater and leggings: a big, attractive girl. Her mother, a youthful looking woman with a hearty laugh, welcomed them inside. Roxanne's twin brother, Alec, stood silently in the entrance hallway, nodding in greeting. They had met Alec before, when he'd come to visit Roxanne in Sutton. He was a nice looking guy, a blue-eyed dirty blond with dark eyebrows and lashes. Quiet, serious. He did some kind of technical work for the utilities company. In Sutton, Roxanne had fixed up Alec and Grace on a double date, which had gone well. Celia suspected part of the invitation for Thanksgiving was for

Roxanne to play cupid. Celia was just there because they couldn't leave her alone for the holiday.

They brought their bags to the guest room, where they changed and returned to the living room for a drink before dinner. Celia tried to make conversation, but found her mind wandering to the Inn and what Jay was doing. He was working Thanksgiving, she knew, but then he said something about helping Owen prepare a dinner for his large, extended family, a reunion of some kind. On Saturday, was it? She was restless, wanting to get up and go outside for air or just to move about. The dress was tugging at her armpits; the tights were intolerable.

Instead, they went into the living room to meet more family, Roxanne's older sister and her trio of fair-haired children. The husband and grandfather had attended the high school football game and just returned with news of a hometown victory. By two o'clock, everyone was ready to eat. Yet, Celia hardly tasted the food. She found herself watching Grace and Alec, seated next to each other. They matched so well in their quiet manner and serious personalities. It was such a natural fit, everything working out as it should. Not like Celia.

In bed that evening, just feet away from Grace, she ruminated about a relationship with Jay—a black boyfriend, from this part of the country, a rural area, and without further education. How would her sister react? Maybe not too surprised; she knew Celia so well, after all. Grace had never met Carlos, but she knew about his Hispanic background, and saw his picture in their living room every day. But, it wasn't the same. That was California. Carlos was an accomplished musician, putting himself through college. He had grown up exposed to arts and culture, and had traveled. And he looked more or less Italian in a snapshot. In Santa Cruz, they were just part of the greater mix of people.

Then another thought occurred to her, and she jerked upright in bed. *What if Jay tells everyone? Would he do that?* Her mind raced, thinking back to the ribbing in the kitchen: Eldridge's warning about "talking about your titties and ass." It would be more than embarrassing; it would be humiliating. Unbearable. She could hear Roland with his sarcastic remarks, and the others laughing along. It was one thing to kid her when they thought she was innocent. It would be another thing if they thought she had fallen.

She turned over in the creaky bed, trying not to wake Grace. The question was, she asked her pillow, would he betray her, turn it all into a big joke?

"I don't think he will," she whispered. "I don't think he will."

The remainder of the weekend passed quickly enough, with trips to the DuPont Estate, parks and museums, things normally Celia enjoyed and had missed in their more isolated life. But most of it was wasted on Celia. She stared mutely out the car window, barely registering the icy raindrops that had begun to fall in downtown Wilmington.

She was in such a hurry to get back to Sutton. For what? Say if Jay decided he wanted to go out, to be her boyfriend. Is that what she wanted? She honestly couldn't say. What kind of couple would they make? Where would they go? Would they be welcome together at the holiday table at Roxanne's house?

And what about Carlos? It had been five months now since she'd heard from him, in June. Almost as long as the time they had been going out. No new information from California. She shook her head, sadly. *Carlos, Carlos, Carlos.*

Grace was upbeat as they packed Sunday morning to return home, humming as they stripped beds and finished packing. Roxanne's family couldn't have been kinder, going out of their way to give two girls away from home a nice family holiday. Celia could see that they felt warmly toward Grace, who shared an interest in quilting and crafting with Roxanne and her mom. As they prepared to depart, Roxanne's mother made a fuss over the two of them: "These girls on their own, working hard, and doing so well for themselves." Celia appreciated the attention and kind words, while another part of her felt like a complete fraud.

The trip home went smoothly, in spite of the holiday traffic and the snow flurries starting to accumulate. Grace yawned at the wheel, genteelly covering her mouth.

"Do you want me to drive?" Celia asked.

"No, I'm fine," Grace answered. "Did you have a good time at Roxanne's?"

"Of course. They're such nice people. And so generous, to put us up like that."

"Good, I'm glad. I wasn't sure. You seemed preoccupied. I thought maybe you were a little under the weather."

"Oh, no," Celia said, clasping her purse in her lap, thinking how to dodge Grace's questions. "It's great to get away. Didn't you think so?"

"Yes, well, Sutton is beautiful and rustic, but there are a lot of long, quiet days in the winter months. Sometimes I don't see much of you during the week—do you ever get a little bored and lonely?"

Celia was surprised at the question. Her eyes followed the windshield wipers, clearing the tracks of snowflakes that melted to rivulets, letting the rhythm soothe her.

"No, I've been all right. I have a few friends from the restaurant. We have fun. You know, Wanda and Warren, and Anita." Probably best not to mention Roland and Tony.

"Any thoughts what you might do next, after the holiday season winds down?"

"Oh, well, yes, of course," Celia said, speaking quickly. In fact, she hadn't thought much at all. "You know, I've been doing really well with my savings. Much better than I thought." She found her mouth running on, "Maybe I could get back to campus for spring semester. By the end of January . . ."

Grace was shaking her head. "Celia, be realistic. Even if you could pay tuition, there's no money for living expenses. You'd end up right back in the same spot."

Grace pursed her lips, focused on the road, a couple of large trucks closing in around them. One of them was for linen delivery, and Celia wondered if it was going to the Grand Marsh Inn. The other truck had a cheerful logo of a smiling mouth about to take a bite of a cupcake. Just for a moment, Celia wondered what it would be like to ride away in a truck like that full of sweet snacks and desserts, making people happy, even if it wasn't good for them.

Away from the truck, Grace glanced over at Celia. "I meant maybe a more permanent job, where you could still take classes at night, some place like Wilmington or Salisbury or even Baltimore that has more jobs and better transportation."

Celia suddenly realized that Grace was trying to tell her something else, something more. Did she want her to leave? Surely, she had not found out about Jay.

"Are you saying it's time for me to go?" Celia asked. They had passed the community college where Grace taught, so it wasn't much farther to Sutton.

"No, I'm not saying that," Grace said. "You can stay as long as you want. I enjoy your company, and I'm glad we've had this time together. I just wonder if it's the best thing for you."

"Is that it?"

"All right. There is something else, but there's no really good way to say it."

"Go ahead. I'm your sister."

"You know Nurse Harrison from downstairs?"

"Yes." Celia rolled her eyes.

Grace sighed. "She said she's seen a number of people in and out of the apartment."

Celia's heart leaped. *Jay?* Was she home? Did she hear them? No, no. Nurse Harrison said "people." It must have been Wanda and Warren, Lacey and Phil A., those guys. A few times, not that many. When she finally got Wanda over her hang-up of entering the apartment.

"Does she know they're my friends?" she got out, through a constricted throat.

"I told her that."

"And?"

"She finds them noisy and disruptive."

"No!"

"She says she hears loud music, and people moving around. She thinks you're having parties up there."

"Well, we're not. Maybe we put on music to dance to a couple times, but there's no drinking or smoking, ever. I swear."

"I believe you," Grace said. "But she says she's nervous now to come to her own house. Apparently, there are some kids who roam the streets after school bothering people, heckling them I guess. She thinks they'll start coming to our neighborhood."

"That's ridiculous." Celia sounded indignant, but immediately she thought of the acorn assault. It wasn't just heckling.

"She saw a man there once, in front of the building, a young black man just standing there, looking up at the apartment. I guess it really frightened her."

Celia gulped. There was such a storm of thoughts that she couldn't answer. She swallowed to wet her throat.

"So what are you saying then? My friends shouldn't come over?"

"Maybe you could find other places to meet, for now, like the pizza place or the bowling alley."

They were passing the mini-mall at the by-pass around the outskirts of Sutton. Grace stayed on the road leading into the center of town. Just before twilight, the landscape was colorless and uninviting.

Grace heaved a sigh. "Celia, I'm sorry. I really am. I wish I didn't have to say anything about it at all. But I'm afraid what Nurse Harrison might say at the hospital about me, and us. I can't afford to lose a job, and I'll probably be here long after you've flown off someplace else."

Celia couldn't argue. She was, after all, a guest in her sister's home. She knew better than anyone how Grace had made her own way, and it wasn't fair for Celia to jeopardize that, even for a principle. She had to work harder at making a plan, having a timeline, or taking some courses. Or finding another job. Which probably meant leaving.

"OK," Celia said, quietly. "I won't have them over anymore. I'm sorry if we caused a problem."

"It's not your fault, Celia. It's nothing you've done, and I know it's not right. The rules are different here, compared to how we were brought up, but I don't see how we're going to change things, right now, just me and you."

They were entering the familiar downtown area, and Celia felt her cloudy thinking starting to clear. What happened with Jay was not going to happen again. Whatever Jay had to say, she would downplay it and let him know it was a slip; a nice slip, but just a one time thing. She would give notice after New Year's, and then start looking for other employment. And this time next year Sutton would be just another chapter in her life.

They passed a blue VW bug driven by a black man. Celia couldn't tell for sure, but she thought it must be Jay. She turned to look after the car, but it had disappeared. Her heart was pounding so hard, she thought Grace would hear it.

"Oh, dear," she groaned to herself. *I'm going to have to see him tomorrow. I've got to say something. I've got to know. What's it going to be?* Then, in distress, she realized she did want to see him again. She couldn't wait to see him again, and it was going to be a hard time waiting.

Monday Celia got to work earlier than usual. She didn't see Jay around at all at first. She busied herself in the dining room, checking back in the kitchen every few minutes. Anita waylaid her on the way back out to the dining room, bright-eyed and energetic.

"You, Celia, I've been looking for you," she started. "When we get a moment, I've got something to tell you that could be verrr–ry interesting. It will take time to explain the details, but I just want to float the idea by you, and get you thinking."

"Anita, what are you talking about?" Celia asked. "You've got me completely mystified."

"Just the way I want you," Anita smiled. "A little business proposition I'm thinking about. You know I've been taking that course, right?"

Celia nodded, dumbly. She might have heard something about it.

"It's going to be good, I think, for both of us, I really think so."

"At least give me a clue."

"It's something that will get you out of here, and will be good for you, in more than one way. I'm talking about another employment possibility. And I think it will be perfect for someone like you, with your talents and charms."

With that, she whirled away, and Celia was left shaking her head. What could it be? Another restaurant somewhere, a little Mom and Pop roadside diner? Celia walked back into the kitchen to put in an order, when she was jolted by seeing Jay already in place on the cooking line.

"Jay!" she said, in some confusion, handing over the order slip.

"You know me," he replied, teasing. "So, what's up, Celia?"

She had nothing prepared. Every thought she had on the way in to work had suddenly vanished. He looked up expectantly, seemingly nonchalant, but shifting his glance from one side to the other.

"Hi, guys," she addressed Phil A., Cuffie, and a new guy. Chef Owen was not in his place, probably in the downstairs kitchen.

"Did you all have a nice Thanksgiving?" she heard herself saying. It came out bright and false.

"Right, we love working four days straight," Cuffie said. "Turkey make me sick." There were shadows under his eyes. No doubt it was constant work over the long weekend. "You missed all the fun."

"Yes, and all the good money," Celia said, realizing that only applied to her, since they were paid the same regardless how busy. Some of the other wait staff had wanted extra hours. She was lucky to get away for a few days, her first real break since she started.

"Hey, Jay," she said briskly. "There's something I wanted to ask you. Do you think we could talk, if you have a few minutes?"

The assistant cooks eyed one another, until finally Phil A. said, "Better keep the ladies happy, Jay man," and they laughed. He was a gentle giant, Phil A., with his meaty arms and the look of a bull-dog, and Celia appreciated his attempt at breeziness.

"Sure, happy to. Just not now. I got to get these boys going before Owen gets back." His tone was light, but Celia could tell he was vexed, and his smile was more sheepish than smooth.

"OK," Celia said, feeling herself blush, but determined to get a more concrete answer. "Let's try to meet up before we leave. I . . . I . . . wanted to get back to you about some of those things you asked me about before . . ." she improvised.

"I'll be here," he said, pleasantly, noncommittally. Celia got the sense he was being evasive, hoping to avoid the conversation she had planned. With that, she got back to work, always a beat or two behind the mark with her duties and her conversations, as she ran over the two ongoing scenarios in her mind: Anita's proposition and Jay's response to her and the situation. Curiosity gnawed at her, and the customers seemed dull and the hours long, until it was time for break.

She saw Jay again, in the kitchen as she passed through looking for Anita. He was still at the grill and did not look up. In the break room, Anita was eating an early dinner, and scribbling notes on the back of her pad. Celia could make out her own name. She hesitated, wondering if Anita might have heard anything about her and Jay. But when Anita looked up, her face was all smiles. Celia took the seat across from her, setting out her fork, knife, and spoon, and placing a napkin on her lap.

"So, what is it? It's not your own restaurant, is it?"

"Hush, girl," Anita said, leaning across the table. "First of all, we've got to keep this quiet. Second, you're out of your mind if you think I want anymore to do with serving food. But you're right. It is a business I'm looking to start, and I'll need some help. You took some dance classes, right, at college?"

"Yes . . ." Celia said. *That news had spread.* She gulped down a glass of milk to quench a powerful thirst.

"You can help me teach exercise classes at our new fitness center."

"Exercise?" Celia said, coughing on the last of her milk. "Fitness?"

"Sure," Anita came back. "Why not? I saw a program on television that said it's one of the fastest growing businesses in the country. Plus, women around here need something to get them off their butts and get in shape."

That sounded strangely like a slogan. Celia wiped the splatter from her mouth.

"They're not fit, like you and me," Anita said. And then, out of nowhere, added, "I played girls' basketball in high school, you know."

Celia could picture it very well, Anita in the little jersey and shorts, the ball between her hands, feinting side to side. Probably aggressive; the kind of girl you didn't want to mess with. At least, not Celia, who was not very competitive, or athletic, really, except for dance, more of the creative kind of thing.

"So," Anita was glaring at her, "do you want to?"

"Well, gosh, that's a lot to take in," Celia said. Her answer apparently didn't appease Anita, whose brows rose. "But I sure want to know more," Celia added as she picked up her fork. She was starving, in need of food, trying to get the seafood casserole in her mouth. "Would you be able to pay me?"

"Of course, fool. It's not a volunteer job. I'm not sure how many hours to start. And I think we will offer commission for each new membership that comes in."

"Oh, I see." Celia nodded approvingly. She continued to chew, but more slowly, turning over the possibilities in her mind. She pictured herself in a leotard, leading classes with music. And then, somehow, asking people to pay them money.

"We really think you would fit in very nicely," Anita went on, encouragingly.

"Who's we?" Celia asked

"My friend, Shelly. We go way back, since high school. She's a white girl, like you." She arched her eyebrows. "We went through integration times together. That'll make you close, if you don't end up hating each other. When I was a little girl, my daddy wasn't allowed in her daddy's restaurant. Now we're going into business together. And the business is only for women. No men to monkey up the works."

An interesting twist. It definitely sounded like it had potential, and it might be fun. She would like the boss, and helping the boss get ahead. Plus the whole thing about empowering women, not to mention crossing the old color lines, all right out in the open. Maybe this is what she needed, the opportunity she had been looking for. She put down her fork, too excited to finish. Another gulp of milk, and then a few bites of the apple tart.

"I'm definitely interested," Celia said.

"I've told Shelly all about your sweet self. I want you to meet her, and we'll show you around a little."

"You've got a place already?"

"We'll get you out to see it."

"Where? Tell me. Don't make me wait—it's cruel!"

A couple of the bus boys entered the break room, carrying food, and then Cuffie and a girl.

Anita leaned over, shielding her mouth with a napkin. "At the strip mall, where the old exercise place used to be, the one that closed down. How about Friday morning? I'll meet you out front of the hotel here and take you over."

"You're on," Celia said, excited to be in on the big secret. As they got up to leave, others were waiting to take their seats.

At the doorway, Anita handed Celia a note, which she only had time to peek at: Anita's phone number and a scribbled "Don't be late."

Celia never got a chance to say more than a couple words to Jay. After a busy dinner shift, the evening was winding down. Her mood had lightened, and although she was still uncertain, she felt more cheerful and energetic than earlier in the day. She finished up a little early, giving her last table to Wanda, and grabbed her jacket and purse, heading Jay off at the exit from the cooking area.

"Jay, how about a ride?" she asked lightly. "I'm totally tired and it's totally freezing out there. Would you mind?"

He didn't answer. For a moment, she thought he was going to ignore her. But when he met her eyes, he looked grave, almost daunted.

She tried again, more like a joke. "Don't you think Anita would like you to help out poor old me?"

"All right, I give you a ride. But . . . but," Jay stalled a moment. "I got to wait for someone."

Celia was disappointed, and slightly annoyed.

"OK." What else could she say? "I'll meet you at the door."

Five minutes later, Jay came to the door, followed by a pale, dark-haired woman Celia vaguely recognized: the girl with the long nails in the Beckers' office. Pauline worked in the banquet area, one of the managers. She didn't look like the type who smiled easily, although she was a pretty girl, heavily made up. When their eyes met, Pauline gave her a sour look, almost hostile. Celia's heart began to pound with embarrassment and an uncertainty that made her feel almost sick. Was she the girlfriend?

Then, out of the blue, Cuffie popped up, sliding into his jacket. "Jay, man," he said. "You drop me home, right?"

Jay shook his head, like a man overburdened. But he waved, "Come on, come on," and pushed open the door. Celia brushed past him and spotted the VW bug in the lot. She arrived first at the car and opened the passenger door, bending the seat forward so that Pauline and Cuffie could climb in the back. She would be the first one out, really only a matter of blocks. Even as she took her seat in the front, she thought, *If only I could jump out and walk away from here—without looking like a fool.* But when she saw the cut-out palm tree hanging from the rearview mirror, her heart beat like crazy, with joy and confusion.

Jay started the car and they pulled out in the direction of Celia's house. They rode in strained silence, not even the radio. Pauline's musky scent filled the car, overpowering the palm tree. Jay dropped Celia at the curb in front of the apartment and said, "Good night." Pauline moved quickly into the empty front seat, and the car sped away.

Celia sighed as she mounted the stairs to their door. She had no more answers and no more resolution than when she'd started out. Jay was acting strangely, but not disrespectful or unkind. The problem was lack of opportunity to communicate normally, because their only point of contact was a busy work place. Otherwise, it was pretty much a normal evening at the Inn, like before things had happened on that Wednesday morning. Except, of course, for Anita's proposition. And the appearance of this stuck-up Pauline, who didn't seem like a girl Jay would go for. Tired and yawning, moving quietly not to disturb Grace, Celia got ready for bed. Then, pulling up the covers in her sofa bed, the place they had been together, she finally had to face facts in the dark: something had changed.

Chapter 12

"Today is another day," Celia told herself on the way to the Inn the next morning. "Maybe it will all make sense today." She was running a bit late, and would have to finish fixing her hair in the ladies' room. Tuesday was a double shift for Celia, although Jay wouldn't be in until three-thirty or four, perhaps for the best, considering her state of mind. For the first time, she wasn't looking forward to going to work. The novelty had worn off, the work was hard, and people and situations were sometimes hard to deal with. Her energy was lagging, and there was this awkward situation with Jay. Or maybe she was just ready for something . . . more.

"Good morning, Miss Celia," James greeted her as usual outside the front entrance. She slowed her steps, knowing she had little time and not sure she wanted James to see her glum expression. Even the thought of chocolates in his pocket couldn't perk her up.

"Good morning, James."

"What's the weather today?" he asked. Celia cocked her head: did she hear right? He was the weather-watcher, not her. Still, she gazed at the sky.

"Overcast," she said. "But I don't think it's supposed to rain."

Still, James didn't smile, but looked at her searchingly. "The weather in here, I mean." He tapped his chest.

Celia managed a small smile. Did he know everything, or was he just good at reading faces?

"Not that good," she admitted. "Unsettled, definitely unsettled. Maybe a storm brewing."

"Don't you worry," he said. "That storm's going to pass. Always does. What's a little rough weather, anyway? Makes life more interesting, right?" Then he dug into his pocket. "I got something here for you." He handed her the bundled napkin. "Apple strudel and a chocolate croissant."

"Ooh," Celia said, her face lighting up. "My favorites." She clucked her tongue as she put the pastries carefully inside her purse. "You're going to spoil me."

He pfff–ed at her. "You're a girl needs a little spoiling now and then."

"James!" she said, embarrassed. *What a thing to for him to say!*

His white glove tapped the watch in his pocket. "Now go, go."

Inside, she made a beeline to the women's bathroom to finish bobby-pinning her hair. The minutes were ticking away, and still she dawdled, reluctant to go out and face staff or guests with a big, fake smile. Finally, she opened the door and headed down the hallway.

"You in big trouble," Josie said to Celia just as she placed her time card into the slot. She appeared to be waiting for her.

Celia spun around, floored. "What are you talking about?"

"Pauline, she so mad at you. She say if she see you, she gonna mess you up."

"Me?" Celia said, a finger to her chest. "Mess me up? What's that supposed to mean?"

"She gonna fight with you. Punch you out."

"No!" Celia couldn't believe her ears. Then, looking at Josie's serious face, she began to wonder. Where on earth had she gotten that idea? It was ludicrous—someone, a girl, wanting to fight her!

"Josie, that can't be right," she started. She glanced down at her drooping apron with a frown and began to retie the knot in back. The collar, too, was probably out of place, she had dressed in such a hurry.

Josie remained fixed in her spot against the wall.

"That what she say. I heard it."

"What exactly did she say?" Celia asked, impatiently.

"She say you too friendly with Jay, that her boyfriend, and you dis her."

"What? How? I never did anything to her," Celia started out loudly, and then lowered her voice. "I'm sure of it. I barely even know her. And I didn't know Jay was her boyfriend. He said . . . well, he . . ."

Josie shook her head again, this time at Celia's appalling ignorance.

"They been together since high school freshman."

Warren had just arrived and joined them in front of the time clock.

"Sophomores," he said. "Off and on, six or seven years now."

"No!" said Celia again, cringing. "Honestly, that's news to me."

Josie wouldn't let her off the hook. "Everybody know it that knows anything. And Owen, he married to Pauline's mother. Owen help Jay about getting a job and being a chef, like him."

"OK, OK, I got it," Celia said, raising a hand. She began putting together pieces of information from past conversations, little details she'd noticed. *What did they know, exactly? Had Jay told all? Why would he? To make more trouble for himself?* It didn't make sense.

She stepped aside while Warren punched his card, and then stood facing them.

"But why does Pauline think I was insulting her? I never said anything against her. I didn't even know about her, or them."

"Cuz you took the front seat," Josie said. "When Jay gave y'all a ride home yesterday."

"You can't be serious!" Celia said, laughing outright. "It didn't mean anything. It just worked out that way." To herself, she was thinking, *It's like a foreign country; nothing makes sense. I can't deal with things on this level.* Her eye went to the clock: 10:58 and she would be working for the next twelve hours. God help her.

"Enough of this nonsense," she said. "Time to get to work, right?" But when she walked to the cashier's station to pick up an order pad, Warren and Josie followed.

"Pauline coming in at noon," Josie said.

"She's got a bad temper," Warren warned her. "Maybe you better lie low for a while."

"I will not!" Celia cried out, and then lowered her voice. "She has no reason to threaten me. If she's mad at anyone, why not Jay? It's up to him how he acts toward me, or anyone."

As she picked up a stack of clean napkins and headed toward the dining room doors, she had a vision of the well-groomed Pauline chasing her across the kitchen while Jay stood silently by watching the action. Striding purposefully through the room, she saw the grill cooks at work; they probably overheard the conversation. Did everyone know everything going on around this place, except her?

What a fool I've been, she told herself. *The question is, how big a fool?*

She looked to see if Anita was working, but then hoped that she wasn't and that she wouldn't hear about this mess. Folding napkins at her station, she nodded to Roland and Tony as they passed, not wanting to engage them in conversation.

The shift went quickly, without incident. Warren tried to joke with her when she came in the kitchen to pick up food. She smiled vacantly, functioning on automatic pilot, going through the motions smoothly and efficiently. She could still make the small talk that earned the good tips, but the charm had worn thin. As she closed down the station for the afternoon break, she saw herself as at a distance, not quite present maybe, numb. She couldn't figure out how she felt or what she wanted to do. Maybe nothing, she said to herself, maybe just let it all unroll around her. In the meantime, she had to count her money, eat a quick meal.

"You OK?" Wanda asked, leaning on the side of the service station. "You don't look right."

"It's something stupid that happened with Pauline. For some reason she's mad at me and out to get me. What's her problem, anyway?"

"She OK. I don't have no business with her, but she seem OK a couple times I worked banquet for her. She know what goin' on, and she fair." She blinked. "I guess she don't like Jay paying attention to you. Just ignore 'em both."

That was about as close to personal as Wanda ever got. And then, true to form, she changed the subject. "Hey, Celia, you been up to Baltimore, right?"

"Yes, I've been there with my sister. Why do you ask?" Celia tried to get her mind on Wanda's question. The napkins were folded; the station was ship-shape. Wanda's eyes were still shy behind the thick rims, but her glance was hopeful.

"You like it up there?"

"Yes, it's nice, I guess, if you like cities."

"How about the Inner Harbor?"

"Now that is nice, a lot of fun to walk around. Why? Are you planning to go?"

"Just wondering. What do they have there?"

"At the Inner Harbor?" Celia asked, and Wanda nodded.

"It's on the waterfront, with lots of shops and some nice restaurants. Busy, crowded, expensive, lots of tourists spending lots of money. Is that what you mean?"

"Yeah, thanks. Just curious."

Then, unexpectedly, Jay came in early at 2:30 pm, during the mid-afternoon break, when only a few tables were open for service. Celia was putting trays away in the kitchen. Without speaking, Celia exited to the dining room and stood at her station, burning hot in the face, a clenched knot in her stomach. The hand that wiped the counter shook, and she felt the brunt of her feelings hit her like an angry wind. For the first time in her experience with men, she wondered if she'd been used. Was it just a way to get his girlfriend jealous? How could she not have guessed? But he had seemed so interested in her history and her plans for the future, didn't he?

There was so much more going on here than she could see, or understand. Almost like a conspiracy. Like she was the butt of some joke: the new girl, the artsy white college girl. Yeah, how entertaining this must be, two white girls fighting over a black guy. That was rich. Suddenly, the images of faces, smiling and joking, seemed menacing to her now, masks. *It's mean,* she said to herself, wallowing in self-pity, *and unfair.*

Don't let them play with you like cats with a mouse . . . Celia remembered Anita's words, from long, long ago—or was it cats with a bird? Something like that. *If you get yourself in trouble, keep your head up.* She said that, too.

This must be what she meant. Anita had been trying to warn her, when Celia had thought there was no danger, no problem. She wished Anita was there, but then again she was glad she wasn't. Anita was too strong and upstanding to have much sympathy. But maybe Celia could salvage things from now on. The problem was she needed to know more, to understand, but she had no one to talk to.

Then she thought of Eldridge: poor, gay, lisping, odd-looking, uneducated, and, oh yes, a smoker, to boot. He was the only one who seemed to always be on level with her, even to the point of explaining his straight-faced lies to the manager. He had even tried, in his way, to defend her honor, or reputation, in the kitchen discussion of her love life a while back. Who else was there?

She knew where to find him. He was taking napkins from used trays, and bundling them for the laundry.

"Eldridge, can I talk to you, in private?"

He turned, one eye cocked. "What can I do for you, baby girl?" He escorted her to one of the back bays where deliveries for the kitchen came in. They could see the side entrance where the customers entered from the parking lot.

"Maybe we should wait," Celia said, anxious not to miss the mid-afternoon diners.

"No, no. We got all the time in the world." Eldridge rested his backside on a stack of empty palettes, relaxed as if he were sitting on a couch. "Wanda cover for you. You know she do that."

"OK, you're right," Celia conceded. "It's just this . . . have you heard about that whole thing of Pauline threatening . . . well, making threats against me?"

"Yeah, I heard it."

"So, what's up with her and Jay? I just don't get it."

"No, it prolly don't make much sense," Eldridge said. "You an outsider here. It's a love thing and a hate thing."

Celia waited while Eldridge crossed a leg, gathering his thoughts.

"I know them all their lives. They two years behind me at school. It's integration times, so we all growed up together, black and white. Not rich white, a'course, from the big houses. They go to private schools. Pauline and Jay, they started sweethearts in high school. Lots a kids done that, too, cause they know each other—and they want to vex folks," he added with a chuckle. "But mostly they done after high school. They go back to they own kind then.

But not Jay and Pauline. They stay strong with each other. She the prettiest girl. She could have any boy, any color."

Eldridge fumbled in his pants pocket, playing with his cigarette lighter.

"She still pretty, but she starting to look hard. Her mom is married to Owen, from the second marriage. I never saw Pauline dad myself. He ain't never been around that I remember."

"And Jay?"

"He think he too big for this small town, back then. He act like he king rooster around school, never mind about teachers and learning. Yeah," he summarized, "he a punk. When he fourteen, fifteen, he go out with his boys, pilfering, breaking down mailboxes and such, 'til he get in trouble with the police. He don't care. But Pauline bring him around. She sensible and she work hard. She know how to deal with black folk, too. Only reason he finish high school 'cause a her."

Celia could barely fit this story to the people she had been dealing with in real life. It was so romantic, almost a fairy tale, everything they had to overcome to stay together. So, what on earth was she doing in the middle of it all? Try as she might, she couldn't see herself as a temptress, or a man stealer. What happened was so, well, unplanned.

Her eye caught movement in the parking lot. Two groups of elderly diners headed toward the entrance.

"We better get back," she said reluctantly. "So, tell me quick. Why's Pauline so mad at me?"

"She think you after her man, and she think he might be goin'."

"Why? Why would she think that? She's never around at all when I'm here."

"She know his boys, Phil A., and Cuffie from the kitchen, and the girls, too, Lacey and Vanessa." Lacey she knew, the dark, bony girl with sharp features and a wide mouth. But Vanessa she only knew from passing, that tall, athletic girl who worked with Lacey, who used to be a basketball player.

Eldridge went on. "They tell her what's going down. Besides," he gestured with an open hand, "everybody know. Everybody can see he pay attention to you, and you nice back. You looking at him."

Celia flushed to her roots, her shoulders tensing. She'd never in her life been so carefully observed and studied. She felt like some kind of specimen on a piece of glass. What happens if we move her here, like this? Or poke her here, like that? But just how carefully had they been watching—that she couldn't tell.

"So why now?"

"She decide she want him back. Same old, same old. First she let out the line, then she reel him back in. That why she so mad. They just get back together at Owen's reunion party, then he let you sit in the front seat of his car. She say, that ain't the way it 'sposed to be."

"Oh," Celia said, picturing it so clearly—the seat pulled back, Pauline's glare. That knot in her abdomen tightened, and then slowly released. Finally, all this was making some kind of sense. She looked past Eldridge down the hallway. "I never would have gone, if anyone bothered to tell me about it." But she could smile, now, a little bit. All this fuss over who sat in the front seat. A comedy, really. There was something hilarious about the whole thing. Except of course the threats.

"Eldridge?" she asked, as they headed through the hallway into the main kitchen. "Do you think she means it, about beating me up?"

Eldridge laughed whole-heartedly. "When she say she gonna mess you up, I don't think she mean her fists. Never mind what they say. Maybe she curse at you. That all."

As Celia took out her pad and pencil to go back to the dining room, he added, "This all blow over, you see. She all noise, I sure about it. One time, Jay took up with a waitress, Penny, white college girl like you. Jay went off with her a couple weeks. Pauline didn't have no fistfight with her."

Another twist in the story. Amazing! "So, what happened?"

"Nothin'," Eldridge said, trying to recollect. "Well, Pauline say Penny a bad waitress, and she get fired."

"No!" cried Celia, stopping short.

"Yeah, but she don't care, Penny. She hate being a waitress, anyway."

"And Jay?"

"She drop him quick. She give him right back to Pauline. I think she bored with this small town life. Everybody say she go back to her daddy house in Baltimore, and she selling clothes or somethin'. But I don't think so. I think she run away with the gypsies come down through the Eastern Shore."

Now he got a smile out of Celia. "Eldridge, I know you're making that up."

"I ain't," he said. "Ask Anita 'bout the gypsies. Or you sister. They tell you."

Wanda appeared with an order slip. "Celia, where'd you disappear to? I got a table for you: four ladies."

"Yikes!" Celia cried. "Wanda, let me finish, and we'll split the tip."

"Nah, you just go ahead."

Eldridge had disappeared, and Celia realized she hadn't thanked him for listening and for the information. She'd try to catch him later. She hurried into the dining room with four bowls of turtle soup plus sherry, slightly flustered but OK. She really was OK, now. It was the uncertainty that was so painful.

"What pretty roses in your cheeks," said an eighty-year-old matron. "Did you just get in from the cold, dear?"

"No." Celia found herself speaking quite naturally. "I just tend to go pink whenever I'm busy, and it's *warm* in that kitchen." It wasn't so hard to be pleasant, like her usual self. The ladies were friendly and in good spirits, out for a good time. Celia completed their order and departed for the kitchen to drop off the slip. Jay was behind the grill organizing utensils. She handed the order to Cuffie.

"Hi, Jay," she said in a friendly voice. He looked up at her with a vacant expression.

She gave him her sweetest smile, with eyebrows raised, before turning and walking away, head up, shoulders straight.

Anita called Celia at home on Thursday to say the meeting about the fitness club was postponed. There was some problem with the business loan, and she and Shelly were meeting with the bank officers on Friday morning.

"I don't know why they're giving us such a hard time," Anita complained. "You won't believe the time I spent over the paperwork. But we've got to get this money in place before anything else happens."

"Oh, yeah," Celia agreed, all sympathy. Although she didn't understand much about financial matters, she had the painful recollection of dealing with her school bill. "Well, just let me know."

"I'll get back to you as soon as I can. And it won't hurt to say a little prayer," Anita put in. Celia was doubtful. She had always believed that it was not right to pray for money directly. Then she considered that maybe Anita meant about their whole business idea generally, not just a check.

She hung up, a little deflated. The news was not terribly good. Anita's dream might be deferred, or worse. And that would leave Celia with no kind of plan of her own.

The weekend rolled by, and Celia didn't even see Pauline, never mind fight with her. Jay was in, but never spoke more than what was necessary. The hullabaloo seemed to have passed. Besides Roland and Tony, no one else mentioned Pauline's threat, and Celia wouldn't rise to their bait, ignoring comments about Amazons and wrestling women.

A tempest in a teapot, thought Celia, on her way home from work on Sunday afternoon. Almost like nothing ever happened. That moment in time with her and Jay had just disappeared—poof! Walking through the remains of dirty, slushy snow, she tried to reason out what must have happened. Reports from the kitchen must have gotten to Pauline, as Eldridge had said. Then Pauline and Jay got back together somehow just after Thanksgiving, a few days after Jay had been to Celia's apartment. Pauline's threat was more or less a warning, following the infamous incident of the car seat, to keep Celia away.

But there was nothing to show that Jay had told Pauline, or anyone, what they had done. More and more, she was convinced. His spies were not as good as they thought. Or else, the event was so spontaneous that no one had caught it. Celia tried to put out of her mind the picture of Phil A. and Cuffie climbing the trees and looking through the apartment window with binoculars. No, they just weren't up to it.

Jay had not told. Pauline didn't know. The little play-show was over, and that was it. Jay must have stronger feelings for Pauline than he could possibly have for her. Pauline was an important part of his history, and also his future, it seemed. They could have a life here, together, like Owen and Fran. He was looking at Celia mainly because Pauline had broken up with him sometime beforehand. He was testing Celia with questions, she realized, because of what had happened with Penny, to see if she, too, would cause him to lose face. In a flash of inspiration, she thought maybe it just happened. Maybe he did like her.

She sighed. *Just one of those things.* Did he feel bad, too? It might make her feel better to know that. He didn't look like he was suffering much. After all, he had his girlfriend back, his consolation. His arms were not empty. She sighed again, kicking up dead, wet leaves.

She had reached the apartment door and went inside. Standing just inside the doorway, she halted. But I did get something. I got him. I got that experience, and that feeling, even if just for a little while. I know what that was like, and no one can take that away.

A couple days later, Celia had a day off, and an agenda. A trip to Salisbury, she decided, to see what she might find for work or school, in case things didn't work out with Anita.

The night before she had called Leona, Roland's theater friend, to see if they could meet. On the phone, Leona said she was happy to offer a tour of Salisbury State where she worked as the Artistic Director. Plus she could make a stop at the employment office. Leona also knew people who might be looking for roommates: theater people, cheap rent. Like Roland, Leona was well-spoken and somewhat dramatic, but a little more down-to-earth. The only weird thing was a little comment she made about "Tony's nose problem."

Celia couldn't tell if it was a problem as in gossiping, or in taking cocaine. Still, when she hung up, she was pretty excited at the possibilities. Celia didn't tell Grace what she was doing, except to ask if she could use the car. It was a straight shot down the highway, forty-five minutes. After dressing and tidying up around the apartment, she got the keys, a map, and checked her wallet for cash. She was pulling on a sweater, when she heard the doorbell ring. It was just after ten in the morning.

Her heart stopped. *Jay! It must be Jay, who else?* She raced downstairs.

Through the peephole, Celia saw a black man, but it wasn't Jay. It was Warren, with that smile of his. She was, all at the same time, disappointed, relieved, happy, and flustered about having company, any company, after her promise to Grace.

"Warren!" Celia exclaimed, standing in the open doorway. He sported a high school team jacket and a bright yellow knit cap. "What are you doing here so early? I'm sorry, but I'm just getting ready to go out."

"Just stopping by," Warren said, but he had a gift bag from Peebles in one hand.

"What'cha got there?" Celia asked, curious in spite of herself.

"Oh, just a little 'show and tell.' Let's see here what it could be."

He reached in the bag to take out a legal-sized envelope, opened, containing a letter. The return address on the envelope was Salisbury State.

"This is it," Warren said, pulling the letter out of the envelope. "Letter of acceptance. I'm going to college, real college."

Celia gaped like a fish out of water. Warren, college. Ahead of Celia. How could that be? But in a second, she recovered herself. "Hey, congratulations!" She raised her hand for a high-five. "Seriously, that's terrific! When do you start? Next fall?"

He looked down at the letter. Maybe he was blushing; it was hard to tell. Then he pointed to the paragraph on the page. "See, it's for next semester, actually. They have a spot for me and a room at the dorm."

Celia glanced at the letter. "Oh!" she said. "January."

"Yeah, I know, kind of a shock."

"That's so soon."

"I'm ready," Warren said, smiling broadly. "I have my money together, and mom and pop are going to help me out. They've seen how hard I've been working. They know I'm serious now. I can still work weekends at the Inn."

"Oh, my."

"Celia," he said, training his big, round eyes on her. "I have to thank you for helping me with all those forms, and the writing. You helped me get this," he said, holding out the letter. "You really did."

125

"No," Celia said, shaking it off. "Come on, stop it. No big deal."

"I got a little something here, show my appreciation."

"No, please, your thanks is enough." Warren took out a small box, a white jewelry box with a red ribbon around it. On the box he had written her name. She had to take it, and then look inside. It was a small, ceramic angel pin, just in time for Christmas.

"Ah, Warren, you're too much. It's . . . it's perfect." Her manner was friendly, peppy, as always, but she felt her throat constrict, as she fingered the pin. Here she was, practically blocking the door to him, and he could not be more thoughtful and generous. Warren, who had been a pal and, really, her champion with some of the hecklers in the kitchen. Who, unexpectedly, had not pressed romance on her—most likely out of self-preservation, preferring to avoid the fuss and bother that seemed to follow her. Who obviously had something on the ball to aspire to college and some kind of life beyond Sutton, and who had a plan in place to get there. Unlike Celia.

Maybe something showed in her face, because Warren said, "And you'll be getting your own good news soon. I'm sure of it, college and you know . . . Carlos." He stopped there. He, too, must have begun to wonder about the long-distant boyfriend. Like any sensible person.

"Ah, yes," said Celia. "Actually, I'm just waiting to hear from a friend in California about him, Carlos." She gestured vaguely, "Some family problems, I think, maybe." She could feel the heat flush up her neck. Suddenly, it all seemed so ridiculous. There was no word about Carlos. At this point, how could the news be anything but bad: that Carlos was in trouble of some kind, or that he had truly turned his back on her? But she resolved in that moment, under Warren's kind gaze, that she would absolutely follow-up with some more phone calls to California and even try to track down Carlos's mother. She needed to know the truth.

"It will all work out, you'll see," Warren said, turning to leave. "I better let you go, then. But thanks, again, Dolphin Girl." He held up the letter, shaking it at her.

"No," she said, with a whisper of a smile. "Thank you, Warren."

After Warren left, Celia returned upstairs to get her things and lock the apartment. She got on the road headed south, hands tight on the steering wheel, seeing little outside the car. Too many things going on all at once to think about. Focus, focus, she told herself, trying to put her mind on the trip to Salisbury, patting the map on the passenger seat and the note with Leona's address on it.

About half a mile out of town, she passed the complex where the new high school had been built, all that money and nothing attractive about it. In the mid-morning, she was surprised to see groups of kids milling about on the front steps and the lawn of dead grass. A fire drill, perhaps, or some kind of outdoor project. Then she noticed a couple school buses ahead of her, waiting to pull up to the school entrance—field trip!

A group of guys were off by themselves, not far from the road where Celia was stopped in traffic, waiting for those buses to turn. One of them looked familiar, or maybe it was the red baseball cap and the backpack he was carrying that caught her eye. *That boy!* That awful boy who had pelted her with acorns on her way home from work. He's the one who told her she didn't belong. She studied the outline of his face a moment, pretty sure: the right height, the right build. And then, by some cosmic coincidence, he turned in her direction, looking straight at her. *The giant B on his sweatshirt!* Celia accidently pressed on the gas pedal, lurching forward a few feet before she hit the brake, squealing.

What an idiot!

When she looked up again, and out the window, he was staring at her. His face was lit up with derision. A few other students turned to look, laughing.

Although the window was closed, she could see the boy mouthing something in her direction, and she was sure it was not something nice.

She drove mindlessly the next mile or so, rattled. In her mind's eye, she went back to the day when she'd first arrived, and how little she knew about the place. And still she seemed to stumble around, not finding her footing.

She had to make a plan. She just had to. She had the money saved up, and there would be even more after Christmas and New Year. It would be enough to pay for an apartment share and cover expenses to start school in Salisbury. She could find a part-time job; waitressing was good money. Back on track in no time, in a situation much more suitable than small-town Sutton. Maybe even making theater connections for the future, even though, of course, she was headed back to Santa Cruz, asap. She could almost see herself, casual and arty, back in the swing of things with a little more life experience and some rather amusing stories–even that unpleasantness about the acorns. Then she scowled; and then she sneezed.

Two things happened, right at the same time. Celia bent down to grab a tissue from a box on the floor between the seats as a great big goose flew up from the side of the road, crossing in front of her. She jammed on the brakes—again. But this time she skidded some ways along the road and then veered to the right, clipping a telephone pole on the passenger side and coming to a halt at the side of the road, slamming her head into the dashboard.

"Whoa," she heard herself say.

She sat up, blinking, tingling as she realized what happened. She checked, had she stopped moving? Was the car in park? Finally, she turned off the engine and sat still, catching her breath. Her vision seemed a little blurry, not quite focused. The hood was dented, and she knew the damage must be worse on the side. By the time she was able to open the car door and swing her feet out, a car had pulled up behind. Celia didn't even hear footsteps and was surprised when a face appeared.

"Sweetie, you all right?" It was like a full, dark moon floating in the air, until Celia realized it was attached to a heavyset woman in hospital blues. The woman bent into the car, taking one of Celia's hands. "You can talk? You can breathe? Nothing hurt?"

Celia nodded. "I'm OK, I think. Just bumped my head a little."

"I'm gonna flag down the next car that comes this way. Tell them to call emergency. They better check you out."

"Oh, no," Celia said. "I can't. I . . . I have to get to Salisbury. Someone is waiting for me."

The woman stepped back onto the road and hailed a car passing in the other direction, toward town. She spoke to the driver a moment; Celia couldn't see who was driving, man or woman. After the car left, the woman came back to Celia's side.

"I'll stay with you 'til they come," she said quietly. "Honey, you're not going anywhere in this car. It's broke but good."

Chapter 13

Remarkably, Celia was fine after the accident. After an embarrassing trip to Sutton Hospital's ER, Celia had nothing but a possible concussion and jammed finger, for which they insisted on taking x-rays. But the car, Grace's car, was wrecked, to the tune of two thousand dollars to repair the wheels, axle, side door, and hood—over a week in the garage. A week without a car for either of them.

Celia paid the thousand-dollar deductible, because she had to, because she was the one who crashed the car. Luckily, Grace had added her as a driver on the insurance in the first place. What really hurt were the charges for the visit to the emergency room, the overnight at the hospital for observation, and the x-rays, right out of Celia's pocket, because Celia had no health insurance.

Grace took the banged up car with good grace, considering it had been her first car and still fairly new. Previously, she had gotten one little scratch on it.

"Thank God you weren't hurt worse," Grace said, over and over. "One medical crisis in this family is enough. Poor Shane. A car can be fixed, and a car feels no pain."

"I know, I know," Celia said. "You're right."

But really, she did feel pain, not bodily pain, but the pain of an empty bank account and the loss of her hopes and plans, even though she had never really been sure what she wanted to do. And worse was the guilt. She was definitely sick with guilt over the car accident and Jay and her noisy friends, and all the other things she had done unwittingly that made life more difficult for both of them.

"I don't know how you put up with me," she said to Grace as they sat in the living room after dinner. "I've been nothing but a nuisance since I got here. I'm surprised you don't hate me," she added, punching a pillow. "I was so spoiled when I was little, but you were always nice to me."

From the rocking chair, Grace gave her a fond, indulgent look. "That's because I was one of the spoilers. Did you ever think of that? Not to say that Mom and Dad weren't good to me. Of course they were. But when you came along, Mom had had the miscarriages. They wanted another child so badly, partly for my sake. And then you came home from the hospital, and we fell in love, all of us, even Grandma and Grandpa who were already pretty ancient."

She was smiling broadly, foolishly. "They let me think I was next in charge, and you were like my own little baby doll to take care of." Grace leaned back, closing her eyes. "Oh, I felt so important then." Grace opened her eyes, looking directly at Celia. "Don't ever forget that, no matter how difficult things might get. You were very much loved, and brought a lot of joy to our family."

Celia knew it was all true, but that didn't make her feel good now. In fact, worse. "Humph," she said, and replaced the pillow.

For one day, Celia moped around the house—"to make sure she was all better." Then, it was back to the Inn—because she was fine, and she needed the money, and she couldn't stand sitting around thinking about how things hadn't worked out.

Later in the week, Grace announced at breakfast that Roxanne had invited her to Wilmington for the weekend, riding in Roxanne's car. Celia was still in pajamas at the table reading the cereal box.

"It's just me, this time. Sorry," Grace said. "Think you'll be all right?"

"Of course," Celia said with an impatient exhale. "I was never not all right, just a little shaken up. No, go. I'm glad she invited you."

Grace's lips twitched, and there was a twinkle in her eyes. "Roxanne is quite the merry matchmaker, me and her brother."

"Is that OK with you?" Celia asked.

"It is. I like him. But I'm afraid of her throwing us together like this. It might work the other way."

"Nah," said Celia, chasing the last Cheerios around her bowl with a spoon. "Not with you two. You're not the kind to get on each other's nerves. It'll be great."

"I hope so." Grace poured out the last of her coffee into the sink and took her coat from the closet. "We're supposed to go out to a fancy restaurant on Saturday night and then to a jazz club."

Celia got up to rinse the bowl. "Nice," she said. "Well, *farewell, adieu, adios,* have a good time. Don't worry about me. I'll be slaving away back at the Inn." And then she closed her eyes, thinking, really, what a terrible thing to say.

At lunch, on the way in to the dining room, Anita grabbed Celia and said, "Let's talk at break. I can fill you in, at least, on what's going on."

It was a busy lunchtime, and profitable. No Jay. No Pauline. Warren was quiet and preoccupied.

She met Anita at the end of the shift, carrying their plates into the break room, mostly deserted by the time they got there. In spite of working so hard, Celia had little appetite for the pork chops in an apricot, mushroom sauce.

"This thing is turning into such a headache," Anita began, after a short prayer. "But I am determined, one way or the other, that this is going to happen. We haven't forgotten you. This time next month the doors will be open, I promise."

"So, what's the hold up, anyway?"

"Oh, it's too stupid. I can hardly even say it without getting all steamed up. I told you about the bank loan, right?"

Celia nodded, chewing slowly.

"I've had my savings and checking account with this bank since I was ten years old. I have saved up quite a little sum over the years, and I have never bounced a check. But they won't give me credit, not on my own. They're saying I have to have my father co-sign the loan for me. I'm thirty-five years old! Ugh!"

Her eyes were blazing. But now Celia knew how old she was, if she was telling the truth. . . .

"What about that other woman, Shelly?" Celia asked.

"She's just recently divorced and all her credit was in her husband's name. They said we don't have enough credit in our own names. She's got to get her father to co-sign, too. It's humiliating, and it's wrong. We're not irresponsible. We're . . . we're mothers, for God's sake." Then she blinked. "Forgive me, Lord."

This was all very interesting to Celia, who had little knowledge of the business world.

"So, will they?" she asked. "Will your dads sign the loan?"

"Well, yes they will. But that's beside the point. And that's not even the worst of it. When we take over the lease of the store at the strip mall, the landlord says he won't meet with us unless there's a responsible male present. Just in case 'we don't understand' what we're doing. It makes me so mad, I could spit. But I keep having to tell myself, 'keep your eyes on the prize,' just do whatever has to be done to get started, and give the rest over to Jesus."

Celia nodded in sympathy. If it was as difficult as this just to get started, she wondered if they really could make it. For a moment she sat silently, wondering about this whole thing about credit and loans. And then there was an interesting image of Jesus sitting in at the meeting about workouts and fitness equipment; maybe he could be the responsible male.

"I hope it all works out," she said. "Just keep me informed and let me know if there's anything I can do."

"Thanks, sweetie," said Anita. "I will."

Celia tried to catch Wanda on the way out, to ask if she might be interested in hanging out over the weekend—maybe a movie or bowling—but she had left early. Following a hunch, Celia headed toward the pub. Sure enough, she found Wanda's dark head bent over the Pac-Man table with that fellow Larry, evidently still around. Celia stood in the doorway a moment, undecided, and then turned to leave, not wanting to disturb them. Wanda must have seen her, because moments later she came out of the doorway, pulling her coat on and hurrying to catch up.

"Celia, wait up," she said.

Celia turned around quickly. "Wanda, I swear, ten seconds ago you were deep in the middle of one of those crazy games with that guy. What did you do, leave him high and dry?"

"No," Wanda smiled. "I told him I wanted to catch you."

"Why didn't you say so at work?"

"You were busy," she said, a little shyly. "Talking something with Anita."

Oh, she had noticed. Well, didn't everybody notice everything?

"All right, then, what's up? Shall we go back to the pub?"

"No," Wanda said. "It's a little private. I was wondering if we could maybe go back to your place."

Celia stopped walking. "Well," she said, with a slight hesitation, "it's not a good time." Now, what would Wanda make of that? They were having their carpets cleaned, perhaps? They had set off a flea bomb? Not having pets, that would be strange. Or, her sister was having an afternoon rendezvous? That was in the realm of the absurd, for her sister, she thought, if not herself. She sighed.

"Let's go to the library; we can talk there."

They followed the familiar road to the familiar walkway and entered the library, quiet in mid-afternoon. They found an empty table in the non-fiction section where they could talk among books on conservation and gardening. No takers this afternoon. A copy of the *Baltimore Sun* was on the table, open to the sports section. Celia pushed the paper aside.

"What's up?" she prompted. From Wanda's expression—and her willingness to go to the apartment—it must be serious.

"I'm leaving," said Wanda, her face set. "I'm going to Baltimore. On Sunday, I'm going."

Celia was stunned, and a little alarmed. Where had this come from? She vaguely recalled Wanda's questions about the city and the Inner Harbor. For a visit, she thought.

"It's like this," Wanda said. "My aunt's coming to stay with my mom and my brothers. Now I can go. I got a job lined up, starting Tuesday, and a place to live. I wanted to tell you, but I wasn't sure about it until now."

Celia exhaled a long breath. "Wow. So soon." She glanced right and left. Still no patrons. Just silent shelves with large books on growing plants and flowers. "Well, that's good, I guess," she said slowly. "But, how did it happen? I thought you've never even been to Baltimore."

"I ain't. This is my first time," Wanda said. "You know Larry from the pub. He got me a job at Poseidon Restaurant at the Inner Harbor." Her eyes widened. "You been there?"

"No," Celia said. A fish place probably. She and Grace had eaten at a hamburger joint. "I'm sure it's nice, and the tips will be good. But, I don't get it. You're leaving here to work at a restaurant there? And, where are you going to live?"

"With him, with Larry." Wanda blinked, looking away. "He always had a roommate, but now the roommate is gone. I can stay there and pay him when the money comes in. And . . . ," she continued, barely able to contain her excitement. "He's giving me a loan to take a class, a computer class."

Celia didn't know what to say. It all seemed so farfetched. Wanda must be out of her mind, taking a huge risk on one guy's say-so.

"Wanda," she said, picking her words carefully. "It sounds very exciting and I know how much you want to go. Are you sure this is the best way? It seems a little . . . strange to me."

"I'm not asking your permission," Wanda said, sitting back in the chair. That defiant, mulish expression appeared. But then her lip trembled. "I already made up my mind, I'm going. This is the only way it's going to happen. I'm taking my chance."

An elderly man with glasses shuffled toward them. Surely not a gardener? But he passed on his way to the local history section, giving a friendly nod.

"But what do you really know about this guy, Larry?"

"Oh, he's all right," Wanda said, unconcerned. "He wants to help me. His job here is almost finished, and he's going back to Baltimore at the end of January."

"Then why are you going now?"

"They need help for the holidays. If I can prove myself, I'll have a foot in the door. If not, there's other jobs." She shrugged, bending forward to look at the newspaper. "There's always waitress jobs. Besides, I got some money saved."

A bell went off in Celia's head. "Does Larry know you've got money?"

Wanda laughed, her eyes on the headline. *Golfer Putts Gold.* As if she knew a thing about golf, or cared. "He don't care—I mean, doesn't care. He's got lots of money, him and his family, from selling belts and ladies handbags. He sure doesn't need mine." She moistened a finger to turn the page.

Celia sighed, looking at the rack of books on display nearby, with titles like *Modern Day Mulching, Organic Gardening,* and something about building a compost pile. No help there.

"I'm sorry, Wanda," she said after a minute. She couldn't help it, that warning note. "I just don't get it. I'm afraid he might have something else in mind. Maybe he's going to . . . oh, I don't know, use you, do you wrong."

"Don't you fret, girl," Wanda said, using the familiar address. "I'm twice his size. If he raises a hand to me, I'll pull it behind his back." Wanda looked directly at her, the paper forgotten. "He's nice to me. He likes me because we play games together. It's not my African princess looks he's after. You know, it's not all jungle fever . . ."

"OK, OK." Celia held up her hands. No way she wanted to go down that road. "If it's what you want, then I'm happy for you. Maybe I can come up and visit after you're settled. But . . ." She couldn't quite let it go. "But I just wouldn't want him to . . . hurt you, in any way. Disappoint you, take advantage . . ."

Above Wanda's head was a large book displayed on the shelf. *Save the Earth, One Tree at a Time,* right next to the *Whole Earth Catalog. Oh, brother.* Where were books that could give guidance, at a time like this?

"Don't you worry about me," Wanda said, tipping her head side to side with a swagger. But Celia could see that her eyes were glistening. She had thought Wanda's tear factory was closed down, but apparently it wasn't.

Wanda and Celia agreed to meet at the Grand Marsh Inn on Friday afternoon to go clothes shopping. Celia had brought a change of clothes for after her shift, plus a warm sweater and gloves. Without a car, it was a bit of a trek to the department store in the new mall on the outskirts of town, about a twenty-five minute walk

"I need serious clothes," Wanda said, as they traipsed along the bypass road in the late afternoon sunshine. "You know, for interviews and such. I'm not staying a waitress forever. Larry thinks I could get a job card punching as soon as I can get through the course. There's gonna be lots of jobs for people can do that."

"I'm not sure if I'm the best one about picking out clothes." Celia held out her arms to display the stretched out wool cardigan and jeans with worn knees. "Look at the stuff I wear."

"That's all right," Wanda said, stepping over an empty fast-food bag. "We try."

At the department store, they went to the women's department. Wanda was actually between a size fourteen and sixteen, and maybe five feet eight or nine inches tall. She picked out mostly dark colors and conservative looking skirts and blouses, but they only made her look middle-aged and dowdy. Celia felt she needed more trendy clothes, so she picked things with brighter colors, thinking that Wanda could wear just about any color against her dark skin, but that turned out not to be true. She got excited about one outfit, a carnival print skirt and top that looked so flattering on the hanger. After Wanda put it on, they both started giggling, getting punchy.

"Too costumey, I guess," Celia admitted, outside the dressing room.

"What you trying to do to me? I look like I'm ready for the fun house," Wanda complained. "It's . . ." she searched for the word as she frowned into the mirror. "Outlandish."

"I'm sorry, Wanda, I'm no good at this." She thrust forward a white blouse. "Here, at least we know this looks good on you."

"Yeah, I'll get the jobs if that's all I'm wearing," Wanda teased.

"It's a start," Celia defended herself. They put the rejected clothes on a rack and left the dressing room.

The shopping expedition was not going well. In a state of inertia, they sat on a bench outside the dressing room. Celia was thinking of rescheduling when Grace could join them, when she realized with a pang there wasn't enough time. It was now or never, and hope was fading. Unexpectedly, an older, experienced sales lady came along, seeming to size up the situation, and offered to help. Within forty-five minutes, she had a suit put together, accessorized, led them personally to the shoe department, and totaled up the sale.

That kind of success deserved a burger and a shake at the food court. Well done.

Out in the parking lot, they deliberated whether to walk back along the well-lit bypass or take the less traveled shortcut to the center of town. It was full darkness now, but clear with some moonlight.

"What do you think?" Celia asked Wanda.

"Either way," Wanda said, unhelpfully.

"Wait," Celia said, turning her head to listen down the darkened side street. "I hear a dog."

"That dog stay chained. Won't bother us."

Celia shrugged, "It's just a little after six. I think we'll be all right."

"All right."

Celia started walking in the direction of Prince Street, the shortcut. She'd driven it many times in the daylight. There was never anyone about.

About halfway, just past the barking dog, the headlights of a car shone from the direction of the bypass. Even from a distance, the girls could hear music playing on the car radio, the bass booming. The car veered suddenly to the right, and then to the left, followed by laughter—young men. As the car came up behind, it slowed, putting Celia and Wanda directly into the beams of light, throwing long shadows. It pulled over next to them, forcing Celia and Wanda onto the grassy shoulder.

"What's up, ladies?"

Without looking, Celia could picture the speaker, young, mocking, wearing one of those baseball caps and a gold chain at his neck, out for a good time on a Friday night.

The girls kept walking on the grass and tried to ignore the boys in the car, four or five of them. The car windows were rolled part way down, the music blaring, and the smell of reefer in the air.

"I want me the big-ass sister," someone said. "Whitey, she ain't got no body."

Celia looked at Wanda, wondering if they should be concerned or just annoyed. Wanda had her defiant face on, looking straight ahead. Then the car started pulling off the road in front of them, so they'd either have to stop or walk around the car by going into the road. Now the music was lowered, and a voice called out, low, soft, and menacing. The voice sounded familiar, but Celia couldn't match it to any of the young guys at the Inn.

"Hey, Goldilocks, you afraid of the big, bad wolf?"

The laughter had quieted, and everyone was waiting for some reaction. Wanda pulled on Celia's elbow, and Celia started to walk with her into the middle of the road. When they passed the car, it started cruising after them, and then beside them, the voices, more than just the one, calling out "Goldilocks, Goldilocks" in high falsetto. *Idiots! Not even the right fairy tale.*

"It's the wrong story," Celia finally turned and yelled.

"Say what?"

"What she sayin'?" someone else asked.

"Goldilocks and the Bears. There's no wolf."

Rather than shutting them up, Celia's words made the boys break out in more laughter. Wanda gave her a warning look.

"Oh, yes, there a wolf," that low voice said, "a whole pack of wolves. And we're going to eat you up."

And then the howling began: four voices, or five, at the top of their lungs. It was frightening, although totally ridiculous. Wanda and Celia kept walking, their eyes on the stream of traffic coming from the cross street in the distance. One of those cars turned and took the right onto the short cut road, heading toward them. The girls scurried to the opposite side of the street, as the car approached, and the baying of the wolves came to a stop. As they tried to distance themselves from the car with the boys, they heard the sound of a bottle smashing on the road some ten feet behind them.

Wanda pushed Celia to the side, and strode to the car, a dark silhouette, taut with anger. The shopping bag was still in her hand. Celia stood spellbound, wondering if Wanda was going to hit someone over the head.

"Who did that?" Wanda yelled. "Who in this car? That Ronnie Whitaker there? I know your sister, and I tell her what you done. Who else? Andre, Morris, Sam? I know y'all, and I will tell the police if any one of you tries some other stupid thing. That's assault you throw a bottle. Just get out of here, leave us be, I'm so disgusted with y'all."

"Cool down, sister," one voice spoke out. "We just playing with ya. That one there," he pointed at Celia, "got an attitude."

Wanda backed away to give the driver room to pull into the lane, and as the car passed her, picking up speed, a hand reached out from the back seat and batted Wanda's shopping bag out of her hand, sending it flying into the middle of the road where the clothes spilled out. Wanda glared, sucking in her lips.

"Those horrible boys," Celia said as the car sped away, leaving them in the dark.

Wanda didn't speak as she picked up the bag and her clothes from the road.

They trudged in silence to the intersection near the post office where they were to part ways.

"I couldn't really see the suit," Celia said. "Maybe it's nothing. Or else, I bet the dry cleaners can take care of it."

Wanda nodded. She'd gone back in her shell, that quiet, distant place. In her mind, she was probably already far away from small-town Sutton at the Inner Harbor looking out over all that water.

"Oh, come on," Celia chided. "It will be all right. No real harm. Just boys being idiots. Besides, we stood right up to them, didn't we?" After the fact, it was kind of exciting, not that Celia wanted to go through it again. "You're pretty fierce, Wanda," she said, trying to provoke a reaction.

Wanda gazed at the ground, twisting the shopping bag by its handle. Was she nervous about the move? Or rattled by their encounter with the boys? Sometimes it was so hard to tell with her. She didn't make it easy.

"So, will I see you before you leave?" Celia asked, finally.

"Probably not," Wanda said, her tone flat.

Celia geared up for good-bye. She didn't like it, but the manners were ingrained.

"Then, I guess I'll see you later. And good luck! I really am rooting for you to make it, you know. Make sure you come by to see us when you're back in Sutton. Oh, wait," Celia said. "Hold on one little second." She scrounged in her purse for a pen and scrap of paper, the back of a receipt. She scribbled on the paper held against her thigh. "Here's my name and address, so you don't forget. Just send me a post card, so I know you made it. And send me your address, too, when you're settled. I'll come visit, and you can show me around. OK?"

Wanda took the paper, but she wouldn't look her in the eye.

"What's so hard about that?" Celia said, exasperated. "A postcard. It won't kill you."

"OK, OK," Wanda said, not smiling. And then she said, "Bye, Celia. You take care of yourself," and walked away quickly. If a back could talk, and the way a person walked, Wanda was shouting that she could not wait to see the last of Sutton. But not Celia, of course. That was different. They had been friends. Kind of. Hadn't they?

Celia had a quiet weekend at the apartment, and for the first time she felt bored and lonely, with Grace gone, Wanda leaving, and Warren preoccupied with making his own plans for the future. Of course, she could catch up on her reading, and maybe write a letter to Janelle. By late Sunday afternoon, the stillness in the apartment drove her outside into a drizzly, gray day, with no destination and no money in her pocket. Force of habit led her to the Inn, which she circled on the far side of the street, noting the well-dressed groups and couples going for early dinner. At the rear of the building, near the staff entrance and the loading dock, she watched from a distance, but there was little to see. Passing the dumpster, though, she wrinkled her nose at the smells of old fish and rotten eggs—the day before trash pick-up.

Back in the center, she dawdled at the shop windows, but nothing interested her, nothing. Of course, she had no money. But more than that, what use would those things be to her, anyhow, without a social life or a love life, or a place of her own? Except a car. A car that would take her anywhere she wanted to go, that could take her away from here, fast. Just ahead on the quiet side street, she spotted a sporty red two-door Sedan parked at the curb. She stopped to peer inside—clean, neat, new. A department store shopping bag was on the back seat—a woman's car, no question. But no keys dangled from the ignition, so there would be no fast and furious get away. Celia straightened with a smile of self-mockery when she heard the click-click of heels on the sidewalk. A dark-haired woman turned the corner, coming into view, and Celia walked quickly away, but not before glimpsing her face—Pauline! From the doorway of a tobacco shop, Celia saw Pauline stopping at the car, and then opening the door to put something inside. Within a few seconds, she had left again, this time crossing the street and disappearing into a gift shop.

Out of sight, behind a tree, Celia stomped her foot at the unfairness of it all. That hard-faced, sharp-clawed Pauline had what she wanted—a nice car, and Jay. It was too much, really too much. Celia felt a sensation of pressure growing from her chest to her throat, as if she was about to roar, or throw up. In her pocket, she fingered the keys to the apartment, and her feet began moving in the direction of Pauline's car, unable to stop. Within a few seconds she was at the passenger side door, jabbing the car door, waist-level. Two or three scratches, hardly visible. She stepped back, raising her arm to mark X's—*wrong, wrong, wrong.* But then she caught her reflection in the glass, a silent screaming banshee, and she faltered, shocked. Her hand dropped to her side, and she closed her eyes, feeling presences: her mother, her dead father and grandparents, all of them right behind her on the sidewalk, staying her hand.

Well, yes, she thought, the bitter taste of bile in her mouth. They ruled her still, with their high standards and great hopes for her to be something special, something rather grand. Only, they didn't quite provide the means to achieve these things, or even to help her keep afloat in rough waters. Where were they, really, when she needed them? How had their Celia, so loved and cared for, ever come to this?

She spun around on the sidewalk, making a beeline for home before she was overcome with any other craziness. She was pursued by images of Pauline at the wheel of the sporty car, and Jay beside her. Then the two of them in some nice room, somewhere, making love. Blech . . . it was making her sick. Passing the dumpster again, she caught a whiff of rotten food. The rest of her walk home she entertained another satisfying fantasy: putting something putrid inside Pauline's car, out of sight under the seat, where it would permeate the interior with the most horrible smell. And then ants, or flies, or something . . . maybe a mouse, or even a rat. And Pauline would scream, and Jay would be grossed out. Deserved it, too. Stupid Jay. What did he see in Pauline, anyway, besides her nice car, and good job, and sexy clothes, and ambitious ways?

By the time she was safely inside the apartment, she was feeling better and actually starting to get hungry. Finally, she could laugh—a little—at herself and the stupidity of it all. But, it had been a little scary, that blind, raw fury. Afterwards, when she was finally able to relax a bit in front of the TV, another kind of gnawing, buzzing feeling remained. A love scene came on the program she was watching, and she felt her body heat up and start to tingle—it was sex she wanted, someone to kiss and make love with, someone's arms around her, someone wanting her. Jay, Carlos, somebody. How was it, with all her supposedly great qualities, and the way that all kinds of men paid her attention, that she was still on her own?

By nighttime, after supper, when Grace walked in the door, Celia was surprised how glad she was to see her. She looked up from the comics with a happy, "Hey there!" Searching her sister's face, she wondered how the weekend had gone. Grace's expression was calm, but rather serious. She came over to the kitchen table, pulling out a chair to sit across from Celia. The keys were still in her hand.

"Everything OK here?" she asked. "You look rather perky."

"Oh," Celia said. "Just happy to see you. Quiet weekend. Nothing to tell." She was not going to mention the incident with Pauline's car. Besides, nothing really happened. Or, not much, unless you were really looking.

"Well," Grace said, drawing in a breath, "there's something I wanted to say to you, right away."

Celia tilted her chin, mystified. "What is it?"

"About what I said a while back, about you not having friends over." Grace stopped to clear her throat. "I want to take that back. You can have people over, any time, as long as you're all considerate of others, of course. And I know you will be."

Celia's eyebrows went up in surprise. "Well, thanks, Grace. That means a lot. What changed your mind?"

Grace turned in her chair, opening her purse to put the keys away. "I did a lot of thinking while I was gone, and I don't want to be that kind of person. This is not going to be my life forever. I've already shown them at work what kind of person I am. If they really want to judge me by personal business that harms no one, instead of by the kind of worker I am, I don't want to work there. I can find another job somewhere."

Celia was moved and embarrassed. She touched the still-warm cup of tea, next to the spread out newspaper. Her stomach was full and she had this clean, comfy place to live in. All thanks to Grace. What a good person her sister was, and what a nuisance Celia was for putting her through so much trouble—the money problems, the car, the troublesome friends.

Then she realized that perhaps it didn't matter anymore. There was no one left, really, who was likely to come for a visit. At the moment, she had no friends left.

Chapter 14

Christmas was fast approaching but promised to be quiet, since Celia and Grace were not going to California for the holidays. Money was still an issue, and Shane's health problems were not resolved. On the other hand, Wanda's leaving meant more hours for Celia. Mrs. Becker was only too happy to fill in her schedule. The Inn had become short-staffed during the week leading up to Christmas: Tony was out sick and some of the workers were going away for the holidays, a number of them headed south.

Meanwhile, Anita invited Celia and Grace to join her family for Christmas service at their church. Celia said she'd like to go, thinking it would be an interesting cultural experience, and that it wouldn't hurt to have a little religious observance. She was pretty sure the church would be all-black, but the idea of home-cooked food and Christmas hymns sung by the choir sounded pretty good. It was a while, she reflected, since she'd been inside a church. Grace was waiting to hear if Alec might be down for the weekend.

The Wednesday before Christmas was full-on, wave after wave of holiday groups, and the occasional party of hunters who didn't mind the cold. The lunch shift started early, at ten, to get ahead of the swelling crowds. Twenty minutes before opening time, Celia saw Tony for the first time after a two week absence. He'd lost weight, his skin was pale, and he was sniffling with a red and runny nose.

"Hi, Tony," Celia said warmly, joining him at the prep station. "Long time, no see. How's your foot?" Roland had said something about Tony missing a step on the stairs.

Tony stared blankly. "Oh, yeah," he said in a hoarse voice. "It's the ankle, actually, and it's still a little creaky." He swiveled his left foot side to side to demonstrate, but Celia had a suspicion maybe the ankle wasn't the real problem.

"Where's Roland?"

"Working banquet. Pauline asked him. She didn't ask me."

Celia was finished with her prep and took silverware from Tony's tray to wipe off the water marks. Roland sometimes worked extra shifts, but she almost never saw Tony without Roland, almost like his white shadow. Celia glanced around the dining room. Brenda, Pam, and Anita were at their stations, but no one had a table yet. Celia headed into the bar area to get a glass of ice water. Turning in surprise, she found Tony at her elbow.

"Celia," he said, "there's something I wanted to tell you . . ." His expression was so grave, Celia wondered what it could be.

"Sure, Tony," she said. "What's the matter?"

"Roland," he started, "and me. We . . . well, no, I . . . I . . ." Poor Tony stammered

"Friends of the Library here," Eldridge boomed at the entrance to the bar. Of course he would know where she was. "You got tables." Celia and Tony met eyes, and then walked silently toward the entrance to the dining room.

"Oh, my," said Celia at the open doorway, surveying the crowd in the dining room. "It got busy." Tony looked ashen. "Later," she said to him, "when we have a few minutes."

"OK," Tony said, and then, under his breath, "oh, shit."

But after that, it was all-out, and Celia never had a down moment until almost four. She had one last order for the single gentleman who lived at the Inn and took his dinner in the dining room. He always ordered the same thing: London broil, mashed potatoes, and green beans. On the way to the kitchen, she passed Brenda who was ready to hand in her order pad for the day.

"Have you seen Tony?"

"Gone home sick," Brenda said, breezing by, still peppy after six hours on her feet. Or, maybe she was just happy about heading home to her family with all that money in her purse. Celia only wished she looked as bright and perky. Or that she, too, was almost done.

Brenda was shaking her head. "He looked awful, shouldn't have come in."

Celia walked blindly into the kitchen, not registering, for once, that it was Jay who took the order from her hand. She turned on her heel, suddenly overcome with drowsiness, lack of energy, and a desire to lie down on the floor and cover her eyes. Instead, she went to get a drink, not her usual milk, but a Coke—a little caffeine jolt to the system.

At the soft drink counter, she got something better than caffeine: Anita in a good mood.

"Girl, when things slow down, come find me. I've got something to tell you." When Anita was in a good mood, her every movement was like dancing. You could sit and watch her like a show. Celia could use some of that energy.

"Well, some good news at last," Anita told Celia, late in the dinner hour when the room was almost empty. She was resetting the table nearest Celia's. "Those old farts at the bank finally got back to us and said things look good to go forward. After we straighten out things with the former owner of the business, we want to get ready to open by end of January. Still with us?"

"Oh, sure. I just wish it could be sooner."

"Yeah, I know, girl. This place gets to you after a while. You've been looking a little wilted lately."

"Who, me?" Celia straightened herself up. She took some silverware for her own table. "I'm fine. Maybe I just need a little more exercise."

"That's what we're trying to do, honey. Just be patient. Do you want to come with me when we meet the owner, to decide what to do about the old equipment? Friday after New Year's, sometime in the morning."

"Can we look inside? I know where it is, but the blinds are all down."

"Call me if you can make it. Here's my number again." Anita jotted it down on her order pad, and handed it to Celia, before crossing the room to her own station. A moment later, she was back.

"You got any creamers?" she asked Celia.

"Sure, help yourself."

Anita glanced over to her last table of three, lingering over dessert coffees.

"I hope you can make it Sunday, for service," she said, resting the tray against her hip. "It's going to be something special. You've really got to see a down-home black church service before you die. The food, the music, the praying. You won't forget it."

Celia could all too easily imagine Anita in a full-length choir robe, singing away. "I'm sure."

"Besides," Anita added, "yours truly is speaking from the pulpit, a special holiday message."

Celia had to laugh. "Why am I not surprised? I'm only surprised you're not running the place. Don't they allow female ministers at your church?" She was only half teasing. Surely others had come under Anita's charismatic spell.

Anita's brow wrinkled. "You're not making fun, are you?"

"Not at all. Why would you think that?"

"I get enough nonsense from some of the people here about my expression of faith."

She looked over to her table and nodded, smiling pleasantly.

"All right, all right, I'm coming," she muttered. "Later," she said to Celia as she left, "I've got a story to tell you about the owner, some funny business he was up to."

But they never had another chance to chat. Celia was so glad to finish up for the day, over twelve hours. It had been very profitable, but her head was starting to feel fuzzy and she couldn't wait to get home and crawl in bed. No TV, no book, no nothing.

She had just settled with the cashier and passed through the kitchen to get her coat in the back hallway. The scarf kept getting caught inside the sleeve. Suddenly, Jay was behind her, plucking out the scarf and placing it over her shoulders.

"Thanks," Celia mumbled.

"You come with me," he said, more statement than question. He took her elbow and steered her down the hall that led to the side entrance, deserted at this late hour. Celia was too tired to even guess what he might say. At the doorway, she stood in silence, waiting for him to speak.

"You working hard, girl," he started. "You all red and shiny on your face. Saving up and all, right?"

She nodded, averting her eyes. She wasn't talking. He's the one who brought her here.

He took a breath. "That's no problem, right, with Pauline? She ain't gonna bother you. That fuss is all over. She don't know nothing, what happened. I didn't say nothing to nobody."

When Celia didn't respond, he continued. "She all right, really. Her mood always changin'. I don't even know what's up with her after all this time."

So, thought Celia, processing this information slowly, he's apologizing for—or defending—Pauline? That's what he's trying to do? *Fine for him. I don't really need to hear it.*

"It's OK," she heard herself saying. "I'm OK." She thought she was smiling but wasn't sure. She seemed to be OK, getting through the days and weeks, accepting how things had changed, moving on.

Well, if that was it, then time to head out. There was no need to give an answer. She turned toward the door, focusing on her hot face in the reflection of the window panes. Wait, was this the way out? Why was her thinking so fuzzy? Why was Jay still here? She put her hands up on the metal door bar without actually pushing it open.

Jay came up behind her, standing close. He bent his head down to her shoulder, his cheek near her ear, his breath in her hair.

"Don't be mad."

Celia thought, Is this a trick? One thing I know for sure, I can't play that game, especially if I don't know the rules. I'm not going for it, she told herself. Then she found herself leaning back against him. His arms went under her elbows and his hands crossed her waist.

It's the flu, she figured out, recognizing the signs. She pressed her backside against him, and felt him harden in response.

Well, he's still attracted at least. She felt a moment of foolish pride, along with the queasiness and light-headedness. *And I'm, I'm . . .* she couldn't finish the thought. She rested a minute, regaining her strength, and then he pressed soft lips to the side of her neck before he stepped back, letting her go. He turned and left, walking not quickly, but deliberately down the hallway. Without his support, she felt like her knees might buckle.

It's too hot, she thought, and pushed open the door. The cool air revived her, and she forced her feet to move toward Main Street, and from there she made it home safely. By the time she arrived, she was shuddering with cold and put her bathrobe on over her clothes. When the warmth began to seep through, she fell to sleep, but woke later in the night hot, too hot, and stripped down to her t-shirt and underwear. She dreamt that night of swimming in water that was too warm, in a place that was scary and unfamiliar with creatures that were alien and threatening.

Celia was sick for about a week, putting a damper on the holiday spirit. Grace got a small, live tree that she placed in the living room, but lights were prohibited in the lease. A nice pile of cards came every day for Grace, from her high school friends, college friends, cousins, colleagues at the hospital, and even some neighbors. For Celia, a few cards. Most people didn't even know she was here. Northing from Carlos, and not from Wanda, either. Celia and Grace had their gifts for each other, of course, and one each from home. Roxanne delivered a couple small, wrapped packages, one for each of them, and another to Grace from Alec.

To brighten the sickroom, Grace put electric candles in the windows and taped holiday cards along the frame of the doorway. One of the last cards to arrive was a photo of Janelle wearing a garland of ivy and feathers, wishing everyone a Happy Solstice. Enclosed in the envelope was a disappointing report on the whereabouts of Carlos. Prompted by Celia, Janelle had located the former roommate, Eddie, now evicted from the apartment.

In Janelle's fat cursive writing, Celia read:

Dear Celia,
Tidings of joy! *Menagerie* was a smash, and I'll call you soon with details. Did I send you reviews from *Romeo and Juliet?* Total stinkbomb. You would have been a much better Juliet.

I stopped by Carlos's old apartment. Eddie the Creep said Carlos called looking for you. He's at his aunt's house in southern Cal recovering from a ruptured appendix when he was at sea. Sorry, sweetie! Eddie couldn't find your new address, which you left him. Idiot! Then he got kicked out of school.

Scoundrel! It's no wonder. The guy has no class. I told him I only came as a favor to you, so then he offers me cocaine if I'll sleep with him.

Hope you're having a great holiday! George and I are off to the spa at Esalen.

Do not doubt you're greatly missed.

Much love,

Janelle

Ruptured appendix! It sounded serious. Terrible. Poor Carlos. She should have tried harder to find him, tried earlier. But maybe it was for the best. If neither one of them found the way, or time, to reach out, then their relationship must not have been strong enough anyway.

This was a new low. She groaned and scrunched up in the fetal position, achy and exhausted. That incident with Jay and her scarf in the hallway, she wasn't sure it had really happened, or was part of a fever dream.

She dozed on and off for several days, only slowly recovering her energy and appetite. She couldn't remember being sick like this for a long time, since she was a little girl. She felt guilty about messing up Grace's plans, and was even more afraid her sister would end up sick, too, though she didn't. Not only that, Grace had to tell Alec that it wasn't a good idea to come, because Celia was so sick. Instead, Grace kept busy with quick errands, watched TV with Celia, and worked on a cross-stitch kit of bees around a hive that she had gotten from Roxanne. There was no Christmas dinner, just pancakes and bacon. And tea.

By week's end, Celia was feeling better and suddenly remembered that she had never let Anita know about the church service, that they couldn't make it. She went through her purse, her uniform pockets, and jacket pockets, but couldn't find the slip of paper with the phone number. She knew they lived in Greenville and looked up the family name in the phone book. Sure enough, there was a listing under Nelson so she called. The woman who answered was not Anita. Celia introduced herself as a friend from work and left a message that she was sorry she hadn't made it on Sunday, because she was ill, but was feeling better now.

To their surprise, Alec called himself and asked if he could visit on the weekend. He would stay with his sister, and asked if Grace wanted to go out Saturday night for an early New Year's celebration. Celia, too, if she was up to it. This was a new development and rather unexpected from the young man who appeared so reserved. And the fact that he included the bothersome younger sister was a point in his favor.

"I guess he missed you," Celia teased, legs folded on the sofa. "He was driven to make the dreaded phone call, and make a plan. I'd say that looks pretty good for the future."

Grace said nothing but began picking up the living room, which had started to look like a war zone. Celia got up off the sofa, folding the extra blankets. She called work to say she was better and could come in on the weekend, lunch and dinner, if they wanted her. If Mrs. Becker had been annoyed about her unexpected absence, she sounded happy to have her back.

It was another busy weekend at the Inn, with little time for chit-chat. Everyone asked Celia what happened to Wanda, but she said simply, "Moved to Baltimore, staying with a friend, got a job at a restaurant." That's all they needed to know. Then, at the end of the week, Roland and Tony disappeared, leaving the dining room in an uproar. They were experienced full-timers, quick and efficient at their jobs. Word was that Tony had ended up in the hospital and they had gone to D.C. Celia was hurt that they hadn't left word, didn't say goodbye, although she wasn't totally surprised by the news. And she wasn't sure it was a strictly-medical problem—although maybe that's what addiction was. Maybe that's what Tony had wanted to tell her that night before she got sick.

On the other hand, Anita was certainly in good spirits "Getting rich, I am. It's not un-Christian to work hard and enjoy your money." She had no problem with Celia missing church. "Yes, I got the message from my mother. When you didn't come in on Friday or Saturday, I knew you weren't going to make it. We'll just have to try another time. Maybe Easter. I will be looking so good in my new spring clothes." One thing about Anita, she didn't lack confidence.

Celia adjusted her apron, glancing around the dining room. Every table was taken, plates in front of every guest. There was an unexpected moment of calm.

"How about Friday," Anita reminded her, "at the coffee shop?"

"I'll be there," Celia said. "What time?"

"Come at ten. The owner's coming at ten-thirty. I'll buy you coffee and fill you in. By the way, you'll need tights and a leotard. I'm going to order some for us, and whoever wants to buy one. Could be a nice little side business."

"Amen," Celia joked, and Anita pretended to scowl, but she couldn't hold back the smile.

A hand waved, diamond flashing. Anita set sail across the room. Celia walked over to Rufus, the oystershucker, at his wheeled cart covered with ice chips to pick up a plate for the man who had ordered oysters for appetizer, entrée, and dessert.

"Here you go, missy," Rufus said, handing her the plate of oysters. The man was one of the darkest people she had ever seen and quick as anything with a knife.

"Damn, we're good," she muttered with Anita at a safe distance. "Everything running like clockwork."

Jay was in charge of the kitchen while the head chefs were working some important banquets. He hardly looked up from his work, except once when Pauline came in to ask him something, and they left together with Pauline holding his arm. Pauline never once looked her way, but Celia couldn't help notice her bright red talons, just the shade of her car.

Only Eldridge seemed the same, unphased by illness, romance, or other people's comings and goings. They sat down together in the break room, still decorated for Christmas, she with a bowl of minestrone, he with an overstuffed corned-beef sandwich. He wore a red bow tie for the holidays, and showed off an elegant, new silver cigarette lighter, which Celia admired.

"Fancy," she said, pointing. "Is that a gift?"

When he only nodded, she pursued it. "From who?"

"That your business?" he said.

"Just asking. All right then, from friend or family?"

"From the one who loves me best," he replied, and Celia's eyes grew large. "So you do have a special someone. I thought you said 'no commitments.'"

"I meant me," he said, serious.

"Eldridge, you're something else."

"Don't I know it. You want to see more, you gotta come out with me." He gave her his most charming smile, a smear of mustard on his lips.

"What?"

Celia was stumped. Eldridge was gay. It couldn't possibly be a come-on. Unless, maybe he was bi-sexual?

She studied Eldridge carefully, in case there was something hidden behind that beaming face, recalling *he may smile and smile and still be a villain.* Hamlet was too right: things were so often not what they appeared to be. But not Eldridge. He was pretty much what no one else would choose to be, so what would he be hiding? He didn't even pretend not to lie. He just lied outright.

At the moment, he was the picture of contentment, not villainous at all. Over his head a paper snowflake dangled from a piece of string. Taped to the wall behind him were an Advent calendar, all doors opened, and a cardboard cut-out of Santa and his elves. Next to it, where the sleigh had been, someone had put up a well-worn poster with a cross, a star, and the words to Luke: "For unto you is born this day in the City of David a Savior, which is Christ the Lord." Celia doubted it was the Beckers' doing, although they had been generous with their Christmas checks and a fresh turkey for every employee. It had to be Anita—who else?

"I know what you looking for," Eldridge declared, breaking into her thoughts. "You bored, lonely, you need something different. You like to see things on the other side, I take you there. We go out one night, over to the Starlight. That's a different world."

"The Starlight!" Celia cried. "Eldridge, my sister heard gunshots from there last summer. What are you thinking?"

"Yeah," he agreed. "They shooting at a goose, crazy drunks. They fight sometimes, but they don't usually got guns, just when those boys come down from the city. Don't you want to see for yourself? I take care of you. I get you back home to your sister."

Celia was dubious. This was just the kind of thing she'd better stay away from, if she didn't want to run into more problems, for herself or her sister. Eldridge continued chewing, unhurriedly, as he looked up at her sideways. Next to his plate were a couple of foil-wrapped chocolates that the Beckers had put out for guests in the front lobby.

"I don't think so, Eldridge, after what all just happened here, you know, the mess I got into. That's the first time in my life a girl ever wanted to fight me. Do you really think it would be a good idea?"

"Yeah, I do," Eldridge said. "Besides, she just say that. She not really gonna do it. Come on now, remember what they say in church," he said, rising and brushing the snowflake with his head. "'What don't kill you make you stronger.'" He cleared his plate to the bussing cart and stuffed the chocolates in his jacket pocket. "Let me know. We can go anytime."

Hm, thought Celia, *that says quite a lot about the state of my social life.* Invited out to the seedy nightclub on the black side of town. Nah . . . not a good idea. For a brief moment, she pictured herself walking into the club, next to Eldridge, all eyes on her cool, white elegance. Now that was a scene from a movie, not necessarily a good one. Whatever made Eldridge want to put such an idea in her head?

Celia was quite impressed with Shelly, when she finally met her with Anita at the coffee shop on Friday before the big meeting. They sat down in a booth, ordering coffees. Shelly was tallish, slim, pale-skinned with reddish brown hair, brown eyes, and large white teeth. Celia knew she was the same age as Anita, since they had been friends in school, but she dressed in a simple, preppy fashion that made her look younger. Anita had also told her Shelly was the mother of twins, eleven-year-olds, a girl and a boy. Last year, she had separated from her husband and was living in her own apartment, while the husband stayed in the house with the children.

"Shelly started out in college a Phys. Ed. major," Anita informed Celia. "But then she switched to business and accounting."

Anita's gaze remained on Celia until she realized she was supposed to make some acknowledgment.

"Oh, I see," Celia said. "Numbers and exercise; that's really good."

Shelly sat across from Celia and Anita, updating them on the situation at the fitness club. Although she was raised on the Eastern Shore, she was college-educated and spoke without the local accent, quick and self-assured as she rattled off numbers and dates.

Like Anita, she said that she wanted white and black women to come to the fitness center and be comfortable there. They were going to advertise in the local papers, stores, and all the black and white venues they could think of. Of course, it made sense to spread the net wide to appeal to as many women as possible. Apparently, the defunct club had been almost exclusively white, the numbers declining as the club went downhill. That was their challenge: to regain the old and attract the new.

"The big question now," Shelly said, putting down her coffee cup, "is whether or not we honor memberships of women who were left hanging when the former business went under."

"Yeah," Anita agreed. "That's a tough one. We don't want to lose them, but we can't give the memberships for free. We'd have no money coming in."

"Well, except for new memberships," Celia pointed out. She had also ordered a grilled corn muffin, which was delivered to the table by a middle-aged man in a stained apron. He returned with coffee for refills. Shelly paused and smiled graciously as he poured, a big, husky fellow, well over six feet with a full beard and an easy manner.

"Anything else I can do for you?" he asked, and they all three looked up to him for a brief moment, as if he could somehow be their fairy god-father, granting wishes and solving problems with his magic coffee pot.

"No, thanks, Russell," Anita said. "But your coffee sure is comfort in a cup."

When he left, she went on. "We're going to have to make some concession, I think; I don't see any way around it."

"A discount, maybe," Shelly mused.

"Equal to everyone, or pro-rated for the value of the old membership?" Anita asked.

It was clear to Celia that this was not going to be an easy transition. Even going into a business under the best of conditions could be tricky for first timers. This situation had all kinds of extra problems. Over her head, for sure. She busied herself brushing the crumbs into a napkin.

"I'll ask my dad what he thinks," Shelly replied, finally. "He's been a small business owner all his life."

Anita stared at Shelly. "Dave would probably know."

There was a slight intake of breath and Shelly's cheeks pinkened. Must be the husband, Celia decided, back on the alert.

"Yes, that's true," Shelly answered, calmly. "But you know this is something I want to do myself, Anita. I don't want to depend on him for anything. Got it?"

Anita sighed, rattling a spoon in her empty cup. "Got it. I guess that means you don't want me to ask him either?"

"No. And don't mention it again, please."

"OK, OK," Anita made a face, then checked her watch. "Ladies, let's go meet this so-called businessman and see what he's going to do for us today. I'll just check myself in the ladies' room."

Shelly shook her head. "Nita, all the charm in the world is not going to sway this guy. He's in a hole and he wants as much money as he can get out of us."

Anita dismissed her with a wave of the hand. "Guys like that, they've got money hidden somewhere else. Just let me try."

"Good luck, ladies," called the man behind the counter, Russell, and they laughed. It would definitely be an experience.

Yet, after a half hour meeting around the desk at New You, it seemed to Celia they were getting nowhere. The sixty-year-old with a Florida tan would not give anything on the cost of the equipment, no matter how hard Anita appealed to his sense of "providing a critical opportunity for today's woman" or "doing the right thing in turning over the business to hardworking newcomers." Even after she got up from the desk to bring water to the table, walking in a way that called attention to her considerable assets, he didn't budge, except for his eyes that followed her every move. Poor Anita! Nothing was working. Celia had no ideas, and sat looking at her hands in her lap.

Only after Shelly cleared her throat and started in on dates and amounts did the man seem to react. In the end, he agreed to a discount on the equipment he was leaving behind in exchange for moving up the closing date, since he was eager to get back to Florida and not have to make a trip back. Of course, Shelly didn't reveal it was no big concession on their part. Her father's lawyer was handling the legal work, and he would pretty much do anything she asked.

They shook hands, and the women returned to the coffee shop to confer. In the end, the new owners of New You had done pretty well for themselves, but it was clear, to Celia at least, that it all came down to dollars and cents, no matter how smart, hardworking, attractive, and well-intentioned they might be.

"We did it, girls," Shelly said, raising her coffee cup.

As they left and walked past the fitness storefront, they were overcome with the impact of it all: soon they would be businesswomen, left to sink or swim on their own. But they were going to give it their best, and why couldn't they have a good time with it?

Celia did a few dance steps on the sidewalk.

"We'll give it a good clean," said Shelly. "Make it shine; make it ours."

"Watch out, Sutton," said Anita, finally able to smile.

The next few weeks were nothing but dreary on the Eastern Shore. There were a couple of snow flurries, but nothing that stayed. With the Christmas lights down, and the seasonal bustle over, it was especially desolate.

Celia met with Anita and Shelly a couple times to make further plans about who would do what, when they finally opened at the beginning of February. One day, as Anita and Shelly went over calendar dates, Celia was thinking how she would deliver the news at the Inn, "I quit." Loudly, or with a smile? New You was exactly what she needed, a fresh start, and a much better use of her talents and personality. Plus, by and large, away from men and out of trouble. It might be a slow start, but she would put her heart into it. Even if she ended up leaving, she would have been part of this new business, getting it off the ground. That was a worthwhile purpose.

But, even before she opened her mouth to share the noble thought, Anita warned her. "Don't give notice yet at the Inn. We may not have money coming in right away, and I can't promise a paycheck for the first couple weeks. I'm pretty confident we can all pay ourselves by the end of February, but we still need to purchase supplies, like pens and paper, tissues, paper towels, cleaners. For heaven's sake, we need a vacuum!"

"Sure, right," Celia said, struggling to cover her disappointment. Then she reminded herself to think of the Big picture, but it wasn't the greatest consolation short-term. The meeting was adjourned and Celia had to go home and deal with a dirty uniform and ruined panty-hose. No fun about it.

These days, she found herself more and more reluctant to get ready for work. Wanda was long gone, and none of the other women seemed interested in friendship, or even just making conversation in the break room. Or, maybe it was something else—some suspicion or dislike of the attention and fuss that seemed to follow Celia.

Things at the Inn had changed in other ways after the holiday season. Virgil was on a reduced schedule after his slow recovery from the same flu that hit Celia and James, the elderly doorman. Celia was shocked when Anita told her that James, now at his daughter's in Virginia, was eighty years old and not likely to come back. Jeremy had gone for an extended stay with family in Georgia, leaving the kitchen quieter and duller.

Many evenings, Jay was in charge. Much of the staff agreed his calm, low-key style was a welcome change from the sometimes cranky Virgil. Everything ran smoothly, all the food out in good time, and the orders accurate. Celia felt that Jay still made a special effort to have her orders ready, so that she never had to wait as they scrambled to fill the plates. Of course, there was less business as well and sometimes slow periods, where the guys in the kitchen would talk and joke among themselves, no longer including Celia or any of the girls.

Pauline often stopped by the kitchen for a quick conversation with Jay, now that they were back together—as if they had reestablished their territory and Celia was just some insignificant outsider. No question about it, Jay's star was rising, and Celia's was not, at least at the moment. It's not that she begrudged him his success. She just didn't enjoy watching the drama play out under her nose.

At the same time, she had become fairly well established as a waitress and given more say about her scheduling. She would need to be available day times when the fitness center opened, and Anita had asked her to put aside some time beforehand to help clean and set up, for which she would eventually be paid. So, she was still stuck on evening shifts, at least for the time being. Counting the days.

After the bank closing to buy New You took place, the women were eager to get in the building and decide what needed to be done. The man who owned the coffee shop, Russell, had taken a liking to the three women and brought over coffee, muffins, and donuts for all.

"Russell, you naughty man," Anita scolded. "Don't you know we're trying to get in shape and take the weight off here? That's what we do."

Russell laughed. "You don't need to worry about that. I'm just trying to give you some energy. Besides, indirectly I'm helping you with your business. They come to me first, and then come here to work off that big honey-glazed donut."

"Oh, so we should pay you commission?" Anita shot back. "Fat chance." No one laughed harder at the pun than she did.

A few of the other store owners came by to introduce themselves. Clearly, their neighbors at the strip mall were curious, and perhaps a little skeptical, about the revamped business, but they were friendly and wished them luck.

June from the beauty parlor had brought a potted plant. She was probably close to sixty, with a plump figure, ultra-blond curls, and rosy lipstick and nails. A rhinestone chain held her glasses on her bosom, and she had a sweet scent—lilacs, perhaps. But her eyes were bright and shrewd, and Celia suspected she didn't miss much.

"No offense, girls," June said. "I'm probably not going to sign up. I hate exercise. It's a hopeless case with me, anyway. The weight never goes anywhere no matter what I do. I'm just about used to myself this way. But at least I can mention you to my clients."

Later, when the visitors cleared out, Shelly put on an aerobics tape that came with a set of illustrations for the exercises. In spite of some disagreement, they had fun figuring out what would work best with the music and still give a good workout. Both Anita and Celia had taken dance classes, and were inclined to go for movement that looked good in the mirror and flowed from one part to the next, while Shelly held out for steps that were more straightforward and repetitive. They finally came up with a scheme that all three could follow, for the sake of consistency, and agreed that no one expected them to do it exactly the same way. Anita suggested that they bring in their own music and make their own tapes, but Celia and Shelly were reluctant to experiment too much right away.

One morning, they met to look over the advertisement that Shelly had put together to run in the local paper. She had a friend who was a graphic artist create a logo of their business name: *New You.*

"It looks great," Anita said, inspecting closely.

"Wow, that's impressive," Celia agreed. "I guess we're really going to have to do this once it's in the newspaper."

"Of course we are," Anita exclaimed. "Who better than us? They need us here. Don't you know that by now?"

They finished examining the copy for the ad then found themselves unsure what to do next. A couple of new pieces of equipment had been delivered, as well as a better sound system, borrowed from Dave, the ex-husband. Someone Anita knew was coming to set them up around noon.

Anita proposed that they change into their leotards and run through a workout. First, they followed the exercise chart with sit-ups, jumping jacks, and leg bends. Then they put on a tape to go through their aerobics routine. They got through the first song pretty smoothly, congratulating themselves on how coordinated they looked in the mirror. Then Anita put on one of her gospel tapes and put the volume to loud. But as inspirational as it was, Celia found it hard to move to. By then, Shelly went to the front office to set up the desk, while Anita and Celia moved on to another tape.

"Celia," Anita said, when they stopped for a water break. "Don't take this the wrong way, but you're looking kind of scrawny lately, since the flu. I can see those two little knobby things sticking up here." She tapped her own more padded collar bone. "You really need to build yourself up a little. We're not trying to promote skinny here, just strong and womanly. Besides, black women will think you're sick or something."

When Celia didn't reply, Anita continued. "Just a word from your mother, since she's not here. Don't get me wrong, girl. You look good, you can move, and we're lucky to have you. But one, you need to take care of yourself. And two, we want these women to shoot for something they can achieve, not the impossible."

"Got the message," Celia replied, sneaking a glance at the mirror, a figure in pink ballet tights and a black leotard. She was always on the thin side. That was nothing new. But her color could be better. *Color.* The thought made her smile.

"One more time, then," Anita said, getting up to press the button on the tape player. "Let's go . . . 5–6–7–8 . . ."

They were just finishing a sequence of steps when the men arrived to set up the equipment. A broad-shouldered man in green overalls entered the workout area, and with him Jay and Cuffie. Celia's jaw dropped; she had never expected *them.* Anita didn't happen to mention *that.* Cuffie had a smirk on his face, while Jay stared stone-faced ahead. Celia realized, of course, they had seen her working out with the tape—in her leotard.

"Ah, Henry, men, speaking of muscles, here they are," Anita greeted them. "Perfect timing. We're all ready for you."

"Ah, excuse me." Celia hurried toward the back. In the changing room, she toweled off and changed into her clothes, all the while thinking, *Head up, head up.* Who knew how long they would take. She couldn't hide in the back forever. Walking carefully through the main room, Celia stopped to watch the work in progress, sections of equipment spread out over the rug. The older man looked up and nodded. Celia said hello to the three men, thanking them, and then made a bee-line into the office with Shelly.

After a few minutes, Anita came in looking for her and Shelly. "They've got everything together. Come out here, so we can decide where to put this stuff."

Shelly must have already known Henry and said hello to Jay by name. Cuffie she just nodded to. After twenty minutes or so, the room was set up, and they stood evaluating the results. Anita still wasn't sure if she wanted to put the member files right outside the office, or near the first station where they did sit-ups and abdominal work.

"Does it really matter?" Jay said with some exasperation.

"Yes, it does. To us it does. Let me see that file cabinet in both places, so I can tell."

When Anita was finally satisfied, she sent Jay and Cuffie to the store to buy some drinks. "Diet drinks for us," she ordered, sounding just like one of those well-manicured women they waited on at the Inn. And belatedly, "Please."

Henry took a seat on one of the exercise benches. He and Anita chatted about church and people they knew. After Jay and Cuffie came back with the drinks, the two younger men spent a few moments trying out the equipment before Henry said it was time to go. Celia and Anita sat down on the exercise bicycles.

"How does he know those guys; Henry, I mean?" Celia had to know.

"Henry, that's Jay's uncle, runs a machine shop in town," Anita said. "Henry and Monique have been friends of mine since high school. I know Jay's mom, Martine, too, but she never comes back this way. They've got to go to Baltimore to see her. They're good, church-going people, and they've done very well by Jay. He gave them a few bad moments, but he's all right now. I've known him since he was a baby, and he was a pretty baby, too."

She smiled at the memory, and then took a long drink.

"Jay goes to your church?" Celia asked.

"He grew up in it, but not now. He'll be back, when he decides to settle. That's when they usually come back."

"You mean with Pauline, from the Inn?"

Anita's expression turned sour.

"I hope not. You don't think I like that girl? She's grasping. She wants things, never happy with what she's got."

"Maybe that's just being ambitious, wanting something better." Celia could hardly believe her own ears. She was defending Pauline?

"Her, no. She just wants to be envied, wants everyone to want what she has."

"I'm not sure I get what you mean."

"Then you don't know the type." She let out a lady-like burp. "Besides, he should marry a black girl."

"What?" For a moment, Celia wasn't sure that she heard right. Some of the soda went down the wrong pipe, making her cough.

"Why do you say that?"

"Nothing against white girls, don't worry. Look at me here with the two of you." She waved at Shelly, who was approaching from the direction of the office. "Black men should help raise black children, and black children need black fathers to raise them, that's all." She looked intently at Celia. "I know what I'm talking about. Remember, I am a single mother, and I know my daughter misses the influence of a father."

"Well, I'm an almost divorced mother," Shelly joined in, straddling the new exercise bench. "And I know my children need the influence of a *good* father."

"He is a good father," Anita retorted.

"He eats, breathes, and sleeps work. He never saw those kids until we split, and he had to under the terms of joint custody," Shelly came back.

"He provides for them. That's what makes him a good father."

"Well, a good provider, maybe."

"You just don't love him anymore, Shelly. You married him for his drive, and now you hold it against him."

Shelly's shoulders drew back, and her expression changed. "Whose side are you on?"

Their voices were getting louder, their faces tense. Celia realized there was a lot of history between these women, good and bad.

"Yours, of course," Anita said. "Who else's? I'm just telling it like I see it. I'm not happy about your divorce, you know that. I wish you would stay together." Then she softened a little. "But I didn't like to see you so unhappy either. So, that's why we're all here, right. To make a new start."

"Amen to that," said Shelly, and when Anita didn't snarl, Celia said "Amen" too.

Chapter 15

As the days passed, Celia found herself caught up in the excitement of opening New You. It was a lot like putting on a play: costumes, parts, a stage, even music and publicity. She volunteered to take flyers to the library and to the hospital, and borrowed Grace's car to drive into Weston to post some flyers there. In the downtown area, she recognized some of the shops and places where she had been with Jay, but that all seemed safely in the past and she went about her business with a feeling of optimism and purpose.

Shelly came up with the idea to hold an Open House the week before officially opening the door on February 1st. They would open from ten until four o'clock for people to stop in and see the place. They printed a schedule of fees and hours of business to put on the door, and for people to take with them. They discussed whether to offer coffee to visitors. Anita objected since someone could easily spill coffee on the newly cleaned rugs, and it was not the healthy drink of choice.

"What do you suggest, then?" Shelly asked.

"Water, I guess, or diet soda. Fresca," Anita said, not too enthusiastically.

"How about lemonade?" Celia suggested.

They considered it—pink or yellow?

"That would be good if it were hot, or if they actually were exercising," Shelly concluded. "But we just want to bring them in off the street or out of the parking lot, as it were. It's February, by golly. I say we give them coffee."

"Oh, all right, fine," Anita conceded. "I'll bring the big urn from church. We can set it up in the lobby, and I'll get a bottle of Resolve. Celia, can you get the cream and sugar?"

Besides a tour of the place, they would offer a demonstration of a class, inviting any future customers who wanted to join in or rounding up volunteers from friends and family. Maybe five minutes or so every half hour, provided anyone was there. Plus, it would be good to have upbeat music playing in the background. Celia said she was willing to do it, since Anita would be working the front area, trying to get people to come in, and Shelly wanted to explain how the membership program worked and answer any questions. After a short debate about putting balloons at the front door—which Anita won—they were ready to go ahead.

"Like planning a party," Shelly said. "Who do you think will come?"

"I would think a lot of the previous members will be curious to see what's going on here, and where they stand," Celia guessed.

"I told all my friends to stop by, even the ones who don't exercise. We've got to look like the happening thing around here," said Anita. "Your kids coming?" she asked Shelly.

"No. I told them to stay away. I'll be too busy. They can come another time." And to this Anita just made a face.

Opening day dawned clear and windy. The women met at nine o'clock to get ready. The strip mall parking lot was practically deserted. The balloons on the door kept whipping against the glass, until they finally brought them inside and hung them from the ceiling. By ten, the parking lot was fairly full, and maybe half a dozen friends had come in to check out the place. Anita kept moving from inside to outside, hailing shoppers from the sidewalk. By quarter of eleven, no potential customers had appeared. Celia had put the music on, but no one was interested in doing an exercise routine, and she didn't see any point in doing it by herself. Finally, after lunch, June walked over from the beauty shop with four women in tow, all white with beautiful hair and nails, comfortably plump.

"I told them to come down here to see you, but they were afraid to come by themselves. I had to bring them myself to show what a nice job you girls have done getting this place ready. And, besides," June said more loudly, "I mentioned that they might even get a discount for signing up early. Isn't that what they usually do in these places?"

Shelly, Anita, and Celia looked at her like she was speaking a foreign language, but then Shelly stepped forward. "Well, sure, that's a great way to get new business. We're offering ten percent off for joining within the next, uh, couple weeks," she said, looking at Anita. "And our rates are very reasonable, considering we're the only and best fitness center for women in this area. Please come on in, and take a look around."

The women looked interested and stepped forward to enter the main workout room. They traveled together, commenting on the appearance of their generous derrieres in the mirror, and what a clean, pleasant room to be in, if they had to go somewhere to exercise. There was less enthusiasm for the exercycles and handweights, which elicited more dubious looks. They took themselves to the back of the club to examine the bright, updated changing rooms and Celia could hear them exclaiming like school children about the whirlpool.

June had stayed behind. "What shall I tell the girls who had memberships before?"

Shelly nodded to Anita and Celia. "June, would you excuse us a moment please? We want to be sure what's the best way to handle this."

Celia brought June a cup of coffee, and the three women went back into the office and took up positions around the desk. It was time to decide whether to go with their previous decision of fifteen percent discount, or something else.

"I don't see why we have to give them a break at all, frankly," Anita said. "It's the old owner who took their money, not us."

"Unfortunately, once burned, twice shy," Shelly answered. "Why should they trust us anymore than him?"

"We're local, roots in the community."

"And we're first time business owners."

"Which is why we have to be fair to ourselves," Anita protested. "We'll give them value for the money."

"If they give us a chance," Shelly said, shaking her head. Celia thought maybe she should just go out and see if anything was going on. She wasn't really a partner in the business end of things. But Shelly was interested in her opinion.

"Celia, if you were a former member, what would you think?"

Put on the spot, Celia had to come up with something.

"Well, I guess I would think I should get a ten percent discount at least, like the new members who sign up early, or make it fifteen percent to make them feel special."

Anita and Shelly nodded silently.

"All right, I guess I can see that, but no double discounts, for signing up early. It's not fair that we're not starting with a clean slate," Anita pouted.

"True, but we're not. Let's see if they go for it." They went back out to where June was waiting.

"We're going to offer a fifteen percent discount to return members, just to welcome them back." Shelly announced cheerfully. June looked a little doubtful, but said, "OK, then, I'll spread the word. Some of them just won't be back, of course, you know, but there's been a few asking."

As the women returned from their tour, one of them said she was ready to sign up, and the other three asked if could they stop in with checks later in the week. Celia offered to show them what a class would be like, but they were ready to go out to lunch, and besides, they had just gotten their hair done.

For the rest of the time, only a few women stopped in with any real interest, including a couple of nurses from the hospital, and three older black women with some kind of town government jobs. A few shoppers picked up flyers, and most of the shopkeepers put in an appearance to see how things were going. Celia wondered if Jay, or anyone from the Inn, would come by, but she didn't see anyone she knew except Grace and Roxanne who brought flowers. Grace spent some time talking with Anita and Shelly about the Eastern Shore, and different spots they enjoyed visiting. Grace and Roxanne had already signed up for a line-dancing class on Saturday afternoons, and that was all the exercise they could fit in.

There was a bubble of activity at the front doorway, and Celia turned to see three young people walk in the door, already in loud conversation. Warren, home for the weekend from college! Followed by Phil A., Tilghman, and Lacey. They hadn't yet spotted Celia, or Anita.

"Look who's here!" Celia said to Anita, beside her at the door to the changing room.

"What do they want to come here for?" Anita said, clearly not as excited as Celia. "Did you invite them?"

"No. Didn't you?"

"No. Probably just here for the free food, and the booty-watching," Anita muttered, none to graciously. Admittedly, young Tilghman was having a good look around.

"Not Lacey," Celia protested. And then catching a bright spot of color in Warren's hands, "And not Warren, either. Look, he's brought flowers!"

Celia bee-lined over to the front, where they finally caught sight of her, waving. "Hey, girl!"

Warren pushed the flowers into her hands. "For you all. Good luck. Nice place you have here—really fine."

Celia was touched. "Thank you, and thank you so much." And then, after a second, "But how did you know about this," she gestured around the room, "or us?"

Phil A. shook his head. "Ain't no secrets here, Dolphin Girl. Should know that by now."

Yes, she should know, or at least assume so, most of the time.

"Did you see the flyers?"

That met a blank response.

"We saw you with your heads together at the Inn," Lacey said, all cozy in her down coat and jeans, and the brightest scarf imaginable. "And everyone see you in and out of this place the last weeks."

"Cuffie told us," Warren admitted. "When he and Jay came by to set this stuff up."

Celia could only smile. Of course he did. And, why not?

"Well, come on then," she said, putting the welcome on, "Check out the equipment, look out back—see our Jacuzzi." She pointed at the food table, "And coffee, treats, help yourself."

"Oh, we will," Phil A. said, winking.

Turning to Lacey, Celia's eyebrows lifted. "Any chance you might want to join?"

Lacey laughed, and they all did, a little excessively. "No, thanks," she said finally. "No offense. I work hard at the Inn; you know that. Why am I going to pay money to work out here? Don't make no sense that I can see."

Well, of course, Lacey was young and fit—now. She just didn't get the greater point of it all.

"OK, well," said Celia, deflecting. "Just make sure to tell Anita how good everything looks—professional—and don't spill anything on the carpet."

After three o'clock, it became clear no one else was coming for the Open House, so they started cleaning up. An old Dodge pulled up outside the door, and an older woman, a teenage girl, and a couple of women with small children unloaded.

"Here they are," Anita announced. Her mother, daughter, sister, and cousins and neighbors had made a road trip to New You. They hauled in bags of chicken and side dishes, and Anita pulled out the contents, exclaiming how hungry she was. She set the food out in the office on the desk and a side table—enough to serve twenty people, and they began an impromptu picnic. Everyone knew Shelly, and Anita introduced Celia to her family and friends.

"No food or stains on the carpet, or I'll paddle somebody's fanny," Anita threatened.

Anita's daughter was fifteen, sweet looking, still in that awkward stage of too long and too thin. Her face had the same shape as Anita's, and her hair the same degree of curl, but her skin was lighter. Her eyes were closer to green than brown, and she had freckles. Celia wondered if Shelly knew the father or knew the story behind the daughter's birth, and felt sure that she did, but that she would not be the one to tell Celia.

Celia got up to turn the lights on, as the sky got dark in the early twilight of winter. She stepped outside to pull down the poster for the Open House, and looked back in through the plate glass window at the family-style party. She wasn't sure it was the sort of scene to inspire starting a fitness program, but it was certainly a lively good time, as well as a celebration. And warm, with good food.

The next week, things were up and running at New You. To all appearances, they were business women who were serious about fitness. Over twenty women joined, including three of the women who June had brought over. From examining the files, however, Shelly told them that very few were former members. Either they were not happy about the rejoining discount, or they were waiting to see how the new owners were going to do.

The members were rarely present at the same time, which made for small classes and unused equipment, not the kind of excitement they had hoped to generate. Too often, the place was empty, and they found themselves sitting around the office looking at each other, waiting to hear the jangle of the bell on the door.

At daily strategy sessions, they brainstormed what else they could do to get things rolling. Everyone who walked in was greeted immediately. The women who came to exercise seemed happy with the individual attention and the sparkling clean state of the facility. Word of mouth had to be positive. Finally, June relayed the news from the beauty parlor grape vine: the discount was the sticking point that kept former members from joining up. Finally, Anita and Shelly had to agree they had a problem on their hands.

Anita was mad, but she couldn't ignore the reality, and prayer was just not enough. "So, what do we do? They've got us over a barrel. We can't afford to ignore them and just let it go. There just aren't that many women interested in fitness within a reasonable driving area. It's not exactly a boomtown around here. Who else could we get to come here?"

"Men?" Celia asked, innocently.

The women eyed her in disappointment.

"No, we're not doing that."

"Let's ask June," Shelly said. "See if she has any ideas. Come on, Nita. Celia can hold the fort while we're gone." They grabbed their coats and headed out the door. Celia wondered how serious this membership crisis might be. Could it put them out of business? She took the Windex and some paper towels and started wiping the large wall mirrors.

The bell jingled. When Celia turned to look, an unfamiliar woman walked in. Celia dried her hands and went to meet her.

"Hello," the woman said. "Can you give me some information about joining?"

"Oh," Celia said, and then again, "Oh! You mean membership?" When the woman nodded, Celia said, "Yes, I'd be happy to." Thrilled!

Bonnie was an attractive thirty-year-old mother of three, looking to get her figure back after childbirth, and she was ready to pay for a membership. Celia had never taken a membership before. Shelly had prepared a couple of clipboards with all the necessary papers. Perhaps it was self-explanatory. She deliberated running to the beauty shop, but decided to do what she could on her own. She had the woman fill out the forms and make out a check, according to Shelly's chart for new members, including the discount.

Bonnie got up to leave, beaming. She said she would be back in the morning when she had a sitter for her toddler, and the other two were in school.

"I'm so eager to get started," she said. "Truly. I've been waiting for my chance to start getting in shape, and I was so happy to hear New You was going to be run by women."

Celia went back to her mirror washing, spraying, and wiping with enthusiasm. She couldn't wait to tell Shelly and Anita, and hoped they would come back with new inspiration.

They returned with coffee and muffins in hand, and agreed that the news was not great, but not terrible. June thought that most women would rejoin if they could get not just a discount, but credit for some of the time they had remaining on their memberships—that is, a free month or couple of months, and those months could be added on the end, so that they would have to pay some money up-front.

"So, we'll have money coming in, but they may or may not stay to see out the extra time on their memberships—it's up to them. I think it will be OK," Shelly said.

"I wish we could talk it over with Dave," Anita said.

"Oh, all right," Shelly said, a bit sourly. "I guess we can ask his opinion. It's not so much that they don't trust us, but they do feel injured, and want some compensation. It's not really fair to us, but we don't have much choice. Maybe we should have asked around first," Shelly went on. "Oh, well, live and learn. I'll call Dave tonight."

"Oh, ah, ladies," Celia interjected. She brought out the clipboard and check that she had gotten from Bonnie. "While you were gone . . ." Anita didn't register right away, but Shelly knew what it was.

"You sold a membership!"

"I did, I did," crowed Celia. "All by myself." And then, "I hope it's right."

"Two hundred and fifty smackeroos," said Shelly. "That's great!"

"That's toilet paper, towels, the phone bill, and a dehumidifier," said Anita.

They were on their feet, hands clasped in the air, a little happy dance—the three Graces . . .

When Dave OK'd the plan, they went back to June, who further suggested that they make a big fuss, and create flyers she could hand out, announcing "Welcome Back Day for Former Members."

"Aim for Valentine's Day. Do it up in red," June said. "That will remind them of love and romance, and that spring's around the corner. Time to be thinking about sleeveless tops and shorts. That will bring them in. You've got the season on your side. They really do want to come back."

June was right. Within a week of the Valentine's Day special, sixty former members signed up under the new terms. Every one of them came through the door with the same comment: "Well, everything looks great. I only hope it's better run than the last time."

By far, most of them were white, between twenty and fifty years old, and many seemed to know each other and Shelly and Anita. At first they resisted the idea of starting over, with a new fitness assessment and new program, along with the demonstrations of the equipment, but as the owners explained, "We have to start over, so we can get to know you. And also, so we're sure you're using the equipment properly, so that we don't have any injuries."

By March, they were busy, mainly in the morning from nine until one o'clock or so, and then again late in the afternoon. They rotated through teaching the classes, once an hour for about forty minutes each, which they soon found to be pretty tiring. Mid-afternoon, there was a lull, so they could get lunch and do cleaning and catch up work. They each had their "housekeeping" chores: Anita was a vacuum fanatic; Celia was put in charge of the toilets and sink in the back; and it was Shelly's self-appointed job to keep the glass and mirrors sparkling and fingerprint-free. There was some back and forth over the music played on the sound system between classes: Celia and Shelly were pretty good with the current pop hits: .

They discussed changing the hours to offer some later times, staying open until six-thirty or seven o'clock for the after-work crowd. But Anita didn't want to give up her shifts at the Inn, and Shelly had her children two nights a week. Celia still worked a few evenings at the Inn, since she'd given up the lunch shifts. So, for now, it was no go.

Anita must have been talking up the health club to friends, acquaintances, and church members because more black women stopped by, asking to see Anita, who toured them around. To Celia, they appeared slightly embarrassed about the idea of changing clothes and exercising in front of other people, but Anita was nothing if not persuasive: "for the good of your health, for more energy, for the good of your love life." It was hard to say no to those kinds of arguments.

"It sounds like more work," one large lady complained. "I work too hard already."

"Yes," said Anita patiently. "That's why it's called a workout. But it will give you more energy later on. Besides," she went on slyly, "it's fun. It's time for women to be together, right girls?" she called out to the five or six women working at the exercise stations. "Right," they panted back.

Due, no doubt, to Anita's influence, more black women joined, almost all of them first-timers. They would not wear leotards and came already dressed in a variety of sweat shirts and sweat pants, until they realized they would get too hot, and switched to shorts and tee shirts, worn under their winter coats. A few of the new members laughed when Celia started them on arm lifts with the two- and five-pound weights.

"That's no weight at all," a forty-year-old nurse's aide complained. "I can't even feel it. Little girl, I move two hundred pound men off their beds every day. This ain't gonna do nothing for me."

A few women came regularly at ten-thirty, when Celia was scheduled to teach, but waited around after finishing their individual programs until Anita's class at 11:30. They tended to group around the weight benches, passing time, and calling out to Anita to hurry up, since she sometimes started late.

"Stop your nagging," Anita said finally, walking over to where they stood. "You've got no reason to be waiting on me. Why didn't you take class before with Celia? She knows the routine just as well as I do."

When no one answered, she said, "You know what, Celia's taking over for me this morning, so I guess you'll have to give her a try. Celia, you can you do that for me, right? I've got to go out for a bit, important business." Celia looked up from putting the hand weights in order on the rack, and said, "OK, I guess so," all too aware she was being set up, but helpless to resist. She went over to the tape player to see if the music was set to go. Anita, of course, hadn't stirred, waiting for everyone to take a place on the floor.

They didn't move.

"She too hard to follow," one woman said, a tough-looking girl. "I can't understand what she say."

"Just stop talking and watch," Anita said impatiently. To Celia, she said, "Maybe you could speak up more, or give them signals when you're starting the next step."

"I'll try," said Celia, more and more uncomfortable. They clearly did not want to take class with her.

"What's the matter with you all?" Anita scolded the five women, finally. "If you think you have to go with me, you're wrong. It's not like that here. We're all women; we all have bodies to work on. Look at her." She gestured in the direction of Celia, who was stretching, and trying to remember the count to a section of the tape she always seemed to get wrong. Suddenly she became aware of six pairs of eyes on her, and straightened up, alert, looking back at the group through the reflection in the mirror.

"This girl, Celia, she's strong, you better believe it. You should see her carry those big, heavy trays at that fancy dining establishment up the center of town. Check out those muscles. What's the matter with that? You just do the work, and don't worry who you're here with. You could be just like that."

Her speech was followed by silence, and then laughter broke out, loud throaty yelps and screams of laughter.

Anita got angry. "What is your problem?"

"We never gonna look like that," one girl replied. "Not in a million years. No matter how hard we try. Not that color, not that shape. It take two of her to make one of us."

Even Celia had to smile at the truth of it, but Anita did not like her words being taken as a joke.

"I was so glad when you joined," she said, in a threatening tone. "But we don't need members that come with an attitude. Would you all like a refund, if you don't like the way we do things here?" Celia started getting alarmed. Anita shouldn't risk turning away business. They were the customers. They could choose whom they liked to have class with.

"OK, OK," one woman conceded, and the others followed her over to the open class space. "We'll take the class with her," she said pointing her thumb at Celia. "It's not like that, anyway. We just like your style better, that's all," she said to Anita.

"But not your tone," another muttered, which Celia could hear.

"Let's go, then," Celia said, quickly. "I'll try to be clearer. I'll hold up a finger when we're about to change up the step. And just stop me, if you're lost." She pressed the play button on the tape player, and the routine began.

During the period that Celia worked nights as well as teaching classes, she became physically exhausted. All she wanted to do was go home and sleep. But it was too hard to let go of the security of the money from the Inn, diminished although it was from hunting season and the holidays. She had the job down by this point, and often found herself going through the motions on auto-pilot, still outwardly smiling and cheerful. If she was keeping a distance at the Inn, the other kitchen and dining room staff were perfectly fine, seeming to appreciate her efficient, willing ways. No fuss, no drama, no real pals, since she and Anita rarely worked the same shifts. In a weird way, she missed Eldridge, who mostly worked daytimes, except for special occasions.

By this time, too, she'd had enough room-service orders to know the drill: getting the food and drinks together, and placing the trays on a cart that she took up on the elevator into the hotel rooms. Mostly it was small groups of men, playing cards or talking business. The hardest part was entering a room full of smoke and trying not to cough. A few couples ordered room service, mostly just coming to the door and taking the trays. They didn't tip as well as the men. The man who ran the elevator was a little fresh, but she could handle him.

"You got something sweet there for me?" he asked, every time. She blew him a kiss, saying, "That's all there is."

Despite Anita's repeated warnings to "be on guard," nobody had given Celia trouble when she delivered orders to the rooms. So when it happened, she was taken by surprise. She had an order of whiskeys and bourbons, sandwiches and chips for Room 426. She knocked at the open door to find four men playing poker, while another stood in a corner talking on the phone. She left the cart in the hall, and carried the trays inside. They wanted the drinks, and had her leave the sandwiches on a side-table. One of them signed the order slip, and she was getting ready to leave, when the man on the phone asked if she would take his drink and sandwich to the room next door.

"It's open," he mouthed. "Mine's a Reuben."

She nodded, putting the glass of whiskey and the sandwich back on a tray. She carried it to the room next door, pushing open the door with her foot. In a moment, she heard footsteps, and then the sound of the door being closed. With her back turned, she was carefully placing the drink on the table, and then the sandwich plate with a basket of chips next to it. Suddenly, the man was behind her, rubbing up against her with his whole body.

"Hey!" she said, straightening up, but he didn't stop.

"I saw you earlier," he said. "I was hoping they would send you up." His arms had circled her waist, traveling up to her breasts. He pulled her tight, breathing alcohol fumes across her cheek, while his lips wet the side of her neck.

"Stop it," she said, trying to twist away.

"It will be worth your while, I promise. Isn't that what room service is for? Easy money for a kiss and a grab."

He was too strong for her. One hand snaked down to her crotch.

"Come on, sweetheart."

She pushed an elbow into his chest and grabbed for the glass of whiskey on the table, knocking the food to the floor. She aimed, intending to throw the contents at him, but the whole glass left her hand and went flying over his shoulder and shattered on the uncarpeted floor.

He stepped back. Now that she was facing him, he must have seen the flash of defiance on her face.

"You little bitch," he snarled.

Her heart was pumping, but she said nothing, edging toward the door.

"What the hell is wrong with you? Look at this fucking mess." As she reached the door he said, "Somebody better clean this up. And listen to me; if you say anything, I'm going to say you were coming on to me, trying to get a few dollars. You hear that?"

By then she was out the door, and pushing the cart blindly down the hall toward the elevator. She jabbed repeatedly at the button, and when the door finally opened, she stepped in, bumping into a man with a suitcase who was trying to exit.

"Hold on, there, Missy," the elevator operator said, his brow furrowed. "Let the gentleman pass."

After he left, the elevator man held the door for Celia. "You OK?"

But she couldn't talk. Furious with herself, tears started to slide down her cheeks.

"Somebody hurt you?"

She shook her head *No.*

"Sometimes they mean," he said sympathetically. And then, "Sometimes they just dirty old men."

Celia dropped off the cart and went right to the Beckers' office. In all this time, she hadn't been back inside the room since the day of the interview.

Mrs. Becker was at the desk and did not look pleased to see her.

"What is it? Can't it wait until the end of the shift?"

"No," she said, finally getting a word out. "That man, the man upstairs . . . he came up behind me while I was putting out the food . . . and he . . ." For someone so used to memorizing speeches and delivering her lines with powerful effect, she couldn't make a complete sentence.

But now she had Mrs. Becker's attention.

"Come inside," she said, while going around her to close the door. "Please, try to speak clearly."

Celia stood in front of the desk, not invited to sit.

"I was on room service," she said. "On the fourth floor, 426. They were drinking and playing cards. One of the men . . . we went next door . . . he came up behind me, and pushed himself on me, and . . . and groped me." Groped—awful word. She had never used it before.

She waited for a response.

"So?"

She was dumbfounded. "He was being rude, and inappropriate, and saying things. He was . . . he was touching me . . ."

Mrs. Becker looked down. When she looked up again, she was shaking her head with what looked like disappointment.

"You should not have gone into that room. You should have told him you would leave the tray at his door."

"But, but, the door was open. So I went in. And I was just going to leave the food there and go. But he came in after me, and, and started doing . . . what he was doing to me."

Once again, she shook her head.

"And what then?"

She blushed. She couldn't help herself. "Well, I pushed my elbow into him, and then I turned and threw his drink at him."

Now Mrs. Becker's eyebrows shot up. "You threw the glass at him?"

Celia nodded. "It didn't hit him, but the whiskey spilled on him. And . . ." she might as well finish, "I knocked the food off the table. It fell on the floor, the sandwich and the chips . . . I guess," she finished lamely, "someone needs to clean it up."

For a second, Mrs. Becker looked like she was going to slap her. A flash of strong emotion crossed her face, and she, too, got pretty red. But her voice, when she spoke, was quiet.

"Foolish girl," she said. "You seem to have so little judgment."

"But, I . . . I didn't think—"

She cut her off, "No, you don't think. That is the trouble, as I feared from the beginning. You are not careful, and you do not think about the consequences of your actions. I've seen you make so many little mistakes, but always you are forgiven, because the people seem to like you. But this time, it was a bigger mistake, and you should have known better."

"Me?"

"It is expected that you look out for yourself in these situations. Now there is a problem with an unhappy guest, and a mess that must be cleaned up."

Celia was shocked. "That's not right. He . . . he touched me."

"So, he touched you. You are supposed to be a grown woman who can handle these things."

"What about him? Aren't you going to say something to him?"

"There is nothing to say, except apologize for the food and drink."

"Then I quit!" The words came out of her mouth even before she knew she was going to say them.

She marched out of the office, heading toward the kitchen, and then through to the break room. She put away her things and disappeared into the bathroom to wipe her face with a damp, cool paper towel. When she felt calmer, she left the bathroom and went to find Anita, who was working an extra shift during the three-day convention.

"I'm leaving," Celia said. "I had it out with Mrs. Becker. This guy cornered me up in a room. He..... But she didn't take my side at all. She acted like it was my fault."

Anita was upset. "Oh, don't let her make you quit. She's a hard-hearted such-and-such. How many times have I told you to watch out with those guys, especially when they've been drinking? You can give it back to them, say anything you want. They won't complain. They know they're in the wrong. You've got the power, not them."

Celia shook her head, looking at the floor.

"Seriously," Anita went on, "think about it. You'll miss the money." She took a breath. "You know what, honey, I bet in a few days, they'll take you back again, if you just say you were upset, it was an impulsive reaction, that kind of thing."

"No. I've had it. I don't want to work at a place like this."

"OK, sweetie. I know you're tired. Go right home and get in bed. I'll see you tomorrow at you-know-where." Just as Celia was turning to leave, Anita asked for her order pad. "I'll turn it in," she said while her eyes scanned the last orders, stopping at Room 426 with a scowl.

After getting her coat, Celia stopped and looked around again, this time for Eldridge. She found him wheeling away the cart with the dropped food and the broken glass.

"Eldridge, I just wanted to tell you I'm leaving," she said. "I mean, for good. I quit."

"Yeah, I heard it. I'm the one cleaned up your mess."

"I . . . I." Celia didn't know quite how to continue. "I'm not sure when I'll see you again." She closed her eyes, shaking her head. "I don't know how I did it, but I messed everything up—again." She opened her eyes, searching Eldridge's face. "What's wrong with me?"

"There, there, sweet girl," Eldridge clucked. "You fine. You better than fine. They just not ready for you, yet. That all."

Watching her, a slow smile came to his face. "It's time," he said. "You need something different from all this. You need some lights and music and fun."

Her eyes widened. "You mean . . ."

"It's time we go to the Starlight. Then you see, then you understand."

"You really think it's safe?"

"Honey, they's no place really safe. I take care of you."

She held his eyes a moment. "You're right. I need something else in my life right now, besides work, work, work." She gave him a wry smile. "We can celebrate my release from this place, anyway."

"You better meet me here," Eldridge directed her. "About ten o'clock Saturday night."

"Aren't you working?"

He shrugged. "A couple hours; no big deal. I leave when I want."

Celia stared long and hard into his endlessly deep, dark eyes.

"Are you sure about this?" she asked.

"Sure as anything." He smiled a broad, gap-tooth smile. "We going to the Starlight."

Chapter 16

At home in the apartment, Celia found it hard to believe she had told Eldridge she wanted to go to the Starlight Lounge. But she had, although she'd never have said yes if Grace wasn't away for the weekend. It was a risk; but a pretty low one, hopefully. According to Eldridge, the Starlight was quiet this time of year; only local people. They would be traveling by foot, so no car accidents. The Starlight was not five minutes away through the marsh, if she had to get home in a hurry. Right or wrong, she trusted Eldridge on this. And she needed something—fun, energy, letting loose, or just forgetting her troubles.

Saturday night, Celia headed out the apartment door toward the Inn in her improvised club wear: black stretch pants with foot straps and a long-sleeved purple dance leotard. She wrapped a white scarf around her waist, gypsy-style, for a pop. A pair of ballet slippers and a jacket for the cool nighttime air. She didn't want to overdress; they were going dancing. She had no big gold hoops, like Vanessa and Lacey wore, but she found a pair of dangly silver earrings she had not worn since California.

At the Inn, she kept in the shadows by the back entrance until she saw Eldridge in uniform, ten minutes late, emerging from the doorway, pulling a pack of cigarettes out of his pocket.

"I was beginning to wonder," Celia chided, waiting for him to light up and take a drag.

"I don't hurry for no one," Eldridge said, taking long-legged strides back the way Celia had come. "Not even you, baby doll."

They followed Main Street to the intersection with Franklin Road where the Starlight was. The next right after that, Hopewell, led to the apartment complex.

"I got to stop by the house and change these clothes," Eldridge said, as they headed down Franklin. In less than a quarter mile, he turned into the front walk of a single story house, gray in the moonlight, without shutters on the windows or bushes in the yard.

"I can see our place from here," Celia said, on tip-toes at the top of the walk. "Except for that big marshy area, the back of the apartment is right across from the back of your house. What do you think of that?"

"Don't leave the shades up when you dress." Eldridge was at the front steps, which were missing a railing on one side. As Celia approached, she saw its outline on the ground, dead grass and weeds poking through the bars.

Eldridge led Celia into a hall, where they stood in the dark.

"Wait here," he said. "I'll get the light."

The house was quiet, no music or voices. Celia wasn't sure who Eldridge lived with—his mom, maybe. Then she heard the sound of a baby, crying softly. Whose, she wondered. Certainly not his mother's; she must be at least in her mid-forties. Or could it be?

A light came on and Eldridge brought her to a room off the hall, maybe a porch or deck that had been enclosed and now was used for storage. Open cardboard boxes lined the walls along with plastic bags stuffed with clothes. The room was damp and retained the deep chill of winter. The whole place smelled sour and musty. Celia closed her jacket and stepped foot to foot to keep warm. In a few moments, Eldridge came back wearing his dancing clothes—black pants and a button-down white shirt, along with a dark sports jacket.

"I heard a baby," she whispered.

He lifted his chin, motioning her toward the back of the house.

"That's a baby won't sleep nights," he said. "Come on."

They entered the kitchen at the back of the house, where the light was on. A young woman, long and bony like Eldridge, sat at the table with a baby in her lap. The mother, Celia supposed it was the mother, was in a thin robe, with her hair sticking out, a bored, grumpy look on her face. One knee was exposed, gray and ashy. The young mother tested a full milk bottle against her wrist, and then returned it to the table.

"This my sister, Eleanor, and that her baby, Leon," Eldridge introduced them. Eleanor looked up briefly, but didn't smile when Celia said hello. They stood a moment watching the baby fuss weakly.

"Get me a spit cloth," Eleanor said to Eldridge, and he bent down to rummage in a plastic laundry basket. Silently, Celia took in the rest of the room. A crack in the window was repaired with duct tape, but she could still feel a draft. There were no cabinets to speak of, just a few shelves holding chipped mugs and plates. All the food stuff was set out along the countertops and rows of cans were stacked up against the wall beneath the window: that was the pantry.

Everything in the kitchen was worn, in all stages of deterioration, holes and scratches everywhere. The kitchen had no design, no decoration, and looked barely functional. Even the cooking pans were beat up. More than that, the room itself was badly constructed, crooked and unfinished. Eldridge's home was barely a shelter. Celia's mother would be shocked to think someone lived here. Celia was shocked.

"This Celia. We going to the Starlight," he told Eleanor. "Where's Ma?"

"She in bed, and she say she not getting up for this baby," Eleanor pouted. She didn't even look curious about this pink-faced white girl in her kitchen.

"He yours, sister," Eldridge said. "You got to stay home with him sometimes. Come on, Celia, we going." Celia realized with a start that it was the only time she could remember him calling her by name.

Years of training made her reply automatically. "Good-bye, Eleanor, it was nice to meet you." Here, the words sounded fake, almost mocking, although they weren't meant to be.

Eleanor placed the spit cloth on her shoulder and picked up the bottle again. Her glance flickered briefly in the direction of Celia, but never met her eyes. With a flash of pity, Celia turned away. She wondered why Eldridge had invited her in at all.

Celia and Eldridge stepped back outside into a clear and starry, early spring evening. Peepers sounded from the marsh. They could hear music from the Starlight, and in a matter of minutes, they were at the door.

The Starlight Lounge was smaller than Celia had expected, really just the bottom floor of an old house that had been converted to a club. There was a bar along the right wall, and the rest of the long, narrow room was crammed with mismatched tables and chairs, except for the very back where there was an area for dancing, not very big either. The bar and tables were already fairly full of men and women, all black. The music was playing, not too loud, and no one was dancing yet. Celia was sort of disappointed not to see any tough-looking characters, mostly just folks in their forties or fifties, making small talk or nursing drinks on their own. A few women were made up, with flashy jewelry or some cleavage, but most sat big and comfortable in their chairs. Celia realized that she and Eldridge were on the younger side. She also realized, by now, that every person had noted her presence without so much as a blink.

She smiled to herself. *So what?*

"It's kind of small," she commented.

"Yeah, but it get a lot of action. You see, in a while. They go out back, too, for a toke."

"You mean, drugs?"

"Weed. If they do coke, they stay in the bathroom," Eldridge explained, weaving through the room. He was aiming for two stools at the bar, nearest the dance floor—the end seat for Celia while he took the one next to her. A protective barrier, Celia thought, with amusement. The stone-faced, tattooed bartender nodded to Eldridge, with barely a glance at Celia, and took their drink orders: a gin and tonic for him, a rum and coke for her. Celia told Eldridge she would pay for herself, but he slapped her hand when she tried to put down the money.

"This my world," he said. "I'm in charge here."

They sipped drinks and looked around, cigarette smoke swirling under the lights of the low-ceilinged room. The mirror behind the bar was tarnished and cracked, making a kaleidoscope of their reflections.

"When does the dancing start?" Celia asked, poking at the ice in her glass with a stirrer.

"Oh, not for a while. They got to get juiced up first. Just relax."

"I am relaxed," she said, stretching an arm with a pretend yawn.

"Yeah," Eldridge gazed at her. "How you fit right in here, it's a miracle. All the way from California." He looked, somehow, like a proud uncle, his long cheeks creased with lines.

Celia broke apart some ice cubes. "How about you, Eldridge? Have you ever traveled anywhere?"

"Nope. I ain't been nowhere; I ain't goin' nowhere."

A few more sips of the tasty rum, and Celia was ready to argue a little, playfully.

"Come on, Eldridge. Aren't you curious to see Baltimore or Philadelphia? Or how about New York? You've got to see New York someday. The streets, the parks, all the stores. Skyscrapers so tall you can't even see the top. And at night, all the lights. It's so amazing!"

"Not me. I don't want to go to no cities. Too many people, too much noise."

Celia pointed the stirrer accusingly. "Eldridge, you sound like an old man." Another man passed, younger with a low brow and darting eyes, checking out Celia. But she didn't care.

"And you just a baby girl, in this world," Eldridge told her.

"Don't be ridiculous. You're five years older than me, same as my sister."

"I an old man inside," he said, tapping his chest. "Can't you see? That's why I so wise. I don't need to go nowhere. Everything happens here same as anywhere, the good and the bad."

Celia must have looked unconvinced, because he went on, "What I mean, I seen enough how people act, they's no surprises left."

"Oh, yeah?" she said, wagging her head. "Sure there are. How about me?" She raised her eyebrows at him, a bit obnoxious. "I know you haven't met too many college dropouts from California who want to be an actress."

"Yeah," he said, beaming. "There's you, little blue-eye bird." He held up his drink, "You new, and now you came to this world, too. See, I'm right."

Celia raised her glass to her lips, hiding her smile. Damn, he got her there. Sometimes she had trouble with people's logic down here, but Eldridge always made his reasoning perfectly clear.

"Well, I disagree," Celia said, putting her glass down. Surprisingly, it was empty. "There's a big world out there."

"Ready and waiting for a black fag like me?" Eldridge shook his head, but his tone was not bitter. His eyes were sweeping right and left, looking, checking, on duty.

"There are places where gay people live together and have good lives. Seriously. I mean it."

"Here is OK. I know where I'm at, what I can do."

"You could go," Celia insisted. Out of nowhere, another drink had appeared and a small dish of peanuts. How did that happen? Celia took a few and pushed the dish over to Eldridge. The nuts were salty and biting on her lips.

"I don't wanna go," he said, Mr. Stubborn. "It's not so bad. Girl, look how you struggling for something better."

He'd turned the table on her, again. She stopped chewing and stared, focused, once again, on the black hole of his smile.

"Me?" she said, ready to refute. But she knew the truth when she heard it. "All right, maybe it is a struggle sometimes, but I'm still positive and optimistic and . . . I still know how to have a good time."

"Me too," Eldridge said. Then putting his drink down, he declared, "Enough talking, Miss Thang. Time to dance."

Eldridge and Celia were the first ones on the dance floor, but in a matter of minutes others had joined them. The music got louder, many of the songs familiar to Celia from hearing them on the local radio stations for so many months. Celia was inspired to give Eldridge some dance lessons, starting with a three-step waltz. For such a tall, angular fellow, he picked it up surprisingly well, moving elegantly with Celia about the floor. Next was the cha-cha to a Latin-beat, which was another thing altogether. Eldridge's upper body traveled a beat behind his feet, and the whole effect was comical. Celia squeezed her legs together, afraid she might pee from laughing so hard.

The dance floor filled up, and quickly it seemed like a big, noisy conversation had broken out in the air above them, people yelling, shouting, hooting, and hollering.

"Hey, hey-ah."

"Uh, uh, uh."

"Get down on it."

Celia laughed at the show-offs, putting on their best moves. She liked how it became a whole group thing, not just pairs coupled off here and there. After a few songs, Eldridge took off his jacket, taking a handkerchief from his pocket to wipe the sweat off his face. After a while, he signaled Celia, ready for a break and a drink.

"It's a lot of fun here," Celia said, back on the bar stool. She took a long gulp. "I'm glad we came."

Just then, she spotted Phil A. and Cuffie from the Inn, along with Vanessa and another girl with big puffy hair and huge gold earrings: Lacey! Celia almost didn't recognize her. Celia jumped up, waving in excitement.

"Hey, Dolphin Girl," said Cuffie with a quick squeeze of Celia's shoulder. His gold tooth flashed under the lights. "Where you been at? What's the matter, you don't like us no more? Up and quit just like that." He snapped his fingers.

"Not you guys," Celia protested. "There was this man . . . but Mrs. Becker . . ."

Cuffie put up his hand. "Just teasing with you. We know how it is. Surprised you stay long as you did." He looked around the bar area, which had filled and someone had turned up the music. "Nothing but good times tonight. Right?"

"So, how you like the Starlight?" Phil A. asked, bending down to speak in Celia's ear. He sported a sleeveless red basketball jersey, showing off his thick neck and biceps. Behind him, Vanessa nodded, and Lacey wobbled in spikey heels. Celia smiled happily at familiar faces, everyone in fun, bright colors and glittery jewelry, so different than at the Inn. And hair, too!

"It's great," she said. "I love to dance." As, apparently, they all knew.

"Oh, yeah, then dance with me." A sly grin spread across Phil A's face. Celia hesitated.

"Go ahead," Eldridge said, swirling the contents in his drink. "I ain't got a key on you. Dance with the boy."

The five of them, without Eldridge, went on the dance floor, laughing and clowning around. After a couple songs, Celia started to excuse herself, thinking it wasn't nice to leave Eldridge alone, but he was deep in conversation with a man who had taken her stool. She stayed on the dance floor until the taped music came to an end.

"Excuse me," she shouted. "I'm going back."

She went to the stool to get her purse, which held a few dollars, a lipstick, and a comb, and asked Eldridge where the restroom was. He pointed to a back corner, past the crowded dance floor, and told her to wait. He waved at Lacey to come over.

"Go with her," he told her.

"That's OK," Celia said, embarrassed. "I'm not one of those girls who needs a pal to go to the bathroom." But Lacey said, "The door don't lock. I'll keep it closed for you."

"OK, OK," Celia conceded, tucking the purse under her arm.

On the way to the ladies' room, Celia noticed that the talking had gotten louder and the air denser, smokier, more charged. A couple of men made remarks to the girls as they passed, and Lacey turned and glared at one. "Keep your hands offa me."

Outside the ladies' room, Celia could hear voices and shuffling inside. Lacey pounded on the door. "Hurry up. We need to get in."

"Why they have to be so stupid?" she complained. "Why they want to do their business in a filthy john, especially when other people have to use it?"

Finally, two women and a man came out, wiping their noses. Celia and Lace took turns peeing in the single stall, and then Celia washed her hands and pulled out the ponytail holder and bobby pins, giving her hair a good shake. She held the pins in her mouth, while she fished for a comb.

"Don't tie it up," Lacey said. "Let it go free. The boys like that. Hold on a sec." She had a pick in her back pocket. "Going fluff you up, give it some volume." Then she stood back to admire. "Like a cloud of gold."

When the girls returned, Eldridge interrupted his conversation, his face almost merry. Phil A. and Cuffie were chatting with some other guys, who came over to the bar.

"That's fine," Phil A. said to Celia. "Real fine."

"Like a natural woman," said Cuffie, approvingly.

"Ra-puzzle, Ra-puzzle, let down your golden hair," said another guy, a cute one in a white polo shirt. Not from the Inn, though. Apparently, a high school friend.

Celia gulped down her drink and found herself back on the sticky dance floor, a little warm, a little dizzy, unthinking and unworried. When she glanced at the bar, Eldridge was alone now, watching her with an air of satisfaction. Celia smiled back, and let the music take her. It was too bad Carlos wasn't here, she mused, or even Jay. Could Jay dance? Maybe a little too proud, too stiff, to be a really good dancer. But he was so handsome, she fantasized, and gentle. Yes, gentle and slow and sexy. She closed her eyes, feeling herself floating and free.

Cuffie wanted a dance, and then Phil A., mostly during the faster songs, when she could simply hold their hands and move to the rhythm together.

Celia could tell, of course, that they would have liked to dance like the other couples around them, bodies pressed together and grinding, but they didn't. The other boy, the one in the white polo, held her for a close dance. His skin was brown and his hair tight and curly, but his eyes were blue and full of fun. Celia could feel her body responding but she held herself away—no fooling around. No, that wouldn't do. She was here with Eldridge, sort of. But he was cute, this boy, and those blue eyes.

A song came on that she recognized from a tape they sometimes used at New You, more jazz than rhythm and blues. The dance floor cleared except for a few diehards, and Celia. Her pals had gone to sit down, including the blue-eyed boy. But Celia couldn't resist. Her arms and legs started following the steps of the routine, doing the counts automatically in her head. Even when she realized that most everyone had gone, and she was on her own, she kept moving, the music directing her, performing like on a stage.

Soon the comments started, along with the hoots and hollers. "Hey, girl, you go." And then, "Go, Celia; go, Celia," from Cuffie and company. Still, she kept going, with all that room around her to move. The scarf came off; she could whisk it dramatically through the air. Four steps back, turn, and step-step-step.

How she loved to dance, using her body. It was so much better than talking, listening, thinking. Hot as she was, heart pounding and breathing fast, she felt so light. The music played on, but something had changed: no more workout tape, no more choreographed steps. Something else had taken possession of her. Eyes closed, she had this awareness of her feet skipping quickly over something deep and heavy, dangerous to land on or sink into, something to do with pain and grief. And then, just as surely, she was pulled upwards as if her arms, hands, shoulders were attached to strings, and that was something very blessed and wonderful. When she opened her eyes, she was still at the Starlight at the center of the dance floor with a newfound, unexpected freedom—from worry, judgment, embarrassment, and even the heartache of love.

The song came to an end, and finally, she stopped. As she stepped off the dance floor, her foot caught in a hole in the linoleum and she tripped, landing rather gracefully on her butt. At that point, everyone clapped and shouted. Cuffie came out on the floor to give her a hand up, and Celia rose to her feet, bowing, curtsying. What else could she do? Celia laughed along, fanning her hot face, sweat dripping down her arms and back as she made her way to the empty stools, looking for Eldridge, who was not to be seen. For a moment she looked around, confused. Had he left her there? But then, from the corner of her eye, she saw him making his way from the front of the room, focused directly on her, his eyes laughing, but his mouth set. He must have seen her performance and also her exit from the dance floor.

"This way, missy," Eldridge said, taking her arm and helping her to her feet. She bent over to pick up her purse and jacket from the floor and almost blacked out. Then she was stumbling loose-legged away from the bar.

"Got to go," Celia called out to her friends, turning back, and then blew a kiss to the boy with the blue eyes.

Almost at the exit, Celia's eye was caught by a flash of white—a woman's blouse. Seated at one of the tables on the right was an attractive woman with a big guy in a tight shirt, showing off his massive chest. When they looked up at Celia and Eldridge passing, the woman's eyes opened in shocked surprise.

"Anita!" Celia cried out. "Eldridge, wait. Look who's here." At the table, Celia dropped into an empty chair, while Eldridge remained on his feet.

"What are you doing here?" she asked. Anita was nursing an amber drink with a bright red cherry. How did she always manage to get special treatment?

"What do you think? I'm out with my friend here, Frank. Frank, this is Celia and Eldridge."

Frank looked at them doubtfully, an odd couple, for sure: one large, black, and missing a front tooth; the other red and sweaty with a mass of wild yellow hair.

"From church?" he asked.

"No, no." Anita's tone was not the most patient. "From work, from the Inn, you know. And Celia works with me at the health club."

"Oh," Frank nodded, "I see." Clearly, he was not a friend from church. What then? A good time date or serious material? Taking in his form-fitting shirt and gold jewelry, she decided most likely a night out. *Ho, ho,* she thought. *Or did she say it?*

"I should be asking, what are *you* doing here?" Anita said. "Eldridge, was this your idea?"

Celia didn't let him answer. "I wanted to come. I just wanted to get out, hear some music and go dancing, so Eldridge said he'd take me. That's all. And we had a great time, dancing up a storm." She pointed toward the dance floor.

"But now you're leaving," Anita continued.

"We don't have to go," Celia said. "We could stay a little longer." Eldridge and Anita traded looks, but Eldridge just said, "I be right back."

Celia settled in, putting her jacket over the back of the chair, and placing her elbows on the table.

Anita, here, of all places!

Anita's glass was printed with bright lipstick, and she was dressed in a way that showed off her shape, pushing her cleavage just into view. Then it occurred to Celia that they were on a date, and she had kind of dropped in on them. Ah, well, she was here now, and couldn't go anywhere until Eldridge came back, so she sat with a friendly smile.

"So, Frank," Celia started, conversationally. "Have you ever seen Anita teach an exercise class? She's amazing. Sometimes I take her classes, too, besides teaching my own, which she doesn't take, usually. Not that I would expect her to."

Frank looked confused.

Anita said, "So, you've had a few drinks, Celia?"

"Oh, just a couple, maybe a few. But it's all right as long as you're dancing, right, so you can sweat it out?"

"How about Frank gets you a coke?" Anita nodded at Frank, who got up and went to the bar.

"Girl, it's getting late. How you getting home?"

"Eldridge will walk me back to the apartment."

"Um . . . hm," Anita nodded. Frank returned with the soft drink. "Here's for the little miss," he said, smiling. He was not that great looking, Celia decided, but attractive in his way, and also very fit.

"So, you were saying, Celia," he went on, apparently interested, "about the exercise classes."

"Oh, yes!" she said, sitting forward. "At the club. New You, I mean, the fitness club, not a night club, of course." She giggled. "But the classes, with the music and the steps, sometimes it really is like dancing. You should come by some time," she concluded, "to see what we do."

Anita frowned. "Celia, it's not a place for men to come watch women. Remember?"

"Oh, right. Yes, I know that," Celia said. "But Anita, you're really great. I think you should make exercise videos, like that woman, what's her name?" She paused, concentrating.

"Jane Fonda?" Frank supplied.

"Yeah, her. But, I think Anita's better. Like I said, it's more like between exercise and dance. She's got this one move, like a transition between the side to side steps, and going into the knee lifts that is so cool." She started to get up. "Like this."

Celia stood, pushing back her chair, which somehow tipped away from under her before she was upright. Frank grabbed the chair before it hit the ground. Then Celia was on her feet, but a little woozy, holding on to the back of the chair. A second later, her stomach caught up, lurching up toward her throat.

"Time to go," Anita announced. "Eldridge!" she stood and shouted over the noise of the crowd. Finally, he appeared, eyes wide, but in no more hurry than usual. He put his just-lit cigarette into his mouth and picked up Celia's jacket and purse from the chair, holding on to her elbow.

"I guess I'm going," Celia smiled, a little disappointed. She was better now, not so wavery. "It was nice to meet you, Frank." And then she whispered, loudly, "You really should come by some day, if you want to see some strong women." He waved as they departed, Anita holding her by one arm, and Eldridge by the other. They made their way, three abreast, through the crowded doorway, and finally down the front steps and onto the street.

When the night air hit her, Celia realized just how fatigued she had become, her ears ringing, and her eyes stinging from the cigarette smoke. They said goodnight to Anita, who waited at the doorway to see them off.

Slowly, Celia became aware of the clear night sky and the stars. The air was cool, but she was sweating and overheated. They got almost to the end of Franklin Street, where it connected to Main Street, when she realized she was going to throw up. She turned to face a straggly bush.

"That nasty," Eldridge commented, wrinkling his nose.

"I'm sorry," Celia said, swallowing. "I guess I overdid it. Can we stop a moment, until my stomach settles?"

She sat down on the curb, knees on elbows, and lowered her head to ward off the dizziness. After a moment, Eldridge folded his long legs, brushed some gravel and dead leaves out of the way, and sat down next to her.

"But it was still a good night out," Celia insisted, dabbing the handkerchief at her mouth. "Great."

"I told you so."

They sat in silence a few moments. Although Celia's stomach still gurgled, her head had started to clear. But as she started to rise, the nausea returned.

"Hang on, girl," Eldridge said. "There ain't no fire."

Celia leaned closer to whisper, "It's so embarrassing to get sick in front of someone's house. I hope no one heard me." She glanced through the chain link fence to a desolate, empty yard with a blank-faced house. A dim light shone out a side window through the branches of a struggling, young tree.

"That Wanda's house," Eldridge informed her with a hint of malice.

"No! It can't be." Celia protested. "She told me she lived outside of town."

"That her house."

"Then she lied to me."

"Maybe."

There was no reason for Eldridge to lie. The house was worse than Eldridge's. One of the worst houses on one of the worst streets in town. But it was so close, as the crow flies, to the apartment and the hospital.

"She don't want you to think bad about her," Eldridge said softly.

Celia sighed. "I don't get it. I thought we were friends."

"And you don't keep no secrets from her?"

That Eldridge, Celia thought, he is too wise for his years. Or else, he sure knows how to read me like a book.

Celia rubbed her eyes and put her forehead on her arms, crossed over her knees. She heard Eldridge strike a match. He blew smoke outward forming a graceful plume.

Celia waved the smoke away. "Eldridge, smoking is what's going to get you."

He just laughed softly. Celia looked at his profile, so calm and dark and otherworldly, and wondered how it should be that he of all people was the one she should feel closest to. She shifted weight from one butt cheek to the other, and noticed the cold seeping through her clothes.

"I wish you wouldn't talk that way," she continued. "You know, what you were saying back there, at the Starlight."

"Then don't pay no never mind," he said.

"But you sound so serious," Celia went on. "Like there's nothing better than this, nothing to hope for. Is that what you think?"

"That's not your worry, lamb," he said, and then, unexpectedly, "ain't nothing can harm me. My heart is pure."

Her mouth opened in delight—*such poetry!*

But now he was straightening up, limb by limb, joint by joint. Celia almost expected to hear him squeak like the tin man from Oz. When she pushed herself up, he took her elbow and propelled her back toward the apartment building, both of them silent.

At the door, Celia said thank you, straightening the welcome mat with her toe.

"Eldridge?" she said, with her hand on the doorknob.

"Yeah?"

"Where's your tooth?" she pointed to her own top teeth. "I mean, what happened to it?"

"That toof gone ten years," he answered. "Never been found, probably buried in the dirt somewhere. Somebody knock it out for me."

"Because you're black?"

"No, not that."

"Because you're gay?"

"Not that, either. I guess they just didn't like my ugly self."

Celia wasn't sure if he was joking. He had the lowest voice of anyone she knew, which made him sound somber even when he wasn't.

"But you're not ugly," she said.

"Bless you, honey-chile."

"Cut it out, Eldridge. I'm not a baby."

"Go on inside now," he said, displaying that gap-tooth smile that was so much a part of him.

"Goodnight, Eldridge. See you around."

Eldridge turned to depart, and checked his watch. Home in ten minutes— if he was going home, that terrible, bleak place. Or was he going back to the Starlight, and one of those anonymous men?

Pausing in the entranceway, Celia had a vision of the three of them, Eldridge, Anita, and herself, ascending into the night sky, she in her nightie, and the two of them with great, gray wings—goose feathers, not swan—her guardian angels. Anita, in her waitress uniform, brandishing a sword at any who dared to approach or get in the way; Eldridge, with his bus boy jacket and a cigarette dangling from his lips, dandy in a 1930s way, flapping slowly but steadily upwards.

Chapter 17

After the weekend, Grace didn't appear to have an inkling about Celia's night out at the Starlight. Strange. Celia couldn't imagine how the word did not get around, somehow. She kept waiting for the shoe to drop, and prepared a brief and duly apologetic response to Grace's possible questions. Or, by some miracle, the timing was just right, and she would not be found out. Instead, it would turn into a telling and humorous anecdote some day in the future when they were looking back at their time on the Eastern Shore.

Anita, however, did not let Celia forget how she had made a fool of herself. Shelly merely shook her head when she heard, but Celia looked on the outing as a night of adventure. Frank, too, had not made a great impression, and was out of the picture. Anita was more close-mouthed about that. Strangely, Anita's whole demeanor seemed to change since that night. She had become even more outspoken about her religious beliefs and kept reminding Celia about coming to Easter service. Celia wasn't sure if it was Celia's soul that Anita was concerned about, or her own, but she kept alluding to "respect" and "dirty business" in a way that made Celia uncomfortable. Shelly took it all in stride. Grace was invited to the service, but already had plans to go to Wilmington for the weekend.

The week before Easter had suddenly become spring, and even attempted to mimic summer, it was so warm. Celia walked to work through town, and then along the road that led to the strip mall. It was unusual to see anyone else walking along the last stretch, passing a gas station and large used car parking lot. But then one day she spotted a young man, black, walking in the same direction, on the other side of the street some distance behind.

Oh, no! Not that awful boy who had followed her and Wanda in the car with his howling friends. The hair, the height, the build, and the color of his skin were similar. But when she took another look, it wasn't him—the face more oval-shaped and the lips fuller. When he caught her looking, he waved and sped up, crossing to meet her. His backpack jangled when he moved: a couple keys on a key chain, next to a brown, furry thing the size of a toe—a rabbit's foot.

"Hello," he said. "What a great day. Do you mind if I join you?"

Celia didn't know what to say. Why on earth would he approach her, just walking along, minding her own business? Was she wearing a sign that said, "Bother Me" or "Looking for Trouble"? He seemed all right—well-groomed, well-spoken, her age, about. Was it her hair, she wondered? Or had she actually developed a reputation as some kind of wild and crazy girl in this small town, where information traveled by invisible wires?

"You can walk wherever you like," she said, not unpleasantly.

A bashful grin appeared. "You don't remember me, do you?" he said. Celia slowed down, facing him. His hair was cropped next to his head, his eyes sort of almond-shaped, a nice nose, and medium dark complexion. He wore a zippered sweatshirt with the University of North Carolina Tarheels logo.

"No, I don't," she answered finally.

"At the Grand Marsh Inn," he said. "I worked there over Christmas."

"Oh, really?"

"Mostly washing dishes after parties in the banquet room," he added helpfully. "But a couple times I bussed tables in the dining room. That's where I saw you."

"Oh, I see," she said. She looked again, more closely. Cute guy, but nothing remarkable. Except the eyes, maybe. Not so much the shape or color, just the expression, alert, friendly, and eager. His gaze was steady, interested, not shy.

She shook her head. "I'm sorry, I don't remember. And, my goodness, it was so busy, and then I got the flu." She made an apologetic face. "I guess I didn't notice."

"I'm at the Eastside Grille now," he went on, just as pleasantly. "Still washing dishes, though. You still at the Inn?"

"No," she replied, thinking how to cut this conversation short. She didn't want to get into *that* discussion. They were stopped at the entrance to the gas station, waiting for a car to pull into traffic.

"I have a new job," she added, after a prolonged silence.

"Over at the health club," the boy said. "I've seen you go in there."

She was taken aback, but just for a moment. He didn't look emotionally disturbed or dangerous, probably just curious, like all these small-town guys looking for the next new thing.

"Yes," she confirmed, "and it's a place just for women."

There were only a few more steps until she turned left into the mall parking lot. Hopefully, he was headed elsewhere.

"Sometimes I stop at the store there." He pointed to the other leg of the mall. "On the way home from school. Senior year." He smiled brightly. "Couple months to graduation."

"Oh, really? And then what?" It was a nosy question, but Celia was always interested in people's business, even when she shouldn't be.

"College, for sure. Just not sure where yet. Got letters from Maryland, Delaware, Salisbury State."

"Congratulations," said Celia, more warmly. "Good for you. Well, I'm cutting across the parking lot here. But good luck . . . ," she realized too late that she had left an opening.

"Alonzo," he filled in. "Alonzo Bailey."

She couldn't very well not return the courtesy. "And I'm Celia Lennon."

His grin grew wide, "Yeah, I know," he said. "From your name tag at the Inn."

But, of course.

"Well then, so long, Alonzo," she said with a wave as she picked up her pace. She hoped that no one, especially Anita, had seen them, and that was the end of that. She caught herself checking to see that he went to the grocery store as he'd said. He did, never looking back.

As she entered the club, Celia could see that class was in session and Anita was in her element. Placing her purse in a desk drawer in the office, Celia stood watching from the doorway. Anita had a group of women on the floor, on their knees, holding one leg in the air until they began to groan. It was a large group, filling the work-out room. Most of them were out of shape and grimacing with effort. Anita commanded them to try harder. She preached at them about the benefits of pushing beyond their limits and feeling the suffering, until they started to collapse and she had to relent. Back on the other knee, she made the leap from exercise to endurance and all its virtues, and then it became clear, to Celia at least, that she had moved into sermon mode, and was chastising them for their weaknesses, physical and moral, and calling them to do better.

"There are no excuses for not being good to yourself," Anita pronounced. "Because God made you, and you are His possession, so you must treat yourself with respect, as you would treat Him. Lunge over, now, on to the right side," she continued without interruption. "Feel that burn. But it is nothing like the burn of desire, which, once you taste it, you are lashed to its wheel."

"White, black, old, young – men, they're all the same with their pants off," Anita told them as they stretched their quadriceps. "They can't resist desire. They don't have it in them. That's why we must be strong, for their sake as well as ours. We are the stronger sex. We must be the stronger sex. Our souls depend on it, and those of our men and our children. We need physical strength and spiritual strength, one leads to the other. Show them your muscles, Celia." She paused a moment, as Celia stood transfixed in the doorway, caught watching. Incapable of resistance, she pulled up her shirt sleeve and flexed.

"Nellie, you're going to run into that wall, if you don't move up a little. OK, everyone, back on your feet now, and march. I mean march, knees up! God loves you for your effort. He really does."

Celia could see that the women, maybe eighteen all together, black and white, were past the stage of thinking. They followed blindly, mesmerized. Celia herself was fascinated, although she knew that Shelly had asked Anita a few times to tone down the religious stuff or they might lose customers. But Anita wouldn't budge. She was utterly convinced that fitness was an all-encompassing idea, inside and out, and that she was coaching these women's spirits as well as bodies.

"I'm just the vessel," is all she would say, and Shelly shrugged her shoulders, muttering, "This too shall pass," when Anita was out of earshot.

Celia studied Anita's style with interest. There were days she found herself waving her hands in the air to "Great Getting Up Morning," Anita's favorite warm-up gospel tune, as she passed behind the class in session, and even singing out, "Blow on your trumpet, Joshua!" along with the tape. A couple of times, finding the tape in the player, she used the song in her own classes, until one of the older women, Mabel, who was generally soft-spoken and reserved, mentioned to her after class that it was a song they sang in choir and it referred to the slaves awaiting their earthly as well as heavenly liberation. Celia took that to mean Mabel found it inappropriate for her, a white girl, to use in class, so she stopped. But one day, to her surprise, she saw Mabel approach Anita with the same comment.

"It's an on-going process, liberation," Anita said, and she continued to use the song until the tape wore out.

At the end of the work day, the three new businesswomen sat around in the office, too tired even for final clean-up. Shelly reported that the money was coming in fairly well, although only four new members had signed up in the past week. At this point there might not be many others. It would be a matter of the present members renewing their memberships, some of them not for a while, with their extra time tacked on at the end.

"What's the point of worrying?" Anita said dismissively. "Everything is fine for now. It's in God's hands. I'm not losing any sleep over it."

"No, Nita, you're right," Shelly said, leaning back with her feet on the neatly organized desk. "We're not doing badly. I just don't feel like I can go blow some money on myself, like the old days, because I'm just not sure what lies ahead."

Anita swiveled slowly in the chair next to the desk meant for visitors and potential members. Cross-legged on the floor, Celia played with a hole in her tights, making it longer and worse, thinking vaguely about food, ice cream, maybe.

"Shelly, you're making me tired with all that," Anita said, rubbing her temples.

"But, honestly, wouldn't you love to go out for a meal at a nice restaurant?"

"Why, yes. Yes, I would. But I'm not going to sit here and pity myself about it."

Anita made a face as she gathered her stuff to leave for the day. "What you lack is imagination. Where there's a will, there's a way. Well, I'll see you two girls tomorrow," she said as she breezed out the door.

Celia looked at Shelly, curious. "What did she mean?"

"Oh, she sometimes likes to rope men into taking her to dinner. Just because she can. It's just a meal out because she's bored and lonely, and she wants to use her power over someone."

Celia raised her brows, surprised.

"Not that that's so bad. I've known her for a long time, Celia, and she's still looking, but not looking, for a man. She wants someone she can dominate, of course, like she does everyone else, but she wants someone who's strong enough to stand up to her, who's tough, like she is. I don't know if that kind of person exists."

"You think she wants to get married?"

"Part of her, yes. She has a standing offer from one of the men at her church."

"Really? Who?"

"His name is Thomas."

"So, what's wrong with him?"

"Oh, who knows? Not exciting enough, probably. I think the problem is that he won't fight with her, and that's the only way she knows where she stands. He just bides his time, and when she's trying to reform, she spends time with him. Then time passes, and she flies off again. It's been that way for years now."

"What do you think will happen?"

"No idea. Do I look like I know what I'm doing?" Shelly laughed wryly. She looked trim and neat, of course, but tired, and maybe even a few hairs out of place. As they talked, she arranged everything on the desk, except the account book she placed in a bag to take home.

"I'm ready to leave. How about you?"

"I'll lock up," Celia answered. "I have a few more things to do, and I want to change out of these clothes."

"See you tomorrow, then," Shelly said. Celia thought about Shelly's revelation into the life of Anita. Celia could see for the first time that in spite of her charisma, Anita was facing forty by herself, without the intellectual and emotional companionship she desired and deserved.

She finished up and locked the door, looking forward to getting back to the couch and putting her feet up. But at the intersection she had to wait for a break in the line of cars that trolled the mall most evenings at twilight, the teens in town looking for some possible action. It was a custom, someone explained to her, for kids without a lot of places to go or money to spend, to drive round and round, up and down the main commercial thoroughfare. And that's where Cuffie and Co. found her.

"Dolphin Girl!" Cuffie shouted out the window of a black sedan covered with stickers. Celia turned, slowly, a bit reluctant. But she made her way down the line of cars, walking alongside Cuffie's Dodge, at just about the same speed. Beside Cuffie in the passenger seat was Phil A., while Tilghman, the high-schooler, sat in back, with his backpack and an open bag of Oreos on his lap.

"Whatchu up to?" Cuffie asked. "Work?" He gestured at New You.

"Yes," she said a bit breathlessly, "just finished. Headed home." She leaned in the window, "Hi, guys."

"Hop in," Cuffie said. "Tilghman, make some room back there." He jerked his thumb at the backseat.

"Oh," said Celia. "Well, where are you going?"

Cuffie rolled his eyes. "Nowhere. Don't matter where. Just round and round, see and be seen. Come on, don't hold up the parade."

So, entirely pointless and probably not good judgment, in general. But she knew these guys; she didn't want to say No. And she liked the look of those Oreos.

"OK, I guess," Celia said, pulling open the back door and climbing in. Tilghman, chewing, tipped his head and immediately offered the cookies. The car had a pungent smell from the cookies, warm male bodies, hair products and lotions. She took a couple cookies while the car rolled on past the grocery store, the hardware store, and Russell's coffee shop, at about 5 mph.

"So, you like it there?" said Phil A. from the front seat. "Better than the Inn?"

"It's great, really," she said, twisting the cookie apart. "We're getting busy; everything's going really well." She knew that this was, in part, a reconnaissance mission on the part of the boys to report back to the Inn. So, let them know things are pretty darn great.

"Anita just the same?" asked Cuffie. "Bossy Boss."

"Yep," said Celia, licking the frosting. "But then, she is the boss, so it's OK. She, and that other lady, Shelly, they're pretty good businesswomen, and I'm learning a lot from them." Well, a few things.

They had exited the mall lot and turned right going past the car dealerships, now heading toward the center of town.

"That's nice," Cuffie said. "But on the level, not much money, right? Not like you was making at the Inn."

"Well, not the same as Hunting Season, that's for sure."

"You could come back, any time," he said. "Take you back, no question. You should see who they got now on lunch shift. It's sad."

It hadn't really occurred to Celia about new hires—replacements—but with Wanda, Roland, Tony and Celia gone, they needed somebody.

"This one lady come in, think she better than all of us, just since she worked some other place in the city, D.C., I think. She act like we're bunch of ignorant fools, just cause we kid around sometimes."

"And ugly, too," Tilghman added, a few crumbs tumbling from his lips. "You be a lot more fun," which made Celia laugh because part of the fun was at her expense. He held out the cookie bag enticingly, practicing his guy moves. "And better to look at."

She took another cookie, flattered. "So, what else am I missing?" Anita did not spend much time filling her in on these matters.

"Beckers is on a roll," Phil A. said, craning his neck to look behind. "Cracking down on everything and everyone. Jeremy got canned, just for talking nonsense; Eldridge's on warning for too many sick days."

"Ah." Knowing Eldridge, just a few extra days off, not really sick. She wanted to know about Jay, and about Pauline, but she just couldn't ask.

"And Wanda?" Celia asked, not too hopeful. Still, somehow a little hurt.

"Not a word. She shook the dust from this place right off her shoes. Bye-bye."

In the front, Cuffie and Phil A. started fussing with the radio. Celia let her gaze rest on young Tilghman, fifteen maybe, intent on his cookies and strawberry milk. Slowly, slowly the car inched along. Most likely Wanda was doing exactly what she said: waitressing and taking classes, one foot in front of the other toward a careful, hardworking future. Or—maybe something else, something better. Say it was love, and she married that Larry Wolf, converting to Judaism to raise their children. And then she got a job in his family's business, Wolf Leather Goods, running the computer department. There she was in nice office clothes, and matching belt and purse – since that's what they made. And better glasses, of course. A comfortable home, not like that terrible place on Franklin Street. And in the family room, side by side, Pac Man and Lady Pac Man.

Celia's eyes looked out to the darkening sky, swept up in the fantasy. One night, she, Celia, is performing in some good, serious play, in a theater in Baltimore. She looks out into the audience, and who is there to see her but Wanda, and Larry! Who's to say it couldn't happen? Although, at this particular moment, she realized, taking in the ripped upholstery and staticy radio, it didn't seem too likely, too soon..

Oh, my goodness, could they go any slower?

They were stopped again, backed up from the light, almost to the center of town. Celia looked out the back window to see how many cars were still following—plenty. A few cars back, a young man was leaning into the window of a stopped vehicle, passing time. It was only when he straightened, looking ahead, that Celia saw the sweatshirt with a B, and that face, now familiar. The light changed and the cars started rolling. But not before he looked back at her—she was pretty sure.

"Wait! Wait!" Celia cried, up on her knees to get a better view. But they couldn't wait. "That guy next to the car. Tilghman, look," she pointed. Belatedly, he turned, but then shrugged, apologetic. By then they had crossed through the intersection, and the man was lost to sight.

"I couldn't really see," Tilghman said. And then, "Why you care about him?"

Sitting forward again Celia huffed. "He's some nasty kid, in high school, I think, that has been very...rude...to me. For no reason at all. And he always has such a menacing look."

"What he look like?" Cuffie asked, glancing at her through the rearview mirror. "Black boy, right?"

"Well, yes," Celia conceded. She thought a moment, picturing him. "Well, I can't really say exactly. Pretty average, I guess. Short hair, wide eyes, not bad looking, just mean, you know, hard? Oh, and he wears a sweatshirt with a big B on it."

"Hm," Tilghman said, "I can't really tell, just from that."

"That B's for Baltimore," Cuffie put in. "Plenty of folks wear that kind of thing around here."

Celia scrunched down in her seat, disappointed. No, that wasn't much to go on. From the corner of her eye, she saw they were approaching the turn that would lead away from home, back toward the mall. Time, probably, to get out.

"Let me jump out at the next light Cuffie. It's an easy walk from here."

"All righty," he said, pulling to the side of the road. "Sure you're all right?"

"Oh, sure. Don't worry about me; I'm not going anywhere near that guy. Besides, I'm a big, strong girl." She showed an arm muscle, making them smile.

Phil A. turned around. "Miss you, Dolphin Girl," he said, taking her by surprise.

"Really?" Celia said. "That's nice. And I miss you guys, too, but I see you quite a bit, here and there." It was a small town. Their smiles turned slightly hopeful, expectant. If they were hoping for an invitation to stop by the apartment for cards or music or TV, it wasn't going to happen, not tonight.

"Thanks for the ride. See you around." She got out, waving, ten minutes from home. That was nice, she thought, musing on her short, unexpected joy ride. Trudging along the sidewalk, she was pretty sure it was a matter of time before she crossed paths with that strange boy again. What was his problem, anyway? Not that she really wanted to know.

On the day of Easter service at Anita's church, Celia didn't feel particularly religious or like sitting in a hot church with no air conditioning. It might be interesting, but not like the Starlight. Hopefully, the music would be good. And she had to wonder what Anita would be preaching about, since she was apparently speaking from the pulpit while the minister was away. Surely she would not be talking about desire, and men all being the same with their pants off. Not even Anita could hope to carry that off.

She had directions to Anita's house. From there, she would follow the family to the church. Her destination was thirty-five minutes outside of town, and quite rural, more so than Celia had expected. Arriving a few minutes early, she drove past and turned around. The house was surrounded by fields, with a large garden area cleared off to one side. A chicken wire pen was attached to the garage, with a few chickens running around, and a goat. By golly, they had animals, which Anita had never mentioned. However else her father made a living, he was also a small-scale farmer. So, what did that make Anita?

Anita's niece, Charisa, came to the door to let her in. She was maybe seven or eight, in a pink dress with her hair pulled to the side of her head, where it was braided and tied with a bow. A pretty little girl, so neat and well-pressed, every last pleat. She was friendly, too, not shy at all, although she had seen Celia only once at the impromptu picnic at the open house.

"Come to the kitchen," Charisa said, taking her by the hand. "Everyone's waiting for you." Celia wondered who everyone was. Anita was not there, probably still getting ready, but she recognized her mother and father, and her sister, Madeline, Charisa's mother. Anita's daughter was absent, spending the holiday with her grandmother and cousins. Mrs. Nelson was packing food and explained that there would be a meal after the service that she was invited to stay for. It looked like some kind of chicken dish, and Celia flashed back to those hens running around in the pen. She hesitated, unsure what kind of food was to be served, like pigs' feet or such, that she heard the kitchen staff talk about.

"I guess I'll have to see how we're running for time," she answered. "But thank you so much for the invitation."

Anita's father didn't have too much to say, except, "I hope she's not working you too hard down there at that . . . that . . . place." Apparently, the general concept of what they were doing was still not that clear to him.

"It probably seems sort of strange that people actually pay to get exercise," she said aloud without thinking. Mr. Nelson nodded politely, and then slapped his knee when he got what she meant. "You right there. But I guess it's lucky for you all that they do."

"Anita," her mother called out, closing the basket. "Your friend here. Come along."

Anita finally joined them, dressed in a yellow-orange suit, the color of melon sherbet, which went well with her skin tone and fitted her perfectly. Only Anita could find a suit that was cut so conservatively, but still managed to make her look sexy. But it must be warm, on a day like today. Celia felt a little sticky in her short-sleeved cotton dress.

"Where are those sweat traps?" Anita cried. "No way am I going to spoil this suit the first time I wear it." She found them in a drawer, and stuck them in through the front of her blouse under her arms. She patted her hair down, grumbling, "So darn humid." Looking into the mirror next to the door as she led them all out, she made a face, and said, "Bless me, Lord. Give me strength in what I am about to do. Let's go."

The church was small and not too pretty, looking more like a barn than a house of God. It was situated in a grove of mature trees, so perhaps another building had stood in this spot sometime in the past. The parking lot was no more than an area of cleared ground, muddy with spring rain. Stepping carefully in high heels, the women were dressed up, many in hats, while the men wore three-piece suits—a far cry from folk masses with guitars and jeans that Celia had attended for a couple years after the move to California. Several women carried fans, so evidently they expected to be hot. Children looked ready for picture day at school, and ran around on the patchy grass while their parents and grandparents visited outside the church steps. Two church elders stood at the doorway, greeting people as they entered.

Celia went in with the Nelson family, while Anita entered through another door, since, as a deacon, she would be seated up front. Mr. Nelson introduced Celia to the elders at the door, who shook her hand and said, "Welcome," like it was not an unusual thing that she was there, the only white person perhaps for miles.

They took seats about halfway up, out of maybe twenty rows of pews. Thankfully, there was a floor fan on each side, and the windows were left open. Anita looked reverent and preoccupied seated up in front with a pew Bible in her lap. A middle-aged man announced that the minister was away on a family matter so they would be led by the deacons and Miss Anita Nelson, who would be giving the sermon. They opened with an old hymn, which was beautiful and soulful: "My Shepherd Will Supply My Need." But Celia was disappointed not to hear a lively gospel song.

While the service proceeded, Celia gazed around discretely, in case there was someone she might recognize, but no. Not Jay, not even his uncle. Mostly there were older folks and women, and young couples with children, who stayed through the service, not leaving for Sunday school. Mainly, the children attended in respectful silence, but Celia picked up a few secret glances and hand signals.

When Anita got up to speak, more than a few congregants stirred in their seats. Celia knew that Anita had spoken before, and suspected that the sermon was not going to be all sunshine and rainbows. The church moderator who introduced her said the topic of her sermon was "Oppression," and Celia could tell that she was not the only one puzzled, and maybe a little uneasy. It could be a bit of a downer. Mr. Nelson sighed and closed his eyes. Mrs. Nelson sat up straight and alert, ready to follow every word.

"We are all oppressed," Anita began, and paused for effect, not reading her notes on the podium. "We are oppressed by death, our own deaths, the deaths of those we love, and by the thought of death. We are also oppressed by the inescapable will to live, in all but the most hopeless, which is present even in infants who will avoid crawling off the side of a bed, although they cannot understand the idea of death. We are oppressed by our ignorance, by the impossibility of knowing and understanding the significance of our lives, of God's plan for us. Instead, we labor in darkness, knowing already the futility of our earthly labors. We are oppressed by the society we live in, yes, that too;

but we are oppressed not only by our *skins*, but by our sins. We know we are committing sin, but we can not help it. We are not free. Never mind any Proclamation of Emancipation; we are not free. Neither are white people or rich people or any single human being at all. We are not free, and except in God, we can never be free." Some in the congregation looked uncomfortable already, and it had just started. Celia wondered why Anita had wanted her so much to come.

"But, what I want to tell you is that we are blessed with this oppression. We, you and me, are blessed in our knowledge of oppression. We know its taste and feel and look. We know it everyday; we know it in our skins." Here she paused, and one man said, "Amen."

"What we don't know about oppression can't be taught," Anita went on, and there was another, stronger, "Amen."

"We are blessed twice, in the knowledge of oppression, and the endurance to survive oppression. These are our gifts. These are gifts to us, and to others, wherever they are in the world, who have lived with oppression. These are marks of God's love, I'm telling you." She paused again, but this time there were no "Amens."

"I witness to you that I am oppressed. Yes, I was once oppressed by the family in town who would not let me babysit their precious children when I was fourteen because of the color of my skin. And by the man who would not stand by me, when I became pregnant with his child at nineteen, and by the bank owners who would not grant me a loan in my own good name, at thirty-six. But I am also oppressed by doubts, by anger, by jealousy, and by actions I am not proud of. I am wholly imperfect. I am unfree. I am oppressed, and sometimes depressed." There was a slight chuckle.

"Like you, sometimes I do not welcome oppression. I rail against it, or complain about it, am bitter about it, use it as an excuse to do less than my best for myself or for others who need me. It's a heaviness we want to put down. We would cheat oppression, and get our pleasures where we can, and when we can, however we can, justifying any kind of behavior. We would oppress others, because we ourselves are oppressed." Anita took a handkerchief and patted her forehead; she looked hot.

"Pity those who do not know they are oppressed, who think they are self-made, not God-made, and who do not know that their earthly power is finite, and their heavenly power is nothing. They labor under the illusion that they are free, and strong, and their own creation, when they are not any of those things. They think earthly success is a sign of God's favor. It is a favor, if that success is used to help build God's world, and it is a dreadful curse for those who would hide from the oppression of being mortal."

Some of the older church members were showing signs of distress, their lips moving and shaking their head, but others were unable to break their gaze at the pulpit. The room was silent except for the whir of the fans.

"It is our work to learn oppression, and to teach it, to our children and to those who are seekers of God's truth. We are not Christians who can sit here on a Sunday and congratulate ourselves for being mainly good-hearted people, who haven't done anything too terrible. That's not enough. We have a mission. We cannot keep this secret to ourselves; that we are oppressed; we are all oppressed, by our humanity, by our mortality. We cannot free ourselves; no manner of acceptance and success can free us, so we must rely on God. God has great love for us, to give us this charge. Our task is great, and many will be lost. But we are strong, so strong, what we have endured, the love we still bear in our hearts.

"We cannot rise up out of this world, not yet, not on our own. We have God's holy work to do. You feel that heaviness on your back, on your shoulders. You think it is the burden of oppression, making life hard for you. No!" She thundered out the word. Then she stopped again, and no one moved, hardly breathed. She commenced, however, quite softly, like parent to child. "Those are your wings, not yet unfurled. That is the weight that you carry. You, me—we are God's dark-skinned angels on earth. How blessed I am to come before you. When I look at you, I see your wings."

Celia felt her throat getting tight, and her heart beating faster. Others sat with mouths open, and some were weeping. It was no revivalist meeting, with shouting and testimonials, wailing and moaning. They looked stunned, as if a meteor had flashed into their presence, tearing a hole through the ceiling, landing amongst them and disappearing into silence.

The moderator cleared his throat, finally, and called them to the last hymn. "His Eye is On the Sparrow." Some sparrow! Not exactly the kind of bird that Anita brought to mind, more like a hawk, or an eagle. They started weak and uneven, but grew louder with each verse. When it was over, and the moderator dismissed them, Celia was still unsure what to make of it all. Like the others, she gave Anita a wide berth as they gathered outside the front door steps, staying alongside Charisa and the family. Several folks came over to speak to Mr. and Mrs. Nelson, with a nod of acknowledgment to Celia.

"She a powerful speaker," one man said to Mr. Nelson, who raised his shoulders.

"She raise the roof with that," said another. "I waiting for the whirlwind to descend."

A well-dressed woman, flashing a gold tooth and some gold bracelets told Anita's mother, "That girl can preach. Why she can't be a minister? They need somebody like that in the city, can straighten out those poor folk."

"I thought we trying to fight oppression," Celia heard a young woman mutter. "I don't know why she like it so much."

"You think she talking about all us, or just the chillun, can be angels?" asked one gray-haired matron of another. "They do look so pretty in they Sunday clothes."

Out on the grass, in the shade of a tall oak, Anita stood with her face tipped to the sky. A tall and slender well-dressed man walked up to her, waiting until she turned to look at him. This must be Thomas, the wooer.

"What did you think?" Anita's voice carried.

"It was brave, disturbing, and beautiful—like you," he said calmly, evenly.

Anita pursed her lips. "Do you agree with what I said?"

"I do. It is true, and you have made me think seriously today about my own oppression." Anita seemed to take this as an achievement and smiled.

"Well, then," she said. "I'm pleased that you responded to the message. It's not my truth, after all. I am simply the vessel. Shall we eat?" She took his arm, and they walked to the stairway leading to the basement where the noon meal was being set up. At the top of the steps, Anita turned back, scanning the crowd. She spotted Celia, beckoning her.

"Are you staying, Celia?" she asked. "Charisa will tell you what's good to eat." A smile played at her lips, and her cheeks dimpled. "This is Thomas. Thomas, Celia." They bowed their heads to each other, silently. "A new experience for you, right, Celia? I hope I didn't make you too uncomfortable in there."

"Yes, I mean, no." Celia stumbled over her words, aware that Thomas was watching. "That was great, Anita, really . . . something. . . . You were like Joan of Arc up there, you know, the saint, the girl soldier—only no one would ever, well . . . It's strange; I had a dream once, about you, with wings . . ." She stopped, realizing she wasn't making sense. The faces passing them looked on with interest, probably thinking, "The poor girl lost her wits."

"I'd love to stay for lunch, thank you." She really would have preferred to go, to digest the whole episode in quiet. But somehow it felt like the acceptance of food was related to the acceptance of the sermon, so she decided she'd better stay. And she was hungry.

Anita continued deep in discussion with Thomas downstairs, seeming to forget about Celia. Under Charisa's direction, Celia filled her plate at the buffet table and sat between her and Mrs. Nelson at a long table with other friends and family. After a quick grace over the food, God's name was not mentioned again, nor anything related to church. The talk turned to weather, the Baltimore Orioles, and what was happening on the daytime soap operas. Anita's mother had a flair for storytelling, as did Charisa, when it was her turn to talk, and Celia contributed comments on some movies she had seen lately. *Jaws* had scared the pants off of her, she volunteered, and she was a little afraid to go back in the ocean, although normally, she loved to swim. They all agreed that *Star Wars* was powerful movie making, and all in all, it was better to live now than in the future.

Celia finished her food and whispered to Charisa, "Is it all right to go for more?" Charisa laughed at her. "Everybody wants you to eat their food. It makes them proud if there's nothing left." And she got up to go back with her, leading her like a large, not-too-well-trained dog. And then, at the dessert table, Celia almost swooned; the best, sweetest looking homemade cakes and pies she'd ever seen, never mind the Grand Marsh Inn.

After two helpings of sweet potato pie and a cup of coffee, Celia was ready to head home—she thought. Then Mrs. Nelson insisted on packing some food to go, "for you and your sister," plenty of everything. Grace would be so pleased—no cooking!

And then, with her cardboard tray of food in hand, Celia went to say good-bye to Anita, now more or less making the social rounds, while Thomas, the suitor, had disappeared.

Anita said, "I won't be but a minute."

Celia knew better. Anita was not a stickler for time, except for delivering her orders at the Inn, or keeping the pace in her exercise classes. She herself called it "Black People Time," although Celia noticed that many of their black clients were quite punctual. So Celia looked at her watch. Ten minutes at least. She put the food on the passenger side seat of the car and circled around to the driver's side to get in. But Anita was blocking the door.

"Good food, right? Didn't I tell you?"

"Delicious." Celia pointed inside the car. "Your mother made me take all this home. I told her how grateful I was . . . am." Anita tapped a foot, impatiently. "And, thanks to you, of course, for inviting me and sharing this . . . whole . . . experience. You spoke so well up there," she went on. "And looked great, too. Yes," she concluded, "very inspiring."

"Oh, come on," Anita said. "Why do you think I wanted you to come?"

Oooh. Just what Celia hoped to avoid, Anita's questions. And she so nearly made a clean getaway. Looking down, she stifled a yawn, ready for a mid-day nap.

"Well, for spiritual reasons, of course." Too general. "And maybe because you were afraid I might be going down the wrong track, or trying to encourage me with things not going so well, money-wise, and school, and, uh, love."

"Oh, please," Anita said. "I'm always after you for that."

Celia took a gamble. "So I could see everybody, and, and meet Thomas?"

"Are you simple?"

"No, I am not. I just don't know what you're getting at. Maybe I really didn't understand all of it, the sermon."

Anita's smile was tender. "Struggling's just life, honey, for most people most of the time. I thought you would understand what it's like to be judged and treated a certain way because of how you look, how you appear—that kind of oppression."

Celia drew a blank. But people always admired her yellow hair, and praised her pink cheeks, and loved her blue eyes. Like some kind of doll.

And then she got it.

"Yes," she said to Anita, with a note of wonder. "I do know what that's like."

"'Course you do. You think you're wasting your time here, just passing through, hoping for something better. Am I right?"

Celia hesitated and nodded.

"What you do here is important, even if you don't see it." Anita started counting off on fingers. "You are helping fat women get healthier and feel better about themselves; you are helping Shelly and me make our dream come true; you keep your sister company, and help each other. Mostly, you're just yourself whoever you're with, and that's something special. Everyone wants some of that sweetness. They want to be better, act better around you."

"I'm not sure about that," Celia said, abashed. "But I get it, what you're saying; I should make the best of it while I'm here?"

"Don't be waiting for your life to get back on track. You don't know where it's going, nobody does. And that's a good thing. And besides, if you went back now, to California, you'd be a different person, anyway. Am I right?"

Celia nodded somberly. "Right."

"There is a special purpose for you being here," Anita pronounced, and Celia's heart began to swell with hope.

"What is it?" Celia asked.

Anita's wry expression returned. "Oh, honey, I don't know. You have to find it yourself, whatever it is. But it's here."

"Oh."

Then Anita pinched her on the bicep. "Strong in body. Strong in heart. That's my next sermon." When Celia didn't respond, she said, "It's a joke."

A slow smile came to Celia's lips. "Oh, I get it. You mean New You."

"That's my girl." Anita had already started to turn away, lifting a hand to hail a woman in yellow with a very large black hat.

Chapter 18

During April, Celia enjoyed walking to work through the center of town, passing daffodils and tulips in gardens and storefront window boxes before the long, ugly stretch to the strip mall. On Thursdays, she came in early for the weekly meeting, arriving just before eight o'clock. Not a morning person, she was generally quiet, even after a half-hour walk. Shelly was always there first, and Anita arrived a few minutes late, often grumbling about her daughter or her sister and their trying ways. Celia tended to sit and sip coffee as Shelly reported on their financial status, and Anita drew up a list of things to do or items to buy. Thursday was also payday, when Shelly handed out the checks in a windowed envelope that looked promising, but was a bit disappointing, after withholdings, compared to earnings at the Inn. Still, it was something, enough to get by and an investment in the future of New You—she hoped.

A kind of routine developed where Shelly picked up coffee and muffins from Russell's shop and left them on the desk while Celia and Anita reviewed the weekly reports. Meanwhile, Shelly took the time to touch herself up in the mirror on the back of the office door. At some point, Celia and Anita gave up on the reports, and instead watched Shelly combing and reparting her silky, fine reddish brown locks: "every hair in place." And then, always, the straightening of the eyebrows over long-lashed hazel eyes, followed by the pearl pink lipstick.

A couple of times when Shelly complained of the heat and humidity, Anita French-braided her hair, something they had clearly done in the past. The result was striking, sexy, but Shelly pulled it out by noon, complaining it was too tight and gave her a headache. Then one day, Anita's eye wandered to Celia's head. When asked, Celia was happy to have her hair done, even just for the day. As Shelly went over the accounts, Anita combed and braided Celia's hair. As Anita worked, she hummed under her breath while Celia listened to the reports with closed eyes. For weeks, the ritual endured, coffee, combing, and accounts, in spite of the fact that they were never quite done when the bell on the front door jangled, signaling the first member of the day.

On her way to one of those eight o'clock meetings, Celia was startled to see Alonzo again, gaining from behind. He waved and hurried to catch up.

Dressed for the warmer weather, he wore a striped t-shirt and cut-off jeans. A bit taller, too. New shoes, maybe.

"Hello, Celia," he said.

Celia was suspicious about his appearance on the road, like he was lying in wait. She would have to take stronger measures to keep him from getting any ideas.

"Oh, hi, Alonzo. Aren't you supposed to be in school?"

"Yes, and no," he replied. "I'm on my way to the hardware store to get supplies for a project. I thought I might see you, and I did." He looked quite pleased.

"Alonzo," she said, stopping to face him. He halted, an expectant look on his face. The problem was that he was just too friendly, but she didn't want it to turn into a familiarity or come-on thing. She had enough going on at the moment.

"I know, I know," he started, while she was still thinking. "You don't want me hanging around."

"Well . . ." Celia said, the wind taken out of her sails. "I don't mean to be rude. It's just . . . just, well, there's no point."

"I don't want to bother you," Alonzo said, not at all offended. "I just came to tell you something. Show you something, really."

"Oh?" Celia said, surprised again.

Alonzo slipped his backpack off his shoulder and rested it on the ground while he pulled open the zipper. Inside, Celia could see worksheets, an Algebra textbook, and a tattered copy of *Great Expectations.* He pulled out a folded community newspaper and a bright yellow flyer.

"Here," he said, pointing toward a circled ad in the notices section: "*Our Town*; we're doing it at the high school."

Celia looked over the ad. Sure enough, Thorton Wilder's play. *Our Town* was one of her favorites. She had played the part of Emily Webb herself. But maybe it was better not to share that.

"Oh, I see," she said, handing back the paper. "Are you in it?"

"Just back stage crew, building the set. Not that there's much. No budget." He wagged the paper. "And publicity. We're all supposed to get the word out. I got a flyer here, maybe you or some of the ladies would like to go." He gestured in the direction of New You. "I heard," he said, then stopped.

"Heard what?"

"They said you were an actress, back at the Inn, and a dancer, too."

She had to laugh. "Oh, did they?" *Honest to God.* "Well, thanks, Alonzo. Hm . . . I do like *Our Town.* . ." She stopped herself. "Next month?" She reached out her hand to take the yellow flyer, examining it. "You know," she said, "I bet my sister would like to go. Maybe I'll ask her."

Alonzo nodded, hiking the backpack in place and turning to leave. "Well, I'll see you around, then."

"Hold on," she said. "Give me a few more flyers, why don't you. I can leave a couple out at New You, and drop some at the coffee shop and the beauty parlor. I know you want a good audience."

"That's so kind of you," Alonzo said, kind of old-fashioned, like one of the elderly lady customers at the Inn. He stopped again, kneeling on the sidewalk to get out the flyers from his pack.

"Anything for the theater," she replied mock-archly.

Funny guy, she thought, as he walked away, backpack swaying side to side.

Later at home, Celia invited Grace to the play, her treat, and Grace said she would be happy to go.

Sunday, New You was closed. Both Shelly and Celia felt that some women might like to exercise on a quiet Sunday afternoon, but Anita wouldn't hear of it. It was the Lord's day of rest, and theirs also. Before the weekend, Anita had asked Celia to take her Monday afternoon shift so that she could get to her daughter's basketball game. Celia was glad for the hours since she was still on a part-time schedule, varying week to week, according to New You's demands. Only Anita worked a full forty-hour week and still put in a couple night shifts at the Inn. She had a lot of energy for someone her age, thought Celia, who often napped on her days off. After wasting half a day looking through old pictures and playbills, Celia headed out for work just before two o'clock, hurrying to make up for a late start. By the time the shopping mall was in sight, she had peeled off her sweatshirt, perspiring through the leotard.

Shelly met Celia at the door. "Good, you're here. Don't change yet. Just put your stuff down and come with me. We need to pick up a few things at the store. I told Anita we'd run over. She's in the middle of something with one of the new clients."

"OK," Celia said, placing her tote bag under one of the chairs in the office. "What do we need?"

"Come on. I'll tell you on the way."

Toilet paper, paper towels, sponges, a dust mop, and air freshener. They headed outside, walking toward the grocery store. Right outside Russell's coffee shop, Shelly stopped, looking through the glass door. She must have spotted Russell, or someone, and gave a quick wave.

"Just a sec," Shelly said, a sheepish look on her face. "I'm going to pop in. You go ahead; I'll catch up in a minute."

"OK."

It was just a minute before Shelly caught up with Celia; good thing, because she had the list. Her lips were working, trying to suppress a smile, and she looked even more sheepish.

"Sorry," she said, and then laughed. "I feel so foolish, it's ridiculous."

Celia looked at Shelly with interest. Was there some romance brewing, along with the coffee?

"Last weekend," Shelly said, looking around furtively as they approached the bowling alley, "I went out with Russell. On a date."

Celia's eyes widened with mirth, not at all surprised. "So?" she prompted. "He seems like a nice guy."

"He is a nice guy," Shelly said, the blush growing in her cheeks. "But Anita's going to give me heck. She can't let go of the dream of me and Dave back together. 'What are you doing with him?'" She imitated Anita's voice. "'He's not educated enough, successful enough, polished enough.' Blah . . . blah . . . blah."

Celia had to agree; Anita would say that.

Shelly pushed a wayward shopping cart out of the way. "It's like being eighteen again, worried about getting in trouble for staying out late. I don't care, though. I'm a thirty-five-year-old woman, and I'm going to do what I want, no matter what she says. She'll find out; it's just a matter of time. And it won't be pleasant, or private, either, probably. I can just see her praying in the workout room that I repent and find my way back. At least you're getting it first from me. You know," she said with a giggle. "I'm so old, I can hardly remember what it's like to date, what I should do. I married Dave right out of high school, and that was it. You probably have more experience in romance than I do."

Ha! Perhaps true, but not all of it good.

Celia selected a cart from the line outside the door and turned to look at Shelly. In spite of her concerns, she looked especially pretty, her red-brown hair tied back in a pink bow, so trim in her spotless white warm-up suit. A certain energy in her step and voice, a kind of glow. New love, Celia decided with a pang of jealousy.

"I don't know what to say, Shelly. I wish you both luck, I mean, you and Russell. Yeah, Anita will probably put in her two cents, but then the storm will pass. There's really nothing she can do about it."

"Except make my life miserable."

"There's that," Celia agreed with a grin.

They entered the store through the automatic doors, and Celia pushed the cart while Shelly put in things from the list. Within ten minutes, they were in the check-out line, especially long and slow for some reason. Shelly groaned. "I said I'd stop the coffee shop by on the way back; it's better than him coming to New You. But this is taking forever."

"I can take it from here," Celia said, eyeing the load in the basket, bulky rather than heavy. "If you want to give me the cash."

"I won't be long," Shelly said, handing over the money. "Can I bring you back anything?"

"No, that's all right."

"I really appreciate it." And she did look very grateful, and full of longing.

"No problem."

"Thanks, Celia." And she was gone.

Finally, the line began to move. Celia paid for the groceries and pushed the empty cart back in place, carrying the loaded paper bags like two babies in her arms. She exited through the automatic doorway, only to pass Alonzo coming in from the opposite direction. At least she thought so. Her eye caught the black backpack with a rabbit's foot. It had to be him.

"Hi!" she called out. "Alonzo!" He stopped, and then waved when he saw her. He must have done a 180-degree turn, because he reappeared outside almost immediately, directly behind her. They shuffled a few steps to the side as another customer approached.

"Hey," he said. "Would you like some help?"

"Oh, no thanks. I'm fine. I just wanted to tell you my sister and I are planning to see the play. I'm going to stop by the high school tomorrow to get tickets."

Unexpectedly, his face fell. "Well, I don't know about that."

"Why not? Is there a problem?"

He looked past her into the parking lot, and then back. "Looks like it might not happen."

"Oh, no!" said Celia. "That's terrible." She held his eyes, proclaiming, "'The show *must* go on.' Seriously, what's wrong?"

"Mostly it's the kids. They mess around at rehearsal, and don't listen to Mr. Timilty. He's the director. English teacher, kind of an old guy, but he's trying his best." Alonzo's face bunched up. "No one keeps track when they're supposed to come and go on stage, and there's so many of them."

"Seventeen," she confirmed.

"Huh?"

"Seventeen parts," she explained. "I've . . . well, I've been in the play myself. It's a lot to keep track of. Isn't anyone in charge of the actors back stage?"

Alonzo shrugged. "That's it. There's no one back stage. There's a girl supposed to be the moderator . . ." His words slowed to a halt.

"Manager?" Celia guessed. "You mean, the stage manager?"

"Yeah, that's it. But she's always talking and flirting. She doesn't really care for the play. A lot of the kids don't. They think it's stupid. They're just doing it for credit."

Celia's mouth opened in protest. "No! It's a beautiful play, perfect for young people growing up in a small town. It might seem corny, because it's set in the old days, but it's very serious and real."

Across the plaza, Celia saw the door to New You swing open and Anita looking around, probably for her and Shelly. Obscured by a vending machine, Celia missed detection, and Anita went back inside. But she had to get going. Shifting the bags in her arms, a package of toilet paper nearly fell out, but Alonzo moved quickly to tuck it back in.

"Well, I'm sorry to hear it," Celia said to Alonzo, "but that happens a lot. Eventually, something gets worked out. I'll wait another week before I go for the tickets. By then I bet you'll be back on track."

"Thanks," he said, stepping once again toward the entrance door. "I hope so." But he didn't sound optimistic.

June was right about being busy in the spring, everyone working on their figures. Some of them were coming right along, too, including Bonnie, the mother of three, who was showing off a good shape these days. Another woman, Zelda, came nearly every day. She was probably fifty, a light-skinned woman who was determined to build up her slender calves, which she was strangely obsessed with. Finally Anita, who worked the most with Zelda, reached the end of her patience and said, loudly, "That's the way God made them. They're not getting any larger unless all of you gets larger, and maybe not then."

Celia came over to take Zelda off of Anita's hands, realizing she must be tired after teaching two classes straight, her own and the one that Shelly had missed. Shelly didn't really like teaching, and tried to avoid it when she could. She was often in the office doing paper work, or would go on an errand to the bank or post office, probably stopping to see Russell along the way. Celia hadn't said anything, but it seemed likely that the cat would be out of the bag soon. When Anita disappeared to the back for some routine Jacuzzi maintenance, Celia felt she should mention to Shelly that Anita was starting to grumble about her absences.

"I know. I've been meaning to bring it up, too. I do stop to see Russell occasionally. But mainly I am getting work done. The busier we are, the more business there is to keep track of. I like it and I'm good at it. Maybe we should start thinking about hiring another person. "

"Really? Do you think we're ready for that?"

"We should talk about it anyway."

That would be interesting. "In the meanwhile," Celia said. "I think Anita's probably getting a little suspicious, about, you know what...."

Shelly smiled. "Oh, no. She knows. I told her."

Celia was genuinely surprised. "And"

"Not as bad as I though it would be, although, of course, she couldn't possibly approve or be happy about it. Still mulling it over, I think. But he's such a nice guy, I think she'll...."

Then, looking behind Celia, she smiled, wide and radiant. "Speaking of the devil, here he is. Hello, Russell. Are you looking for me?"

"Of course." He walked over to her side, but refrained from a kiss. "And to say hello to Celia here, that I haven't seen in a while. How you doing, sweetheart?"

"Fine, thank you."

"Great. Well, I'd like very much to take this young lady out for lunch." he said, rather grandly, and Celia was stumped for a second, thinking it meant her. But then he reached out a hand to Shelly's arm, and it was obvious. "It is our one month anniversary." He was as corny and sentimental as any girl.

Celia lifted her eyebrows. "Somewhere nice, I hope. How about the Inn?" That was just silly, as they weren't dressed for it, and probably wouldn't appreciate the atmosphere.

"Oh, no," Russell said. "We're in the mood for chow mein."

It took Shelly no more than a second to grab her purse, and they quickly departed. Almost on cue, Anita came out from the back, her chore completed, and ready for lunch. Celia and Anita sat down at the desk to eat their tuna fish sandwiches, courtesy of Mrs. Nelson, closing the door for privacy. Celia deliberated mentioning Shelly's idea about hiring someone. Maybe not, at least until after they'd eaten. There was no telling how Anita would react. While Celia swiveled in her chair to get the drinks out of the mini-fridge, Anita pulled out a bag of chips from the bottom desk drawer. She had a weakness for salty things. No purist herself, Celia took a handful. They chewed in silence. Celia could see from Anita's face that something was up. Then Anita sighed, and Celia knew. Had she thought for a moment that Anita didn't see or hear when Russell stopped by?

"I just don't know what Shelly is thinking, going out with that guy." Anita's tone was relatively calm. "There's certainly no future there that I can see. Could they be any more different?"

Celia hazarded a reply. "Well . . . they have some things in common: same age, both divorced, with children, grew up around here, and um . . ." She took a quick breath. "And, they're friendly and hardworking, and they both have businesses right here at the mall."

Anita shook her head, as expected.

"I mean things like education, values, family background. There's nothing there. I don't know for sure if Russell finished high school."

It seemed better not to mention that he had earned his G.E.D., which was not such an easy thing to do, according to what Russell had told Celia on this very subject.

"Well, think about it. Everyone thought that Shelly and Dave were a perfect match, right? Look what happened there. It's not enough, I guess. There's got to be something else to it. Maybe a little difference gives the relationship some zest. That guy I was seeing in California, Carlos, he and I were from very different worlds, but that's partly why we were so attracted to each other."

"Didn't exactly hold up, though, did it?"

Celia turned red, but didn't take the bait. "What I meant was, I just don't know if there's such a thing as a perfect match."

Anita continued to brood over her sandwich and chips, while Celia hoped for a phone call, or the jingle of the front door bell. It remained quiet until Anita spoke again, pensively. "Everyone seems to think that Thomas and I are a perfect match—everyone but me, that is. My mother, my sister, all the ladies at church, even my daughter thinks he's something special. I don't know why I don't feel that way about him. What is it? What do *you* think? Same as everyone else, probably."

"I have no idea," Celia protested, wiping her lips with a napkin. "I barely met him."

"Then, what's your *impression* of him?"

"Oh, that." Celia knew she was entering dangerous waters. "He seems pleasant, considerate, intelligent . . ."

"Blah-blah-blah. Stop all the nicey-nice; I want the bottom line, your gut feeling."

"Oh, all right, all right. I'll try." Celia twisted in her chair, not unlike a fish on a hook. "He appears very calm, rational, and sure of himself. It seems like he really likes you, appreciates your good qualities, but . . . but . . ."

"But what?"

211

"I don't know." Celia scrunched up her face. "Maybe he seems a little superior somehow. Like he's always been in the right and if he waits long enough, you'll see the light. It's like a person who's never really had doubts about himself, who never really got into a bad situation, so they didn't have to get themselves out."

"That's it!" Anita shouted, hands on the arms of her chair. "You're on to it. He does think he's superior, because he's never sinned—like me coming back home with my baby from a man who ran off on me. Thomas said he'd marry me then, but I honestly thought that the father would come looking for me. But I was wrong." She stopped, inhaling deeply. "We were in love, her father and I, but he had no guts. After he told his parents, they sent a check for the baby and asked me to let him finish graduate school, and move on. They gave me their address, not his, in case I needed money or if I had to contact him."

"I'm sorry," Celia said.

"I'm not sorry!" Anita exclaimed, pushing her chair back from the desk. "My child is a gift, not a burden. She has given me strength and purpose."

"Well, yes, of course."

"So, he was right, Thomas, about that situation," Anita said. "But he never went through what I went through, never had a clue how it might feel. He has never suffered one minute of failure, has never put himself out there, risking all. And that's what stands between us."

Celia squirmed. She didn't like to argue, especially with Anita in a righteous mood, but she didn't think that it was fair to Thomas, either.

"I don't know about that," she said, getting in a quick sip. "He's been waiting for you all this time, right? That's taking a risk. And he didn't go off and marry someone else, did he? I'm sure he could find someone who's a better match." Hastily, she added, "More obliging, I mean, and um . . ."

Anita's eyes widened. "What? What are you saying?"

Celia blew out a breath. "OK, let's put it this way: from his point of view, he has had adversity. It's like, you are his trial or burden in life, if you see what I mean. And he has failed, after all these years, to get you." She raised a finger in the air. "So, that's failure."

Anita continued to stare. Then, her eyes narrowed and she leaned out of her chair toward Celia, who drew back, thinking she might slap her. But instead, Anita's cheeks dimpled and she laughed, a big, full-throated laugh.

"Are you saying I'm a b-i-t-c-h?"

"No! I don't even like that word. Maybe not the easiest person in the world to be in love with, that's all I'm saying." And then, solemnly, "Thomas must have a lot of strength to last this long."

Anita's lips parted, soundless. Then she rose to her feet, the bag of chips spilling to the floor. Crossing the rug, she took Celia's face in her hands, gazing into her eyes.

"From the mouths of babes and fools," she said, looming inches away.

"What?" Celia could smell the tuna on Anita's breath

Anita loosened her hold, stepping back and nodding slowly. "A message from God," she murmured. "Straight from your lips."

"Me?" Celia demurred. "Oh, I don't know about that...." She tried a small smile, but there was no joking.

And then, more to herself than Celia, Anita pronounced, "The Lord moves in mysterious ways." She blinked once, twice, and then pivoted, returning to pick up the litter and straighten the chair.

"My, oh, my," she said. "Time to get back to work." With that, Anita disappeared into the back area.

Celia shook her head, blowing out air. What a woman, what a place she'd come to. She got up slowly, feeling more exhausted and less excited than when she came in. But then, there was still the file to put away and lobby to sweep. She yawned, thinking she'd really rather take a nice nap. Yes, yes, it was nice to be appreciated, but she didn't have much to show for it. New You wasn't her business and not her future. The money was coming along ever so slowly. If only she had a few friends more her own age, without houses and kids to worry about. And nowhere was there a boyfriend waiting years for her to come around.

She deposited her leftovers in the trash, and then stood looking at herself in the mirror behind the door. Pretty girl, lovely hair, a healthy glow, and building some nice muscles. But as for love, well, that looked like an impossible dream at the moment.

"Look at me," she said to herself. "Going nowhere fast."

Chapter 19

Strangely, Grace didn't notice Celia's flagging spirits for some time, probably because she was so busy herself. She was teaching another night course at the community college with students who weren't very motivated. A couple of times, she had to go to Washington, D.C., for professional conferences, and had traveled to Philadelphia for the wedding of a college friend. Also, a new hospital administrator had come from New York and was making changes that were not, in Grace's opinion, helpful or necessary. And, those several urgent calls from home, Mom wanting to consult Grace on yet another experimental therapy for Shane. On the other hand, things with Alec were going well. Having observed him over the last few months, Celia appreciated his intelligence and quiet humor, and especially the way he treated her sister.

"What's up, over there?" Grace asked one evening at home in the apartment. She was seated at the kitchen table leafing through newspapers and nursing journals, making notes. Celia reclined on the sofa, pillow on her stomach, gazing around the room: framed photos, a needlework project stuffed in a bag beside the easy chair, Grace's weighty biographies from the library, and newly polished black pumps drying on a towel, all evidence of Grace's busy, productive life. Celia sighed, unable to imagine the day she could afford a place of her own.

"Are you OK?" Grace asked again, when she got no reply. "Not sick, are you? I wouldn't be surprised if you were run down from all that exercise. You are supposed to take a break between workouts, you know."

"Healthy as a horse. Don't worry, no repeats of Christmas," Celia said—that nasty flu bug, when she had been sprawled out on the sofa for days. "Just pooped."

But Grace wasn't ready to leave it at that. "Is there a problem at work?"

"No." Celia rolled on to her side. "Things are fine. I really love it there. I only wish the money was better, but we're just trying to get off the ground."

"Didn't you say Shelly and Anita were having a conflict?"

"Oh, that. Yeah, about Shelly being out of the club so much. They always have a conflict about something. It doesn't mean anything; they just fight like sisters." She paused, struck by her words. "Not like us, of course. But yeah, things are going pretty well, as far as I can tell. In fact, we're talking about hiring someone new." Maybe that would create a nice diversion.

"Hmm . . ." said Grace. "I don't see how you could pay for someone else, since you're not making much money yourselves."

"It would be an investment," Celia improvised. "In order to grow and make more money. Besides, I think Shelly's father would loan us money, if we needed it."

It was Grace's turn to sigh. "It must be nice to have your own personal bank. Well, I still don't really see the long term prospects for you."

"I know, I know," Celia said. "I don't know what I want. That's the whole problem."

She got up off the sofa and went to the table, taking a seat and looking through the papers and journals, while Grace continued writing in her notebook. She had marked some ads for employment, and was copying down addresses of hospitals and health care facilities in Atlanta, Georgia, of all places.

"Are you looking for a new job?" Celia asked, taken aback.

Grace looked up. "Yes, I am."

"But why would you want to go to Atlanta?"

Grace put down her pen. "It's supposed to be a nice city, you know. Actually, Alec is applying for jobs there, and if he goes, I might go, too. That's what I'm looking for, jobs in nursing. Looks like quite a few. It's a big city."

"But, but . . ." Celia stammered. "I didn't think you liked the South that much."

"I never said that," Grace protested, a half-smile at her lips. "I just didn't like the views of some people living around here. I'm sure Atlanta is more up-to-date."

Celia found herself surprisingly distressed. For one thing, it would certainly force her to make some changes of her own. But more than that, what was her sister thinking of? This seemed so unlike her.

"Are you going to live with him?"

"I'm planning to get my own place, hopefully near him. And who knows what the future will bring." She looked almost amused at Celia's open-mouthed expression. "I'm a big girl, Celia. What do you think; you're the only one who can take risks? I've put in my time here, and gotten some good experience. You know I haven't been that happy at work lately. It's not like we're making wedding plans or anything, but there's something about Alec I really like, and I think he's 'for real,' if you know what I mean."

This news should not have come as such a surprise. While she had been going through all her ups and downs, life went on, people made plans, things changed. Grace was always a planner, and motivated.

"Well, I suppose so," Celia said lamely.

"And another thing, Celia," Grace said, pushing the papers aside and putting her arms on the table. "You should make some plans as well. Not just because I'm thinking of moving. You could stay on here without me, maybe get a roommate. I'm sure the landlord would let you take over the lease. But would you really want to? Is there enough here for you on the Eastern Shore?"

"No, not really." Celia slumped forward on the table, and then straightened up with a sigh. "So you think it's time for me to go?"

"I think you should be looking for other jobs in other places, yes. Go ahead and start with the theater or arts if you want, but you may have to compromise, and find some other area. You can always take night classes to finish your degree, and see how things stand then."

Suddenly, Celia knew Grace was right. That's exactly what she needed to do. Only, for some reason, she wasn't quite ready. Her time was fairly consumed with being part of a new business. She didn't want to leave Shelly and Anita after only a couple months. It took time and money to travel places and apply for jobs, which she didn't have much of. And, a kind of inertia had taken hold, an anticlimax after the Inn. But there was more than that, too, she realized, something about this drama she was living out about different types of people meeting and mixing, the good and the bad. She found that interesting.

"How soon do you think you might . . . leave?"

"Most likely by the fall. And of course I'm waiting to hear what turns up for Alec." She hesitated. "Don't think I'm throwing you out. I've enjoyed having you here. Sometimes I have felt so far away from family. And, well, it reminds me of earlier times, good times, before Dad passed and all."

You're too good, Celia thought, humbled, and then said rather vaguely, but in all sincerity, "I can never make it up to you."

Celia wasn't on the lookout for Alonzo, exactly, but she found that she was noticing young men whom she happened to pass on the way to work. There weren't too many of them. She surmised that he went to the grocery story on a regular basis, maybe twice a week, usually in the afternoon.

Mid-week, she saw him a few hundred yards ahead, recognizing his backpack and his distinctive gait. Resisting the urge to yell, she trotted ahead until she was in reasonable distance.

"Alonzo, wait up," she called out, panting a little.

He turned, surprised, and waited for her. His look was more concern than welcome. Maybe he thought he'd done something wrong.

"I was just wondering about the play. How's it going?"

His face remained a blank, puzzled.

"You know, how I was planning to buy tickets, but then you said maybe I should wait?"

Light dawned, but no smile. "I remember. Maybe you better forget it."

"Really?"

"Yeah, it's not going very well. Mr. Timilty says that if we don't have it together for a full run-through by the weekend, he's going to cancel." He shook his head. "Doesn't look promising. Misfortunate, I'd say."

Celia held back a smile, unwilling to correct him—*misfortunate*, it certainly gave the idea. She looked into his eyes, a soft, light brown. He seemed genuinely disappointed. A horn beeped. A long line of traffic was stopped at a light, a weathered pick-up truck at the rear, just a few feet ahead of them. Country music played on the radio, and a man in a baseball cap sat at the wheel.

"He bothering you, sweetheart?" he called out the window. Celia grimaced; how embarrassing.

"No!" she said, swinging away.

"You want a ride?"

"No!" she shouted. Not likely.

The line was moving again. The man shrugged, and then put his foot on the gas, leaving a puff of exhaust.

Alonzo was staring off in the distance, miles away.

Celia gave a little snort. "Some people," she said, covering the moment. "So, you're telling me they can't put on the show for the lack of a stage manager? I can't believe they couldn't get someone else."

"Nope," Alonzo said. "No volunteers." He hesitated. "That's not the whole thing. Some kids hang around at rehearsal, watching. And then they tease the kids who are trying to say their lines. Stupid, kid stuff."

"Terrible," Celia said, fired up with people's bad manners. "They should get a swift kick in the butt. I could . . ." She stopped talking, but she was thinking.

"The kids in the play aren't motivated," he offered. "They're just not into it, can't relate to it. They rather do something else."

"Yes, you said. What do you think of it?"

"It's OK. Yeah, I guess it's nice. Not my first choice." Then he shrugged. "Nothing for me to do, really, just stand around. I'm supposed to run the

217

lights, eventually. I wanted to build something—you know, steps and platforms, that's why I joined up. My grandfather taught me carpentry; he used to make furniture. I like working with my hands." He turned over his hands, showing her his palms, muscular and lightly calloused. "I guess I won't be doing that."

Celia scrutinized his face, a dark shadow of whiskers over his lip and framing his jaw, giving him a mature, serious look.

Alonzo glanced up toward the plaza. "You going this way?"

"Yes," she said. "Work."

They walked in silence, side by side, the short distance remaining.

"So, what's his name again, the director?" Celia asked.

"Mr. Timilty."

"And when do you guys rehearse?"

Alonzo looked reluctant to tell her. But he was too polite not to answer.

"Monday and Tuesday afternoons and Thursday night."

At the high school, obviously. Celia nodded.

"OK, then," Alonzo said.

"So long, Alonzo," Celia said. "Too bad about this whole thing."

He shook his head in resignation. "All our efforts in the re-fuse pile."

Celia's lips turned up at the way he pronounced the word: like, to not accept something. Or, did he mean it, literally, a pile of refusals to cooperate on the play? Kind of cute, really, and it showed he had an appreciation, if not perfect command, of language.

After lunch, Shelly took off on some errands, and there was the customary midday lull at New You. A few women moved quietly from machine to machine, at their own pace, no desire for advice from "the General" or her assistant. Anita was developing a new routine, set to a gospel song which she was eager to try out. Celia liked the song but had her doubts about using it for exercise. It was Celia's job to perform each step as directed, while Anita operated the tape recorder and made notes and stick drawings. The song was surging and powerful, and gradually Celia got caught up in the music, raising a fist to the driving chorus and singing out, "Right On, King Jesus."

"It's *Ride On*," Anita shouted at Celia over the music.

"What?" Celia shouted back.

Anita stopped the tape. "It's *Ride On*," she repeated. "Not *Right On*, like 'power to the people.'" She imitated the fist movement. "That doesn't look right, what you're doing."

"Oh," Celia said. She had never seen the written words, just hearing them on tape. "Are you sure?"

Anita sat back on her heels. Celia dared to question her on Biblical, never mind black spiritual, matters? "Riding on a milk white horse," she sang, emphasizing the "riding."

"But Jesus doesn't ride a horse," Celia countered. "He rides a mule. Right? On the way from Bethlehem to Egypt, a mule. Riding into Jerusalem with all the palms, a mule. I don't remember him riding a horse anywhere."

"It's not Jerusalem," Anita said, trying for patience. "It's the River Jordan."

"I don't know," Celia said, after a moment. "Why would he be riding a horse to the river? I don't think that's right. If he's riding anything, it's a mule. I believe, out of humility, Jesus rides on a small brown mule."

"Five minutes ago, you didn't think it was about riding at all," Anita said loudly. "It's definitely a horse, a milk white horse! That's what the song says."

"I'm sure I would remember hearing about Jesus on a horse."

"It's a spiritual horse!" Anita exclaimed. Now they were both on their feet, hands on hips. "Big and white and powerful."

They had come to a standstill, locked in argument. Celia knew it was pointless to continue, but she couldn't help herself. Why did Anita have to be so bossy all the time, correcting everyone right out in public? Why couldn't she be more accepting of things the way they were. Celia may have had a few missteps, but she was not a child.

"So, you're saying the song is about empowerment, just as I was trying to show."

All exercise had ceased. Somebody, somewhere, giggled. Celia saw they had landed themselves in a ridiculous situation, but she couldn't see a way out. Darn that Anita for being so stubborn; no way in the world would she back down.

Suddenly, a woman appeared from the back of the club, hurrying through the swinging doors, wrapped in a towel.

"Anita, Celia," she said. "Come quick. There's a leak in the Jacuzzi, and water is spilling on the floor."

"Oh, my Lord," Anita exclaimed, reasserting her claim on God. "What now?"

They made their way to the back, where the water had already spread over most of the tile floor surrounding the Jacuzzi and on to some of the carpet. There was a small crack in one of the fiberglass pipes connecting the Jacuzzi to the wall.

"We'll put some duct tape around it, until the repair guy can get here," Anita said. The argument, it seemed, was past. "I'm sure there's some in the office. Celia, honey, can you get it from that shoe box where we keep the hammer and such?"

Celia got the duct tape and returned only to find Anita ranting about the old mop in the cleaning closet. "This piece of junk; why'd he even leave it behind? Should have gone in the garbage. We need a good mop for this job." She put the mop aside, while the two of them cut and wrapped the tape around the leaky pipe. Anita pulled out a couple of spare towels from the closet and put them down in the wettest areas.

"Now, where's the paperwork for all this?" Anita did not handle small emergencies well. She seemed to take these normal, mechanical type problems personally.

"Shelly probably has it filed in the desk," Celia answered. "But look, here's a service number printed on the side of the panel."

"All right, all right," Anita said. "I'll call them, and tell them they better get over here before this carpet is ruined." She was clearly looking forward to the battle, although Celia thought a calm approach might work just as well. She picked up the towels Anita had put down and took them out back to wring. When she returned, Anita was copying down the number, and turned to her. "Run up to the store, sweetie, and get us a good mop. Quick, quick. The water's still spreading, and we're out of towels. There's money in petty cash."

Still in her leotard, Celia took ten dollars from the box, unsure of the cost of a mop, having never bought one before. She walked quickly along the plaza, turning the corner to the other leg of the L, past the bowling alley to the grocery store. Inside, at the aisle with cleaning supplies, she couldn't decide which mop to purchase. How would she know a good mop if she saw one? Finally, she asked an older woman who looked like she would know, and went to pay.

She stepped outside into the bright sunlight. In the doorway of the bowling alley stood four young men, all shades of black, all looking in her direction. She braced herself, not from fear but embarrassment at passing a pack of guys while in her tights and leotard, carrying a mop. As she got closer, she recognized Jay and some of his pals with a quick, sharp breath.

Head up, head up, she told herself. Jay was leaning up against one of the vending machines, watching her approach. She met his eyes; she couldn't help it.

"Hey, Cinderella," he said. "Where's the ball at?"

Celia blushed. She could only imagine how she looked with her sweaty leotard, shiny face, and messy hair.

"Hello, Jay," she replied with a tight smile, not slowing her pace.

"What, you not gonna talk to me anymore?" he said, stepping out in front of her on the sidewalk, and motioning his crew back inside with a flick of his head.

"I'm in a hurry," Celia said, slowing her pace and holding up the mop. "There's a leak in the Jacuzzi."

Jay smiled. "You can wait up a minute. I'm sure it ain't no flood, and the ark not gonna leave without you."

Celia had stopped in front of him. He moved in closer, just two feet away. Why was her heart racing like this? Why did she feel like this after all this time? Against her better judgment, she smiled.

"So, you liking it down there?" he asked, gesturing toward New You.

"Yes, I do. It's been great."

"You looking good, filled out nice." Jay nodded appreciatively— obviously a come on, but why? Did he think she was going to go for it, after everything that had happened?

"Well, thank you," Celia said graciously. "I feel good. And I am in pretty good shape, from working out so much." And then, to change the subject. "So, how are things at the Inn?"

"Same old, same old. Nothing new under the sun," Jay replied.

Still in her polite voice, Celia continued. "And how about you and Pauline?" Some devil made her add, "Will there be wedding bells any time soon?"

Jay flinched, not expecting the challenge. Then he shrugged if off. "Not too good there. That's the whole problem. She always acting like we already married. I ain't ready for all that."

"Sorry, Jay," she said, a bit breathlessly. "I just can't feel too bad for you." And then, after a pause, "I'd better get going." She shifted the mop from one hand to the other, just starting to turn.

"Wait up," Jay got out quickly. He took her by the wrist. "I wish we had another chance," he said softly.

A jolt, like electricity, went up her arm into her elbow. How could it be that she still had such strong feelings? "Fat chance," she tried to say, but she couldn't. She stayed rooted to the spot, and when his hand slid down to her hand, she found her fingers laced with his. *God help me,* she thought, and she knew that if he asked her to meet him somewhere, she would go.

Instead, she heard her name being called. "Cel-ia! Cel-ia!" She recognized Anita's voice without looking, and they dropped hands and turned. Anita, an apron over her leotard and her hair in a kerchief, came at a trot through the parking lot, cutting the corner. Some distance away, she shouted, "We need you back with that mop."

Even after Celia waved, Anita kept on coming, obviously annoyed. Celia had already started over to meet her, glancing back once at Jay. When they met, Anita hardly looked at her but motioned her to keep going. "You'll see what needs to be done. And look out for the repair guy. I'll be right back."

Anita made a beeline for Jay. All Celia could hear as she hurried away was, "I told you . . ." and everything else was lost. Told him what? It must have been something about her. Pausing once behind a pick-up truck, she saw Jay looking down at the ground as Anita spoke.

At New You, Celia took the plastic wrap off the mop and began to sponge up water, then rinsing in the bucket. Her thoughts circled round and round as she worked. Why the come on? Why now? She had looked in his eyes and knew for certain that he knew, had already known, the truth about her feelings. But what about him? What did he feel? Try as she might, she found no clue how he really felt about her. And she had to wonder, did he even know himself, or could he read her like a map but have no insight into his own heart?

Mopping furiously, she pictured Anita, that avenging angel, arriving so exactly at the right—or was it the wrong—time? No, it was right. It was. Celia felt a wave of relief, huge relief. He hadn't broken up with Pauline, or moved, or found another job. There was no reason to think things had changed. This time she was not ignorant, or innocent. She wasn't going for the same thing twice. Yet she almost had. Celia put the mop down, and sat on the steps up to the Jacuzzi, her head in her hands.

What was Anita's part in all of this? Did she know more than Celia had realized? Was she just trying to protect her, keep Jay away? It wasn't that Anita liked Pauline; Celia knew that. It wasn't jealousy, either, or dislike. No one had done more for Celia since she moved here than Anita, except, of course, Grace. But there was something else, something not seen, and it bothered Celia to think that there was something going on behind her back.

Celia heard the front door open and a man and woman speaking. The repair guy? It sounded more like Shelly and Russell. She got up, realizing she would have to go be the bearer of bad news. Then she heard Anita's voice, relating the story in high drama.

She closed her eyes and acknowledged fully, for the first time, that she was somehow hung up on Jay, although she couldn't say why. Suddenly she remembered her ride with Jay in his VW bug to Weston, and how sitting there with him, with their burgers, the world had seemed so rich and complete for that moment. She decided their time together wasn't just a mistake. Something had been lost, a connection severed. But she knew, just as certainly, that there was no chance, and never would be. She picked up the mop again, just as Russell, Shelly, Anita, and the service repairman came through the doorway to see the leaky Jacuzzi and the wet floor.

Celia stood back, mop in hand, as Anita drilled the repairman about how long and how much, with Shelly putting in an occasional word of reason, and Russell answering questions when deferred to. Finally, the man was left to work in peace, and Anita's attention came back to Celia.

"Oh, cheer up, buttercup," she scolded. "You won't be on mop duty all day."

Celia turned her face from Anita, attacking the floor with a vengeance. That Anita better not get too close, or she'd get a good whack on the head.

God in heaven, Celia prayed. Help me. I need something else, something more, something to hold onto, so that I don't slip.

And then, like an answer to a prayer, she knew exactly what—the theater. The high school play, *Our Town.* She would do whatever she could to help save it. And it would be her salvation.

At Sutton High School, ten minutes before eight in the morning, the front office secretary told Celia that Mr. Timilty could be found in Room 125, first floor, B Wing. The halls were quiet; Celia was ahead of the students.

"Yes, dear," he said, looking up from his desk. An older fellow with a double chin, a bow tie, and an excessive amount of hair. Celia's costume shop experience told her immediately: toupee. But he smiled pleasantly, as so many people did when Celia entered a room.

"I'm Celia Lennon," she said, "and I live here in Sutton. I wanted to talk to you about the play."

His chest seemed to deflate.

"Ah, yes. The play. I'm not selling tickets, and I can't promise there will be a show."

"Yes, I know. Here." She thrust a piece of paper at him: her resume with its limited education credentials and long list of productions she had been in since junior high school, including *Our Town,* bolded. "I want to help."

He took his time to look at the resume, and then sat back, resting his hands on his generous mid-section.

"I see," he said, his bright eyes narrowing with interest.

She looked around. There were only student desks, except the one chair pushed into the corner. "Do you mind?"

"Not at all. But time is short before the invasion of the hordes."

In spite of his sarcasm, she rather liked his delivery, a touch of panache.

"I met a young man recently, Alonzo Bailey, who goes to school here."

She waited for a sign of recognition, and then went on. "He was delivering flyers for the show, which I was interested in seeing. Then, later, he said there were problems with the rehearsal, kids not taking it seriously, a lot of fooling around backstage, that kind of thing."

"All true. And so . . ."

Celia took the plunge. "I want to volunteer to be stage manager. I have a lot of theater experience, as you can see."

His eyes crinkled. "Ah, another theater lover. I should have known." Then his smile turned sad, looking down at the paper. "So kind of you. And I'm sure you're just delightful. But, I believe at this point, it's rather pointless. We're scheduled to rehearse Thursday night, but I think that's the end of it. I said one more chance, and if it's still a mess, which I believe it will be, it's off for this year."

"Yes, but, but . . ." Celia said. "There are still a few weeks. Miracles have happened in less time."

"It would take more than a miracle."

"Do you mind if I come and watch? Then, maybe, if there's any progress, I can start helping."

The bell rang, loudly, ear-splitting.

"Certainly. At the least, you'll see for yourself what a state we're in."

Celia was on her feet as students started entering the room, louder even than the bell. One after another, they tramped in, almost every one of them black. Finally, a few white faces, and one young Asian man. As she left the building, she realized there was some diversity at the school, but not much. This was a primarily black school. And of course that meant, the students in *Our Town* were likely to be black, too.

Hm . . . she thought . . . that's a little different spin on an all-American play. As she departed the school, she had to admit that the situation did not look promising. And yet, and yet, she would love nothing more than getting totally involved in the world of a play, at least for a little while.

Thursday night, Celia realized she didn't have to go to the rehearsal at the high school. No one was expecting her, really. The play was doomed, it sounded like. Still, she found herself changing into nice pants and a light sweater, taking a pad of paper, hitching her purse on her shoulder and turning right rather than left when she got to the end of the street. *Why?* It was theater. She needed something consuming and distracting.

Grace had the car, so Celia gave herself time to walk to the school, which was not far. She'd driven by it many times and once attended a choral concert there. So she knew where the auditorium was. At seven o'clock on the dot, she was there—at the public entrance to the auditorium. The lights were on, but she didn't see anyone.

Had it been called off?

Then she heard a few voices back stage, and from a side entrance, Mr. Timilty strode in carrying a clipboard and what looked like a copy of the script.

Then a figure crossed the stage, large, dark, with a looming shadow—Alonzo. He was checking lights and microphones, talking to someone who remained off-stage.

Three more figures rambled onto the stage, chatting—two young women and a young man. From the other public entrance to the auditorium, a cluster of young people came in, two of the boys dressed for basketball. They approached the stage, laughing and shouting greetings.

This, apparently, was the cast.

"Now or never," boomed Mr. Timilty, and the chatter slowed to a reluctant stop. "Gather here a moment before we proceed."

At the back of the auditorium, Celia had no trouble hearing him speak. While they were focused on him, she moved a few rows closer.

"This is it," Mr. Timilty pronounced. "Sink or swim. If it doesn't go tonight, it doesn't go at all."

Mutterings.

"Now, who is here?" Mr. Timilty said. "And, more to the point, who is not?" He really did have a fine, carrying voice, Celia thought, and excellent diction.

"No Nina, no Bobby, and no Tyrone." He jerked his thumb. "They're out."

He looked at the figures circled around him. "The rest of you are here, and some of you want to be. Let's see how far we get, and that will make our decision for us. If we can't get a single run through, that's the message: time to stop."

Celia took a seat, waiting to hear the familiar lines.

The actors went on stage, the boy playing the character of stage manager staying out front. They carried scripts, although they were meant to have their lines memorized.

"Now, ladies and gentleman," cued Mr. Timilty. "*Our Town.*"

The play began. The first actor was fine. He must be one of the committed ones—a play, if not his first choice. The other actors came in on their cues, and the first scenes went smoothly—probably that old adrenaline rush of stepping up when the stakes were high.

And then, one actress faltered. Not a big deal, but she was rattled and left before her last lines. A verbal disagreement could be heard backstage.

Just into the second act, everything started to collapse. Like a virus, the hesitancy, the lapses and the wrong starts took over. On stage, the actors froze, one after another. Whispering and stifled shouts escaped from behind the curtain.

"Well," Mr. Timilty said, finally. "Is that it? Act One? Not bad, but the audience will be expecting more. They'll be expecting Act Two and an ending. Sorry, this doesn't cut it. Everyone, out front."

He got to his feet, waving the actors off the stage to the seats around him. "This is my point exactly. You can do it, but you won't."

No one answered. Meanwhile, though, Alonzo had come out from back stage and was making his way down the side steps when he caught sight of Celia out in the audience. His face registered surprise, then wonder.

A hand lifted in a wave, and she waved back.

A few heads swiveled round but Mr. Timilty cleared his throat, and Alonzo continued toward the assembled group.

"So, we stop here. Or, does anyone see a reason to go on?"

Finally, one of the boys said, "We give up. We don't like the play. Never did. Not saying it's a bad play. Maybe it's good for someone else, but just doesn't mean anything to us. Our heart's not in it."

"We tried, Mr. Timilty," another girl said. "At first we really did. But even when we were trying, it was bad. Nobody wants to see us do it."

Now Mr. Timilty responded with some heat. "You mean, those louts who sit in the back of the auditorium and snicker? You can't pay attention to them. They have no appreciation for any of the arts. They're just here to mock, no matter what you do. So, don't even think about them."

"But, Mr. Timilty . . ." One of the girls began, a big girl with lots of braids. "We brought you the play that we wanted to do. We would have done it, no matter. It's a good play, and it's about us and our lives, at least, back in the old days."

Celia sat up, curious.

But Mr. Timilty was shaking his head.

"I told you before and I'll tell you again, we can't do it. First of all, it's not appropriate for families—think of it." He started counting off fingers, "Violence and mayhem, murder, rape, incest, fratricide, betrayal. And it all comes to such a terrible, bloody end."

"But that's the truth of it," the girl persisted. "That's how it was."

"And, language," Mr. Timilty would not relent. "Nigger this, nigger that. There's no bleeping it and there's no substitute for it. Plus, the names and places are very connected to this area—they would have to be changed. There are people who still live here with those names, and they would be highly offended."

"But . . ."

"I'm sorry," Mr. Timilty said, and he seemed genuinely disappointed. "The play has merit, and some very compelling scenes, I grant you that. But the script is a mess. There are pages missing, and scenes that make no sense. People leave to do something, and we never find out what happens. It lacks unity and artistic integrity. If the playwright were still able to revise it, that would be one thing. But apparently, that's not the case. So, the play simply cannot be done, not here, not by us. Do you understand?"

No one answered.

Mr. Timilty rose to his feet. "So, are we decided then? Or shall we take a vote?"

The students all rose as well. "No vote," the tall, imposing girl said. "We're through."

And with that, they filed out, dropping their scripts in a pile on the stage. Alonzo returned to the back of the stage, and one by one the lights shut off, until there were just the house lights in the auditorium. Mr. Timilty left in a discussion with the big girl, and perhaps had not seen Celia at all. Just as well.

Celia waited until everyone left, looking to where Alonzo had disappeared. She walked up to the front row.

"Alonzo," she called out, and he came out from the side of the stage, down the steps, to where she stood in the open space in front of the stage.

"You came?" he said, shaking his head.

"I did."

"Why?"

"Why?" she repeated with a half-smile. "Well, because of what you told me: you needed a good stage manager. And since I used to do a lot of theater, I thought I might help. So I talked to Mr. Timilty earlier in the week, and he said I could come and see for myself." She laughed wryly. "He wasn't very hopeful, and I guess it's all over now."

Alonzo nodded soberly. Still, when he looked up, his eyes seemed to shine, as disappointing as the rehearsal was.

"You, you want to . . ." he began.

But Celia had a bee in her bonnet.

"That other play," she said, interrupting him. "What is it called, and what's it about? Something to do with black people and slavery, I'm guessing?"

"Chesapeake Uprising," he said, then stopped. He seemed to be considering his words. "The play is about slavery days. It was written by somebody who used to go to school here, but he moved away to D.C. He was living in a bad place, and he got killed." He paused, awaiting Celia's reaction.

"Killed? Murdered, you mean?"

He held her eyes. "Looks like."

"Wow. So, what does that mean, in terms of the play?"

"His sister goes to school here. She's the one who wants us to put it on, Desiree. The story is about a slave rebellion that takes place on the Eastern Shore. There's two brothers, half-brothers from the same slave mother, living at two different plantations. One is for the rebellion, and the other tries to stop it. That's the main conflict, see?"

"You mean, fighting, not just trying to escape?"

"Armed rebellion—guns, shovels, knives, and machetes."

Celia's eyes widened. "Oh, I see." She shook her head slowly. "I guess it doesn't have a happy ending."

"No, the rebels are caught, and the one brother kills the other brother and then he escapes with the help of his lover, the plantation owner's daughter."

"Quite the drama," Celia considered.

Alonzo held her eyes for a long moment. "It's a family story, see? The white girl is the half-sister of the slave who betrays the rebellion. They have the same father, the man who owns the plantation, only they don't know it, of course. The slave's mother was sold away to another plantation where she had another son by a black man. He's the one who starts the rebellion. So, he's half-brother to the betrayer, I mean, betraitor."

"Just traitor," Celia corrected him gently. But she was stupefied. "It's not real?"

"You won't find it in the history books."

"How many acts?"

"Just one."

"How many characters?"

"Seven. No, eight."

"Hm . . ." Celia mused. "I'd like to read it."

Alonzo stared at her. "You mean that?"

"Yes, I do."

"I have a copy in my backpack," Alonzo said. "We all do, us in the play. It's the one we wanted to do. We even practiced some scenes for Timilty. But you heard what he said."

He unzipped one of the pockets of the backpack and brought out a rolled up bundle of papers. She scanned it, flipping dog-eared pages.

"Hm . . . I'm not so sure it can't be done. Let me read it, and I'll let you know what I think." Her forehead wrinkled, and she murmured, "How is it any worse than the Greek tragedies or Shakespeare?"

"So, how will I hear from you," Alonzo asked, "when you're finished?"

Celia scanned the empty rows of seats, considering. Not New You. And probably not on the sidewalk, where Eagle-Eye Anita might see them. "How about next Thursday, after school—say two-thirty at the bowling alley—in the back by the vending machines. OK?"

"I'll be there."

"If you can't make it," she started, and then blanked. "Well, never mind, just be there."

She tucked the script in her bag and buttoned her sweater as he stood, watching.

"You feel like a slice of pizza?" he said. "Or, you want me to walk you home?"

Celia fixed him with a warning look. "Oh, no, no," He was sweet, but there would be no confusion about this. "You know this isn't a date, right?"

"Just being polite," he said, his smile fading.

"You're a senior, right? How old are you anyway?"

"Seventeen. Eighteen in a couple months." His hand started for his back pants pocket. "I can show you my driver's license. . . ."

Celia shooed that away, for some reason a bit surprised that he could drive. "Well, I'm nineteen. And I am a college student—just on break. I've lived all over the country, and have a lot more experience of the world than you do, I'm pretty sure. See what I'm getting at?"

"Sure, sure," he said, deferentially.

"OK, then. So, no thank you; I don't need you to walk me home. Besides," she added more lightly. "I'll be there in a jiffy."

"A jiffy," he repeated. "I guess that's pretty quick. OK, then. I'll see you Thursday." He didn't seem offended by the turn of conversation, if maybe a little disappointed.

"Thursday it is," Celia said, rather grandly making her exit.

At home at the kitchen table, still in her dressy clothes, Celia read *Chesapeake Uprising* in one sitting. It wasn't long—running time probably less than an hour. Mr. Timilty was right about the violence, family secrets, the local names and places, and the fact that the script was a mess.

But there was something to it. It *was* like a Greek tragedy in its depiction of seething anger, abuse of power, revenge, betrayal, and doomed love. The dialogue was a little over the top, and there were some logical inconsistencies. The characters, however, were strongly drawn and clearly motivated; the scenes were well structured, and the climax—well, the climax was a doozy. *Holy cow!*

But she had an idea. Putting down the script, she got her little address book and found the name she was looking for: Leona Jones. If anyone could help, it would have to be someone like Leona—theater-oriented and used to dealing with students. True, Celia had never actually met her, since her accident on her way to their meeting, but they had talked on the phone. And there was their mutual friend—Roland, the Rogue, wherever he was.

Chapter 20

The following Thursday, Celia ducked into the bowling alley, dark as night coming in from the sunshine. Midafternoon, it was quiet as a tomb. It never seemed very busy except for morning or after-work leagues, and sometimes on the weekends.

Alonzo was there before her, studying the selections in the vending machines. The lights were on at the snack bar at the far side of the room, but no one was at the counter. The back seating area was separated off from the bowling lanes by partial walls.

He turned and saw her, giving a wave. His backpack was on one of the tables, where she walked over to meet him, sort of looming in the dim light.

"Good afternoon," he said, with his usual calm cheer.

"Hi there, Alonzo. So, great, you're here. I wasn't sure if you, well, if this really . . ." And then, seeing his confusion, she switched gears. "It's good news—I think. I've been talking with someone who could help make this happen."

"Really?" He didn't look skeptical as much as someone trying not to look skeptical.

"Sit down, and I'll tell you what's what." Out of her tote bag she took the script he had given her, and a Xeroxed copy, read and marked up by Leona, with some cover notes. "Her name is Leona, and I met her through a mutual friend. She works in the Theater Department at Salisbury State." She did not mention that she had not actually met Leona until Saturday, when she'd driven down to Salisbury to give her the script to read.

Next to her, Alonzo said nothing, but nodded, looking at her rather than the script.

"Leona really likes the play," Celia said. "That is, she thinks it has merit, and she thinks it should be produced. She read it, made comments and suggestions, and has done some rewrites herself to make it more, well, clear and complete."

Alonzo didn't have to speak. His face showed more dismay than joy.

"What's the matter?"

"That's very generous of her, and all. But I don't think she can just rewrite the play over—it's somebody's words and ideas. Even if he's dead, I think we should respect that."

Celia sat back, taking in his words. "Well, of course you're right. I really think Leona is just shaping it up, getting it ready to go on stage. She wouldn't change anything fundamental."

He still didn't look convinced.

"She's . . ." Celia started, and then stopped. "Let's go over her suggestions, you and me. Then you take the script with her edits and rewrites and see what you and the others think."

She handed the marked script to him. "I think they're pretty good, and faithful to the original."

He seemed so lukewarm about all this, strangely.

"Leona's got a lot of theater experience," she prodded. "Acting, directing, backstage, lights, props: she's done it all."

He looked up from the script, staring, mute.

A light went on in Celia's head. "She's from the Eastern Shore, you know."

Now his mouth began to open, as if in surprise.

And then Celia got it, what had not occurred to her before.

"And she's black—African American." She pursed her lips wryly. "Does that help?"

He nodded, his jaw more relaxed.

"Read it," Celia urged. "See what she's done. I think you'll like it."

He nodded again

"This play can be done," Celia said earnestly. "I really think so. With Leona's help. And all you actors. And I'll be the stage manager and do publicity. Whatever."

Now he was smiling.

"But," Celia cautioned. "We've got no money. And we have to find a place to hold it. Not the high school, I guess."

"Not there," Alonzo agreed. "But we'll find somewhere. There are places in town we can try, several avenues—church halls, Elks Hall and such."

Celia laughed; she couldn't help it. "Not avenues, Alonzo. That would be holding it on the street. Venues, I think that's what you mean—locations. Right?"

"Venues," he repeated, unperturbed. "That's it."

"OK, then," Celia said, taking out her pen. "Let's get to it. We need a plan of action. First, you can contact the others and tell them about Leona and show them the changes in the play."

He nodded.

"And then a meeting for everyone, with Leona, to decide the time and the place—before the end of school. That gives us over six weeks. We can meet here for the first time, I guess." She scanned the large, deserted space. "It's usually pretty quiet. As long as we buy some fries and drinks, they won't care. Let's say Monday after school, at three, if Leona's free."

She looked up, and Alonzo was beaming, with hope or amusement, it was hard to say.

"Well, I say," he drawled, reaching into his own bag for a pen. "It sounds like we're going to have a play here."

Celia flipped to the first page of the script. "Let's get to it."

With Leona on board, *Chesapeake Uprising* suddenly seemed very real, rather overwhelming, and coming up quickly. A dozen of the students from *Our Town* showed up at the meeting, ready to see what was going on with the revised play and new director. It didn't take long for them to get the idea that Leona was serious—about the play, and about her time not being wasted. She was in her mid-twenties, small and athletic, with short hair and expressive eyes. Unlike Anita, she didn't use feminine wiles, softening her statements with teasing and smiles. She was direct and to the point, and her language was not delicate. Well, she was not a teacher. But she did understand theater and kids.

First thing, she wanted to do a read-through of the entire script, assigning parts at random. Business later, she said, which seemed a bit odd to Celia, who thought the kids wanted to know what she was planning and what was required of them.

"This play has to stand on its own," Leona said, looking around. They were seated at two adjacent tables, chairs pulled over, and Celia sitting mostly silent next to Leona. "It has to *carry,* all by itself. Never mind the other stuff; that doesn't mean a thing if the play doesn't work. Let's see what's in the words. I'll read Mariah, the old slave mother; Celia, you read stage directions."

Leona began:

Listen, chillen. Gather round, my dark beauties, my pale lovelies, all you my chillen, and grandchillen, and great-great grandchillen. I got something to tell. Don't matter I'm dead now all these years, since "that" time, 1835. I know it all; everything that happen. I knew it then, but I larn young not to tell all I know. Then things happened 'fore I could pass it on to them that needed to know. They gone or they dead. The uprising. That's the story I gonna tell you, how it come about, who was there, what happen, what followed. But that not all; otherwise, you think it's just some sad story about people who try to break away, but they fail. This the story behind that story, you see? Is a family story; everybody in it family. Everyone who live and die. Every single one, family; you unnerstan? And everyone in this room here with me; you family, too; this you story.

The students, all of them black except two white boys and a girl, twittered once during the reading, when the plantation owner's daughter, Laurette, vowed she would have Milo, the slave, no matter what—*the most handsome man on the Eastern Shore, of more value than any other.* Her speech sent a ripple through the group—mockery, contempt—but it didn't happen again, after Leona made it clear they could stop any time. She was small, but like a lion, fierce and scary.

At the end of the play, after Mariah's speech about future generations on the Eastern Shore, there was silence. Celia was stunned, almost, with the poetry of the spoken language and the harsh reality depicted. The students looked like awe-struck children at a magic show, or witnesses to something much deeper and more disturbing. One of the girls, the big one with long, beaded braids, wept, putting her hands to her face.

Leona waited a long moment before she asked, "You tell me; does it carry?"

All of them, Celia included, nodded yes. Even in this unpolished state, the story carried all the power and emotion that Celia could recall from any drama—high school, college, or other—that she had ever seen. And, looking around again, she realized that for some of the students, the story was close to home and maybe personal. Her own heart was pounding from the realization that this play could really happen.

"Good news," Leona said, standing up. "We can borrow lights, props, and costumes from the theater department at Salisbury. That's my say-so. Bad news, we don't have a dime to rent space, do publicity, or pay me for my services, as cheap as they come. If we're going to do this play, we do it right, and we make some money. Not a lot. Just enough to cover our asses. It's theater, not charity, and not a private grievance meeting. Do you get what I'm saying?"

They nodded, whether they did or not.

"Some people are not going to like the play, and that's fine. They can stay home. But you know people just have to shoot their mouths, so don't be surprised if you hear some shit going down."

Leona turned to Celia. "We need a venue and we need it fast. See if we can get it donated, or at least at a nominal sum. One of these kids can help you."

Celia met Alonzo's eyes, and he nodded. Looked like they would be partners in this crime.

Leona addressed the students. "Next meeting I'm going to hear you that want to act—I mean audition, and take it seriously. We also need all brothers and sisters to work on sets and on publicity. I can get plywood and paint, and paper for flyers. My girl Drew will help with construction, but you all have to come up with ideas. Bring tools, and be prepared to work."

She was bossy, this Leona, but all the kids, including the chatty-Cathy's, were struck silent.

"It's good, this play," Leona concluded. "It's important what it has to say. You want to be part of this."

And there was no question, they did. Suddenly, the room was full of excited voices.

"One more thing," Leona said, holding up a hand for silence. "We've got to change the title. It's not going to work."

This time there was grumbling and protest. It was Alonzo who spoke. "That's Neely's title, the one he gave it."

Leona was ready. "Maybe that would be the best name if it wasn't a new play, being done here, by us. So, hear me out. We got this play. We want an audience, right, to come and hear what we've got to say all the way to the end? That word 'uprising' will keep people away, just by itself. Some people don't want to hear about all that old slavery crap." She made a face. "White or black. They say it's all past, past history. But that's not what we're saying. Check this out: we got pitchforks, shovels, and axes in this play. So what, they're make believe? That's enough to scare some people shitless."

The faces around Celia were rapt. Leona wasn't talking to them like their teachers or parents or preachers or bosses. It was like some new language.

"They might run out of the place before we're done."

No one smiled.

"So," Leona concluded. "I propose we call it *Anticus* after the rebel leader. His act; his name."

A few heads nodded, thoughtfully.

"*Anticus,*" Celia repeated. She liked the sound of it, classical and dignified.

So it was agreed.

Then it was on to casting and rehearsal schedules, with Leona in charge. The next meeting was planned for Thursday night, back at the bowling alley, where they would be awaiting news of their new performance home.

Yikes, thought Celia, a little pressure!

By some miracle, a place to rehearse and hold the show dropped into their laps, and it wasn't Celia's doing, or Alonzo's. The next day when Celia met Alonzo at the bowling alley, he had good news. One of the girls asked her uncle, who was custodian of the former opera house in the center of town, to find out if they could use the place. The building was empty while the owner decided how to renovate—into a movie theater, or some type of multi-shop arcade. And the answer was yes—in return for a favor. He needed some "healthy young folks" to move out debris from the backstage area—which they had to do anyway, in order to use it.

"Sweat equality," said Alonzo, fingering the fringe on his notebook, while his knee beat time under the table.

"Ah, Mr. Big Words," Celia teased, happy to have such a good prospect so quickly. It felt like karma, almost. "So close, Alonzo: sweat *equity*."

He looked away, across the lanes. "I'm just trying to improve myself."

"And you are," Celia said, encouragingly. "One word at a time." She gave him a pat on the arm. "Let's check it out, this so-called opera house. And if it's basically decent, we'll tell Leona. Wow, wouldn't that be something?"

"Now?"

"Come on, partner, let's go."

Once in the town center, it took only a minute to find the janitor to let them in and to take a look around. It was dark and dusty and smelled like mildew, but it was a grand, old place, and it was perfect for *Anticus*. Eyes and mouths wide open, Celia and Alonzo turned to each other.

Score!

The next task was for the more artistically minded—design ideas for the set, which Leona put Celia in charge of, with any students inclined toward drawing or sketching. Celia knew what was needed, she knew a good set when she saw it, but drawing was not her strength. Initially, no one stepped forward to work with her. Alonzo, however, said that he had taken drafting in school, liked to build things, and was willing to try.

Celia and Alonzo agreed to meet after Celia's Friday shift. She was adamant about him not coming to New You, reluctant to deal with Anita's reaction. Also, of course, it was not a place where men were encouraged to hang out, inside or outside the plate glass windows. After a moment's hesitation, she gave him her address. Grace knew about the play and that some people might come by to work on it. She was fine, more than fine—happy that Celia had a project she was so excited about. Grace's mind was focused elsewhere these days; she didn't need to know the particulars.

Right at the appointed time, Alonzo arrived on Friday, Celia meeting him at the downstairs doorway to escort him, quietly, up the stairs. At the kitchen table, Alonzo set down a roll of largish papers bound in a rubber band next to his backpack. "Let me show you some sketches," he said, slipping off the rubber band and flattening the papers. "Not too bad." He grinned, affecting a high-brow tone. "Rather artistic, if I may say so myself."

Celia laughed. "You know," she said to him across the table, "if I closed my eyes, I might think you were white, the way you speak and the things you come out with."

"No danger of that," he replied evenly, but the smile had disappeared.

"Oh," Celia said quickly, realizing that "no harm meant" was not the same as "no harm done."

"I'm sorry. I shouldn't have said that."

"No problem," Alonzo responded. He yawned, maybe the schoolwork and job catching up with him. And then, after a pause, "Growing up, I spent a lot of time with a white kid, Brett, and his family. His father is a judge at the court house. Maybe I picked up on some of that."

"Oh, I see," she said. She got up to pour drinks, a quick diversion. "Iced tea?" She handed him a glass, which he put to the side.

"Here's what I got," Alonzo said, spreading the drawings across the table, three of them, each depicting the two plantations: the mansion house at Rosebush and the slave quarters at Willowbend, with the suggestion of a field and road between. One was quite fantastical, like something from *The Hobbit;* the second was a little Disney; but the third was cool, restrained, classical—a porch with slender white columns overlooking a yard; and, on the other side of the stage, a rustic hut or shed.

"This one," Celia said, tapping the last. "This looks just right." She bent, looking closer at the fine pencil work. "Nice. I could never do that."

"Thanks. Well, like I said, I took a class."

He took out a pencil case with a bunch of colored pencils. "Let me finish this up, make it look good for Leona. Not much to it, really: the platform for the porch and a rail, three columns, some steps. The yard is nothing but some hay and grass, really. And the shack isn't much more than a little closet." He was talking more to himself than to her as he worked.

Celia took out her own notebook, and started jotting down the information to give to Leona, in terms of building materials. Then, as he shaded in the sketch, she started on the list of places to put up flyers, calculating how many they would need. Leona had also asked her to draft a press release to send to the local paper, but Celia wondered how to word it, considering the play was not affiliated with any school, college, or known community organization. Perhaps they should give themselves a name, she mused. Why not? The Tidewater Players, perhaps? Or Marshland Actors Group? Not quite right.

She put down her pen and watched Alonzo. Everything about him looked warm, from his hair to his skin to his eyes, like he could never really be cold. There was a little gap in his front teeth, but nothing like Eldridge, and his lips were nicely formed, shapely. Good for kissing, you would imagine, and there was something tender—what was the word? endearing?—about how his lashes, short and curly, lay down over his cheeks as he bent over his papers.

She sat up abruptly, stifling a cough.

Alonzo looked up.

"Cookies?" she asked.

"No thanks."

Celia put her notepad aside, watching him work. "So," she said, conversationally, "this friend of yours, Brett? What kind of things did you guys do?"

"Lots of stuff."

"Like?"

"Oh, boating, fishing, camping, hiking, that kind of thing."

"And, where did you go—out on the boat?"

He reflected, running his fingers over the columns on the sketch.

"Um . . . all over the Chesapeake on his dad's boat—both sides from Havre de Grace about down to the Atlantic, under the big bridge that goes to Virginia. Lots and lots of little ports." He raised his eyebrows. "Some of them have restaurants you can pull the boat right up to."

"Really?"

With a half-smile, Alonzo put down his pencil. He, too, was going to have a break. "You know what, I'll have one of those cookies, if you don't mind."

Celia jumped up from the table and got the tin of oatmeal raisin cookies, putting them on a plate.

"Nice," he said, taking one. "Homemade?"

"Grace, my sister." Celia took one also, then another. "They are good, aren't they?"

Alonzo's gaze traveled to the needlepoint sampler of a rooster on the wall over Celia's head.

"My Gran did lots of needle work," Alonzo said, making small talk. "And quilting, too, before her fingers got stiff." He got to his feet to look closer, examining the workmanship. "Somebody did a good job on this."

Honesty compelled Celia to admit, "Yes, Grace did that—too." All that homey, crafty stuff that Celia didn't do, had never bothered to learn. Alonzo was obviously impressed with craftsmanship of all kinds. Celia felt a twinge of something. Jealousy, or envy, maybe? She was never sure of the difference. Just the idea that she was lacking something that Alonzo admired.

Alonzo was back at the table, finishing his drink.

"Yeah, we went a lot of places," he said, picking up the topic. "Little trips, with Brett's family. Baltimore, the Aquarium, and all that. I've been to D.C. maybe five or six times, including school trips. Could probably show you around."

"Sounds like you covered some ground . . . and water."

"Oh, we did. Annapolis, the Naval Academy. Saw the Orioles at Camden Yard. That was fun."

He began to shade the roof of the shed, the shack—whatever it was. Back to work.

"So, what happened to this Brett, then? Did he move?"

He shrugged, not looking up. "Family's still here. He went away to private school, boarding school, and after that, just lost track, I guess."

Celia made a face. "That's too bad. It sounds like you were pretty good friends for a while."

"We were," Alonzo looked at her as he spoke, but she couldn't interpret his expression. "Things change. We both changed. It made me feel bad for a while, but now it's OK." He had moved on to trees and greenery for background on the set.

After a moment, Celia crossed her arms and put her head down on the table.

Alonzo looked up. "Celia?"

"Just resting," she replied, turning her face to see him.

He looked doubtful.

"I don't know what's wrong with me today," Celia confessed. "Can't focus. Maybe some fresh air . . . do you want to take a walk?"

Alonzo checked the wall clock, and shook his head. "I have to go to the library. Research paper; it's got to turn out good."

Almost from habit, or maybe just another diversion, Celia asked. "What's it about?"

He made a funny face, not humorous, just unfathomable. "Fred...Frederick Douglass. You know that name?"

Celia sat up again, her chin in her hands. "I've heard of him. Something about slavery, right?"

He nodded. "Abolitionist, but he was a slave first. Grew up right around here."

"Well, that's good for you. Lots of information, good sources. I imagine." Alonzo tipped his head, yes and no, but nothing further.

"But you've already been accepted to college, right?" Celia went on. "It's not like you won't get in."

"Yeah, I know, but I've got to show I can really do the work, or I'll look like a fool when I get to college. Besides, Mrs. Matthews is riding me pretty hard. She thinks I can make honor roll."

"Really?" Celia said with some surprise. She hadn't thought much about Alonzo's academic aspirations. "I hope you make it. Is she one of your teachers, Mrs. Matthews?"

"No, guidance counselor. She kind of took an interest in me after my mom moved away." Alonzo went on, after some hesitation. "In middle school, she moved to North Carolina with my half-sister to live with the baby's father. I stayed back here with my grandma and uncle. Mrs. Matthews checks with me on school stuff, and other stuff, too. Helped me get my driver's license." He chuckled to himself. "Even though I have no car to drive."

He started collecting his things. "Better get going, I guess. This is pretty much finished, if you want to show Leona before the weekend." He rolled up the drawing, and held it while she got the rubber band.

Just as he was ready to leave, Alonzo asked, "So, you want to work on the set with us, build something with your own hands?"

Celia held the rolled sketch across her arm like a baton. "Me? I'm not great at, you know, making things. That is, cutting, measuring, anything with details."

"I could show you," Alonzo said with his slow smile. "Need the help. We got a lot of work ahead of us. Saturday, we're meeting at ten, a few of us. We cleared out the junk, and now it's time to get building."

"OK, then," Celia said brightly. She tapped the back of a chair with the rolled sketch for emphasis. "Sign me up." Maybe she could do something useful, learn to use her hands. Or help Alonzo, at the least.

Chapter 21

Suddenly, like magic, Celia was back in the world of theater with so much to do and not enough time to do it: really a second job. She told Anita and Shelly about the play right away; there was no keeping it secret, and she would need time off as the date got nearer: one weekend, Friday and Saturday nights, at the end of May, at the old Sutton Opera House, eight dollars for adults; five for children and seniors. Shelly was fine with the news, and departed for coffee.

"Yes, so, what's it about?" Anita wanted to know. It was early, a couple curlers remained in her hair; she was looking at mail at the desk in the office.

"Historical drama," Celia said, leaning in the doorway. "Slaves trying to escape to freedom."

"Oh, that," Anita looked over her reading glasses. "Harriet Tubman, you mean, and the Underground Railroad? I've seen it. It's good."

"No, something new." Celia hedged. "Made up, really. One of the student's brothers wrote it." She did of course want Anita to come and support the play, but she didn't want any, well, interference. "I'll get you good seats," she promised. "Especially if you place an ad in the program." Laying out the program happened to be one of Celia's jobs.

Now Anita was smiling. "Good girl, taking care of business. Sure, put an ad in for us, the smallest; you know we don't have money lying around."

First sale!

In her free hours, Celia skittered about town, putting up flyers, soliciting ads, purchasing supplies for the set and the box office, and crossing items off her list of props to be collected or made for the play. On top of the list were shovel, ax, and pitchfork. At first, Celia assumed they could borrow the real things—why not? They were easy to obtain and obviously more realistic. But Leona wouldn't have it. They had to be constructed, even the shovel, with cardboard and duct tape if need be.

"No accidents," she said. "And no heart attacks."

When it was quiet at New You, Celia would leave early or take an hour off to do her theater business. She waited until Shelly was at her desk doing paperwork, and there were no classes scheduled. It pained her a little to deduct the time, but she was willing, in the name of theater.

Her travels took her into the center of Sutton, to the printers and the paint store, and the little old-fashioned hardware store she enjoyed poking around. Somehow, she often found herself crossing the block behind the Grand Marsh Inn. More than once, she wandered by the dumpster, looking to see who was coming and going from the staff entrance—someone she knew like Eldridge, Lacey, or Cuffie. Looking, really, for Jay. She only saw him once, and he was with two other guys, so she wouldn't dream of making herself known. Instead, she ducked behind the dumpster, embarrassed. What if she did run into him, anyway? What else, but embarrassment or rejection. In her fantasy, Jay turned to her and said, "Finally, I'm free. Let's take a chance, see what happens." And then, kissing and more, although it wasn't clear just where this was taking place. It seemed to be a room at the Inn, not that that was likely. None of it was likely. Still, she couldn't keep her feet from taking her past the Inn, and sometimes stopping, looking, hoping, dreaming.

On an afternoon break, Celia was at the mall grocery store, her last stop before New You. She had run out of tape for the flyers. In addition, she needed a box of tampons. With a few spare minutes, she thought of picking up a magazine for home. Turning the corner to the magazine aisle, she spotted a large, dark, childlike shape on the floor, legs sprawled, turning the pages of a comic book. It was a face and shape she knew: Josie, from the Inn.

"Josie!" she called out, coming closer. "How are you?" Disturbed from her reading, Josie looked up with a frown, and fixed Celia with the eye that did not wander. Celia stooped down next to her. It was the first time she'd ever seen Josie in jeans and tennis shoes, her midsection wide and comfortable, relaxed and taking up plenty of space.

"It's Celia, from the Inn. Remember? I used to be a waitress."

The light dawned ever so slowly, and Celia was rewarded by a smile of recognition, and hopefully, good associations.

"You that yellow hair girl that wears the fish," Josie declared.

"That's me," Celia agreed. "So how have you been?"

This question was a stumper. Either Josie wasn't asked often or she didn't think much about her state of being. She gazed down the aisle, contemplating.

"OK, I guess," she finally answered, glancing at *Snoopy and Peanuts,* like that might put an end to the small talk.

"How's Eldridge?" Celia tried jogging the conversation.

Surprisingly, Josie's face tightened with some unrecognizable emotion. "Not so good. He moving slower and slower, and he call in sick some time."

Strange. He certainly was well when they had gone out at the Starlight, tiring only just before Celia did on the dance floor.

"What's wrong with him; do you know?"

"Nobody know."

"That's too bad. If you see him, could you please say hello for me?" Josie's wandering eye found Celia's face, and then roamed away. OK, not likely "Well, how about Cuffie, Phil, Lacey, and all of them?"

"Same. Same."

Casually, lightly, she went on. "And what about Jay and Pauline? Are they still together?" Here was her opportunity to find out what she couldn't otherwise ask, shamelessly pumping the slow-witted girl.

"You afraid she gonna fight with you?" Josie asked, grinning broadly. Maybe she wasn't so slow after all.

Celia frowned. "No, no. That's all over with. I was just asking how they were doing."

"Had a big fight," Josie announced. "She threw a water pitcher at him, and she got him, too."

"Really?" How interesting. Celia leaned in closer. She could smell Josie's combination of bubble gum and hair oil. "Were you there?"

"Right in the kitchen," Josie confirmed. "She yelling and yelling, and he tell her to get out of there."

"What was it about?" It was terrible to gossip like this, and kind of awkward to keep bent over, especially when other shoppers passed with their carts. More than one middle-aged housewife gave them the once-over: a white girl in sweats carrying Scotch tape and a box of tampons, and a black girl on the floor with a comic book, engaged in some kind of social conversation.

Josie shrugged.

"Was he messing around with some other girl?" Celia kept pushing, although it pained her to say the words.

"Don't know," Josie said. She scrunched up her face, trying to recall. "She tell him grow up," she said finally.

"And what did he say?" Celia asked, staring intensely into Josie's eyes. Her knees hurt but she ignored the pain.

"Get off my back," Josie said, scowling, with some heat. Celia's eyes widened, thinking first that the words were meant for her. "We trying to work here." Josie went on, a pretty good imitation of Jay. "That's when she throwed the pitcher at him. She turned back to Celia, smiling. "She tough. She could whoop you, no problem." Clearly, Josie had a lot of confidence in Pauline the Ferocious.

Well, well, well. Whatever it meant—the final end, or just another chapter in the ongoing love/hate battle—Celia found the news immensely satisfying.

"Got to go," she said, getting up stiffly from her crouch and starting to hurry away. Then, feeling a twinge, she turned back. "It was nice to see you, Josie. Take care of yourself. " But Josie had already returned to the comic book.

Celia paid for her purchases and walked out with a light, quick step, buoyed by Josie's interesting news.

Later in the evening, Celia put down her mystery, getting ready for sleep. Her thoughts returned to the encounter with Josie at the supermarket—and the news about Jay and Pauline. It wasn't very nice of her, really, to probe Josie like that. And, she had been enjoying someone else's adversity, their conflicts and troubles. But when she closed her eyes, there was a smile on her face. So, the high and mighty are not so high and mighty anymore. She turned over on her stomach, burrowing into the pillow, reviewing her own status. Grace was great, and Celia had a comfy place to stay. Her health was good, and she was stronger and fitter every day. Work was fine; money trickling in. And this play was shaping up nicely, better than she could have imagined. Thank God for Leona. The script was more than good; it was commanding. And she had brought a truckload of costumes and materials they could use for the set. Some of the kids were stand-offish with Celia, but she was comfortable working with Alonzo, and the others would come around. It was going to be awesome, and Celia would be part of it.

So what, she had no savings and was no closer to college? Or the fact that there was no boyfriend, black or white, at present. Probably better that way. Otherwise, at the moment, things were not so bad in the life of Celia Lennon; in fact, rather exciting. And yet, as she slipped toward sleep, there was this strange undercurrent of something else: anxiety, nervousness, even fear. That maybe she was wading into murky waters, taking this on as she was, still an outsider, still unaware of all going on around her, except to know that some folks, black and white, would not like it, or her.

On Saturday morning, Celia arrived at the make-shift shop at the back of the theater. She had picked up donuts, coffee, and juice on the way. Alonzo was already at work building a platform. All his tools were assembled on a counter, ready at hand, like a dentist. Behind him, on a rope suspended between two walls, were the backdrops, one a night sky pinned with foil stars and the other blue with small white waves to represent the water.

"Ah, bright and early," Alonzo said when he saw her.

"Reporting for duty," she said, putting down her bags with the goodies. "I brought something for the troops."

His slow smile spread. "Yes, well, they'll be here in a bit. I like an early start."

"Me, too. I'm ready to go. Just tell me what to do, and I'll try my best."

Mostly Celia held boards on the saw-horse or handed over tools to Alonzo, who briefly explained what he was doing, while Celia decided she'd rather watch than handle a power saw. Periodically, she swept up wood shavings on the floor. Between times, she sat on a stool near the counter, sipping coffee and chatting about her family and life in Santa Cruz. Alonzo listened with a half-smile, and Celia thought it might be nice for him to hear about what might be in store for him at college. Somehow, she found herself relating various plays she had been in: Shakespeare's *Much Ado about Nothing,* and *Midsummer Night's Dream,* and a Greek comedy called *Lysistrata* in which she and the other female characters vowed not to have sex with their husbands until they give up going to war.

"Those are some good stories," Alonzo said, during a break. He took a long drink of the apple juice, wiping sweat from his forehead. "That's really something, they were thinking about things like that way back then."

"I know," Celia said. "Some things really haven't changed all that much. It makes you think and it makes you feel, right? That's why it's so powerful." She sighed. "I love the theater. I know it's not a great way to make a living, but it just means so much to me. You know?"

He didn't look too clear.

"Well, what I mean is that the people in the theater at school became like a family for me, especially after we moved to California, and I had to start all over, knowing nobody. I'll be the first to admit some theater folks are kooks, and totally hung up on themselves—narcissists." She paused, letting him add a new word to his vocabulary. "Or else, they're *extremely* insecure and always looking for attention. That's why they—maybe I should say we—act, instead of sports or academics, or whatever. But, for the most part, they, we, are very accepting and tolerant, because everyone's struggling to be accepted in some way."

"Even you?" Alonzo said. "With your golden hair and pretty smile?"

Celia's mouth opened to protest, but she stopped herself, realizing that his question was genuine, and that he had paid her a compliment. Then she was a bit flummoxed—another good vocabulary word—how to reply.

"Even me," she said, finally. "Don't get me wrong. It's not like we were a bunch of losers. It's just that theater is so challenging and demanding, and gives you a purpose, and you all have to work together, and then it's all over."

She snapped her fingers. "Like that, it's gone. And all the magic: I love getting dressed up and putting on make-up, strolling under the lights for everyone to see and wonder about. I've miss that," she said with a sigh. "I really have."

Alonzo nodded, picking up a piece of sandpaper. They heard the sound of footsteps and voices behind them, coming in through the back door to the theater, off a little alley way. Big, braided Bettina, it sounded like, and a couple of guys.

"Here to help," Bettina said, as she appeared through the doorway. Her expression darkened slightly at the sight of Alonzo at work while Celia sat dreamily with a coffee and donut. The guys shuffled in behind her, two boys from the cast and a couple new recruits. Bettina, with her loud voice and commanding presence, had a persuasive way. Plus the fact that she was bigger and taller than some of them.

Alonzo paused to show them the column he had started on and to give instructions to finish the platform. Bettina had come specifically to work on the trees and bushes, and Celia said she'd help.

"Full speed ahead," Celia cajoled the group. "Leona's coming by at one o'clock, and she's bringing somebody named Drew to check on us. A real tech expert, I guess." She made a slight face. "I don't even know if it's a girl or guy, to tell you the truth. What kind of name is that?"

No one answered, not even a shrug.

"But it doesn't matter one bit," Celia said. "Let's show them what we can do."

They broke only once for a snack, and worked through until they heard Leona's voice in the back hallway.

She strode in with Drew right behind her. They made quite a pair, Drew looming over Leona, sporting a pale blond buzz-cut, a plaid shirt, cargo pants, and work boots. Suddenly, Leona the lion didn't seem quite so scary. They stood in the center of the room, gazing critically at the work in progress.

Leona turned to Drew. "What do you think?"

Drew walked over to Alonzo's column, running a hand over the long curves.

"Not bad," she said.

She bounced on the newly completed platform, which did not give way.

"It'll do."

She examined the decorated drop cloths and beginnings of the field/garden. "Fair enough."

They had passed the test. With few words, Drew took over the set building and kept them at it for a couple more hours. A platform with steps and a couple columns were erected—the outline of the plantation house. At four-thirty, Celia said she had to leave.

"Grace needs the car," she said to Alonzo. "Are you going to be here tomorrow?"

He nodded. "And you?"

"Maybe. I'll try, but I have a couple other things to take care of."

As she was leaving, Alonzo put down the sandpaper and followed her out to the back door.

"What is it?" she asked.

"Just a question," he said, then stopped to wet his lips. "Do you think you might like to go to the prom with me, end of school?"

Celia was stunned. Where did that come from?

"The prom?"

"Sutton High senior prom. I thought you might like it—you know, get all dressed up nice, put on some make up, fancy shoes. Lights, dancing, music." His face contracted with mischievous humor. "Everyone looking at you, wondering about you, the beautiful debutande."

"Debutante," she corrected automatically. "Yes, that's me. But Alonzo," she started in on him, "what are you thinking? That's crazy talk."

He put a hand in the air. "You can think about it, tell me later."

"Alonzo," again. "Seriously . . ." And then she stopped herself. What was so wrong with the idea? She did love getting dressed up, performing, so to speak. She had told him so herself.

Her head wagged back and forth. "Alonzo," she said, "you just might be as foolish as I am. But, OK, I'll think about it. Right now, though, this play. Right?" Then, before she turned away, "Thanks for the invitation."

Just as the elements of the play were coming together, trouble began. Not one thing, Celia reflected, but battalions, like it said in *Hamlet*—or something like that. The first of the problems was relatively, and literally, small: mice. They were all over the abandoned opera building, particularly backstage where they left their droppings scattered like brown rice. They got into a bag of snacks that Celia had left for the crew who was working so industriously on the set. At night, during rehearsals, one might steal across the stage, or a couple might pop out from behind the curtains. And while the mice didn't make much noise, the humans got pretty worked up. Plus, the audience might not appreciate small furry creatures scurrying through the aisles or over their toes during the performance, especially in the dark. Celia and Leona concluded they had to do something, starting with traps.

"Thankfully, not rats," Leona commented. "They say children and animals don't belong on stage—too distracting, you know? A rat would clear the house. Mice are bad enough."

Even with the traps, which they could hear snapping shut from time to time, the mice made their occasional appearances.

Again, Celia turned to Alonzo, anything he could think of to control the problem. His answer: cats. From somewhere, he brought in Smoky and Soot, two dusky feline brothers, setting them up with water and food, keeping them busy on mice patrol. Pretty effective they were, too. One time, just before rehearsal, Celia found Alonzo scattering some kind of dry, light brown substance at the corners of the stage and backstage. She thought for sure it was some kind of rodent control, but he said no. When she pressed him, he said, "Tobacco, for good luck. That's all, no harm done, and it might help." She had nothing to say to that, honestly stumped by Alonzo's odd fits of superstition, when he seemed otherwise such a rational young man.

The next development, out of the blue, was a phone call just after dinner at the apartment. Celia and Grace were at the table just waiting for their tea to cool.

When the phone rang, the two girls looked at each other. Their mother would not likely call at this time, unless it was an emergency.

Grace got up from the table. She said hello; a deep male voice reached Celia's ear.

"Yes, it is," Grace said into the phone. "Oh, yes. Of course I remember. Jimmy was such a brave boy. He's OK, I hope?"

The male voice again, while Celia looked on full of curiosity. *Who could this little boy be?*

"Great, great," Grace responded, and then listened some more. And then some more.

"Oh," said Grace, her brow furrowed. "I see. Well, she's right here." She put her hand over the receiver. "Mr. Tanner, the principal at the high school. He wants to talk to you." Then, whispering with a kind of warning look, "His son was my patient."

Celia's jaw dropped. What could it be—except the play? She got up from the table, taking the receiver from Grace.

"Hello," she said into the phone. "This is Celia."

"Yes, hello." It was a deep, pleasant voice; not hostile, anyway. "Bill Tanner here, from the high school. Do you have a minute we could talk a little about this play you're involved in?"

"Ye-es," Celia said. "I guess so." Her eyes met Grace's, and she mouthed, "The play." Grace's lips tightened, as she took her seat back at the table.

"Here's the thing, Celia." He cleared his throat. "I got your name from Brad Timilty, the English teacher. He said you might know what's going on. He told me he'd met you, and that you were a level-headed young woman, a theater professional. He also said he heard you were involved in this new play, about slavery. Is that correct?"

"Yes," she said, and stopped there. Let him say what he wanted. Her eyes flickered to Grace, who was stirring honey into her tea, listening.

"So, Celia, there are rumors going around school about the play, some of them quite disturbing, but it's my job to get to the root of things. Believe me, I've been around long enough to know that rumors are often way off-base, but maybe I can put a stop to this before it gets to be a problem for us or for the people putting on the play."

"What are they saying, exactly?" she asked.

"That the play is anti-white, that it promotes armed resistance, that it contains rape and violence, it uses the word 'Nigger.' Actually, Brad told me he'd read the script, and most of that action isn't on the stage, but the concepts, apparently, are represented—at least in the version he read. What's your take on this?"

It's all true, Celia thought, a pit in her stomach. On face, it probably didn't sound very good.

"It's been changed, rewritten quite a lot," she said, carefully. "The focus is more on the relationships and motivations, not so much about the, well, uprising itself." That was not bad, for off the cuff. At the table, Grace was listening intently with little expression. Probably at the end of her rope. *This is it,* thought Celia, *she's had enough of me, and I'll be packing my bags to leave. And I'll understand completely.* But, not until after the play. Surely, Grace could see how important this was to Celia, and to all these kids.

The principal, Bill, went on. "I see. I see. Well, it's not my place or my call to tell you and your fellow thespians what to do. After all, there is such a thing as freedom of speech, and it is outside of school. But, they are my students, and it's becoming an issue for other students. And then one of the parents called. So, that makes it my problem. My thought is this: what if we have Brad Timilty read over the new script, and see what he thinks, his view on the current state of things."

"Hm . . . I don't know . . ."

"He can advise you, perhaps, to make the rough edges more smooth, and he can let me and the rest of us know what's actually in the play—not a call to violent protest, I assume, as some of the kids are saying."

"No!" Celia said, her heart starting to race. "I mean, that's not the intent of it at all. It takes place over a hundred years ago. It's about what happened in the past, a situation some people were in, what they did, and what the consequences of it were. That's what a play is. *I* can tell you that. Mr. Timilty doesn't need to check it out."

It was quiet on the other end of the line. "Yes, well. A specific objection, if I may say so, is that there are no positive white characters, and that the slave masters' son and daughter are terrible, morally reprehensible people."

Celia was starting to vibrate with emotion, willing her voice not to shake. She knew this was trouble, and that it was more than she could expect Grace to deal with. But she had to fight for *Anticus;* she had to.

"It's a story, not real life."

"Still, well, don't we want something that is uplifting and inspiring for our young people?"

She took a breath.

"Who says it's not—for some *young people?*"

The principal sighed. "Celia, I'm going to have to trust you on this. But I'm afraid you will bring down the wrath of some of the people in this town, students and parents, if the play is as offensive as the kids seem to think."

"Let them come see it for themselves, and then decide," Celia got out. "It's going to be good, very good."

"I will certainly make every effort to be there," he said. "And I wish you the best. But, maybe going forward, you might keep some of this in mind, what we've talked about. And I'll be sure to emphasize it's a historical play— in costume, I presume?"

"Yes."

"In some unspecified town."

"Yes."

"And not a rally of any sort."

"No."

Unless you mean a rally to face an ugly past, Celia said to herself.

"And listen," Bill, said. "We're really very grateful to have someone like you take an interest in our students and in this kind of undertaking. If things don't work out . . . as well as you hope . . . with this production, we could really use your services in some other capacity down the line, next year's production. There could be a small stipend . . ."

"Good night, Mr. Tanner, and thanks for the thought."

"Yes, good night, Celia. I'm glad we had this chance to talk."

When Celia hung up the phone, Grace was gazing at her, hands around a tea mug that was already empty "Well?" she said.

Celia sighed, sinking into her chair. What could she say?

"There's a problem, I take it," Grace said, her expression grave. "How serious is it?"

"I'm not sure. Really." She slapped the table with her hand. "The play is really good, if people would just give it a chance, instead of just trying to stir up bad feelings. You know how hard we've been working on this. We believe in it."

Grace put her hands to her face, silent, thinking. Not very happy thoughts, it appeared. "So, he was trying to talk you out of it?" she asked, finally.

"Or change it, or have one of the teachers edit out the disturbing parts."

Grace heaved a sigh, closing her eyes. "This town," she said, "not eager to change, is it?" Her eyes blinked open. "He wasn't threatening you, was he, Principal Tanner? He's a nice man, from my experience with his son, and people say he's been a good principal."

Celia considered. "No, he was perfectly pleasant. It was more like a bribe—they 'might' have a job for me in the future, if this play doesn't work out."

"Oh, my," Grace said, a small smile breaking out. "That would be interesting." Then a cloud crossed her face. "But I don't see that happening."

Celia swallowed. "You mean, I'll be gone by then?"

"We'll most likely both be gone by then."

"But you're not saying . . . you're not telling me you want me to leave, right now?"

"No, I'm not saying that. But maybe you should think about what he said, Principal Tanner. Maybe it's not the place for you, this play or this town. I know you want to be involved in the show and see it succeed, but you could just stay in the background, like a supporter." She leveled her gaze. "This play really should come from the black kids, don't you think?"

Celia sat quietly, rubbing the surface of the old table, the center of family life for so many years. She didn't want to give the play up; she was so sure it was the right thing, for her, for the kids, for everybody.

"It's just going to make things harder," Grace said, standing up and resting a hand on the back of her chair. "For both of us—in the relatively short time we have left here. Why stir the pot? Why cause unnecessary problems? Don't you think we have enough to deal with just carrying on our lives?"

"I have to do it," Celia said, staring at her own stilled hands. "I just have to."

Grace sighed, turning away toward the sink.

"Don't worry," Celia said after her. "It'll be all right, you'll see. It'll be great."

At the opera house, rehearsals were going full speed ahead, and Celia didn't tell anyone about the principal's phone call, not even Leona. It was like a dream, though not a good one. Celia refused to be sidetracked, or let anyone else be. It was challenging keeping up at New You, and then all the extra hours spent on the play, all-consuming as it always was before opening day. In addition, Celia was sore all over from a new program Anita had insisted on incorporating, a series of calisthenics straight out of the Army Field Manual. "If they can do it, so can we," was Anita's motto. But it was hard, and not that fun, although Celia had to admit it got results. Fortunately, perhaps, the masses revolted, and except for a couple of fitness buffs, none of the women liked the program, and either complained or stopped coming until Anita, finally, conceded defeat. Otherwise, the fitness classes were routine by now, and Celia went through the steps, her mind engaged elsewhere, on the stage and the set. Sometimes, she was in the story of *Anticus* itself, far back in time, although not so far away in place.

And then, two weeks before the show was due to open, a crisis: the white girl backed out. She didn't want to play the white girl in the play, Laurette. "Too time-consuming," she said, and she "didn't really like the character."

"I suspected it," Leona told Celia at the beginning of the next rehearsal.

"You did? But she was doing great. And it's a good part, important."

Leona wrinkled her nose. "She was uncomfortable, I could tell. When it came to picturing herself up there on stage in front of friends and family, declaring her passion for this black man who is a slave, and all the things she's willing to do to be with him, she just couldn't do it." She expelled a breath. "Not that I really blame her. It takes maturity and commitment and guts."

Celia was surprised. Leona, MizHard Core, was letting the girl off the hook—until they locked eyes.

"You're going to have to do it, Celia," she said.

"No, I don't think so." The idea had crossed Celia's mind earlier, certainly. Why wouldn't it? She just had a very sure conviction that she should stay behind the curtain.

"Or, the show doesn't go on."

"It will do more harm than good," Celia said. "Some people are going to have a problem with me on stage—an outsider, you know." Really, she was thinking how much it would upset Grace; how upset Grace would be with her.

"So what? Like we should be afraid of stepping on people's toes? Forget it. We can't find anyone else now, and they'd probably have the same reaction." She tipped her head, the light glinting off her small, dark eyes. "You want the show to go on?"

Celia nodded.

"And you can act, can't you?"

Put that way, the only answer was, "Yes."

"Then, it's got to be you. Get your lines down for next rehearsal. Costume's no problem; you can wear the same clothes."

Celia looked at the floor, feeling the adrenaline rush. "Well, OK, I guess."

"Step up, girl," Leona said. "Two weeks, we're on."

Chapter 22

Two weeks were not enough, and yet more than enough for Celia to get ready for the play. There was the same intensity she remembered from other productions, the focus, the repetition, the endless rehearsals that went on late into the night,. But something was different, obviously. Two weeks to nail down a part, difficult in that Laurette was essentially the villainess—she causes Milo to betray Anticus, his unknown half-brother, and the rebellion, and his own sense of honor. All in all, not a very likeable girl. Celia struggled to make the role work, knowing she had to make Laurette something more than the caricature of a spoiled, rich girl. The first rehearsal was not promising; Celia could feel it herself—no matter how haughty and highbrow she played it, Laurette's lines came out flat. Halfway through the scene, Leona called a break and took Celia aside.

"It's just empty," Leona said, running a hand through her short-cropped hair. "Sound and fury, signifying nothing."

Celia was devastated. She didn't think it was that bad. But Leona's words recalled something the reviewer had said about her back in Santa Cruz all those months ago. "Frothy, lightweight."

"You've got to channel your inner bitch," Leona advised. Celia stared open-mouthed, fearing that the truth was, maybe she didn't have one.

"It's in there somewhere. No woman gets through life without the ugly monster rearing its head. Just think of something, sometime that really pissed you off; something that was just not right, just not right." Still not much response. "Parent bullshit; a guy dumps you; a girlfriend crosses you. Tap it, Celia," Leona went on. "Righteous anger about the unfairness of the universe; something done wrong to someone you love."

And, of course, that was it, what Leona said. How everything had shifted and slipped since Celia's father had died, and her mother had stumbled, and Grace had to be practical, and Celia couldn't finish college. That was all grossly unfair, and she was mad about it. Not to mention Jay and his mixed messages; and how the Beckers had treated her at the Grand Marsh Inn; and that despicable man in the hotel room. And Pauline who wanted to fight her. And those boys who mocked and taunted her and Wanda. What about the acorns! Never mind the fact that she was exhausted and had dropped a two-pound weight on her toe and it was throbbing.

A smiled crossed Celia's face; the bitch was there. That angry, desperate creature who couldn't get what she wanted and needed, and was ready to attack anyone in her way.

Leona smiled, too. They were ready to get back to work on the scene. Only thing was that Laurette was now raging and vicious, an unredeemable harpy, which wasn't quite what Leona wanted either. Finally, Leona said to Celia, "You know, the girl is human. Laurette thinks she's in love. And, in the end, what she feels is love for Milo, not just lust. Her final action is for his benefit, not hers. Try to keep that in mind."

As they got nearer to opening night, they all had to face the fact that the play packed a powerful message that would not be welcomed by all. Celia was not even sure what Grace or the women from New You would make of it. In the last days, she found she was in a kind of sensory overload, taking in so many words and images from the play, yet still leading three and sometimes four fitness classes a day. And registering new clients. And cleaning and vacuuming. With a sore toe.

Celia found out that Alonzo's birthday was three days before opening night. She didn't hear it from him; some of the other actors and crew members teased him about getting drunk on his eighteenth birthday. Certainly, he didn't expect anything from Celia. Yet, she wanted to acknowledge that it was a special day, and that he had become something more than a high school pest following her down the road.

Celia had only two scenes on stage. Otherwise, she was to the side, out of sight, as the stage manager, cueing the other actors. There was little time during the course of the play that she wasn't focused on the action, as actress, prompter, and line feeder, learning almost everyone's lines by heart. They all stumbled occasionally; only the tiny, frail-looking girl who played Mariah was flawless; an odd choice, Celia thought, for the powerful grandmother figure, but Leona was adamant that she was the one.

The actor who played Milo was a very light-skinned, good-looking fellow, but not nearly as compelling as Anticus, a short, wiry boy who held his own with his on-stage wife, Tabitha, played by Bettina, twice his size. "Milo" was also the boyfriend of Desiree, the playwright's sister and a driving force behind the play. At first, Celia held back when Laurette and Milo kissed in a passionate embrace.

"No one's buying that," Leona said from the front row.

So Celia closed her eyes and let her lips find Milo's, only it was Carlos she was kissing, and then Jay, then Alonzo. Her eyes fluttered open, not at all what she expected. Only, of course, it was Milo, who was a pretty good kisser after all.

"Ooh, that's hot," said a stage hand, watching the run-through next to Leona.

"Too hot," said Desiree, a dark-skinned girl with short, stylish hair and arty, ethnic clothes. "Make sure it's just acting."

"That will do," said Leona.

The matter of Alonzo's birthday kept Celia awake one night, along with everything else. His eighteenth, it was a pretty big deal. Besides the teasing, she didn't think anyone else was planning a celebration. Bettina or Desiree, perhaps? But they were busy themselves with school and the play. It wasn't Celia's place to organize a cake and a party, if he even wanted something like that.

"A bottle of champagne," Celia decided finally, straightening the bed sheets. She could pick it up at the liquor store on her way to New You. "That's what I'll do. We can open it, share a glass, and make a toast."

On the day of Alonzo's birthday, she brought the bottle and some plastic cups in a paper bag to rehearsal.

Just after Leona dismissed them for the evening, she found Alonzo in the light booth. "Hey, you," she said. "I hear it's your special day. Just wanted to say 'Happy Birthday.'"

He looked up, surprised. He had been winding electrical wires into a loop. "Yeah, eighteen, finally." His smile spread. "Thanks a lot; appreciate it."

"Well," she said, holding up the bag. "I got a little something for you. But it had to wait until after rehearsal."

"Such a kind and magnanimous lady," he said, bowing from the waist. "So, what you got there?"

"Champagne!" she said, as she drew the bottle from the bag. She had to suppress a giggle, feeling a little like a high schooler herself. "And a couple of plastic cups. I thought we could go out in the back alley and have a little toast to you and your future."

He couldn't have looked more pleased. And then his face started to contract. "That sounds great. But, um, just one thing. Some of the guys, and the girls, they're waiting for me, to take me out for a beer at the Pizza Palace. Same idea, I guess."

"Oh great!" Celia exclaimed, pleased for him. But still, a little disappointed. She hadn't been invited, of course. She wasn't really part of that world, or one of them. "You should do that. Just take the bottle with you." She thrust the bag toward him.

He was standing in front of her now. "No, I want that toast with you. I'll tell them to go ahead; I can join them in a bit." His eyebrows lifted, "Would you want to come, too?"

"Oh, no," she said, flustered. "I don't want to butt in. I . . . well. I don't think it would feel right, do you?"

"Alonzo!" They heard Desiree's voice. "We're waiting on you. Come on before they change the drinking age. Any minute now." Desiree walked through the doorway of the booth, now rather crowded with the three of them. Behind her appeared Bettina's head, then several others.

"I'll stay back here a minute," Alonzo said. "Celia brought me something for my birthday, and I want to take some time to enjoy it, and show my appreciation."

It wasn't badly worded, but it couldn't stop the twittering. Desiree's face clouded, and then, she shook her head with a wry smile. "Suit yourself. You know where we'll be." Then she turned to Celia. "No reason you can't come with us."

Celia's face lit up, grateful. "Thanks, Desiree, but no thanks. We won't be long."

A few side-glances, but the crowd turned and left.

Celia and Alonzo went out through the back door into the cool evening air. The one spotlight shining into the alley made everything lose color, only black and white remaining, and all the shades of gray.

"Just pop it," Celia said, suddenly giddy even without a drink.

Alonzo got the cork off, the explosion followed by the sound of little critters scampering in the alley, making them laugh. Champagne spilled out the open bottle top.

Alonzo poured while Celia held the cups. They held the cups in the air, and mock-clinked together. With his first taste, Alonzo sputtered a little.

"Hope you like it," she said, a bit at a loss for words. "It's a bit on the sweet side."

"The sweet side," he repeated. "It's the best I've ever had."

"The only champagne you've ever had. Right?"

She took another sip, the bubbles so cool on her parched throat. Alonzo took another, slower drink, which left his lips wet and glistening in the light. He finished his cup and she poured him another. She closed her eyes a moment, letting the silence of the night take over, after the constant sound of voices on stage, speaking and shouting. Only, it wasn't quiet long. A siren sounded from the direction of the hospital, and then drew closer. She opened her eyes again to find Alonzo looking at her, his eyes soft and watchful.

Celia slapped the side of her head. "Oh, I forgot, the birthday song. No, really, I have to." She wanted to sing it for him, and not in a silly way. At least, not too silly. As she finished, and he applauded, blue and white lights flashed, lighting up the alley walls, like a festive party or a disco club.

The siren, the lights . . . police. Something was up, not that there was much crime in Sutton.

"Happy eighteenth birthday, Alonzo," she said. She stepped in closer, ready to kiss him. Just a birthday kiss, of course. There really couldn't be anything more, under the circumstances. Her head tipped back, eyes wide open, feeling the power she had over him, and wishing quite sincerely that it was power for good.

Then came the sound of static and walkie-talkies. And then a figure appeared at the opening of the alley way. The beam from a powerful flashlight blinded their vision.

"Police," said the man, approaching.

The flashlight first caught Alonzo. "Stay where you are."

And then, the beam traveled to Celia and her cup. "What have we here, date night?" When he lowered the flashlight, Celia saw the smirk on the man's face.

"A birthday," Celia said primly.

The police officer guffawed. "No worries, I don't care what you're up to. Has anyone been by here—two, three kids within the last five, ten minutes?"

"No one since we came out. Is it serious?"

"Punks. They smashed a car window. There's been a series of break-ins downtown, mostly cars." His gaze swept the alley and then returned to Celia. "Young lady, this is no place for you, this time of night. Maybe you need an escort home?"

It took a moment to register what he meant, that she wasn't perfectly safe, with Alonzo.

"No, thank you. I'm fine."

The officer turned to leave, and Celia caught Alonzo's expression, anger and resentment.

"Best we be going," he said quietly. "I'll walk you to your car." So much for the champagne. So much for the kiss. So much for Happy Eighteenth Birthday.

So soon it was Thursday, the day before the first performance of *Anticus*. Celia had the day off and was at the apartment, going over her checklist, one more time. One last time. She re-counted the bills in the cash-box, borrowed from New You. In a tote bag, she had a folder of paper signs—Concessions, Rest Rooms, etc. Plus, scissors, tape, markers, pens and pencils, push-pins, more duct tape—whatever might be needed. Another bag with paper towels, cups and snacks for the cast and crew. She checked the kitchen clock—almost 9:30, time to head to the printers to pick up the programs for the play. Afterwards, she was going to drop off tickets for Anita and Shelly and their families at New You—good seats, but not front row. And for Saturday night, as they had agreed, by Celia's request. One thing she wasn't sure she could handle was looking Anita in the eye, as well as everything else, on Opening Night. Grace, too, was coming the second night, with Roxanne and Alec.

One last time, Celia looked over the mock-up of the one-page, folded program she had submitted earlier in the week, running her finger through the text for any possible typo's—too late to change. Her eye caught the words: *Time: sometime in the past, before the end of slavery. Setting, somewhere, anywhere in this country where people sought to escape slavery.* There was a simple graphic, drawn by Desiree, of a black woman holding the hand of two small boys—one black, and one who looked white. Celia wondered if the picture might prove confusing, as the two sons of Mariah, Milo and Anticus, were not brought up together and didn't know they were half-brothers. But all the others had wanted to use it, so she said nothing. In the program, she had spelled out the characters' known and unknown relationships to each other, sensing the audience might get a little lost. It was a bit much: Milo, son of Mariah and the master of Rosebush; Anticus, son of Mariah and a slave on the Willowbend Plantation; and Laurette, the master's daughter at Rosebush, where she had been brought up with Milo, who was her unknown half-brother. And the two plantations, Rosebush and Willowbend, only ten miles apart but different worlds.

Then it was opening night. All that work over the last weeks leading up to this moment. The cast and crew assembled, the audience arrived, and the play began. All Celia was aware of as she stood back stage were the words, poetic and sometimes grandiose, rising and falling like music. She stood in costume on her spot, marked with white tape, a pen flashlight in hand to follow the script, which she knew now by heart.

First, Anticus's wife, Tabitha, after her rape by the master's son at Willowbend, in her tattered skirt, stained in ketchup blood, to her husband: "Fight for us, Anticus. It doesn't matter the cost, only that we try. I would take up arms myself, if I had the strength. I would rather die than continue in this world. When that boy rape me, he had no care for me, nor this babe inside me—our babe. He like to kill me when I hold back from him. I say, 'You gonna lose a slave child you beat me like this,' but he don't stop. He leave me bleeding. You kill him, or you kill me and this babe. I jump in the river; watch me."

Celia's first appearance as Laurette on the porch at Rosebush: in a full-skirted red gown, her hair piled high on her head, gemstones at her neck. Pacing back and forth, a haughty pout on her face: "This rebellion will never happen; I will not let it. When Milo warned me, he thought I would flee. Never! I told him that he must stop it and save himself from certain death. Then, my father will reward him, and we can be together in the only way we can. What else can I do? I must have him or I cannot live. Daddy has never said no, and I have never learned to do without my heart's desire. Milo is my obsession, the strongest, most handsome man in the county who could pass for white any place but here. All he has to do is whisper in Daddy's ear, 'I heard word . . . ' Those, those niggers will be whipped and killed, as they deserve. To think of rising against us! Then things will be as they were, as they're supposed to be. And I will have Milo." As she shakes her head, departing the stage, Celia feels a hot wind of anger and contempt at her back. *This is how it feels to be hated.*

Then Anticus at Willowbend, rallying the other slaves on a dark stage with flashlights in paper bags to mimic torches: "Brothers, we have no other future. Else, we live and die here, this hell on earth, and the same for our children and their children. Who else will help us to freedom but ourselves? We have our will, our tools, and boats that wait for us. I will put a knife into the overseer, and then all that remains is master and son. Their women and young ones are gone to the city. Everything must be done quickly and in silence. Then on to Rosebush, where brothers watch for our sign. Between us, we will slay those who oppose us and escape to the shore, where our women and children wait, and the small boats that will take us North, all in silence so that no one knows we're gone until we're safe away."

The betrayal outside of Rosebush: Anticus, carrying a painted plastic shovel, scouts ahead of the others, whispering behind. Milo, ax in hand, appears alone, welcomed first as an ally. He reaches a hand to Anticus, but instead knocks the shovel away, and raises the ax, with its blade of roof tiles and duct tape, over Anticus's head. "Anticus, I cannot spare you. This is too far gone. The master knows all and has gathered others. It could never have prospered, this dream of escape. The whole wide world is a net to catch you and return you back. I spare you that agony. Do not damn me my chance to live, a man as light in color and as able as my master's sons, with only the sin of being born to a slave woman."

Milo pauses, the cue for sound effects. Instead, dead silence, for one beat, two, three. Then the boy working the tape recorder presses the button, full volume, and a pack of dogs was unleashed with blood-curdling cries. Celia felt a gasp in the auditorium, and could only wonder how that terrible noise was captured in the first place. The volume was adjusted, and human shouts began, off-stage. Milo resumes: "I hear the master's men. The guns are loaded. They await my signal. You are first to die, Anticus, but the others meet certain death in moments to come. Farewell." (swings ax; lights out.) This, unfortunately, was when the head of the ax detached and went flying, landing with a plonk, lost in the sounds of the uprising.

Then Celia's last turn as Laurette, after the uprising, about blinded by the stage lights: "Milo is my heaven and hell. He was the sun of my life, and now he is gone. I helped him escape during the uprising, just at the end, when the slaughter was over. He that betrayed his brothers was also betrayed by my father, who had seen my unquenchable love for Milo. Now he's gone on a boat across the bay, and I will never see him again. He would not let me follow; too many would suffer in revenge for me. So, I stood at the edge of the bay ready to slip under the water. Yet, I stopped, for the life within me—his seed, a piece of him growing inside of me. So, I returned to my family, caring only to survive that his child be born. That is all."

They had reached the homestretch, Mariah's final speech to her audience family: "Children, do not weep. Not for me. You think my life nothing but pain and sorrow. My mother die at Rosebush while I young; true. And my first born, Milo, my beauty, my treasure, he stay behind when they sell me to Willowbend. Anticus, my secondborn, love of my heart, soul of my soul, loses his good father when the cart overturns. Me, born a slave, die a slave, forty-two, worn out from work and care. My two sons, arms raised against the other, both gone. But death give a second-sight, and this what I seen: my Anticus baby with Tabitha, that boy live a long life and die a happy man, father of nine children from three mothers. That nine children had a passel of children, and them children, too, spread and spread, up and down the shore—all the same family. Laurette's baby from Milo, she born a white girl raised by country folk when Laurette die from the birth, her soul already gone. Blue-eye, yellow-hair baby grew up to have nine children of her own, all pass for white. Generations now, they live here, too, white folk that farm and fish for their living. Hundreds and hundreds children come down from me, and from my two sons, the one led the uprising, and the other one that stopped him.

"We still here, we with you, we in you; and you brothers and sisters to each other, unknown. That's what I come back to tell you. When you hate the one don't look like you, still might be your kin. Look at me, black as night, but my father a white man took a black woman, and I the grand-daughter of the richest man in the county. Don't pity me; my blood still flowing in your veins and my greatest joy is you have a good life. A good life. That is all a mother wants for her chillun. God Bless."

After the lights went out for Mariah, there was silence in the audience, a certain awe and uncertainty. *Was that it?* Then the clapping began and the shouting. Not so much words as hooting and hollering, as if the heroine in the action film had dodged the last bullet, and against all odds, walked smiling into the sunset. So, despite the memory lapses, the flying ax, and the murmuring audience, the play was over, and it had "carried." Celia had to believe everyone on stage and in the audience would agree the play was a "blow upside the head," "a smack in the face," "a turning on end." However you wanted to put it; the playwright's words had made people see that former world in a different way.

The cast, including Celia, came to the front of the stage for bows. Flowers and programs were thrown at their feet, as the younger members of the audience, fellow students, shouted out the cast members' names. The parents and teachers stood back, seeming stunned by the sudden revelation of their children's performance and their commitment to that strange, disturbing story. This was the moment that Anticus was meant to call up Leona for acknowledgment, but the wave of people rushing the stage was too much. Cameras began flashing. The audience had breached the stage: hugs, kisses, tears, and high fives—the place was a free-for-all.

But no Alonzo. Looking around quickly, Celia could not spot him, and she started to head backstage to drag him out front. Then she remembered, there was no family to see him, and he had begged Mr. and Mrs. Matthews to wait until the second night, when all the kinks would be worked out.

"Alonzo!" she yelled above the din, when she saw his form emerging from the hallway leading to the lighting booth. He halted and she ran up to meet him, leaving some of the light and chaos behind.

"We did it!" she said. "Honest to God, we really did it."

His face broke into a smile, and she could see the tracks of perspiration from his hot work. "Yeah, we did," he said. He pointed at her in her costumed glory, "And you're the one got us there."

He took her hands, and they stood together, swaying with energy and excitement until he stepped in, pulling her close. Just for a second, they hovered face to face, and then they kissed, his hands dropping to her waist. His lips were as soft as she'd imagined. His mouth tasted salty from the sweat and like the chocolate bars they'd had in the cast room. And his body was so warm, so alive, and everything she needed and wanted.

She pulled back to look at him, feeling his hands loosen, and knowing that though they were strong from physical work, they were trembling.

"Celia," he said, shaking his head. "Celia."

"What?"

"You are something . . . something else. I never knew . . ."

"Knew what?"

"You were like that on stage, so different."

"That's acting, silly!"

"I know, but you got those people freaked out there, hating you like you were some nasty piece of work, when really, you're so . . . so . . ."

"But Alonzo, we all have good and bad in us. Me, too."

Still, he shook his head. "You almost had me believing you could be that Laurette. You were that good—I mean, bad. That's some talent you have, to act that way when I know how good you are in your heart."

"Alonzo! What? We . . ." Celia remembered about the play, and everyone around them. "We, we should go." She pointed toward the stage, but she couldn't step away or let go of his hands. Instead, she moved back into his embrace, lifting her face for another kiss. Then they heard voices, and the stomping of feet headed backstage, moving toward them and the cast room.

Celia noticed smears of color on Alonzo's face—her lipstick and foundation.

"Hold up," she said, reaching to erase the tell-tale marks.

"We did it," Alonzo whispered, and then they separated, already walking, until they were swallowed up in the crowd.

"Notes," came Leona's commanding voice. "Green room, everybody. In five minutes. Tech, too. Just cause we kicked ass, doesn't mean we didn't screw up a few times. I don't even want to hear 'party' tonight. That's not happening. Tomorrow's show is it; the best we can do. No mumbled lines, no sneezing, no tripping on the set, and no flying axes. God in heaven, you people gave me a scare."

Alonzo and Celia went along to the cast room, where they took seats awaiting Leona's comments, like everyone else. Celia's stage management was appreciated, except for a couple of audible "hushes" to nervous cast members waiting to come on stage. Alonzo's lights were too dim on the night scenes—people were tripping and, frankly, it was sometimes hard to see who was talking. And the set for Rosebush was not angled properly. Celia didn't hear anything else. She was exhausted, really, with work and the play. And at the same time, her whole body was buzzing with adrenaline—the thrill of the play, and desire. No more sore muscles; no more bruised toe; only bubbling joy and happiness.

She looked at Alonzo and looked away.

Crazy, she said to herself. I'm crazy. This whole place is crazy. After the play, I'll figure it out. After tomorrow night. We have this play to get through, and it has to be good. He'll be here, and I'll be here, and we have to do our parts. Then I can think about it.

The second night at the theater was a more solemn affair. Celia noticed right away that the cast was unusually quiet, focused, no joking around. Mr. Timilty was coming tonight, and the principal, Mr. Tanner. Grace would be there with Roxanne and Alec, Shelly, Russell, and Anita. Some of the folks from New You and the Inn. Leona had gotten a reporter from the Salisbury newspaper to come, arguing that it was a Salisbury State-affiliated event; and one of the students had arranged to have his father videotape the show. Clearly, there was reason to be nervous and self-conscious; but most of all, no one wanted to be the one to screw things up. Everyone wanted the audience to see what was good in this play.

The cast room was quiet, everyone ready and waiting well before the ten minute warning, and then the five minute warning. The noise was all out in the front of the house, which was packed and already warm. Celia asked Leona if she wanted her to set up fans in the aisles, but she said they would all suffer the heat together.

Mariah waited at the side of the stage, rocking on her feet. Celia told Desiree to tell the girls in the lobby to close the auditorium doors. The lights went out in the house, a single spotlight lit center stage. Mariah shuffled across, her tiny, stooped figure with a head wrap and a dark shawl.

"Listen, chillen," she began, then stopped, her hand to her mouth to cover a cough. But it wouldn't stop and she went on coughing. Must have been the dust or dryness of the place. *Disaster! At the very first moment.* Mariah turned sideways, when a young woman in the front row called out. "Granny, you need some water?"

"Yes, chile," Mariah got out. "Water, please."

"I'll get it," Celia said, sparked into action. She left her spot, hastily filling a cup from the sink in the cast room, and carried it to the girl who had offered, while the audience waited.

Mariah drank. "Thank you, chile," she said, all in character. "You bring comfort to an old woman." And then she went on.

Celia brought her hands to her own face, relieved almost to tears.

The play began, growing in heat and passion. The actors, all of them, were steadfast, becoming somehow older, burdened and constrained by the lives they portrayed. Every word was full of purpose, conviction, eerily like voices from the past in desperate conversations. The lighting, the sets, everything added to the suspense, the awful action to come.

And then the uprising began. Anticus approached Rosebush, and Milo stepped out of the darkness, ax upraised, and making his speech. Following, the sounds of gunfire, dogs barking, shouting from backstage.

And from the back of the audience.

Celia suddenly became aware of the noise from the back rows, young, male voices: "Kill them!" "Stab them." "Cut them down." Loud, vicious taunts reverberated through the room. And then the howling began, like wild dogs— or wolves, reverberating throughout the auditorium. The actors froze. Audience members craned to look behind, unsure if the noise was part of the show. Then some of them raising their own voices, chastising the boys, until a din filled the room.

"Silence!" Leona stood up and shouted from her seat on the aisle. "Quiet, everyone!"

It was over, like that. The boys now were laughing, but settling down. From the side stage, Celia could see them all quite clearly, one face in particular. Red hat, wide eyes. menace.

Him, thought Celia, her heart thumping.

The actors on stage looked to Celia, seeking direction. She waved them to exit, even before the final words of the scene, when Anticus says with his dying breath, "We are valiant, but betrayed. Let the story tell that we risked everything." Without a cue, Alonzo cut the stage lights, and the actors scampered off. Music began playing, the haunting tune that had begun the scene. Alonzo turned the volume to high while it played on, filling the time until Celia could get in place for Laurette's final speech.

Celia couldn't get her feet to move. Unbidden came the image of walking with Wanda on the side of the road, the car following them, the sounds of howling and of broken glass. Eyes closed, she saw Wanda, straight-backed and fierce, approaching the car with the boys. Paralyzing fear began to turn to anger, and she looked out past the curtain. Leona was speaking to the boys in the back. First one stood up, and then another four or five, proceeding out the row and departing the theater. Leona turned, her eyes seeking Alonzo in his booth, and she held up a finger. When she got back to her seat, the music died out, and the audience sat in dark silence.

Celia walked to the center of the stage, feeling the beam of the spotlight hit the top of her head, and then descend around her.

"He was my heaven and my hell," Laurette said, but the fire was gone out of her. Let them hate her, she was beyond that now. Hard to breathe, hard to stand, full of anguish and pain. Only Alonzo's spotlight held her upright. Heartache, disappointment, disillusion, and loss: everything flowed out. But there was no answering contempt from the audience, only something soft and warm, like pity.

Celia left the stage, searching blindly for a wall to steady herself. Tabitha passed her going toward the light. Celia listened to Tabitha's lines, how proud she was of Atticus and his sacred sacrifice, and that she would ensure that his unborn child would live and grow to be a man, hearing stories of his noble father, and bear the seed of uprising in his own heart. Atticus's wife left to vigorous applause, and then all that was left was Mariah, who shuffled on stage, older than the hills, no larger than a child, with a drink of water in her hand to end the play with a blessing on her multitude of descendants.

The audience departed quietly in small groups, no crowding the stage this time. The parents, many of whom had come the first night, knew that the cast was staying for a pizza party. As they assembled backstage, the cast and crew, too, were subdued.

"Assholes," cried Milo. "Why they had to carry on like that, scared everyone half to death. Never gave Anticus a chance to finish."

"Yeah, they just here to mock us," Bettina complained. "They don't care about no play."

Leona, surprisingly, shrugged it off. "Anything can happen. It's live theater. Got a reaction, anyhow. Like it or not, it was powerful theater. People will be talking. They won't forget. And," she turned to her cast and crew, "you won't forget, either. This is part of you now." They stood in silence, unmoving.

"Come on," Leona said. "It's our night. Wash up and change before the pizza gets here. Party all you want, but don't forget, tomorrow noon, we strike the set, and I better see your asses back here, every one of you."

A few of the cast and crew had already headed to the small wash rooms, so Celia went still in costume and make-up to the back alley with Alonzo, Bettina, Desiree, and a couple other girls for some cool air while they waited their turns. One of the girls lit a joint while Desiree passed around a bottle of wine. They closed the door so the smoke wouldn't drift inside, just in case.

Still, they couldn't let it go, how the play had been violated. Celia was no longer manager, just one of the exhausted, wrung out cast. "That guy, the leader, with the red hat?" she asked, taking a swig from the bottle, and wiping her wet chin. "What's wrong with him?"

The high schoolers ha-rumphed.

"That Morris. He think he in charge," reported Bettina. "And he got his crew to go with him. He come down from Balimore a couple years ago, cause he running with a bad crowd. He always sayin, 'When I go back to Balimore . . . blah . . . blah . . . blah.' I wish he would go back there."

"He carry a knife," Desiree said, not smiling.

Celia looked from her to Bettina, and then to Alonzo, who was staring upwards, at the little slice of sky.

"Yeah, he do," confirmed Bettina. "I seen it." Pause. "He ain't ever used it, though, that I know. He just take it out to show around. Punk. But he get those other kids to go around with him."

They were just passing the joint around again when they heard voices from the top of the alley and hurriedly hid it, thinking it was parents or teachers.

But it was Morris and his pals, seeking them out by some sure instinct.

"Oh, shit," said Bettina. "Why the hell he has to bother us here. What for?" She pulled at the door, but it wouldn't budge. "Oh, shit," she said again. She banged a couple times, shouting to no effect. On the other hand, they weren't about to run out the end of the alley. Morris approached, the smile on his face made more sinister by the sharp light. Only two friends accompanied him. Perhaps the others had enough theater for one evening.

Celia had never really seen Morris close up. He was a bit shorter than Alonzo, maybe a little more muscular and trim. His features, too, were a little sharper. There was no trace of boy left in that face. Handsome? Not like Jay. On stage, it might be a face that looked noble in battle. Here, it looked sour with some unknown grievance against the world.

"Ain't you a vision," came out of Morris's mouth, leering at Celia in her tacky red satin dress. His eyes traveled to Alonzo. "Now look what we have here. It's the Oreo side-by-side with Vanilla Wafer." There was no one who didn't know what he meant; even Celia could appreciate the metaphor.

"He rubbing up next to you, sweetheart?" Morris continued, looking at Celia. "That so he can get a little white on him. He been trying ever so long, but nothing just won't work."

"Shut up, Morris," said Bettina, who was almost as big as he was, and looked quite frightening in her torn, bloodied slave garments.

He turned slowly to her with a slight frown. "Shut up, yourself, fat cow."

Alonzo sighed. "You don't have to speak to her like that."

"I ain't talking to you, or you." He gestured back at Bettina. "I'm talking to Vanilla here. What I was trying to tell you," he addressed Celia directly now, "is to watch out, or some of that black might rub off on you."

Celia knew to ignore him. How long could he go on, if he got no good reaction? But in spite of herself, she heard herself speak. "I'm not worried." Bettina and Desiree were grim-faced and watchful.

Morris was delighted. "Sugar, you be much happier you want to rub against me, I promise you." This Celia ignored. Braggarts were no real threat. She had pretty much got used to the sexual bragging that was part of the everyday conversation at the Grand Marsh Inn kitchen. Morris's pals also seemed to recognize this as run-of-the-mill business, and shifted restlessly, ready to move along. But not Morris.

"What you doing with this fool, anyway? You could do better, if you looking for a black dude. Girls be looking for a man can satisfy. Not him; he wasting away from the white disease."

The hair on Celia's neck prickled—from anger and now fear that things might get physical. She understood the nature of Morris's insults to Alonzo, but not what he was referring to, specifically. From the first, she knew there was something about Alonzo that set him apart: a general reserve with the others, a low-key presence in the group, more often hanging back and listening to the banter, rather than joining in. Not that they excluded him; they didn't. And they more than appreciated his building skills and dedication. He wasn't actually shy, not with Celia, and not in voicing an opinion. But here it was, again, some other unseen current of out some mysterious past that she didn't get.

"I don't care what you say to me," Alonzo said softly. "But leave the girls out of this. There's no need for rudeness and vulgarness here."

"Hear him roar," Morris said. He appeared to be joking, but there was no humor in his eyes. "I been wondering about you, boy. I wonder what you gonna do if I punch you in the nose. What you think, homeboys? He gonna fight back, or he gonna back down? He look big and strong, but maybe he just gonna cry."

Celia could feel Alonzo tense. He had to do something, either confront Morris or find a way to leave. Clearly, Morris had no intention of giving up on this little scene. No way was Celia going to stay to witness to a fight. But what could she do, scream? It was as if time had slowed to a stop, and they were all paralyzed there in the back alley as the rest of the town was going about its business.

A spot of yellow caught her eye, a dandelion pushing through the pavement. Celia became aware, as she stared at the ground, that next to her, Alonzo had begun to move, pulling back as if to drive forward.

Then, the back door swung open, spilling out noise and light and voices coming toward them.

"Hey! I smell weed." And then, "Hey, what's up? What's going on out here?"

Maybe half a dozen others had joined them in the alley, ten or so theater folks staring across the alley at the three bad boys.

"Is there a problem?" Anticus asked, the steeliness of his character coming through.

Morris lifted empty hands. "No problem, no problem," he said, taking in the newcomers with a shrug. "Enough fun for today, I guess." He looked at Celia. "Sorry, darlin'; another time."

The moment had passed, and already the two other boys made motions to leave. Morris turned, sauntering behind them until they reached the opening to the alley and disappeared, turning left

"If I had a brick," muttered Bettina, "I'd throw it square at his head."

"Just heckling, same old shit," said Desiree. "He's gone now, anyhow. Let's go back in."

No one said anything about Alonzo, who stood motionless.

While the others filed in through the back door, Celia stayed behind with Alonzo. Then Alonzo started down the alleyway. Celia trailed him to the street, dragging her long skirts.

"Alonzo, please, wait," Celia said, catching up to him under the streetlight. "Don't just go off like this. Talk to me." She could feel his humiliation radiating like heat.

"He's just a bully," she said. "You can't let him get to you. Don't give him that power. We didn't go down to his level. You stood up to him, for me and those girls."

He shook his head, not agreeing.

"Alonzo," she said, "you don't think I care about anything he said. It means nothing to me. You're so much better than him." That's all she could think of to say, and it didn't seem to make any difference at all. "Come on;

let's go somewhere, just us. How about the Pizza Palace? I'll buy you a drink. Or, we can just take a walk, anywhere."

"Leave me be." He held up a hand. "Please." He looked at her once, briefly, and then turned and walked to the street, turning right—away from the boys.

She knew not to follow. But neither could she leave. It was like that nightmare of being frozen on stage, all lines forgotten, while emotions flowed like magma through her veins. A car passed, two faces turned to stare at her finery. Finally, she turned, willing herself into motion. She entered through the back door, propped open with a brick, weaving blindly through groups of people toward the wash room.

Before she got there, Leona stopped her, putting a hand on her arm. "We've been looking for you," she said. "Photo op. The reporter from Salisbury wants a few pictures—in costume."

Celia let herself be led to the front of the stage, where the other cast members were already assembled. She was paired up with Milo, naturally, and tried to make happy for the camera, but she was feeling slightly sick to her stomach. They grouped and posed four or five times. Each time the camera flashed, it felt like a blow. The reporter took down names, and finally they were allowed to disperse. Except for Celia.

The photographer grinned at her. "One by yourself, gorgeous." Celia was too taken aback to be affronted. "Seriously, you killed them tonight. Or, I should say, they wanted to kill you. I'm Doug, by the way, and Leona said you might be headed to Salisbury one of these days." He handed her a business card. "How about I take a couple extra shots for your portfolio? Sound OK?"

"Well, thank you," she said, stiffly, finding it hard to smile naturally as he snapped away.

And then the reporter was done.

But not Celia. Someone else was waiting for her, a tall, fair-haired man in a sports jacket.

"Bill Tanner," he introduced himself. And then when she stood there blankly, he added, "Principal, Sutton High School. We spoke."

"Oh, yes, of course."

"I'm sorry," he said. "I have the advantage. I know who you are from the program. I'm just here to say congratulations. The show was excellent in so many ways. I didn't think these kids had it in them to carry it off, but it truly worked. And, I must say, you were outstanding. Really. I'm a little awe-struck. I didn't realize that you were also acting a part in the play. What a very talented young woman you are, and I hope you go far in your career."

Celia was close to tears. She wasn't prepared for this. All she could think about was Alonzo, and that awful Morris. "Thank you, thank you so much."

He tipped his head. "I want to apologize about sounding the alarm. And I'm sorry about the disruptive students. Unfortunately, that goes with the territory. But I want to thank you most sincerely for doing this. We needed this; we all needed this."

Mr. Tanner departed, and already Celia could hear the dance music from backstage. Someone shouted, "Pizza!" and Celia climbed the steps to get back on stage, seeking out Desiree who had the cash box, so she could pay the delivery guy. The crowd parted to let her through, a group of freshly scrubbed, jubilant, excited high school kids getting ready to party. The celebration was going forward, even without Alonzo, and Celia needed to be part of it. But as Anticus grabbed her hand for a swing around the stage, she about tripped over her skirts. She got the smile in place, but her heart just wasn't in it.

"Let me change first," she said, and then headed to the wash room. She changed into her own clothes, hanging the red dress over the door to the bathroom stall. At the sink, the basin was filthy with grime, hairs, wet towels, and petroleum jelly. Turning the faucet on full, Celia splashed water on her face, rubbing in the soap and letting it mix with hot tears.

Chapter 23

Alonzo didn't appear on Sunday to strike the set. His absence made the work take longer, and was more arduous for those who didn't have his strength and experience. But no one said a word about him or the incident with Morris. Whether Bettina, Desiree, or the others had discussed it amongst themselves, Celia wasn't sure. But she was willing to bet that everyone knew. Nobody was talking, and Celia understood it was a way of letting time pass and letting him save face. Likely, he needed a few days to cool off. But then a few days turned into several, and she hadn't seen him and had no one to ask about him. Of course, he was angry. So was she. But why should that stop them from spending time together or interfere with their, well, friendship.

Friday marked one week before the prom, and Celia hadn't seen Alonzo once, not even on the street. She had looked for him at the strip mall a couple of afternoons, to see if he'd come over to pick up groceries. On a chance, she went by his grandmother's house in the "short-cut" neighborhood, two blocks from the acorn assault. But the house, humble and unpainted, behind a wild, unkempt garden, was quiet. If the grandmother or uncle were in, they were not answering the door. Only a female neighbor looked out the window when Celia called out Alonzo's name. Too late, she thought of a pencil and paper to write a note. Uneasily, she walked back the way she came.

She decided, somewhat reluctantly, to try the high school at the end of the day as the students left. She felt like a bit of a stalker, hanging out at the bottom of the steps to front entrance. And the last thing she wanted was a run-in with, or even the sight of, Morris. But maybe from the cast or crew, someone who might know about Alonzo.

In her peripheral vision, Celia saw a blur in turquoise and a dark head with cornrow braids down to her shoulders: Bettina. Celia hurried to catch her.

"Bettina, wait up." Bettina's head swiveled, looking for the voice that was calling, and then her eyes widened in surprise.

"What you doing here?"

"Looking for Alonzo. Have you seen him?"

Bettina shook her head, making the braids twitch. "Not today. Not here, I don't think. There's no more classes; we only come for exams."

Celia swallowed, thinking. "Do you know where he might be?"

She could tell by Bettina's expression that she was a bit hesitant. Some doubts, perhaps, about Celia? Or, the thought occurred, maybe some feelings about Alonzo herself? "At work, maybe. You know that place, Eastside Grille."

"Thank you, Bettina. Thank you."

She zipped home in ten short minutes, making a plan. Grace had taken the car to Weston, so Celia would have to ride Grace's bike the four or five miles to the Eastside Grille. Inside, she grabbed her keys and a few dollars, leaving a note for Grace about taking a bike ride. She skipped down the stairs, took the bicycle from the storage area, and jumped on, peddling like crazy until she realized she'd be exhausted before she got halfway there.

Once she arrived at the restaurant, Celia hopped off the bike, deciding how to enter. The Eastside Grille was a weathered, one-story building with a gravel parking lot and inviting front porch. It wouldn't be busy, this time of day. But looking down at her sweaty tee shirt and jean shorts, she headed around the corner to a side door, which was open. No one was in the short hallway, so she went farther along into the kitchen, hot, small and crowded. There were four men working, but no Alonzo.

"Excuse me," she said. "I'm looking for Alonzo Bailey. Is he here?"

"Out back with the trash," one man replied without expression. Celia followed his thumb through another doorway that led to small yard. Next to a smelly dumpster, Alonzo was bent over cutting and flattening cardboard boxes.

"Alonzo?" she said, suddenly awkward, feeling very much out of place.

He looked up. "Celia." He sounded more disturbed than pleased. "What are you doing here?"

"I . . . I didn't know how to reach you. I wanted to talk to you, about, you know, what happened at the play, and . . . and . . . to tell you about the prom, that I want to go, if you still want to go with me."

Alonzo took a moment to respond. "You sure about that?"

"I am. I'm sure." Her eyes widened. "That's what I came to tell you." The words rushed out of her mouth. "You know how much I like to dress up, right? Actually, I never got to go to my own high school prom, for various reasons. And that was just a couple years ago. Really, I am only a year or so older than you, according to our birth dates." Here she took a breath. "And, it turns out, maybe I'm not so worldly-wise as I thought I was. And," she swallowed. "You've been through a lot yourself, seen a few things. So, maybe we're not so different. And, and. . . . I'd just really like to go with you."

Then he shook his head and laughed. "Well, then I'm glad."

"I'm glad too." Celia felt her heart turning around inside her chest, out of happiness and confusion. "I was worried, when I didn't see you . . ."

Alonzo held up a hand, looking around. "Not here, Celia."

"Right, of course. Tomorrow, when you're free, can you come by the apartment?"

He held her eyes. "OK. Has to be early though. I'm working at eleven."

"Fine. No problem. Come at nine; we can talk."

Slowly, with a sigh, he nodded.

"You'll come?"

"I'll come," he said. "I promise."

She wanted more than anything to go up to him and put her arms around him. But his eyes flicked to the back door, and he tipped his head—time for her to leave.

"Well, then, I'll get out of here now," Celia looked around, trying to decide which way to exit.

He pointed toward a walkway. "That way to the parking lot," he said. "And thanks for coming." His hand, sticky with ketchup and grease, started to rise, but he pulled it back. "I only wish I was done, and could get a ride back with you."

"But I'm on my bike," Celia exclaimed.

"You are?" Alonzo's whole face brightened. "Girl, you really are crazy about that fitness stuff."

Celia decided to leave it at that.

The next morning, Celia met Alonzo at the bottom of the stairs, where he stood with little expression on his face. In the morning light, he seemed different, more of a stranger. It occurred to her that he had grown some since they first met, and filled out, more like a man. Then he spoke, that same light tenor, and it was the real Alonzo, the same soul who had become so familiar over the past months.

"There's something I want to show you, a place. We can talk there." His voice was soft, but there was something in it that was pressing, if not exactly urgent.

"OK, sure. Where is it? I mean how far?"

"Maybe two or three miles from here, past the Quaker Meetinghouse. Kind of a back road."

"Should we take the car? Grace doesn't need it."

"Probably easiest."

She ran back upstairs to get the keys, retuning and handing them to Alonzo, who took them, surprised. "You have your license, right?"

He nodded.

"You know the way, and Grace won't mind," she said, meeting his gaze. "Let's go."

South out of town, they took a right onto an unpaved road, with high grass between the ruts, clearly unused for some time. At one point the road split, and the path to the right disappeared completely into a stand of thick, tall brush. A wooden marker with a rough drawn cross pointed the way.

"Where does that go?" Celia craned her head to see. "Looks rather mysterious."

"You are a curious gal," Alonzo commented, without slowing. "I'll tell you later, if you still want to know."

Celia knew that closed look. He wasn't going to say anymore.

The path to the left wound further through tall trees, finally ending in a bright clearing, right at the water's edge. A large, two-story structure, weathered but intact, stood close to the riverbank. It had a pitched roof, a couple of long, narrow windows on the side, and the faded remains of gray blue paint.

"Where are we?" Celia asked, as the car rolled to a stop.

"At the river that leads to the Bay."

She pointed to the building. "And what's that? A barn?" She didn't really think so, since it had windows. "It looks almost like a chapel, a chapel in the woods."

"Neither of those. Come see."

They got out of the car and walked around the side of the building. At the river's edge, it was elevated a few feet, away from the water's changing levels. A huge double door stood over a smooth, packed stone surface ending right in the water—a ramp. The doorway was quite grand, with a couple of bird decoys mounted on each side of a sign: "The Waterway."

"A boathouse," said Celia, in wonder. "But it's charming, so . . . quaint."

"Yep," Alonzo said, smiling widely. "Built around the turn of the century. And wait until you see what's inside." He took a couple of steps away from the ramp and bent over, feeling along the support timbers.

"Are we supposed to be here?"

He didn't answer, continuing his search down on his knees to reach farther underneath.

In a moment, he came up with a set of keys on a keychain.

"Got it," he said. "Still there, after all these years." He came to Celia's side, meeting her eyes. "This is Brett's place, the boy I told you about. We used to ride our bikes out here when we were kids. I don't think anyone comes here now. Kind of neglected, looks like. Plus, the big boat stays at the marina at St. Andrews. These are just the little ones, for fishing, messing around in."

"So, we are trespassing," she said gently, not wanting to spoil things, but not up to any more drama, either.

"Guess so. But I doubt anyone would be upset if they found out it was me. In fact, they'd probably invite us up to the house." His eyebrows went up. "The big house."

"A mansion?"

He nodded, "An old one, too."

"So, this is the family estate?"

"So many questions," he sighed good-humoredly. "His mom's side of the family. Even had a name, Belle Grove. That's way back, of course. They've sold off most of the land by now, but not here by the river. This is still theirs."

"Oh, I see," Celia said, musing.

"Want to go inside?" Alonzo asked, his eyes twinkling as he brandished the key.

"Course I do. You know how curious I am. Said so yourself."

The key was sticky in the lock, but finally it turned, and Alonzo swung open the doors, creaking on their hinges. The interior was not dark, as Celia expected, but full of light from the windows and two skylights overhead. Motes of dust floated through the sunlight; otherwise the place was neat and tidy—*shipshape.* On each side of the open central area, large racks were mounted on the walls to hold the watercraft: two canoes; a kayak; a small, maybe ten-foot row boat; and what looked like a tiny sailboat—*Sunfish,* Celia read on its side.

"Holy cow," she said. "Just look at all this stuff. So, these are the boats you used to take out, you and Brett, and 'mess around in'?" She wagged her head, imitating his words.

"This is the boat I learned to sail in," Alonzo said, pointing to the *Sunfish.* Then turning to the rowboat, "We caught lots of turtles and frogs in this old tub. And we explored the bay in the canoe. The kayaks came later."

"Good memories," she said, reading his face.

"Lots of good memories."

Celia wandered to the back of the boathouse where deep wooden shelves and hooks held nets and buckets, fishing rods, tackle boxes, life vests, paddles, and oars.

Celia returned to Alonzo's side, squeezing his arm. "This is so cool. I'm really glad you brought me here."

His eyebrows rose. "There's more."

"More?"

She followed him to the far side of the boathouse, away from the driveway, to a rustic porch, facing into a stand of pine trees. They mounted a couple of steps to the deck, set with a table and chairs created from branches and sticks and unplaned pieces of wood. From the porch, one view was over the water, and the other into sun-dappled woods, the ground covered with pine needles.

"It's lovely," Celia said. "What a perfect spot for a picnic."

"We built it, Brett and me" Alonzo said. "Well, mostly me. When we were twelve. It took us all summer."

"Oh, my goodness." Celia pulled out a chair to examine the workmanship.

"And the table and chairs, I made those." He smiled with unabashed pride.

"They're wonderful," Celia said. "I mean it. You're very talented."

"Thanks. I learned from my grandfather; he could build anything. But he never saw this, what I made; he was gone by then." Alonzo stopped and cleared his throat. "There's something else," he said. "Kind of silly. Come with me." He led Celia off the porch and down a short path into the woods where he stopped, pointing. "Check this out."

It was a tall, full-bodied oak tree. On the trunk about five feet up rough letters were carved: *A-man, BreRabbtt, and Benjulum.*

"This was our best climbing tree: me, Brett, and another boy, Ben, who moved away in fourth grade. Ben was white, too, but his parents were regular folks. His dad was a guard at the lock-up at the courthouse, where Brett's dad worked. We were friends from first grade. Can't say why. Active boys, I guess, and we liked the outdoors. Our parents let us run all over town, as long as we were home for supper. This was one of our favorite places."

He looked around. "We built forts and went exploring in the boats, all kind of adventures. Other kids came out sometimes. We had major battles in the woods, mostly acorn fights." His eyes glazed, seeing other faces. "Long time ago now."

Celia sensed, this was it; this was the root of Alonzo's troubles. "So what happened?"

"The family still lives here, in the big house. Brett goes to school in Virginia. He left when we were thirteen, after eighth grade."

"Wasn't that when your mother moved to North Carolina?"

"Yeah, but it's not like she left me behind, or anything like that. She wanted me to go, too, even though that man was not my father. He said I could come."

Celia winced, like he was "allowed," not really wanted or welcome.

But Alonzo went on. "I wanted to stay back here and live with Gran. I didn't want to leave Brett, and my teachers and classmates. I really thought I belonged here. He didn't tell me he was going away to school until the end of summer. I don't think he really wanted to, just his family made him. But then, of course, things changed."

Away from the water, the breeze had died, and Celia was feeling warm and sticky. She moved to a spot in the shade, while Alonzo stood like a schoolteacher, the tree for his chalkboard.

"Morris is right in a way," he said finally. "I liked Brett's world and all the things that went with it. The opportunities he had, and I had, too, for a while. Nice cars that worked. We didn't even have one after my mom left. They had all these boats and fishing gear, trips to the city. At Brett's house, they talked about all kinds of things at the supper table, where they were going, what they were going to do. Partly it was money, I guess. But partly it was just what they thought the world was like, so much bigger than the five square miles of Sutton."

Alonzo looked at Celia, and then toward the river, glinting through the trees.

"The year Brett went to Virginia, I was kind of on my own at school. Once he was gone, the white kids weren't so happy to have me around; and by then, the black kids thought I was weird, like I thought I was better than them. It wasn't too good, but one or two of the girls were nice to me, and I worked hard at my schoolwork, so it was OK.

"I wrote Brett some letters, and he wrote me back a few times, at first, then he stopped. His family went to Florida for Christmas. I saw his dad in town, so I knew he was coming home for break in March. Plus, that's when his birthday is.

"I didn't hear from him, so I waited until his birthday to go over and see him. I had made him a little canoe, carved out of wood, painted just like the one you saw. He wasn't at the house and his mother told me that he had friends down from his new school, and they had gone to the high school to play football. I thought it would be good if they were playing ball; I could drop into the game. But it didn't work out like that.

"They were still there, five or six boys and a couple girls. The girls were sitting on the bleachers, watching the game. When I walked over, Brett saw me and nodded. He came over and I asked about playing, but he said they had already made up the teams. I said, 'No problem,' I could sub. He didn't really give an answer. They called him to play, and he just left me standing there.

"I went to sit up by the girls in the bleachers. All I said was, 'Are you girls enjoying the game or just waiting for them to finish?' That was it; I didn't even sit that close to them.

"One of the girls gave me a dirty look. Funny, she looked so young and sweet, like one of those Raggedy Ann dolls with the two braids and freckles." He ran his fingers across his nose and cheeks. "But I guess she didn't like the look of me. When there was a break in the game, she went over to Brett, complaining about me. She must have been bugging him, though, because I heard him tell her, 'Ssh, you don't have to be that way. He's all right. Just ignore him.'

"Anyway, Brett came over and asked if we could talk, so we went behind the bleachers. He said the girl said I was coming onto them and making them uncomfortable. I told him exactly what I had said, but he just shook his head. She was being a real pain in the ass about it, he said, and that the other guys think it's weird I'm just hanging around. Said now was not a good time; he'd catch me later. . . .

"So I left, and didn't say anything about his birthday or the gift. He didn't call, either. End of the week, all those kids left back for school, and that's when I left too."

Celia gave him a questioning look.

"Left town; left Sutton. I needed to get away, to go somewhere away from here."

"You just left—by yourself?" Celia asked, moving closer.

"I came here." He spread his arms. "The police came looking for me after a couple days. Brett's dad is the one who told them about this place; he came with them." He looked toward the river. "But I wasn't here, just stayed long enough to gather a few supplies. Then I took the canoe out of the boathouse, and loaded it up, heading up the shoreline toward the Bay Bridge. Never made it, though."

Celia looked at the water, too, and imagined Alonzo paddling the canoe with his backpack, some clothes and groceries. How did he ever find his way along the endless inlets and coves of the bigger bay?

"So, they found you, a tiny dot in that great big body of water? Or, did you come back?"

"Neither." He paused, now back in that moment. "A big storm came up. Rain and wind and lightning, too. Might have been a hurricane almost. Too much for me. Too much for anyone. When I saw how dark the sky was in the middle of the day, and the chops on the water, I knew I had to pull out. When the downpour started, I could barely see in front of me, never mind the shore.

And the canoe was taking on water." He smiled wryly. "I thought that was it for me."

"Oh, Alonzo," Celia said, shaking her head. "You out there, just a kid, all alone, and no one knowing where you were."

He almost laughed. "That's the thing. Some people thought I was dead. They really did for a day or two. Thing is, I wasn't sure where I landed. I just hauled out and found a place to wait it out. By then it was dark, so I stayed put under the canoe. The next day I was still sleeping when this dog sniffed me out, a big German shepherd. Then an old man came along, a farmer, must have seen the red of the canoe." He smiled with memory. "I don't know what he thought, this boy washed up on his land. I could barely talk, I was so mixed up. Dehydrated, I guess, and exhausted. I don't believe he knew anything about a kid gone missing from Sutton. But he took me in, put me in dry clothes, and he and his wife gave me food and a bed to sleep in."

A small whirlwind passed, raising leaves and pine needles before it spun away. Alonzo paused to watch. "Sometime in the night, the old woman came in the room where I slept. I don't know what she was saying, but I think it was some *juju.*" He looked up quickly. "Like a spell or a blessing. Next morning, I found that rabbit's foot next to my pillow. She told me at breakfast I should keep it with me, and that things would get better." Now he raised his eyebrows at Celia, who said nothing, whatever she might have thought. "After that, I told them I had to get back to Sutton. We threw the canoe in the back of his truck and dropped it off here. Then the old man took me to Gran's. He never told me his name. And my mind was so fuzzy, I still can't remember where they lived to thank them properly. And that's it, end of story."

Celia considered. "Hm . . . quite an adventure, I guess, now that it's over. What wonderful people, to help you like that. But what about Brett? Did you see him after that? He must have heard what happened, and how it turned out."

Alonzo cleared a spot for himself on the ground and sat down, playing with the pine needles between his fingers. He glanced up at her at last.

"He came around the house once, maybe two years ago. I wasn't there. Gran wouldn't let him in the door, said he was drunk or high."

"Oh, dear."

"Word is he's into that kind of stuff now. Having trouble with his folks. But I don't know for sure."

After a few minutes of silence, Celia sat down next to him. "I'm sorry; sorry about all of it."

He raised a hand. "Don't pity me, please." His voice was thick. "I don't want that. I'm just telling you what happened, so you know what Morris is getting at."

"How did he know? Was he there, at the football field?"

Alonzo shook his head. "Nah. But somebody was. And somebody told somebody. That's how it is in this town. And then it was a big deal when I went missing. Like I said, some thought I was dead."

"Terrible," Celia spat out, and then almost to herself, "I don't know which of them is worse." She didn't have to say their names.

For some time they sat in silence, an occasional pine needle drifting down in the shafts of sunlight, a bird calling in the tree tops. A yellow finch, late for its morning meal, landed on the oak tree. It was so peaceful and quiet here, a welcome relief from the past few months with the play and all that effort, the pressure, the uncertainty of carrying it off and its reception. But they had achieved it, what they set to do, and it was a bit of a miracle, really. Alonzo had given her a lot of the credit for making *Anticus* happen. But, really, it was Alonzo himself who had initiated the idea of the play. He's the one who had solicited Celia to attend a play in the first place, and spread the word. And then saw enough value in the new script to round up the others. Nevermind his drawings for the set, and all his sturdy building. He was the bridge, Alonzo. Or, at least another support of the bridge. There was a kind of hard-won wisdom behind those deep brown eyes, and a lonesomeness, an awareness of being different, yet accepting it.

How had Alonzo come to this state, she wondered, instead of going the other way, toward anger, bitterness and destruction? Gazing at the river and its shiny, changeable nature, she thought maybe it had to do with the water. That story he'd told her, the story of escape in the canoe. Surviving that deluge had transformed him, leaving boyhood behind, strengthening his sense of self and his spirit. And that's what had made him something special.

Back at the boathouse, Celia looked around a last time as Alonzo locked the doors. The day was so mild and beautiful, the water slow-moving and calm. So many good, unexpected, things in her life now, she reflected—New You, the play, their friendship—finally someone in Sutton she could feel at ease with. Those should not be overshadowed by Morris or Brett, or any of the negative people or experiences that came with living in such a challenging place, or really, any place. Then she had an idea, stooping to pick up a fallen pine cone and then a second one.

"Alonzo," she said, as he came up next to her at the river's edge. "See these? These are the past, the bad things that happened." She turned to him, giving him one. "We're going to throw them in the water, and be done with them."

He didn't smile and his eyes were solemn as they cast their pine cones and watched until they disappeared in the lazy current.

"Gone," Celia said, "from our lives. Not really gone, of course, at least not until they fall apart. But we can't see them anymore, and they are not for us to worry about. Agreed?"

"Agreed."

"And now this." Celia bent down to the water. "I wash my hands of all that." She splashed around as if cleaning her hands. "Come on, like me." He knelt to do the same.

"And say it."

"I wash my hands of all that."

Celia got to her feet, wiping her hands on her jeans. Then she spun to face Alonzo, her face brightening. "We do have one thing to worry about." She paused, building suspense, and then felt bad when he looked so concerned. "The prom."

He didn't get that she was teasing.

"Remember?" she said. "The dancing and the music and the fancy clothes? I mean, it's next week. What we're going to wear, and how about some flowers?"

"Flowers?"

"Corsage? Boutonniere? Alonzo, if we're going to do this, we're going to do it right." She fluttered her eyes. "I can't wait for you to see my dance moves. I just hope you can keep up."

Now he was smiling. He had sand on his pants and pine needles in his hair, a creature of the great outdoors.

"Because we're going to have a great time," she said, "and no one's going to stop us."

But he didn't agree right away. "You sure? Not just because you feel bad for me? Or, or, you're afraid to say no to me after all this . . ." He gestured at the river.

"No!" she said, and then stopped. How could she argue? It might seem, *The lady doth protest too much.* "You'll just have to take my word, I guess."

Celia wanted to put her arms around him and comfort him. But she also knew, with some surprising sense, that might just cause other problems that neither of them was ready to deal with.

Celia scooped up another stray pine cone and chucked it in.

"That's for Morris."

Chapter 24

There was no avoiding it. Celia had to break the news about the prom to Grace. She wouldn't keep a secret like that from her sister, and probably couldn't if she tried.

Saturday at suppertime, they were at the table finishing the broccoli and chicken casserole. "Grace, you've got a minute, right?"

"One minute, maybe two. I have a ton of papers to correct. Why, what's up?"

Celia waved her fingers. "A couple little things. First, you're still OK with me taking the car tomorrow? For the beach, I mean."

"Sure, as long as you're back by four. I've got that wedding shower." She put her serious look on Celia. "Really, don't be late. I don't have much time after I get home from work and pick up Alec at Roxanne's." A nurse's life: seven am to three pm shifts, and every other weekend.

"Right, right, no problem."

"And," Grace added. "The gift is already in the trunk, wrapped, so make sure you don't get it wet or sandy. Maybe put a towel over it or something."

"Got it."

Grace didn't ask, and Celia didn't volunteer who was going. She had just said, "Some people were talking about a trip to the beach." Well, those people were Alonzo and herself. She was sure Grace wouldn't object, but maybe wonder.

"Thanks, Grace, really, I appreciate it." Celia paused. "There's another thing. You know Alonzo, right, from the play?"

"Yes."

"Well, the thing is, he's a good guy. I like him."

"Like him? Oh, I see." Grace got up and started clearing the table. "And that means what?"

Celia went over to the sink, filling a basin with soap and water. "Oh, we've been hanging out a little since the play. He's been over here a couple times, and we've gone some places, bowling, bike-riding." She studied Grace's expression. "Friends, acquaintances. You remember Wanda and Warren, right, from the Inn?"

"Except Alonzo's still in high school."

"Why does that make a difference?"

"Because it does." Grace came to the sink, taking a dish cloth from the drawer. "I know this is a different world, but you're still accountable for what you do. It's one thing to be involved in a play with a group of people. But do you really think it's OK to be hanging out with a high school boy, especially a black kid from around here? You might think it's company, but he probably thinks you're leading him on."

"No," Celia said, her hands in the soapy water. "He doesn't think that." She handed Grace the plates to rinse and dry. "What can I say? He befriended *me*. He's kind of a loner here, too, in some ways. And, besides, he's going off to college in the fall. What's the harm in spending time together?"

"I just hope you realize what you're doing, and you think about how he might feel." Grace sighed, drying the silverware. The casserole dish they left to soak. They had returned to the table. "So, is that what you wanted to tell me?"

Celia realized the moment had come. She thought of suggesting dessert. Then she realized she would never enjoy ice cream or cookies, knowing she harbored this secret.

"Now, don't get mad. Just listen."

Grace was standing, hand on hip.

"Maybe you better sit down," Celia suggested, but Grace shook her head. "Alonzo asked me to the senior prom, and I'd like to go. It's next Friday at the high school."

There, it was out. At first, it seemed like Grace just didn't get it. She bent to brush some crumbs into her palm. Celia waited for that deep sigh of disappointment.

"Senior prom?" Grace said, finally, shaking her head. "Celia, Celia, Celia . . . I don't know how you do it. You are like the cat with nine lives, the way you tempt fate."

"Yes," Celia countered. "But things have a way of working out, don't you think? Like at the play." She didn't allude to the encounter with Morris, of course, or all that followed. The play itself was a success. "Sounds crazy, I know," Celia admitted. "But I'm your crazy sister, right? Hear me out. He's a nice guy. He wants to take me. And, as you know, I never got to go to my own prom."

Grace picked up the salt shaker and made like she was going to throw it at Celia. "How about I knock some sense into that head of yours? As I remember it, two guys asked you. Or was it three? But you chose to play the Good Witch at the community theater instead."

"I know! I couldn't do both."

"Well, you made your choice, then."

"Yes," Celia said, lifting her chin, "but now I realize I missed out on one of the most important events of high school. Plus, you know how much I like dressing up and dancing."

"Yes, that I do." They looked at each other a moment in silence. Grace went on, "It's not just a matter of what people might say. Try to think of it from Alonzo's point of view. He does seem like a nice guy, from what I can tell. It's not fair that you use your charms on him, just for a fun time and chance to show off."

"But it's a fun time for him, too!" Celia protested, her voice rising. Really, what was so wrong about the idea?

"If not you, he might have asked another girl," Grace said. "One of those girls from the play, maybe, who actually lives around here, that he might have a future with."

"Oh, pshaw." Celia waved it away. Who thought about things like that?

"Celia, please, just think things through. Even if your intentions are good, there can be serious consequences. Don't you see that?"

"Yes, yes," Celia said, exasperated. "For heaven's sake, what's the big deal? It's a night out; we're friends; we're both going our different ways before long."

She saw Grace wavering, softening.

"It will be a nice memory for both of us, someday."

"And you've thought about his feelings for you, and your feelings for him, whatever they are?"

"Yes!" Celia practically shouted. "It's fine; we're both fine." Knowing, really, that she didn't know. But she wouldn't give way, she couldn't. She couldn't say *no* now; Alonzo would be so disappointed. And for no good reason, really. In fact, he might think the worst, that Celia had second thoughts about going with him."

"I just wonder if . . ." Grace continued, and then she stopped, exhaling deeply

"I'm going," Celia said, quietly, "with him."

Dead silence, only the tickling of the mantle clock.

"Well, I can't stop you," Grace said, finally. She held up a hand. "Just, please, no drama. Nothing."

The worst had passed. Grace had said her piece, aired her concerns. What would be, would be. Grace went to get her tote bag in the living room, then returned to the table.

"Sorry, Cinderella," she said wryly, "I have nothing suitable for a prom."

"Yeah, that's a problem," Celia agreed, still at the table. "I'm thinking of trying that second-hand store on Grove Street."

Grace was digging in the tote for her teaching folders. A glimmer of a smile came to her eyes. "That's run by the Ladies' Aid at the Hospital, you know. The closest you'll get is a mother-of-the-bride's dress in salmon or turquoise."

Celia must have looked stricken.

"Well, good luck with that," Grace said, pulling off the place mats. "Can you wipe down the table, please? I've got papers to correct."

Finally, Celia got her long-awaited trip to the beach. As a reward for all their hard work on the play, she and Alonzo were going to splash in the water and bask in the sun. Happily, Alonzo knew how to swim and said he liked the sand and surf—unlike Jay. The day started clear and promising, already warm by nine-thirty. Celia packed the trunk of Grace's car with chairs, cooler, blanket, pillows, magazines and towel. To make room, she removed the shower gift, a heavy, cumbersome box of wooden tray tables, wrapped in white and silver paper, putting it in the small storage area under the stairway next to the bike. When Alonzo arrived at ten with the all-purpose backpack, Celia was ready to head out of town, due east to the coast in about an hour's time.

The Delaware Beach was crowded, not surprising for a hot, sticky Sunday. Celia and Alonzo found a spot some distance from the parking lot, hauling the beach stuff between them. By the time they set up, they were sweating, ready to cool off in the water. Celia stripped off her shorts and tank shirt, down to Grace's black one-piece, not much different than a leotard. Only it was, with her arms and legs exposed, and a deeper-cut neckline. Beside her, Alonzo pulled the tee shirt over his head, displaying his abdomen and chest—trim and muscular. Turning her gaze to sea, Celia wondered how she had not realized they were spending the day in bathing suits.

After a quick dip, they were chased out of the water by masses of tiny, stinging jelly fish. The waves were disappointingly flat, in any case. Celia resigned herself to lying on her back on the blanket. Under sunglasses, she could see Alonzo in her peripheral vision, legs stretched out from the beach chair, face tipped to the sky. He looked good—handsome, sexy. Girls walking along the shore tittered as they passed. Unexpectedly, Celia found herself agitated, restless, even annoyed. After a bit, she sat in a chair, trying to read, but couldn't focus on the pages, fighting the beginnings of a headache.

Around one they ate the sandwiches and chips, drinking lemonade out of paper cups. By then, Alonzo was ready for another swim, but Celia was feeling drowsy. She flopped over on her stomach and fell asleep, dozing and waking to see Alonzo in his chair, and then later, next to her on the blanket, inches away. At one point, she felt a wet cloth on her shoulders and then a cool hand on her cheek, but she could barely manage to mumble thanks. When it was time to leave, she was still in a daze, and Alonzo took the keys from her purse, driving them home just as Celia's sunburn began to really bloom. They had talked about going out for pizza, but she wasn't hungry and couldn't make any decisions until she had showered.

They got back to the apartment just before four. Celia, in sunburned misery, tromped upstairs, forgetting all about the tray tables. Grace was on the phone in heated conversation with Alec, who apparently had to cancel last minute due to a work emergency. Her face was also red, and she didn't look at all happy as she took the keys from Alonzo—not that she was mad at him. Celia headed immediately to the bathroom for some aspirin and a cold shower. At four-thirty, she was on the sofa bed while Alonzo sat at the kitchen table looking through a magazine, an icy drink at his elbow. Celia couldn't decide whether to offer Alonzo a chance to rinse off in the shower. He was coated with sand and smelled a bit ripe. Of course, it would be fine; but maybe, somehow, not good judgment on her part to have him here alone, wet, and in a towel. She groaned, second guessing herself, thinking, *What would Grace do?* But, of course, Grace never found herself in these situations.

The phone rang. Grace was calling from the bridal shower, looking for the trays. The box was missing from the trunk. Did Celia know what happened to them?

She certainly did. The problem was, there was no car to transport the tray tables to the party. But Grace, both annoyed and relieved, had already worked out a plan. If Celia knew where the box was, which Grace assumed she did, Grace would call Roxanne to ask if Celia could borrow her car for the half-hour ride to Chestertown. Roxanne wouldn't mind, if she wasn't otherwise using it. Grace would call back as soon as she reached Roxanne—or didn't.

Celia leaned back on the sofa bed, her wet hair in a towel, appalled. It was just the kind of thoughtlessness that she dreaded showing toward her sister. Such a little thing to expect: the gift in the car, where it belonged. When she told Alonzo what Grace had called about, her voice sounded whiny and fretful.

"Nobody died," Alonzo said, putting down the magazine. He sat on a folded towel since his trunks were still damp. The dark shadows at his knees and elbows glistened from baby oil, and there were patches of sand coating his calves and ankles. "If you want, I'll run it up there for you. Just get me the directions."

Celia thought before answering. It was tempting. She was so tired and so burned, even her eyeballs felt dried out. Alonzo liked driving and he was careful. But no, it wasn't Grace's car; it was Roxanne's. And once at the party, what would Grace think if he showed up by himself, in his trunks and muscle shirt? Or the hostess, or the other party guests? But it made her feel like crying, she was so uncomfortable and so mad at herself.

"No. I've got to go. I'm the one that made the mistake. But would you mind driving? I'll just run in and leave off the box. It won't take a minute."

"Sure. Ready any time. Just say the word."

"We still have to see if I can use Roxanne's car. Grace . . ." Celia broke off as the phone rang. It was Grace, and Roxanne was happy to let her borrow the car, just two blocks away.

"Oh, great," Celia muttered, hanging up the phone. "We're on." She had kind of hoped the car wasn't available, and Grace would just have to explain about her spacey sister and give an IOU. Make it a joke. It was an honest mistake, after all. But no, she had to make things right. Celia got up to change again. With that crowd, she had to look presentable. It was the least she owed Grace not to show up sloppy and braless.

There was a pink dress in Grace's closet in a light fabric with short sleeves. She grabbed Grace's bone pumps, but could not bear the thought of stockings. A dab of lipstick, no blush needed. In her rush, a hack job with the mascara. Alonzo was waiting when she emerged and wanted to know if Roxanne's car was air-conditioned.

"It better be," Celia exclaimed. But it wasn't.

The ride north was so quiet, Celia dozed again. Alonzo didn't even bother to put the music on, preoccupied with his own thoughts. Off the highway, they made a wrong turn, stopping at a gas station for directions. From the center of Chestertown, it was a short distance to the stately house with a long, narrow driveway and beautiful, landscaped gardens. There were so many cars already that they had to park on the street.

"Why don't I pull up to the front and let you out? That box is heavy," he said. He was the one who replaced it in the trunk.

"Nonsense," Celia said, somehow more uneasy now they had arrived. It was an imposing house. The bride-to-be, Meredith, had come from money. She was a nurse at the hospital, and a good one, according to Grace. And pretty, too. Celia had met her once. Not surprisingly, Meredith was marrying a doctor, who likely made a great deal of money, not to mention the good salary that she earned. They could probably count on a bright future, worthy and comfortable.

"I can carry it. I haven't been working out all these months for nothing." Celia climbed out of the car, and went around to the back where Alonzo had popped open the trunk. He pulled out the package, slightly crinkled from where it had stood on the floor of the storage area.

"At least let me carry it to the door for you," he said, watching as Celia struggled to balance the package. Celia could see the wide bay windows at the front of the house and heads and shoulders of men and women at the party. They, too, could see anyone approaching the front of the house.

"No, I can manage," she said, a bit terse. When he looked puzzled, she added, "I got myself into this mess; I have to fix it."

"But I went with you to the beach," he protested. Celia shook her head again. "No." He stared at her and then dropped his gaze, returning to the driver's side of the car.

"Alonzo . . ." She stood paralyzed in the hot sun with a twenty-pound weight in her arms. But it was no time to explain, or to argue.

"It's fine," he said.

She turned and walked toward the house as quickly as possible in the low heels. As she mounted the steps, someone opened the door to let her in. Someone who must have seen her coming. By this point, she was sweating like a pig through her dress, and feeling a little light-headed from the exertion.

"Thank you," she grunted, walking into the cool front hall.

"A little thing like you handling a big package like that." A sweet-smelling, matronly woman in white frowned sympathetically. "Honey, you should have asked for help with that big bundle. Just put it down and come in. One of the men will get it."

"Oh," said Celia, putting down the box and straightening her dress. "I'm not a guest. Just the delivery girl. I took the present out of my sister's car to pack my beach things."

The woman smiled, amused. She had bright blue eyes and few wrinkles for an older lady, forty or fifty or sixty. "Oh, you must be Celia we heard about. I'm Meredith's Aunt Lily. Of course you're a guest, now you've come all this way. Let's get you a drink, sweetheart. There's a wonderful punch."

The cool air and delicious smells, her parched throat: Celia couldn't say no.

"Just a soft drink for me," she said. "Then back on the road."

Celia followed Aunt Lily into the living room, hung with crepe paper streamers and paper swans, a little too elegant for balloons. She looked around for Grace, but she must have been in one of the back rooms.

"Here's Celia, in the nick of time, with present safely delivered," Aunt Lily announced to the room. Twenty heads, male and female, in the large front room turned to look. Celia had never been so hot in the face. Meredith, the niece, with her neat ash-blond hair and perfect make-up and pale blue dress came up next to Aunt Lily. She caught Celia's eye and began to laugh, and soon the room was filled with good-natured laughter.

"Grace is in the sunroom," Meredith said, escorting her to the back of the house. "We heard about your little dilemma. You really didn't have to come. We could have made other arrangements."

"Oh, yes, I did have to come," Celia said. "I would have been in the dog house for months, and deserved it, too."

"Now that you're here, please stay," Meredith said. "There are probably a number of people you know. And way too much food."

A woman approached, rather similar to Aunt Lily. Meredith's mother, perhaps. Clearly a relative. Clearly a matter of business.

"I'm sorry," Meredith said to Celia, "I've got to go. There's Grace by the fern tree. Do stay."

Celia nodded her thanks without answering. She just wanted to find Grace, tell her about the gift, get back to the car, and go home. The sunroom was larger than their apartment and filled to its high ceiling with potted trees and plants. Grace stood in a small group of women, a couple of whom she had met before. Waving, Celia made her way over.

"I'm here. I'm here," she called out. "Sorry I messed up."

Grace didn't look all that pleased to see her. She had a right to be mad. Plus, of course, the worry that someone might have broken into her car, perhaps bringing up some unpleasant speculation about Celia and who she was associating with. But there was something more; a strained look that didn't seem to have anything to do with Celia. Maybe it was the absent Alec she was really mad at, Celia thought hopefully, and then regretted it. It was strange seeing her sister so formal and made up in a cocktail dress. Like another person, almost, in a costume. And Celia wasn't sure she liked it, even though she loved nothing better than dressing up and trying on different characters herself.

"I guess you managed with Roxanne's car," Grace said.

"Yes, it was no problem." The room was too bright for Celia's eyes. She blinked a couple times, trying to focus.

"What's wrong?" Grace was examining her. "You look a little glassy." She turned to her friends, "Excuse me, please, for a moment."

They moved to a quiet corner and sat down on a plaid-cushioned rattan loveseat amid the lush foliage.

"A little too much sun, I guess," Celia said, slumping into the cushions.

"Did you use sun screen and stay hydrated?"

"Forgot."

Grace sighed. "Maybe you should sit a while. I'll get you a cold drink. I'm sure Meredith won't mind."

Fighting a wave of wooziness, Celia told Grace that Meredith had already invited her to stay, but that she really wanted to get back.

"Maybe some Coke," she said, hesitating. "Or ginger-ale."

"I'll be right back," Grace said, the old, familiar concern returned. She got up, bending over to whisper, "By the way, Celia, you need a slip with that dress. It's see-through against the light."

Celia rolled her eyes.

"Just don't linger by any windows, OK?"

"Anything else?"

"No, I'm just telling you. The dress looks nice, almost matches your skin." Now she was joking; that was better.

Alone on the loveseat, Celia thought about running back to the car to tell Alonzo that she might be a few minutes. But then, if she could get back to the car, he would drive them home. So there really was no problem, except for all these concerned folks. Ah, what to do, what to do? A pleasant scent reached her nose, perhaps one of the greenhouse flowers. Then a shadow passed, and a kind of vision in white. Looking up, she recognized Aunt Lily, who also recognized her.

"Celia, dear, are you all right?"

"Fine, thank you." Technically, that was not true. Still, it was no time to call attention to herself at someone else's special occasion. "What a lovely party."

"It is. Of course, Meredith arranged most of it herself, even though her mother and I are officially the hostesses." A small, social smile appeared at her lips. "That's why it's a Jack and Jill shower. She wanted it that way. Such a modern girl. So capable and independent—knows exactly what she likes." Aunt Lily winced, the smile fading. "I've got to sit down. These shoes are killing me."

Celia pushed over, scanning the room for Grace. No matter how great Meredith's virtues, she didn't have time to appreciate them right now. What if Alonzo got it in his head to come looking for her?

"Yes, she's a terrific nurse, I hear." It was amazing how she could do the small talk, even in times like this. All those years of actor training really paid off.

Aunt Lily pulled off her shoes and was rubbing her feet together, settling in. "Meredith's the best at whatever she does. I really need to find her and ask her about the brie, whether or not it should be heated. But I suppose it can wait. Gracious, look at the food that's out already."

"Yes," Celia answered, dutifully looking and at the same time ransacking her brain for an excuse to get up and leave. But she couldn't do it. She wasn't capable. She might as well be pinned to the cushion. As Aunt Lily adjusted herself, she placed a cool, dry hand on Celia's arm for balance. It was such a soft and soothing sensation, Celia found herself drawn toward Aunt Lily, attracted to the wide, ample bosom. Like a pillow, gently powdered flesh and white silk. How nice it would be to rest her head there and close her eyes. The sweetened breath, the effusive manner; Celia realized that Aunt Lily already had a few glasses of wine. She straightened up again, pulling herself to attention.

"Everything she does, she does well, Meredith," Aunt Lily went on. Yet, somehow it sounded more like grievance than praise. "She's got it all: brains, looks, and all the social graces."

Celia nodded dumbly, beginning to drift. Outside the sunroom was a tiered patio and an in-ground pool, set against a tall hedge.

"There's no need for her to work so hard, no need to work at all. Her father, you know, is a professor, a very well-respected legal scholar, made a name for himself in administrative law. Many articles published; many."

Yes, money in the family, Celia thought dreamily. No, she hadn't known about Meredith's father, the famous professor.

"She could have been a society lady, like her mother. But no, she would have a career. And a difficult, challenging career as well, nursing. She's got these ideas about things, you know, men and women and work and so forth."

Celia reminded herself to stay alert, look out for Grace. No dozing.

"Of course, I'm old-fashioned," Aunt Lily acknowledged, pushing her feet back into her shoes. "Now why she wanted to invite them I'll never understand." She motioned with no great subtlety across the room to where two black women and a man stood together, balancing drinks and plates. Celia hadn't noticed them before, what with all the people, decorations, and plant life.

"They work at the hospital. I was introduced, but I don't remember their names," Aunt Lily confessed. "It's so awkward for them, too."

Celia said nothing.

"Oh, goodness, I'll never get these shoes back on." Aunt Lily struggled to dig her feet in. "I'd better see about the brie and such other useless duties as Meredith's seen fit to give me." She turned to squeeze Celia's arm. "Thanks for letting an old lady bend your ear." She started to rise. "Oh, and you might like to freshen up in the bathroom. There are some nice young, single men here that Meredith would be happy to introduce you to."

"Oh, certainly," Celia smiled vacantly. Honestly, what was the woman going on about? In the front room, Meredith had stopped to speak to a guest.

"Just look at her," Aunt Lily beamed. "Isn't she a vision? You know, Celia, honey, blue is the color for you blondes. Leave the pinks and roses to the dark-haired girls." She winked. "Some free advice from your Aunt Lily." Patting her on the head, Aunt Lily tottered off. Celia looked rapidly about, wondering if she was steady enough to get up and go find Grace.

But luck was not on her side. In another second, Grace was back with the admirable Meredith in tow, her face full of sympathy.

"It could be heatstroke." Meredith felt Celia's forehead and the back of her neck.

"You're warm," she pronounced. "And probably dehydrated. Here, drink up." She took the glass of ginger ale from Grace and watched Celia sip it down. Grace handed Celia a damp wad of napkins for her face, while Meredith took her pulse. It was like being sent to the nurse's office. Meredith stood over her, her pretty brow furrowed.

"Nauseous?" she asked, which Celia was slightly, but didn't want to say so.

"It's hard to say." Meredith shook her head. "I'm not that familiar with heatstroke. Are you, Grace?"

What would Grace know of heatstroke, who always wore hats and that sticky sun screen in the summer?

"Not really."

Meredith snapped her fingers. "What am I thinking? Here we are standing in a room full of doctors, one of whom I'm going to marry, so he'd better be good." She swiveled on her foot to call across the room. "Dr. Campbell, Dr. Fenton, can you come here, please, and render assistance?"

Celia groaned, although she didn't mean to. The doctors appeared at Meredith's side, ready to do their best.

"Are you ill?" the first asked, big forehead, glasses.

"No. Meredith is just fussing because of my red face."

"Do you think it might be heatstroke, sweetheart?" Meredith asked the other doctor, who was tall, dark, and handsome. When she turned her head, an earring twinkled, sapphire blue to match her dress and eyes.

"Hm . . ." Dr. Sweetheart took a closer look. "Maybe. But that's a bad burn, the kind that can lead to skin cancer later in life." He looked meaningfully at Celia. "You should be more careful."

"Oh, I will. I will," she promised, in agony. She was stuck, out of ideas. The sun must have pulverized her brain. How she would love to lie down. Perhaps she could just expire here on the loveseat. That would solve all her problems, and give them something useful to do. They were already present and circled around her to perform the autopsy: death from sunburn and embarrassment. But no, Alonzo might still show up, creating all manner of speculation.

"My advice: stay cool, relax a while, and nibble at some crackers or even the finger sandwiches, if your stomach is OK. An hour or so, you should be fine." Dr. Fiancé was speaking in his medical voice.

"I can't stay," Celia cried out. The ginger-ale and adrenaline had started to kick in. "I've got to get home, so I can change and, uh, rest."

"You can rest here. And borrow a nightie, if you like," Meredith urged. "I don't think it's a good idea for you to drive back right now. What's the harm?"

"I . . . I . . . I brought a friend," Celia got out. "And . . . this . . . friend will drive me home."

"Let's bring her right inside, then. She can help us celebrate while you recover. The more the merrier. For heaven's sake, did you leave her sitting in a hot car? I'll send someone out."

"No!" Celia pleaded. "Please don't. I can go myself."

Grace was giving her a strange look. *What friend? Alonzo, who else?* There was a remote chance it could have been Shelly or Anita, or some woman friend from the club, but not likely.

"You know," Grace said in a matter-of-fact tone as her eyes met Celia's, "the car is borrowed from my friend Roxanne," she explained. "They really should get it back. I'm sure she's got evening plans."

"We said we'd have the car back right away, by . . ." Celia's muddled mind couldn't even fabricate what time the car hypothetically had to be returned. "You're all so kind," she heard herself saying. "Meredith, you'll be the best wife, I just can tell. And, Dr. um, it's wonderful how you will be able to take care of each other—medically, of course, and emotionally." That was probably just about the nuttiest thing she had ever said, but they smiled with good grace. And then they departed, finally, leaving Celia with Grace, her poor sister.

Through the window of the front room, Celia saw a movement. A dark shape was making its way slowly and cautiously up the line of nine or ten cars in the driveway. Alonzo. In dismay, she lurched from her seat and spilled the drink.

"Celia!" Grace said.

"What a klutz. I'm so sorry. "

Grace bent over to scoop up the ice cubes and pat the wet spot with a napkin. She looked up, expecting Celia to join her, but instead Celia blurted, "Grace, I've got to run. Right now, this minute. Sorry!"

Sitting back on her heels, Grace nodded, knowing, because she knew her sister, that some craziness was going on. She called out to Celia's back, "Take care of yourself, for heaven's sake. And get that car back safely."

Celia was almost sprinting, high-stepping awkwardly in the too-small sandals along the driveway. When Alonzo saw her, he stopped until she reached him and motioned him back toward the car. When he started to speak, she turned her face away and silenced him with a wave of her arm. A couple of tears spilled down her cheeks that she did not want him to see. The slanting sun was still hot and stabbed at the back of her neck. It was like an electric prod, pushing her forward, away from the cool haven of Meredith's house.

A picture came into her mind: Adam and Eve banished from Eden for eating the apple, one of those old museum-type paintings she'd seen somewhere, maybe in a book. The two of them were downcast, full of guilt, attempting to cover their private parts, while an angel hovered above with a flaming sword. Like that was really needed. Out, out they were driven, like stupid cattle. No more icy drinks, tasty tid-bits, ferns, and soft cushions in the sunroom for Celia, or Alonzo, either, for that matter. In the picture, Adam now had brown skin and sandy knees and Eve was sweaty and burned with disheveled hair.

Finally, they arrived at the car, out of sight of the house. Alonzo paused at the driver's door, clearly confused.

"What happened to you? You were gone so long, I thought there was a problem."

"Yeah," agreed Celia, out of breath, sweat trickling down her knees and back. "There was a problem: me. Stupid me."

"What do you mean?"

"Nothing. Never mind. Let's just get out of here." In the passenger seat, Celia saw that she had spilled ginger ale on the dress, and it was now on Roxanne's upholstery. "I'm sorry you had to wait," she said.

"It's OK," Alonzo said

"I don't feel good." Celia slid down in her seat, wrapping the wet part of her skirt over her knees.

"Are you going to throw up?"

"No, just . . . bleh."

"Let's stop for water and some ice," Alonzo said. "My throat is parched, and you look like you need something cold and wet." He started the car and drove to the gas station where they had stopped for directions. The middle-

295

aged pump attendant saw they weren't looking for a fill up and pointed at the quick-stop next door. His gaze took in the two of them with a curious frown, and Celia dreaded whatever ugly words were going to come out of his mouth. But, looking at Celia, all he said was, "She looks poorly. Maybe you want some Alka Seltzer."

"Celia?" Alonzo asked, but she shook her head no. Alonzo went inside, returning with a bottle of water, paper towels, some Cokes, and a bag of ice. As he got back to the car, the attendant approached again, looking through the window at Celia slumped in her seat.

"Better get her home quick," the man said to Alonzo. "She needs a cool shower and a fan."

"I've got it," Alonzo replied, as he started the car and pulled away.

On the highway, they sipped their drinks, not talking. Celia held a packet of ice wrapped in a paper towel next to her forehead. She stared at the fabric upholstery of the roof, images flashing in rapid succession: the steps to Meredith's house; the bouncing streamers; the glint of light on the pool; Meredith's face, slightly freckled.

Then she recalled another detail: Meredith's earrings, sapphires surrounded by tiny seed pearls. Celia had seen those before or something very like them at Peebles, real gemstones, not faux. She had seen them and wanted them, but at four hundred dollars, she could not afford them, not now and maybe never. But Meredith had them. She had everything, Celia thought, fighting back tears.

There was some kind of terrible mix-up. Meredith had somehow gotten Celia's life, the life that she was supposed to have. Her successful father, her big house, the nice man that Celia should have been engaged to. More than that, her security and peace of mind. All the good things. Not to mention the brie and the crabmeat sandwiches.

And then, looking out the window, she had another thought. It wasn't her life that Meredith had taken; it was Grace's. Grace was the independent go-getter, the capable and professional one. The one who worked in the medical field, not the struggling artist with undeveloped talent. It was Grace who had struggled so hard to get a good job and a place to live, and a solid, steadfast guy to go out with. Who lived well and dressed well and took care of people.

And then, her thoughts turned to Alonzo, baking out in this hot car, uninvited in, by her, for some cool air and refreshment. Because of, because of . . . More tears slipped down her face. In the driver's seat, Alonzo sat upright, focused on the road. He should be angry with her, how she had treated him. But instead he said to the man at the gas station, "I've got it."

After half an hour, Celia started feeling better, her skin not so hot and her head not so achy. By the time they arrived in Sutton, the weather had cooled. They parked the car at Roxanne's apartment, Celia rang the bell and gave her back the keys, saying it had all worked out, but she was burned from the beach and couldn't stop in.

At the apartment, Alonzo helped get her set up with a fan, wet cloths, and an ice pack wrapped in a dishcloth for her shoulders. Still, she didn't feel good.

"Alonzo." She had to say something before he left. "I'm sorry. . . . I should have . . ."

"We don't need to talk about it now. You're not yourself. Get some rest."

"Alonzo, I shouldn't have done that, making you wait like that for so long."

"You didn't do anything wrong."

"I didn't do something right. I have no excuse." And then she tried to explain. "I just felt so bad, you know, my head, my skin. They were all being so . . . well, nice . . . they were all around me, trying to help me. It was like I was trapped, and, and . . ."

Alonzo held up a hand, shaking his head. "Enough."

"I was afraid if they saw you coming up the driveway like that . . ."

"Let it go." His raised his voice, more commanding.

She met his eyes, and gave up. "OK."

He was on his feet, headed toward the door. "I'll be going now."

"Wait."

He stopped, turning, and Celia took a quick breath, "But we're still on for the prom, right?"

He gave a quick nod.

"No. It's important," Celia said. "Please say yes, you still want to go with me."

Still he looked a bit impatient. "Yes, I do want to."

"Sure?"

"Sure." He didn't look very enthusiastic. Or, maybe he was just hot, tired, and hungry himself.

Now she was sitting upright, the icepack slipping off. "I'll make it up to you, all fun and good times—you'll see."

He waved it off, but then stopped, giving her a lingering look before he walked out the door on his way home.

At night, Celia lay awake, listening for the sound of Grace's car. As the headlights swung across the ceiling, she finally found the words. "I'm ashamed," she said out loud. "Ashamed of myself. What was I thinking?" Her whole body flushed with heat, her skin aflame. The entire mess-up was her fault. First, her carelessness about the trays. And then, her fear of embarrassing Grace, making Grace lose face somehow—as if Grace needed to measure up to Meredith and her friends. All Celia had to do was let Alonzo carry the box to the front door, where she could leave a message, and then they could go. Instead, that foolish charade—trying to hide Alonzo's presence, leaving him to suffer in that car.

When she heard Grace's keys turning in the downstairs lock, she turned over, closing her eyes. In the darkened room, she felt like a dying ember. When Grace opened the door, all she would find was Celia's ashes. *If only!* Celia couldn't face her sister, or anyone; not yet. Even with sunburn and heatstroke, she should have known better. As the door swung open, letting in the hall light, Celia promised herself she would find a way to make things right. She would talk things over with Grace, slow down, and be upfront. As for Alonzo, she would be the best date ever at the prom—her most beautiful, obliging, charming self. He could hold her tight as they danced. And, if he wanted, he could kiss her, there on the dance floor, or anywhere, in front of anyone. It wasn't just making it up to him; she wanted to be with him, she wanted him to be happy—happy with her.

Chapter 25

At New You, the week started off with a bang. Things were hopping. A new group of women, mostly from the hospital, had joined and were coming on a regular basis. Several nurses requested a three-thirty class, after they got off the seven to three shift. Celia had picked up more hours to cover for Shelly and also a couple of evenings when they decided to extend hours. She was tired when she got home, but the money was slowly adding up.

Celia was filling out a new client form when she heard Anita clear her throat in the front lobby.

"Attention, please. I have an announcement to make," Anita said, so that everyone could hear, inside the office and out. "We have hired a new associate, starting tomorrow, and you will all love her. Her name is Tammy, and she is terrific. With Tammy on board, we can offer more hours and a greater range of classes. Please be sure to welcome her when you see her."

At their desks, Celia laughed and Shelly rolled her eyes. Of course, it was news to them, too, but they were not hugely surprised. They had been discussing getting another person for some time. Typical Anita to make a splash. No doubt Tammy was a good find. Anita had an eye for people.

"So, where did you find her?" Celia asked when Anita stepped into the office to drop off some files.

"The Inn, where else?" The Inn, very interesting. And, Celia wanted to know, what was she like? Young, or not so young? Local or from away? lack or white? Pretty?

"And, so, what's she like?"

"She's coming by this afternoon; you can meet her."

Later in the morning, Anita came over to observe as Celia worked with June from the beauty salon—a reluctant exerciser who had fitness thrust upon her in the form of a gift certificate from her daughter, worried about her mother's high blood pressure.

"Oh, don't let her near me," June exclaimed, looking over Celia's shoulder at Anita. "She's got no compassion, whatsoever, for the out of shape. I'll stick with you, dear." She smiled at Celia. "She's a good girl, Anita, and she's nice to people. You're lucky to have her."

"I know that." Anita feigned insult. "I'm the one who found her." Then she smiled too. "She's got a good head on her shoulders, and I'm trying my best to put God in her heart."

"I hope the new one is good," June said. "I mean with fat women."

"Of course," Anita said. "Come back later and find out for yourself."

The new girl, Tammy, was a hot ticket. A college student home for the summer, she was white, a dirty-blonde with her hair in a ponytail, a little shorter than Celia and more athletically built. Cute, but not as pretty as Celia. She lived with her parents, sister, and brother in town, and had attended Sutton High School, where her dad was a gym teacher. Nothing Anita said or did disturbed her in the least. And she was pretty good with fat women too.

After a couple days, Celia started to think here was someone, finally, that it would be easy to make friends with: similar age, single, active, some college experience, loved music and dancing. Furthermore, Tammy knew her way around the area—and she worked a couple nights a week at the Inn and knew everyone there, every single one. She'd worked there the past two summers. From what Celia could tell, she had lots of friends across the color lines. Friendly and outgoing, a little fresh and a lot of fun. Thank you, Anita!

Celia ended up asking ask Tammy if she would cover for her on Friday afternoon, day of the prom, since she was leaving early. Normally she was the only one there from four to six, because Anita worked at the Inn and Shelly picked up the twins for the weekend. Tammy was happy to take the hours; otherwise, they'd have to close early.

"Big date? Come on, tell," Tammy prodded. It was late afternoon on Wednesday; they were alone and Celia was deciding what music to play for the four o'clock aerobics class. Tammy was in Shelly's chair, sucking on a Tootsie pop, although candy was expressly forbidden. "I haven't got anything going on and I'm dying to meet somebody. I don't even care if he's dumb. I was going out with this boy at school—yeah, smart guy all right, but so controlling, like there was always a right way to do things, and then my way. Oh, spare me. I'm too young for goals and plans. I just want a honey I can hug and squeeze. Thank goodness for our friend, the little white pill. Wouldn't it be awful to live in a time without birth control?"

Celia's eyebrows lifted, but there didn't seem any need to answer. "I really appreciate you covering for me, Tammy. Ask me, anytime."

"Just a little minute. You didn't tell me your plans. Yeah, I'm nosy. I don't deny it."

"I am going out," Celia conceded.

"Sounds like some kind of special occasion."

Celia was tempted to tell Tammy about the prom, but decided it was probably better to be discrete. She barely knew the girl—or what she was likely to pass on

A couple files needed to be put away. They heard the front door bell jangle, but it was just one of the ladies leaving for the day.

"Well?" Tammy said, as Celia took a timer from the desk drawer.

"I'm afraid to say any more. If it goes well, I'll tell you afterwards, OK?"

"Is it a married man?"

"No, it is not."

"Black guy?"

Celia was taken aback. She didn't expect to be asked so directly. "I have to plead the Fifth, Tammy, you know because of Anita and her policy on these things."

"Now we're getting somewhere. Yes, Anita has shared her dating philosophy with me on several occasions. Yet, things happen, sometimes under her very own nose. You know her daughter started seeing a white boy at school?"

"No!"

"She kept it hidden as long as she could, but Anita found out. Of course, the harder she tries to pressure her, the harder she'll push back. Just human nature." Tammy was rummaging for more snacks and found some pretzels.

"But," Celia said, "it seems like she never had much luck about breaking up Jay and Pauline. That's supposed to be her best friend's nephew, and a family that goes to her church."

"Oh, those two." Tammy's eyes twinkled. "Don't think she hasn't tried. But they've survived her best efforts—until now, of course, they're split up. But that wasn't her doing. I don't know what finally did them in." She laughed. "Maybe I'll get a chance with Jay now. Do you think that's naughty? I'll tell you what. It might almost be worth my job here. I did kiss him once, in ninth grade, before Pauline moved in and took over."

Celia stood open-mouthed.

"Don't tell me you're shocked. I thought you were Miss California Love and Peace."

"It's not that."

"What is it then? You look like a fish waiting for a worm."

"I slept with him, with Jay, just once." Celia couldn't believe she was saying it, for the first time, to another human being.

"No way!" Tammy shouted. She drummed the desk in excitement.

Celia nodded.

"How the hell did that happen?"

"I don't know, exactly. Kind of a mistake, in a way. I mean, it was when he and Pauline were split up, only I didn't even know about her, and then they got back together again, right afterwards. I almost can't believe it really happened."

Tammy looked awestruck. "If you had any idea how many girls in our school wanted that boy . . . Well, was it as great as we all imagined it to be?"

"Don't ask me that," Celia said. "He was very nice at the time, that's all I'm going to say."

The bell jangled once, then again. Celia and Tammy looked at the clock. The women were beginning to arrive for class.

"Come on," Celia said, picking out one of her favorite music tapes. "If you want to see this routine. We can run through it once, you and me, before class starts." She stopped at the doorway, looking back. "And thanks again, for covering for me on Friday."

She entered the workout area with a little bounce in her step. She was suddenly happier than she had been in a long time. A secret was out. She had a new friend. Jay and Pauline—history! And she was going to the senior prom with a great guy. That was a lot of good stuff, all at once. Why not be happy?

Then it was countdown to the prom. Getting a prom dress had not been too difficult, considering the shortness of time. As Grace had predicted, there was nothing suitable at the consignment shop. But at Peebles, Celia found last year's prom dresses on sale for 70% off. That she could afford. She picked a royal blue dress, fitted in the waist with a medium neckline and short, straight sleeves. It didn't look much on the hanger, but better on. Even Grace agreed it was a good choice when Celia tried it on for her at home.

"Kind of tame for you," Grace observed. "What about ruffles and lace?"

"I'm getting older," Celia said. "And Alonzo appreciates my sophisticated taste."

"Oh, of course."

The truth was, when Celia had tried on some of the more elaborate gowns, she kept seeing Laurette in the mirror. And that was not someone she wanted to emulate. Celia found that she was off red satin, maybe forever. And then, when she'd slipped on a white dress with lace and puffy sleeves, a girl shopping with her mother said, "She looks like a bride." Putting it back, Celia thought she might never be that kind of bride. In the end, she was happy with the blue dress, thinking it made her look mature, even womanly, and she hoped that Alonzo would think so too.

They arranged to meet Thursday at the florist to pick out a corsage and boutonniere. Alonzo took the bill from the attendant.

"Here," said Celia, pulling out her wallet, before he stopped her.

"Please," he said, with a hint of irritation. "Let me do this. OK?"

Outside on the sidewalk, she placed a hand on his arm. "Are you still upset with me about Sunday, the shower? I really am sorry. You didn't really let me apologize properly. I know it was the wrong thing to do. I should have let you help me, instead of leaving you to bake in Roxanne's car."

His look was first puzzled and then almost amused. "Yeah, I know you didn't want to deal with it, explaining about me." He shrugged. "I told you before, let it go. We're none of us perfect." Then he tipped his head. "But I got out of the car and took a nap in the shade. That's where I was, until I realized you were gone so long."

Celia's jaw dropped. Of course—Alonzo was no idiot. And good for him he had a nap. Once again, her assumption had been wrong. But this time, the story was for the better. Her whole face brightened. She hooked her arm through his elbow as they started down the sidewalk. "So, I think we're in pretty good shape, then, for this prom. Don't you?"

"It's going to be something," he agreed, bouncing along next to her. "A once-in-a-lifetime, for sure."

To Celia's surprise, Grace was a big help getting ready for the prom. She had hung the prom dress on back of the bedroom door for the wrinkles to fall out. She had found a small white purse Celia could take instead of her big, floppy handbag. And she brought out some hairspray and put bobby pins in place to secure Celia's updo. Fine details had never been Celia's strong suit. What a sister—to be so supportive in spite of all her misgivings.

At the apartment, Alonzo stood inside the door while Celia showed off the dress, taking a few turns on the rug.

"Isn't she something," Alonzo said to Grace, who nodded. "She looks like a real . . ."

Celia held up a warning hand. "Do not say *princess* or I will have to hurt you."

Alonzo didn't look too surprised or perturbed. But he raised his voice. "Give a body a chance," he said. "You're too quick, sometimes." Which was true.

"Sorry," she said, striking a haughty pose.

"Queen," he said. "I was going to say *queen.*"

"I don't look that old."

"A very young queen," Alonzo continued calmly, "still getting used to the throne, but very kind and just and beautiful."

"Why, Alonzo," Grace turned to him, "that's charming."

"OK," Celia said, blushing. "I'll take that."

After Grace got a few snapshots, they drove the six blocks to the high school, parking in the big lot outside the cafeteria. Couples, black, white, and some mixed, were walking toward the entrance. A big girl passed in a bright pink gown and long black gloves. Celia did a double-take, thinking it was Bettina, but it wasn't.

"Will Bettina and Desiree be here, do you think?" Celia asked Alonzo, getting out of the car.

"They'll be here. Desiree is coming with Laurence, you know, Milo from the play. I don't know who Bettina's date is, but I know she got a dress."

"You do, do you?" Another, not so pleasant, thought occurred. "What about Morris, and his crew—do you think they'll come?"

Alonzo laughed. "Not likely; not them. I'm not saying they won't be by to see the action, but they're not going to buy tickets and tuxes for something like this."

A photographer was taking instamatic pictures as each couple entered the cafeteria. The background was an arched trellis decorated with flowers and a white wicker bench to sit on. The pictures were five dollars each, and Alonzo said he wanted one. They sat, heads touching, and waited for the results—only a mixed success. The flash made her skin colorless and his face too shiny. Still, it was a memento.

"Here, I'll keep it in my purse," Celia said, taking the picture from Alonzo.

They entered the big, darkened cafeteria, disco lights flashing and the heavy bass of dance music. Already it felt warm and humid. The room was not air conditioned, although standing fans were placed in the corners. They stopped at a set of chairs pushed back against the wall, where they watched the crowd already on the dance floor. Celia spotted Desiree and Milo and pulled Alonzo to join them, just a little warm up. At the end of the song, Desiree waved them to the chairs. Milo gave Celia a big smile—they had been sweethearts on stage, after all. Maybe Desiree placed her hand more firmly on his arm; hard to say. But Celia knew it was nothing. They were so clearly a couple—Desiree in outrageous red, and Milo in navy blue with red accents. A mixed-race couple, Celia would have said, but no one would have agreed. It was a marvel to Celia that Milo could look so light, so white, but everyone knew he was black: the walk, the talk, the food, the friends, the music, the culture. His mom, all black. So, he was black. But, she was sure, as in the play, anywhere else he could pass for white.

"We got some wine in the car," Desiree said, "if you want to come out with us."

Alonzo looked at Celia, who wavered at the unexpected invitation. She would love some wine, and she wanted to be friendly. But a little bell tinkled in her ear: *wine, dancing, girls and boys.* She recalled her time at the Starlight: her solo dance with spectacular stumble; making a fool of herself in front of Anita and Frank; and then, of course, throwing up in Wanda's yard.

"Thanks, that sounds great. Maybe a little later," she replied.

"Suit yourself," Desiree said, pulling Milo along. "By the basketball courts."

After they left, Celia and Alonzo danced to the next song, and the next, fast, bouncy songs. At the end of the second, Alonzo put up a hand.

"Time out," he said. "How about some drinks?" At the refreshments table they picked up cups of Coke and Sprite with melting ice. When they returned to their seats, Alonzo took off his jacket—as most of the boys had already done. Beads of sweat formed on his forehead, and a damp stain was growing up his back.

"Sure you don't want to go out for some air?" he asked. Celia tried to read his face.

"Sure, we can go," she said. Then the music started up again, one of her favorite songs, and she looked back with an apologetic smile. "After this one. I love this song. Please. I have to dance."

"You have to?" he said, getting up and wiping his brow with a napkin.

"I do, or I'll die."

"Well, OK, then."

After that, a slow song started, a good one, and she turned to Alonzo, who stood waiting to see if they were staying or going.

"I like this one too," she said.

"Yeah, all right," Alonzo agreed.

"Open your collar, and roll up your sleeves."

He stepped up to her, putting his arms around her waist, like the other boys were doing. Celia held on to his shoulders lightly, and they took a few steps like this, until Celia leaned in closer, and rested her cheek on his chest, feeling his breath on her face. His body through the pressed shirt was solid, and the skin of his neck was warm and damp where they touched. Without thinking, Celia found her fingers massaging his shoulder muscles and he pulled her to him, their bodies pressed together. Then it wasn't just a dance anymore, but a full embrace. Although they didn't look at each other, they

305

held on tight, dizzy with heat and their racing hearts. And she could feel him, growing and stiffening up against her.

He's mine. We're together, some voice in her head said.

No doubt about it: something had changed. Whether it was a good thing or a bad thing, too late now. They stepped to the music, slowly, unconsciously. Was this what Alonzo was hoping for all along? Or did he, too, wonder what was between them? Celia had rarely felt so at home in a man's arms. No nervousness at all, just happiness and promise—promise of good things. As the song was ending, she sighed, wishing that they could stay right here all evening until the lights went out.

She could tell things had changed for Alonzo, too, as they went back to the chairs. They remained standing.

"Do you still want to go outside?" she asked.

His eyes, deep brown-black, focused on her. The words came out slow, labored. "We don't have to stay, you know."

"What do you mean?" Celia asked. "Where else would we go?"

"Some of the others, they're going to Weston to the Riverside Motel. They said, plenty of rooms there."

"Alonzo!" She rolled her eyes, trying for light and humorous, covering her confused surprise. "It's the prom! We came for the dancing and the music, and to show off our pretty clothes. Right?"

She saw disappointment wash over him like a wave.

"I don't want to leave yet," she said. "I want to enjoy the evening here, with you." She tried to reach for his hand, but he pulled it away.

"I thought you wanted to get closer, that's what you meant."

"I do. You know I do." And then, with some heat, "But not like that, at some sleazy, anonymous hotel."

Alonzo adjusted his pants quickly with one hand and ran the other over his face. "I was just hoping tonight—" and he stopped abruptly with a heavy sigh.

She shrugged, now truly upset.

"When it's right." She cleared her throat. "It's just," and then Grace's face appeared in her mind, followed by Anita's. "But I don't want you to expect too much from me, get close and then be disappointed." His face was shutting, and it became heavy going. Not at all what Celia had hoped for their night out. *Stupid motel.* All she wanted was a good time, and yes, maybe some hugging, kissing, stroking his arms and back, the long lines of his cheeks. A bolt of desire shot through her. But she knew better than to go forward blindly.

"You know, I'll be leaving, eventually," she said. "I can't stay here forever, in Sutton."

Alonzo's jaw clenched. "Yes, and I'll be leaving too. Did you forget?"

He was right; she'd somehow forgotten that he had plans, too, more definite than hers.

"Not now," she repeated, getting anxious. "When it's right, when it's a little more definite what's going on for both of us."

"Yeah, right."

"Alonzo." Couldn't he try to be a bit more understanding?

"What?"

"It's something we need to talk about, so there's no misunderstanding, so . . ." She trailed off. Alonzo looked at her sideways. "I'm going out." His voice wasn't loud, but his tone had changed.

"Wait. Where are you going?"

"I'll catch up with Bettina and them. We can leave whenever you want to."

Celia shrugged. Arguing was not going to help. "All right. I'll be out in a little while, then. Just take it easy. Don't overdo it or anything, OK? You know, the wine, and all that . . ."

He stared, and his expression was blank. "I can make my own decisions." Then he walked away. Celia was tempted to follow, but she didn't. Let him cool off. Let him see the merit in her idea—not because she was older, but because, in the end, it would be better for both of them.

Celia took a seat, holding the purse in her lap. There was a lull: the music had stopped and the room had emptied out through the open doors. A few people remained at the drinks table, but there was no one else nearby. Unexpectedly, she felt alone, and stupid, and out of place. Maybe there was something wrong with her. Why was it, she wondered, that Carlos and Jay had both deserted her? Both were handsome, intelligent, ambitious, and focused on their futures. Both of them had been sweet and loving, but not for the long run. They were important in their worlds, but not really all that interested in her hopes or dreams. *But Alonzo,* she reflected, *Alonzo is different.* Because of Brett, because of what happened afterwards, he had been an outsider. And she, in this place, was an outsider too. . . .

She got up, heading to the ladies room, really just to pass time. The restrooms were located at the end of a long, dimly lit hallway. Inside the bathroom, the two stalls were empty, and no one was at the sinks. Thankfully, the smokers headed outside, rather than hanging out in the closed, musty room. At the sink, Celia stared at herself in the smeary mirror, washed out with the stark overhead light. Her hair, pulled back, was escaping its pins, making a ring of curls around her face. She patted it down, and put on more lipstick. Closing her mouth, she rubbed her lips to spread the color.

Without warning, the door opened wide with a gush of stale air. In the mirror, a male figure appeared, dark-skinned with a white shirt. *Alonzo, looking for her!* Celia started to turn.

But it was not Alonzo. Morris walked in, his eyes on Celia while the door swung closed behind. He took a step back, leaning against the door, barring the exit. No hat, and no sweatshirt, but it was him.

"Hey, girl," he greeted her with an easy drawl. "How you doing?"

Celia turned to face him. His skin was glistening with the heat, and his hair was plastered down close to his head, tight and rippled like a bathing cap. A gold chain glinted around his neck in thick, twisted strands.

"Lover's quarrel?" he asked. "I see Romeo out there, sulking."

"Let me out," Celia said evenly, although her heart was beating like mad. *What's he doing here? What else but trouble.* She thought about the knife. She thought about an attack, here in this grimy girl's room, her prom gown on the dusty floor. "You can't keep me here. Someone will be coming any minute."

"Don't be so sure," he said, and his eyes traveled sideways, just to let her know about his boys waiting somewhere outside, keeping an eye out. Or else, he was bluffing. "I just want to talk with you, ask you something."

There was no noise beyond the buzzing of the exhaust fan. Without the thump-thump-boom of the speakers, it felt like the whole building was empty. It crossed Celia's mind, if she screamed, would anyone hear? Her thoughts were scrambled, making her unable to name her feelings, unsure what to do. She was annoyed, yes. Should she be alarmed too? The situation was so ridiculous, stuck in the girl's room in her discount prom dress with a high school bully. Surely Alonzo would come looking for her, or send Bettina or Desiree to find her. It was only a matter of time before someone came. Or would they? What if . . . ?

Celia had a doubt, and then another. What if Alonzo had gotten so mad, he decided not to come back? Or thought she had left? But not without the car. No, that wouldn't happen; he wouldn't think that. What if she had interpreted everything wrong and they were all against her, and thought it was funny and just what she deserved to be scared out of her wits by Morris? Teach her a lesson.

"Hey," he said, jarring her to attention. "What you come here for?" he asked. "This not your prom; you don't belong here. Something wrong, you don't know better?"

She hunched her shoulders.

"They's somethin' about you, white girl," he said, shaking a finger. "You something else. You just go around doing whatever you feel like. You go where you not supposed to go, walking all over town, wearing those tight clothes. You go to the Starlight, you feel like it. You talk to all the boys, no matter what, even that sorry Negro." He jerked his thumb toward the cafeteria. "You got to be the white girl at the black play. What's up with that? "

No answer.

He straightened himself up and took a step closer. She could see the perspiration on his brow and heard a jangle in his pocket. A sparkle from his earlobe caught her eye, a tiny stud. Just then the sound system started up again, distant, and then the music.

"You wasting your time with that boy. He don't know what he is. I try to tell you before, what you need, somebody like me." He tapped himself on the chest. "It's time you know a real nigger. That's what you here for. Ever since you come skipping down the street in a place you don't belong, money spilling out of your pockets. You 'member?"

Of course she did.

"Well, the time is come—you and me, me and you. Nobody gonna bother us here, I can promise you that."

Celia blinked. Her breath had gotten shallow. If he touched her, she would scream. But would anyone hear from this distance, with the music playing so loudly?

"That would be rape," Celia heard herself say, in a voice that sounded like someone else: a teacher, a parent, a lawyer.

Morris smiled, like he genuinely appreciated her response.

"Oh, really? You think so? But everyone know you like black boys, you hang around school and all, so maybe they think you looking for some action. What else you doing here? Everybody know you some crazy white girl from away looking for a good time, likes to play dangerous, break the rules. So, somethin' happens between us—I say this, you say that—who gonna know the truth about the matter?"

That's a bluff, Celia said to herself. But, what if something happened. Could he be right?

"Wouldn't it be something," Morris asked, tilting his head, "if I got a baby on you, and someday you be the mother of a little Morris, cute little monkey, just like me. Maybe he have your pointy nose and little mouth, but he got to have my eyes. When you looking at him, you be seeing me. Come on, it be fun for you raise a brown baby."

Celia's face must have shown disbelief, like maybe he was actually crazy. He moved in closer, striking distance. She gasped and pulled back.

"What, you scared of me? You think I'm going to hurt you?"

Celia willed herself not to lower her gaze.

He leaned in and thrust out his arm. Her hand flew to her mouth, and she knew then, she couldn't scream; there was no air in her lungs. But there was no knife, and he didn't touch her. He yanked the purse out of her hand.

He turned slightly to rest the purse on the other sink, and then opened it. *For what?* There was no money. Alonzo had the car keys with him. The lipstick, the comb, and the prom picture. That was it.

He dropped the picture on the floor. It was the lipstick he was after, the bright, geranium red she had worn for the occasion, thinking even as she put it on: *maybe too bright.* He took off the cover and screwed out the color tip.

"I ain't goin to hurt you," he chided. "I just gonna mark you." He turned back to her with the lipstick held out like a knife, and in a sudden movement, ran the tip up her bare arm onto the bodice of her dress, leaving a bright red gash.

"Stop it!" She drew back, turning away from him. But he had already stepped away to survey his work.

"I leave my mark, so you don't forget me," he explained as he leaned over the sink, peering at his own reflection in the mirror, lipstick in hand. Carefully, he drew lines up his own cheeks, two on each side. Scars? Some kind of tribal decoration?

"What 'chu think of me now?" he said, his face a grimace. "Your worst nightmare? Bogey man gonna get you, catch you up and steal you away."

For the first time, Celia felt a flash of terror. She could not deny Morris had some kind of power, far beyond his age or size. And for the first time, she knew that no one, not even Alonzo, was coming to her rescue. She closed her eyes, summoning strength.

"You can't harm me," she said evenly, "no matter what you do. My heart..." She swallowed. "My heart is pure."

His eyes widened with surprise, or was it amusement? It was not what he expected. For a long moment, he hesitated, emotions playing over his face. "That right?" he said, rubbing his chin. "You something else, I'll say that; something different." He shook his head, perplexed. Spooked, even, maybe. "I still don't get, why you come here, this town? What for?"

It was a good question. What was the purpose that Anita was so sure that she had?

She met his eyes. "I didn't come to do anything. I just came."

They heard a noise out in the hall, a kind of scampering, but not of mice. Impatient boys, on watch.

"All right," he said, moving away from the sink. "Enough of this. You can leave—after you pay."

"Pay?" she got out. They both knew there was no money in the purse.

"Yeah, that's the thing," he said. "You think you so free to go around how you like, change things. But you ain't free. You get that now?" He paused, his eyes traveling to her hair. "Maybe I cut some of that hair off your head, shines like pure gold. I got a knife here somewhere." He bent as if to pull something out of his pocket, but he didn't. Then he straightened again, his smile cruel.

"Nah, give me a kiss. I wanna see how sweet it is. Yeah, that's it. A kiss, you want to go."

He put his face up next to hers, violent red gashes on the cheeks. Up so close, she could see the whites of his eyes were not so white, more yellowish. She didn't look at him directly, but at their reflection in the mirror.

Like a bad scene in a bad movie, Celia thought. It's all come due. Every wrong step I've taken since I got here. Grace tried to tell me. Anita tried to tell me. There were warnings right and left. But I wouldn't listen. And now this. She sighed. Morris.

But a kiss—that was nothing, really. Suddenly, she realized that the damage was done. Her reputation, such as it was, was already spread around town. Her transgressions were known and public. She had shamed herself in front of Alonzo and been forgiven. There was no place to fall; there was nothing to lose.

She rose to her toes and kissed him on the cheek, right on the lipstick stripes. She stepped back. Now the print of her lips joined the stripes together. He took one look, turning sideways, apparently satisfied.

That was it. He was done with her, bored maybe. Truth was, if she reported an attack, he would pay, one way or another. Arrest, court time, at the least, no matter the outcome. End of his games and his little reign of terror.

He left, the door swinging shut behind. Celia took a wet paper towel to clean her arm. No matter how hard she scrubbed, the stain wouldn't wash completely off her dress. Then she took another towel to wipe her face, but the lipstick tube was destroyed. Finally, she picked up the purse, replacing the picture. Out the door, the hall was empty and dark, no one lurking in the shadows. She paused before walking into the lighted cafeteria, her heart pounding with fear and excitement.

The showdown was over.

"Where have you been?" Alonzo asked, meeting her at the chairs. She could smell wine on his breath, but his eyes showed relief. Did he think she had left?

"In the ladies' room," Celia said, flatly. And then, "Morris came by while you were gone."

Alonzo's eyebrows rose almost to his hairline. "Oh, yeah? Did he bother you?" He looked around, ready to face Morris, and primed with the wine, maybe happy for the chance. "Where's he gone?"

"Forget about him," Celia said, starting for the door. "I need to get out of here." Her voice was calm, but she could picture herself rushing to the safety of the car, and then back to the apartment, in her bed, curled up in the cocoon of her blankets. What happened with Morris was so strange, bizarre, terrifying. Had she screamed and struggled, she believed, it might have gone much differently.

"No, wait; what is it? What happened? Tell me," Alonzo said. His face was close to hers, and he grasped her arm. Reflexively, she pulled away, and hurried to the exit. It was all she could do not to break into a run. Alonzo stood in place, watching her retreat.

Outside, Celia found herself in a swarm of people in the dark, illuminated only by the distant lights of the parking lot. At first, every face was a stranger, and she feared she would see Morris and his mask-face. Instead, trying to focus and remember the direction they had parked, she heard a soft, lilting voice over her shoulder. "You looking for Alonzo?"

It was Bettina in her silver-white gown. With a light wrap over her shoulders, the girl looked robed for a celestial choir.

"He gone back in lookin' for you," Bettina said. Her voice was like a charm, normal and familiar. Celia tried to concentrate on Bettina, shaking off her panic and forcing herself to relax.

"Yes, I know. I saw him. I just had to get out of there. It's so hot and stuffy, I got a little light-headed, you know." Then, following Bettina's gaze, she saw that Alonzo had arrived, close-mouthed, struggling with feelings. For a minute, it didn't look like anyone was going to talk, and Celia was sure that Bettina knew of their earlier spat and assumed that was what had upset her.

Celia turned to Alonzo. "I'm sorry. I don't know what came over me."

"Do you want to leave?"

"Maybe we can just take a walk, a short one, so I can clear my head. Do you mind?" He looked at her, unsure, but fell in step as she started walking. "Excuse us," he said to Bettina.

They headed down one of the paved paths that led from the cafeteria to another wing of the school, the rise and fall of voices fading in the background. Neither spoke until they were out of hearing.

"Alonzo." Celia didn't know how to present things about Morris. She wanted to tell him, but she didn't. She didn't want the incident to take over prom night. "It's not you, what you said, at all," she started. "Morris said some rude things, and it made me mad. But I don't want to tell you, because I don't want you getting involved, and I don't want him to ruin our evening."

"What did he say?"

"The usual stupid things."

"About me?"

"And about me, too—my reputation, I guess. But I don't care."

Celia heard an intake of breath. "I should find him, and call him out."

"No, don't! That's just what I don't want you to do. I'm OK, really. It shook me up a little, but I'll be fine. Just give me a few moments."

They had come to the end of the pavement, where it met a driveway circling the school. They were under a stand of trees and the darkness was complete. Celia's breathing slowed, finally, and she moved closer to Alonzo, brushing his arm with her arm. The scent of him, the wine, the soap, the material of his shirt, what he had for dinner, whatever it was that made him smell the way he did, reached her, along with fragrance of the invisible grass and trees.

He put his arms around her, and she breathed into his chest. It was too dark for him to make out the red stains on her dress, but she knew they were there, tingling, like all of her was tingling.

"I mess up everything, don't I?"

"No, no. Nothing you did." He tightened his embrace and kissed her on the head, making soft, comforting noises.

"Alonzo," Celia said, "I'm a stranger here even after all this time, and I don't always understand what's going on. Sometimes, I'm not even sure who I am anymore. But you still like me, don't you?"

"Course I do," he said gruffly. "I'm crazy about you. That's no secret; never was."

A few tears started to flow, surprising Celia. "Well, the thing is, I need you. I really do. I need you to be my friend, and be there for me, like I'll be there for you, and, and . . ."

"Hush."

"No, no." She made an impatient gesture. "What I mean is, I want you. I want to be with you—a lot. Even though it probably doesn't make sense to other people. But it makes sense to me. I know it's right."

Alonzo put his fingers to her lips, and she kissed them. Then she took his hand in her hands and kissed it, and sought his face, his eyes, his mouth. The restraint was gone. All fears and doubts were peeled away. She would be with him. They would be together, in front of anyone and everyone. Grace was right in some ways: follow your emotions and you may lose some options. But she was wrong, too. Celia thought something was gained, too; something precious that could never be replaced.

She broke away. "Come with me." She led him through the parking lot to Grace's car in a distant, shadowy corner. "We can go to the motel, if you want," she whispered. "I mean it. I'm ready."

He opened his mouth to speak, but she rushed to kiss him, pulling him against the car. She felt her power to arouse him, and how they were getting hotter and hotter, more in synch. Then he straightened up, blowing out air.

"Whoa," he said, but she could tell he was smiling. "I guess you had a change of mind. What happened in there? I don't think Morris was singing my praises."

"No," she admitted, reaching for him. "No, it's how different you are from him. Plus, I don't know; something's changed. I can feel it in here." She brought his two hands to her pounding heart. "Don't ask me to explain."

"But let's forget about the motel. You were right. It's not the time or place."

"But . . . but," she stammered.

"Hold up," Alonzo said. "Tomorrow, let's meet up when it's daylight. We'll talk, whatever you like. I know somewhere better, somewhere special— peaceful, private, by the water."

Celia was mystified, especially since they had no money. "Where's that?"

"The boathouse."

"Oh," she laughed, her humor restored. "That exclusive, romantic getaway. You know what? I'd love to," she said, "even if we are trespassing. So that's it," she said, clutching his hand. "Our first big fight is over?"

"Not so bad. We're all right, right?"

"Yes, we are."

They stood, listening to the last strains of music and then voices of departing prom-goers. Figures moved through the parking lot, laughing and shouting. Then the sound of car doors, engines starting, and headlights piercing the dark.

"It's breaking up, I guess."

"Yup."

"Time to go?"

"I'm ready."

He kissed her softly, again, and she couldn't help herself, wanting more. Then a shadow passed, a darkness in the dark: the memory of Jay, and that dizzy moment, and her falling so quickly into that well of pain and disappointment. But this was not the same; Alonzo was not the same; she was not the same.

Alonzo followed her around to the passenger's side where he opened the door.

"All right, then," she said, still a bit out of breath. "Tomorrow, at the boathouse, a picnic and a blanket."

Around the other side of the car, Alonzo echoed, "Tomorrow."

Chapter 26

Alonzo was at the apartment at noon in jean shorts and a tee shirt with a sailboat. Grace warned of thunderstorms in the afternoon as she gave Celia the car keys, who promptly handed them to Alonzo, their fingers touching. At the moment of contact, there was a spark, like static. Celia picked up the cooler and Alonzo put the plaid blanket over his shoulder, not making eye contact as they said good-bye to Grace. On the way downstairs, Alonzo had a bounce in his step as he jangled the keys. Celia felt it, too, that buzz from last night and that energy that connected them. Still, there was this thing, this uncertainty and expectations of what was between them, hovering, getting in the way of the day and their plans.

Celia sat silently as Alonzo drove to the end of their short road, taking a right on Main Street, heading south. The car was warm from sitting in the sun, and they had rolled up the windows, putting on the air conditioning.

"Alonzo?"

"Yes?"

"About last night. I want to apologize for my crazy behavior." Celia squirmed, trying to find the words. "I try to be thoughtful and calm, like Grace, but for some reason it's hard for me. I just get worked up, and everything comes out. I went totally overboard, first when you said about the hotel and . . . ," she left that unfinished. "And then, afterwards, when I was acting like a wild woman."

"Oh, yeah," he said. "You had a whole lot of emotions going on."

She didn't laugh. "No, I mean it. I was not my best self, as my mom used to say."

"That's fine, that's fine," he said. He was quiet as they followed the road out of town merging onto the highway. The summer landscape was full and lushly green.

Alonzo glanced over. "I've got something to say, too."

"Really?"

"Something happened last night, after I left you and went back to the school."

Celia turned abruptly in her seat. "Oh, no, don't tell me . . ."

He lifted a hand from the steering wheel. "Hear me out. When I got back there, only a few people were still by the cafeteria; the others are all hanging at the basketball courts, drinking. Then I saw Bettina—you know how she is, hard to miss—kind of big with a white dress on. She's having an altercation with Morris."

"No!"

"Yeah, they're yelling back and forth. And that date of hers, nowhere to be found. So," he said, getting to the meat of it, "I see Bettina haul up and slap him, and then he takes a swing at her, knocking her down. I get there quick as I can to help her up, and then Morris comes at me from behind. But I see him out of the corner of my eye. So, I turn last second and punch him, right in the nose. Made it bleed."

Celia's hands went to the sides of her face. "Oh my goodness," she said. "I . . . I . . ." Then she didn't know what to say. She didn't want any violence any time. But if anyone deserved it, it was Morris. And what else could Alonzo do? Still, it was drama of the worst kind, and Celia could only hope none of this would go any further. If Grace…

"So, then what?" she asked.

"Well, then Bettina's back on her feet and she's coming at him with the heel of her shoe, pretty sharp, too. It's two of us, one of him. I don't know where his crew is, drinking, I guess."

If she didn't know better, Celia would have thought there was a smirk on his face. She could just picture Bettina in her fury. Celia certainly would not want to fight her. It had started to seem quite likely that Bettina did like Alonzo—not that she let on. In spite of herself, Celia could barely suppress a smile. How on earth had it come to Celia weighing her odds in a possible girl fight? And yet, there was a certain comfort in knowing that she was pretty strong, for a smallish girl.

"You think it's broken, his nose?" she asked.

"Can't say. After that, he just slipped away in the dark."

They took the turn onto the side road, not far from their destination. Not so far at all, really, from Sutton, but like a world away.

"And Bettina, is she all right?"

"Broke a nail, I guess, and the heel of her shoe." His tone was light, even, but there was some satisfaction there. Celia sensed there was more.

"Well, that's good, I guess. I mean, that it's not worse."

The car bumped and swayed over the uneven ground, and soon they were in the woods, kind of gray and shadowy on the overcast day.

317

"What were they arguing about?" Celia asked suddenly. She knew, of course, there was no love lost between Bettina and Morris. It might have had something to do with the play.

At first, she wasn't sure Alonzo had heard the question. Then he said, simply, "You."

"Me!"

"Yeah, he says you kissed him in the bathroom. He was looking for me, to tell me."

The skin on Celia's face flamed, because it was true, she had kissed him, under duress. But she had no plans to tell anyone about that.

The silence grew as they got closer to the boathouse. Clearly, he was waiting for her to say something. He parked the car in the clearing near the boathouse and turned off the engine.

"Well," Celia said finally, her eyes focused on the rippling water beyond the boathouse, "I did kiss him on the cheek, because he made me, if I wanted him to go away. Which I did. But I don't ever, ever want to see him again." A shadow of something, maybe sadness, crossed Alonzo's face. "But there's nothing more we can do about it. You punched him and Bettina got him with her shoe. Maybe he'll keep that to himself. Not something he wants to spread around." Then she placed a hand on his arm. "I realize that you were standing up for me, as well as defending Bettina. And I have to thank you for that." In fact, there was a tremor of excitement, totally foolish, to think that two men were fighting over her, Celia.

They opened the doors to get out into the humid air. Here, by the water, a breeze fluttered the leaves and pine branches. It felt ten degrees cooler than at home.

Alonzo took out the cooler and the blanket. Celia followed him to the porch on the far side of the boathouse. At the bottom of the steps, he turned to her, "Do you want to sit up here or spread the blanket on the ground?"

She hesitated. The blanket, the ground. She wasn't hungry.

"I know, I know," he said. "You want to talk. I'm just asking."

"Never mind about that," she said. "There's nothing to talk about." She made a comic face. "Just put that stuff down and come here."

She reached out to him, giving him a hug that turned into a kiss and then a deeper kiss. Then their arms were around each other, warmth building. Celia pulled back a few inches to look him in the face.

Her hands stroked his upper arms, and then his back. His hands slipped down her waist and behind.

"The right place, and the right time?"

"Better than some motel."

It was the most beautiful place—outside among the trees, no prying eyes, no scornful comments. Just the two of them, young, healthy, and with good feelings for each other. In front of the porch was a small clearing, covered with pine needles. Alonzo spread the blanket over the ground, taking care to straighten the corners. He moved slowly and deliberately, wetting dry lips, until Celia realized that he was hesitating, perhaps waiting for her cue what to do next. Not nervous, surely. Not with her.

"I'm prepared, you know," she said, trying to sound casual. He looked up, but didn't seem to know what she was talking about. "Birth control," she spelled out. "I'm covered." She almost laughed at his startled expression. "Since I was at college, you silly. I hope you realize I'm a very modern, independent girl."

"Some girl," he said, with his slow smile. But he had stopped moving, sitting on the corner of the blanket. There was no hand, no arm, no tackle. He just sat there.

"What is it?" Celia asked. "You're not . . . it's not . . . your first time?"

He shook his head no, so somber. "But the first time with you. And I . . . I just don't want to do anything wrong."

She laughed; she couldn't help it, though a surge of tenderness welled up in her chest. "There is no wrong," she said. "There's just you and me. Here," she held out a hand, which he took. "Let me start."

She knelt on the blanket next to him, pulling off his sneakers and socks, putting them to the side. Next she worked his tee shirt over his head, beginning with small kisses on his neck and shoulders, pushing him down onto his back so that she could start on his chest, and then his abdomen. A couple times he started to curl up, ticklish, before she made him stretch out again, scolding and teasing. Then, unexpectedly, he took her by the shoulders, pulling her down on top of him, and she could see the strength of his desire taking hold.

"Not too fast," she said.

He released her, pushing himself upright. Slowly, carefully, he unfastened the buttons of her shirt, slipped off one sleeve, then the other. He stared at her silently, until she took his hands, and with him, pulled down the straps of her bra, drawing his face to her bare chest. They lay down together, kissing hungrily, starting to move in rhythm. She could see in his eyes how aroused he was, but wanting to do right by her, to restrain himself and not attack like some wild animal. She knew how hard it was to hold back, but she wanted more like this.

"Now me," she said. "My shorts and panties. And then you can kiss me there."

She wasn't used to telling guys what to do, or asking them. But with Alonzo it was different, not just because he was younger. Because she was so sure and so unafraid, of his expectations or of the future. Everything was OK, everything was enough. It was just here and now, and just them in their own little world. There would be no betrayal, like Jay, because they had already been through the hard things, together, publicly. What else could there be?

Alonzo's shorts came off, and his underwear. Then they were naked on the blanket atop of the pine needles, with the glint of water reflecting off the tree trunks.

He's beautiful, she thought. She climbed on top of him, looking down into his eyes, almost glassy with strangeness and desire. She rocked her hips, teasing, until she realized that he would come quickly, right away, if she kept going. So she rolled off, and waited for him.

He rolled to his side so they were face to face as he caressed her face and arms and neck and breasts.

"I waited for you," he said.

"I'm here," she said with a laugh, but not joking. "Right here, right now. All yours."

He kissed and kissed her, like a drowning man, desperate. Just when she thought he was going to kiss her forever, he got up on top of her. And got inside her—now as ready as ready could be for him. This is it, she thought, making love, as they were laughing, moaning, and kissing. *Making love.*

A cloud put them in momentary shadow, and a breeze passed over their sweaty-sticky bodies.

I don't see how this can be right, Celia thought, looking into the canopy of the trees, but somehow I'm sure that it is. Then she lost her train of thought of right or wrong, good or bad. Between the water, and the sun, the green branches arching over head, and the pleasure of this man inside her, she felt like every atom of her self was dissolving and then re-forming, along with him, into something new. *Thank you,* she heard, though no one had spoken. *Thank you.*

Afterwards, shoulder to shoulder and hip to hip with Alonzo, Celia closed her eyes, listening to the wind in the pine trees.

"You know," she said dreamily, holding his hand across her belly, "this is a different world, isn't it, almost like another country."

Alonzo barely responded, so she poked him in the ribs.

"This building, it's like a doll house, but for grown-ups, right? You could live here, and go fishing for your dinner, make a little campfire and eat it on the porch. Then at night, go to sleep in the boats, each like a little bed." She paused, thinking. "Or, make love in the pine needles if you wanted. Bathe in the river, explore in the canoe . . ."

"That's nice," murmured Alonzo.

"It's so beautiful," Celia said, rubbing up next to him, lightly touching her lips to his chest over his heart. "And you're so beautiful. And everything now is just perfect."

"Everything," he murmured, as they stretched out, relaxing. "Perfect."

But it wasn't long afterwards that the wind shifted, and Celia noticed the clouds getting closer and darker. They ate their picnic on the porch and wandered back inside the boathouse looking at the boats. Even with the door open, they found themselves in deepening shadows, until finally Alonzo announced, "Rain soon."

"No boat ride?"

"Not today."

"When can we come back?" Celia asked, carrying the blanket. Alonzo had the cooler on his shoulder.

"Soon," he said. "Very soon."

As the car rocked its way along the rutted path, a few large drops of rain hit the windshield and then stopped. The wind had come up briskly, but the clouds seemed to have risen, making full, dramatic shapes in the sky. When they got to the intersection with the other path, Celia tapped the window.

"Wait. What's down there? Is it an old church?"

"Not a church," Alonzo said, slowing the car to a stop. "A cemetery."

"Is it far?"

"No, but the road is rough. We probably have to walk part of the way."

Celia scanned the sky. "The rain's holding off. Let's just take a peek. Can we?"

Alonzo exhaled deeply. "Not much to see," he said finally.

"Come on, Alonzo, please," Celia said. "Now I am curious. And we didn't get our boat ride."

Alonzo had to make a couple maneuvers to make the sharp left. The little car bumped along the tracks for a while, once getting stuck. After a few tries, Alonzo was able to rock it out. Shortly beyond, the track narrowed and then quit as the trees grew thicker. Still, there were markers on the trees every once in a while. They parked and got out. The rain continued to spit, but once they were in the woods, they couldn't feel it at all.

"This way," Celia cried, spotting a marker. "Now this way." It was like a game, but how on earth could anyone drive a hearse out this far, even a horse and wagon? It must have been abandoned a long time ago.

Then she couldn't find anymore markers. She stopped, looking around at the downed tree limbs and overgrown brush.

"This is it." Alonzo sounded sure. But Celia didn't see anything like a cemetery, no gate or fence or rows of slab stones.

"Where?"

"All around," Alonzo said, sweeping his arm. "You just have to look."

She took a few more steps on the carpet of dead leaves, peering right and left. "I don't see anything, except rocks and broken branches."

A few rocks were a little larger than you might expect, a foot or more high, standing quite upright, set at somewhat regular distances. Celia walked to one, brushing the leaves and pine needles away. The surface of the rock had been planed smooth, and there were letters—a name: *Corey.* And a number, *18.*

Alonzo had reached her side.

"Slave cemetery," he said.

He followed Celia as she went from stone to stone, clearing debris to make out whatever was written: *Baby; Sampson, kicked by a horse; Emmaline, our mother; Tony, called to Jesus.*

Only a few had dates: 1809, 1830, 1845.

"How many are there?" Celia asked.

"Might be a hundred. I'm not sure."

"But it's not still used? I mean, no one comes here anymore, do they?"

Alonzo tipped his head side to side. "No one's been buried here for many years, I'm sure. Now they get buried next to the church, or in the town cemetery. But I wouldn't say it's not used. People come here. Look closer."

"No flowers," Celia said. But she poked around, carefully. And then she saw things: feathers, small smooth rocks, seashells, coins and other things, more modern things, like a rosary, a rabbit's foot key chain, and some small nip bottles.

"Strange," she called to Alonzo. "I guess you're right. But, they're small things, and easy to miss—if you weren't looking for them."

"Right."

The wind was rushing around in the tress overhead, and they could hear the splatter of rain increasing.

"I suppose we better go before it pours," Celia said, back at Alonzo's side, slipping her hand into his hand. He had said little while she'd been walking from stone to stone. They retraced their steps to the car.

"You've been here before," she said, huffing to keep up.

"Not for a long time. Used to come with my grandpa."

"Do you have family buried here?"

He took a breath. "Yes. I don't remember their names now, or where their stones are. Like I said, I haven't been in years, since I was real little, since he passed."

They were almost at the car now and out of the deep forest. The rain was wetting their faces, as the wind lifted Celia's hair. They jogged the last few steps to the car. Celia felt her lungs working, like she was in fog or smoke, or moving underwater. Looking at Alonzo in the driver's seat, she wondered how it was for him to be here with her. She stopped his hand from turning the key.

"Your ancestors were slaves here, on this farm—Belle Grove?"

He nodded.

"And they were owned by the ancestors of Brett's family?"

"Yup."

Again, that uncertain, shifting feeling like stepping in marshy land that gave way underneath her feet. Here was a reality that she was not prepared for, except that it had been here all along, and must have been inevitable, if she had thought, if anyone had said . . .

"And you knew this—you and Brett?"

"Not when we were kids."

A flash of lightning brightened the path. They hadn't made it to the main road before the downpour began, the water streaming down the windows. Then the whole world outside the car was blurry and gray, like they were being tossed about in the middle of the ocean. Celia had the sense that everything was rushing past, all mixed up, past and present, hers and his, in this crazy time-capsule of a place.

Chapter 27

Celia was undecided how much to tell Tammy about her experiences with Alonzo or the prom or a boy named Morris. She didn't know her well, and wasn't sure how she might react. Tammy was perceptive enough not to corner Celia when she arrived Monday morning in a bit of a daze, as a number of people pointed out. Instead, at the break, Tammy told Anita that they were headed to the coffee shop.

"No loitering," she said.

On the sidewalk, Tammy did a little dance-skip. "So-o, how did the date go?"

"Not exactly as planned," Celia admitted. A silly grin crept over her face. "But it turned out well in the end." They entered the cool, dark coffee shop, where only a few customers remained after the breakfast rush. Russell took their orders himself, pouring the coffee with a wink, and sent the muffins out right away. He knew all about Anita's short leash.

"Oh, something happened; something definitely happened," Tammy said, studying Celia across the booth. "I can see it—something good, and I think I can guess what."

She took a bite of the English muffin, which dripped a golden tear of butter.

"All right." Celia put down the jelly knife. "We were at his senior prom, at the high school . . ."

"Prom!" shouted Tammy, bouncing with excitement. "At the high school!"

"Sh . . . sh," Celia begged, looking quickly around.

"OK, OK," Tammy lowered her voice. "But, what the heck? Girl, that's a little out of the ordinary, especially around here."

"He asked me, Alonzo. I didn't see the harm. And it's his senior year. And . . . well, never mind. That was our date." And then, watching Tammy resume her muffin. "Really, it was a lot of fun. But then there was this guy being a jerk and giving me a hard time about hanging around with black kids, of all stupid things. Then we had a fight—I mean, Alonzo and me. And then we made up. And then I decided that I really like him, you know, as a guy, in spite of our differences."

"And so?"

"Well, so," Celia said primly, "it got romantic."

"Kissing? More?"

"Well, yes and no." Celia appeared to examine the crumbs on her plate for guidance.

"You've got to explain that to me."

"Well, not there and then, at the prom. I mean, what were we going to do, anyway? He had this crazy idea about going to a hotel, but I just couldn't do it. It seemed kind of sleazy or something."

"Sleazy!" Tammy pounded the table, startling the young waitress passing by. "It's a rite of passage. That's what we did at *my* senior prom. Weston, right? It was the first time I went all the way with Kenny Jeffords, although the next day I woke up sick as a dog."

Celia declined to comment. "So, anyway, we didn't do anything then. But the next day, we went to this place he knows, by the river, at this boathouse, very secluded. That's where it happened." She felt the blood in her face, but she couldn't hold back the rush of happiness. "For better or worse—now we're lovers."

"I knew it!" Tammy jumped in her seat, pony-tail swinging. "So, what now, lovebirds?"

"I don't know," Celia confessed. "I really like him, and he really, really likes me . . ." She sighed deeply.

"Hm . . ." Tammy said, smirking. "Some problem." She had finished her muffin and a second cup of coffee. "If you ask me, it sounds like a perfect summer romance."

"That's the thing," Celia said, refusing a refill from the waitress, who came back in a moment with the bill. Outside, a couple largish women passed, but neither was a customer at New You. Still, any moment, Anita might appear at the door, summoning them. Or worse, rapping her knuckles on the window, impossible to ignore. Celia turned the check toward her and pulled out some bills from her pocket. But she wasn't ready to go.

"I don't think it is a summer romance," she said. "It's more than that. I know it sounds crazy. It doesn't make sense to me or to him, either. How can it work out? The only things we have in common are love of theater and lack of money." She smoothed the crumpled napkin. "And the way we feel about each other."

"Ahh . . ." Tammy nodded sympathetically. "Is he going to college in the fall?"

"Somewhere. It's not decided yet."

"And you? You must be heading out of here eventually, right?"

"My sister is leaving at the end of summer; I've got to do something."

Tammy flashed an irreverent smile. "Well, in that case, you have no choice but to make hay while the sun shines."

"But it's going to be so much harder . . ."

Tammy waved a hand. "Oh, please. Don't be such a sissy." She was teasing, but it was like cold water in the face. "You're a fool if you turn away a chance for happiness—and sweet loving, especially with a hot guy, even if he is under age."

"He is not! He's eighteen!" Celia's heart flipped from hope to fear, and back again. "OK, OK,' she said. "I get your message." In the back of her mind, she heard her own words: *Somewhere . . . not decided yet.* And then, *Salisbury* . . . Why not Salisbury?

Tammy broke in, getting to her feet. "Come on, let's go before they come looking." She grabbed the check with Celia's portion. "Sorry, I've got to break a twenty."

As they waited to pay at the register, four people walked by outside, including Anita. But she was deep in conversation with a young woman and didn't look once toward the coffee shop.

"Anita," she hissed at Tammy.

Tammy looked out the window. "Looks like she's going somewhere." In fact, she was in slacks and a blazer, not gym clothes at all. And she carried a purse.

"Isn't that Cuffie and Lacey?" Celia said, pointing at the two other figures.

Tammy put the change away in her purse. "Yep."

"And who's that?" The fourth figure, the young woman talking to Anita, was a stranger to Celia, but absolutely lovely in a pale summer dress. A natural beauty, with every straightened hair in place, a perfect mocha complexion and a bright, heart-melting smile.

"Just a minute, while I leave the tip," Tammy said, and went to put change on the table.

Outside, they watched the four walking away, headed toward the bowling alley. Anita and the new girl parted from Cuffie and Lacey, walking to Anita's car in the lot and driving away. Church, maybe? It seemed the most likely thing. But Anita had mentioned nothing to them about leaving. And why hadn't she come to hound them out of the coffee shop? Strange, indeed.

"Cuffie! Lacey!" Tammy yelled up the sidewalk, and they turned. They waved and strolled back toward the coffee shop, no great hurry.

"Hey, Tam-Tam," Cuffie said. *Tam-Tam*! Of course, they knew Tammy from past summers at the Inn. And from high school, too, come to think of it.

"Dolphin Girl!" Lacey exclaimed, putting her oversize sunglasses on her head. "Where you been hiding at? Ain't seen you since the play."

"We got to call her Movie Star now," said Cuffie, turning to Celia with his sly smile. He was flashing some bicep in a muscle shirt and wore his baseball cap backwards.

"Don't be ridiculous," Celia fake-bristled, secretly pleased. "I'm certainly not a film star; my career is on stage. Live performance; no special effects."

"Well, ex-cuse me," Cuffie went on, and then added. "My moms told me I got to stay away from you."

"What!" Celia seriously thought she didn't hear that right.

"Yeah," Cuffie said. "she saw the play, too. And she warned me, 'Cuffie, don't go near that white girl; she just like poison.'" He sounded so serious.

"No, no, no! Cuffie, you know that's not the real me. That's fake; just acting. Right?" She looked from face to face, a bit perturbed. They did know that, right?

Cuffie broke into a smile. "Just messing with you. We know you alright, Dolphin Girl." Then he shook his head. "But you got my moms spooked."

Celia was still working through her defense when Lacey broke in. "Stop your nonsense, Cuffie." She waved a hand. "Nevermind about all that. You girls might like to come out to Starlight for some dancing?"

Celia clamped her mouth shut. She turned to Tammy, not sure what to expect.

"Tonight?" Tammy asked, perfectly natural.

"Yeah, a bunch of us going out." Lacey smiled her big smile with lots of bright lipstick.

Then Cuffie was back in the game. "This girl here a real hit on the dance floor." He was pointing at Celia. "You got to see those moves." He started to demonstrate, but Lacey poked him, hard.

"Nah," Tammy said. "We're going to a movie, Celia and me, with some other folks." Which was true, they did have plans. "Another time, maybe."

Lacey shrugged, ready to move on. But Cuffie was enjoying his spot in the shade with the three young ladies. Celia glanced at New You, but there was no one coming or going. And now, of course, Anita was gone. She saw her chance. "Any news from the Inn?" she asked. "I mean, besides Mrs. Becker's broken ankle and the fire in the downstairs kitchen." She knew about those from Anita and Tammy. "You know, Eldridge or Warren or Wanda?"

"Well," said Cuffie, taking his hat off and rubbing a hand over his head. "Let's see." Warren was doing well in school, back most weekends, pretty serious with Vanessa. Nothing from Wanda, although one of her brothers said she was still in Baltimore. Eldridge was not around: "He ain't quit, and ain't been fired, but he been out a couple weeks now. He some kind of sick, but no one know what it is."

Tony and Roland had moved back to D.C. permanently. Rumor was that Tony was in rehab for drug addiction and that Roland lived at home and went to see him every day.

Lacey chimed in: Pauline had a new boyfriend from Annapolis, someone she met at the Inn when he stopped there one day. He was supposed to be a successful guy with a big job, maybe a salesman or something, a couple years older than she was.

"And Jay . . ." Cuffie paused for effect. He knew, they all knew, that there had been something between Celia and Jay. "That's Jay's new girl just went by with Anita," he said. "From out of town. Her father the assistant manager of the office supply store. Nice girl, seem like, church-goer. Jay playing quite the gentleman."

Celia felt a pang, in spite of her newfound contentment with Alonzo. Rejection's shadow fell a long way. And then, like a cloud had passed overhead, she had a sensation of things shifting in a deep and serious way. Somehow this young woman's presence in Sutton meant something for all of them. Like a gust of cool autumn air or the distant call of migrating birds, change was coming.

All of a sudden, Shelly stepped out of New You, jangling the bells on the door and looking about like someone emerging from a long sleep, or doing accounts. Apparently, she'd realized she was on her own. She caught sight of Tammy and Celia on the sidewalk, of course, only a short distance away, having a good gab.

"Aren't you coming back?" she said. And they agreed, that was the plan.

Celia followed Tammy to the door, digesting what she had seen and heard. Her eyes took a moment to adjust to the dark inside. There was that off-balance feeling again. That girl, that beautiful girl, had entered the scene and altered everything; she was sure of it. A starring role, it looked like, while Celia was fading out. Cuffie and Lacey, she knew them of course; you might almost say friends. And yet, it was like they had become characters in a play or a story. Tammy, too. And Shelly. People she cared about, but she could only perceive their lives at a distance. Anita could still get under her skin; there was something lasting there. But only Alonzo remained completely real.

If Grace had noticed a change in her sister, she didn't say anything. She was trying to cope with a major development, not to her liking. Alec had gotten a job, a good one, only it wasn't in Atlanta, the land of plentiful hospitals and medical centers. It was in Charleston, South Carolina, which everyone knew was pretty and historical and charming, but did not offer as many employment prospects. Alec told her he really wanted to take the job, although he hadn't yet given his final answer to the company. He wanted to hear Grace's reaction, and she had asked for a few days to think things over. She was disappointed, no question.

"I'm meeting Alonzo at two," Celia told Grace on Thursday morning. "Can I borrow the car? We'll be back by supper." Listening to herself, she sounded like some naive teen. But in reality, not so much.

"Sure. Go ahead," Grace said, pulling on her pantyhose and wiggling her feet into her shoes. "Where's my purse?" She looked around in a distracted way. "Shoot!" she exclaimed. "I didn't know there was a run in these!" She was generally so even-tempered; it was hard for Celia to know how to deal with her sister in this emotional state. At least she knew where the purse was, and got it.

"How about this?" she offered. "I'll make supper, and you can tell me what's going on with you and Alec and work."

"Thanks, Celia; I appreciate it. I just don't know what I want to do, or what I should do. Why did it all have to change around like this? Stupid Charleston." But then she laughed at herself and picked up her purse, ready to go. She paused. "I haven't really seen Alonzo since last weekend. Everything OK with you two?" Maybe she did have an inkling that something was up.

"Oh, fine. Hey, you better get going. It's getting late." It was a clumsy deflection, but Grace said nothing more than "so long" and headed out the door.

Hot summer was upon them, and it was as if time had come to a standstill, one day like the next, the temperature mounting and then a thunderstorm in the late afternoon or evening hours. For Celia, every day was full of work and errands, school catalogs and Alonzo. Sometimes they biked or boated, but mostly they went to the boathouse to talk and daydream and to be with each other.

Sex changes everything, Celia said to herself as they walked to the far side of the boathouse. *And yet everything seems to lead to the same place.* But she wasn't complaining. It was cooler under the pine canopy than it had been in town, and there was that same breeze that found them by the river. Watching Alonzo spread out the blanket carefully, she reflected that it was so much nicer to be with someone who you were yourself with, and relaxed, and not so hard to impress. Briefly, she thought of Carlos and then Jay. Sometimes too much challenge and excitement got in the way of other, sweeter sensations. She smiled, and he asked her why.

"You're not as innocent as you look," she declared, as they sat down.

"No, I'm not," he agreed.

"You probably knew before me that we would end up like this. I mean, being lovers." She shifted her position to her side, next to him, face to face.

"I hoped so."

"And you played your cards right," she continued.

"Nope. No cards. Just patience."

Celia had a thought, and scrutinized his face. "What about *juju?* Did you use that on me?" She was teasing, but not completely.

He didn't smile when he answered. "I would only ever use it to protect you from harm."

"I know, I know." Her voice was light again; she hadn't meant to offend. Then suddenly, she thought about Morris, and what happened at the prom. And how things could have been so much worse, and she began to wonder . . . but no, that was not what brought her and Alonzo together.

"So," she said, drawing a finger around his lips, "when did you fall for me? When we started working on the play?"

"Nope, before that." He bit her finger playfully.

"Oh, you mean when you were stalking me on the road," she said. "Trying to catch up."

Alonzo gave her a funny look, not really what she expected. "I was keeping you company," he said. "Girls don't walk down that road, not by themselves."

"What?" She drew back. "Are you kidding me?"

He shook his head. Celia remembered thinking it was a bit funny that she saw so few people walking that stretch of road, more commercial, less scenic than in town. A few men, yes, including those who she suspected of checking her out. A couple of older ladies pushing their wheeled carriages from home.

"But why not?" she demanded.

"I don't know," he said, stretching out his legs, propped up on his elbows. "It's just not done." When she continued staring, he said, "I guess it's not really cool to walk, especially in warm weather. And, maybe the girls don't want to show themselves off like that."

"Oh," she said, and it suddenly made sense. "I see." She started to laugh, but it wasn't really funny. And she knew, now, that's what Morris was referring to, her parading down the street, sometimes in her leotard. She smacked herself in the head. "My God," she said. "What a clueless wonder. It's a miracle I survived. So, then, you were my gentleman escort?"

"Maybe, the first time."

"Nothing else?"

"After we talked, and you tried to shake me off like you did, but still so polite, and so curious, then I was hooked. I didn't even know what to make of you at first. This is all new for me, to be with somebody like this."

"But you could get used to it," Celia teased, rolling on her back and tugging at his arm, until he collapsed down next to her.

"Every day," he said.

"Every day!" she repeated, and then, "every day." Then she held her next words. It wasn't time for conversation. She worked her way under his arms, starting the dance, their dance.

"Oh, Lordy," he said, rolling to his side so they were nose to nose. "What in heaven's name is going on here?"

"Us," she said. "Just us, doing our thing."

She gave him a few minutes rest, as they lay on the blanket recovering themselves.

"Alonzo?"

"Yes?"

"I was thinking about something, about what's going to happen . . ."

"What do you mean?"

"When college starts."

"Sh, sh . . . ," he said, closing his eyes. "Let's not talk about it."

"No, wait. I want to say something. I have an idea."

He cocked open one eye. "More ideas!" And then, wryly, "What, pen pals?"

"I'm serious," she scolded. "What we can do. We could both go to Salisbury—you to college, and me to find a job and take some classes and work with Leona at the theater. We could, couldn't we, if you decided to enroll at Salisbury State? Wasn't that one of your choices?"

Alonzo pushed himself to his elbow and then sat up, drawing his t-shirt over his lap. "For real? Are you really thinking about that?"

Celia sat up, too, crossing her legs and pulling a corner of blanket over herself. "I am. I mean, I don't have any definite plans. But Grace is leaving soon and I have to do something. It was either stay here and keep working until I have enough money to go back and finish college. Or else move home, where things are still a mess." She looked down at her hands. "Honestly, I don't want to go back. My brother is better, but things are still not good." Taking a breath, she went on, almost deciding as she spoke. "I have been thinking about Salisbury for a while, really. I was on the way there to see about a job when I had the accident."

She couldn't decipher the look in Alonzo's eyes; pleased, concerned, doubtful? Maybe not convinced. And he, more than most people, knew about her impulsive ways.

"No, listen, Alonzo. I'm not just dreaming; it's what I want. I can take over Grace's lease through the end of December, and work nights and weekends at the Inn through hunting season and the holidays."

He tilted his head, dubious, "I thought you quit on them."

"Oh," she said, breathlessly, "they'll take me back. Then, by January, I'll be ready to move and maybe even take a class or two." She trembled with excitement. "Doesn't that sound good?"

"The way you put things, it all sounds good. Do you really think so?"

"I do, Alonzo. I really do. But what about you? You haven't decided yet, have you? You would have told me, right?"

"I haven't put down a deposit anywhere. I couldn't make that decision, couldn't face making a plan to leave. I'm accepted at three places. Mrs. Matthews said I could wait until the end of July."

"But you could go to Salisbury State."

"Yes." He hesitated. "It's not my first choice . . ."

Celia turned away, holding back her first words. "Oh, I see."

He put a hand to her chin, turning her to face him. "But I'll go there if I can see you. I'll tell Mrs. Matthews right now." He gestured like he was getting up, ready to go. "Well, as soon as I'm decent."

"Oh, Alonzo, this is crazy, isn't it? Right, everyone else but us will think it's crazy."

He shook his head. "That's how we do it," he said. "That's how we know it's right, because it is crazy."

Kiss, kiss, kiss. Well, then, they had a plan.

"Too bad someone here has got to work, like tomorrow and Friday." Celia was running her fingers along Alonzo's arm and shoulder. "How about Saturday we'll take one of the boats out?"

Alonzo looked up at the sky, not at her or the water.

"Can't Saturday," he said softly. "That's graduation."

"No!" Celia exclaimed, giving him a love tap. "It can't be. Why didn't you remind me? Every time I asked you, you were so vague about the whole thing." There was something annoying about being caught so off guard.

"I have no more tickets," Alonzo said, looking down. "Just for Granny and my uncle. And my mom. I kept one for her in case she makes it."

Celia was surprised and a little hurt. But she shouldn't be. His mom, after all . . .

"She wants to come for graduation," Alonzo was saying, as he studied the clouds. "And she wants me to make a trip down there."

"Oh, my!" Celia said, taking in these new developments. "Well, that's big news. I hope she makes it, I really do." Then she cleared her throat. "But, when would you be going on this trip? Not right away?"

He looked at her, hesitant. "I haven't picked the date yet. When I get some time off from work."

"No rush," she whispered. "We've got time, so come on." It was the last thing she said, as they put their arms around each other.

The next time they went to the boathouse was an overcast afternoon the week following graduation. Alonzo's mother had not come after all, but she'd sent money, a sizeable check along with a bus schedule to Raleigh, North Carolina. He hadn't invited Celia to use the other graduation ticket, and she didn't press him. She got it—that Alonzo's disappointment was too great, and that it would have been awkward for Celia to be there with his grandmother and uncle, whom she'd only met once, when she'd run into the three of them at the store. The grandmother, short and stooped, had looked her over with a puzzled, doubtful look; and the disabled uncle, more like an oversized ten-year-old, was only interested in his jelly donut.

After a quiet picnic came a long embrace that smelled and tasted like barbeque chicken, and then a nap with an extra blanket pulled around when the wind changed and cool air came off the water. A squabble among crows brought Celia back to wakefulness. Alonzo's eyes were open, and he was staring into the trees.

"Does she know about me, your mother?" Celia asked, stroking his cheeks. He blinked a couple times.

"She does, from Granny, at least that you're in the picture. I haven't really talked to her about it. It's not something you can really explain on the phone."

"I haven't said anything to my mom either, mostly because she's so wrapped up in everything at home." She sighed. "As long as I'm with Grace, she thinks she doesn't have to worry. Poor Mom."

Alonzo's face was drawn, unsmiling. Under the blanket she could feel the tension in his body.

"I'm sorry she didn't come," Celia said quietly. "Work and money?"

Alonzo sighed, facing away. "She doesn't really like to come back. Too many bad memories."

Celia let that sit.

"My father," Alonzo said. "Things didn't end well."

"I see."

"And me, what happened when I left. That put a lot of shame on her, too." Alonzo took another breath, exhaling slowly. "A new man, a new baby, I guess she thought it was a new start."

"But . . ." Celia started, then stopped herself. She was ready to criticize his mother for abandoning her son. Instead, she put an arm over his shoulder. "That doesn't mean she doesn't love you. I'm sure she does. She just couldn't deal with . . ." Her voice faded. "Like my mom, she couldn't, either."

"No, I know she's trying," Alonzo said, still so loyal. Yes, just like Celia's mom was trying, just not very successfully. "She wants what's best for me." Just like Celia's mom.

On the way home with Alonzo at the wheel, Celia pulled a booklet out of her purse. She flipped through the pages before stopping at one marked with a pen. Alonzo's eye caught the motion, and he raised an eyebrow.

"Course catalog," Celia said. "For Salisbury State. I picked it up at the library. Here, let me show you something."

"Supposed to keep my eyes on the road, remember?"

She jabbed him in the ribs, and he swerved the car playfully side to side on the empty road for payback.

"I found something interesting." She raised the splayed booklet in front of him briefly, just so he could see the markings.

"Theater construction and technology," she read, and then almost laughed aloud as she heard the words. *Her, Celia? Construction? Talk about two left thumbs.*

Alonzo chuckled. "Oh, yeah? Interesting. How about a first aid course? That could be useful."

Celia pursed her lips, ready to retort. But he spoke first. "I'm just kidding. I bet you'd get a lot out of it. You could use some of those skills at home— quite practical."

"You think I could do it?"

"I know you could." He reached over to pinch her bicep. "Stronger than you look. And smart, too—when you think things through."

Celia studied the booklet. "It meets Tuesdays and Thursdays at nine-thirty. I could still waitress or whatever. Come January, of course. I'm just looking ahead. Maybe we could take it together. Building, construction—isn't that architecture?"

They were just pulling into the apartment complex. Alonzo would park the car and walk home. It wasn't far, after all. Nurse Harrison's blinds were drawn, but Celia always suspected she was lurking by the windows, watching.

Alonzo turned off the engine and pulled the keys out to give to her. "I'm not sure what it would be. But it would be fun," he said. "Anything with you would be fun."

"And we'd be together," Celia said, turning toward him.

"Together," Alonzo said. He leaned over to kiss her, and it was like it was the first time, finding each other, reaching across the divide, new feelings, new discoveries.

"Oh," said Celia, purring like a cat. "It's probably a pipe dream. I'm kind of a dreamer. Maybe you noticed that by now."

"Let me see what Mrs. Matthews says."

Celia blushed, making a face. "She knows about me, Mrs. Matthews?"

Alonzo nodded. "Of course. Even if I didn't tell her, word gets around this small town."

"And she thinks I'm the devil in disguise, the white devil?"

"Not at all. You've got that wrong." Alonzo's mild face had tightened with emotion. "She said you must be quite remarkable. And I said, yes, you are."

Celia grinned, delighted. "All right, mister, go on," she commanded, and then, nicely, "please." Then she jumped out herself, running to catch him at the back of the car, where she thread her arms around his neck and gave him a full-on kiss—a very public display of affection. From the corner of her eye, she detected a movement at the window of the downstairs apartment.

"Bye," she said, giving Alonzo a tap on the rear. He shook his head, but started off down the road with his easy, bouncy gait.

"See you tomorrow," he called.

Just as Celia was climbing the stairs to the apartment, she heard the phone ring and hurried to unlock the door and let herself in. She answered a bit breathlessly, thinking it might be about an apartment share.

"Celia?" A woman's voice, and then an intake of breath.

"Mom," Celia cried. "What is it?" Their mother never called before Grace got home from work.

"Celia," her mother repeated, but she couldn't go on.

"Is it Shane? You're scaring me."

"No, no." Her mother cleared her throat. "Shane's fine. Nothing's wrong. I'm calling with some good news, for you, at last." And then she started to cry.

"Mom, please, are you OK?"

She heard her mother put down the phone and blow her nose. When she returned, she was breathy, but calmer.

"I'm fine, too." She laughed. "Well, no, I've been a wreck, I know. I'm sorry. But things are a little better. I'm better. So, let me tell you what's happening."

"Go ahead."

"Shane's not well, but not worse, either. So, you could say stable. Gordon's patent issue was finally decided in his favor, and he's got a new investor in the business. Production's been going along pretty well. I'm sure it will be up and down for a while. But that's not why I called. The thing is, last week I called Aunt Clara about you."

"Aunt Clara?" Celia wasn't even sure who she was. She pictured an old lady, a clone of Granny Jones, except skinnier. "You mean, Great-aunt Clara, Grandma's sister?"

"Right. She's in San Francisco, still living on her own at seventy-eight. She was very good to me when I was younger, very supportive, and I decided to tell her about what happened with you leaving college and how terrible I felt about it. I'm afraid I cried through most of the phone call. But, here's the point. Her husband left a nice nest-egg, and she has no children of her own, so I asked her for a loan—for you."

"A loan? Mom, no! I don't want to owe money to someone who might be dead before I can pay it back."

Celia's mother was never one to yell or even scold harshly, but Celia could hear the note of impatience. "Hear me out, Celia. She remembers you, from a Christmas play you were in when you were six, and she was genuinely sorry to hear that you had to leave your theater program. She wants to pay your tuition and fees at college. As she says, like an early inheritance. She would have left some money to us anyway, as next of kin."

Celia felt the floor start to tilt, the braided rug twisting under her feet. She extended the phone cord to sit down. *Back to college. Back to the theater, and acting and plays and rehearsals and first nights.* And then, immediately— *Alonzo!* Her heart thumped painfully.

Her mother's voice came through the line. "She's already sent me the money so I can pay your tuition for September. We've kept your mailing address here for school bills, so you're still an in-state student. The only thing is that she'd like to see you herself before you start. Grace said she's moving on August fifteenth. I think you'd better plan to come home by August 1st, to give yourself a chance to see Aunt Clara and get organized for school."

"Oh, my," Celia said. Her eyes raced from the clock to the calendar. That was no time at all. "Don't you need the money for other things?"

"Aunt Clara can't fix Gordon's business problems. If Gordon's business takes off, we can repay some of the money, but she doesn't expect it. She wants to do this, to pay for your education." Her voice began to falter again. "I told her how hard you've been working, and how you girls have struggled to get by in that place, beyond the beyond. So now, finally, we can help you."

She began weeping again, leaving Celia a moment to think—what to answer? I've made other plans? I found someone I really care about? I want to stay here—beyond the beyond?

"Mom," she said finally. "That's great. Really. That you found this way to help me, and that Aunt Clara is willing to give us the money. But . . . but, it's not so easy for me to say yes. There's something . . . there's somebody I met. And we already sort of started to make plans."

Her mother spoke surprisingly calmly. "Well, I know, honey, at least I gathered from what you've said, about the play and everything, and what Grace's told me. And I don't discount that at all. Really. I loved your father even when my family doubted he would make it through law school and have any kind of career. But he did, and I have no regrets. So, in a sense, I understand. But I also see how difficult it would be for you, for both of you, to carry on a relationship, when you both have such great challenges. Those things, those deprivations and sacrifices can take a toll on a relationship over time. And now you have this opportunity ahead of you. I don't know that Aunt Clara would be as willing to help you all the way across the country, paying out-of-state tuition at a relatively unknown school when she can't share your progress."

Celia had no answer. Was it possible that to return to the university, to follow her dream, meant she had to give up this unexpected good thing that had gotten her through some of the most difficult days of her life?

"Celia, are you there?"

"Yes, Mom."

"I'm sure you need time to think about it. I can't help being excited for you, and so grateful that I'm able to offer you this, but it's up to you. Just promise me one thing, that you'll talk to him . . . ah . . ."

" . . . Alonzo."

"Alonzo, about this news and what it means. OK?"

" . . . OK."

"And Celia?"

"Yeah?"

"Nothing can take away what you have with Alonzo. Nothing can take away what you feel. But it doesn't mean that you can be together always—sometimes it doesn't work out like that. Your father's death left me in great distress, in a terrible state. But I had my time with him, and those memories, and you girls. And, on the other hand, it's always possible that life could bring you back together again, later. But, to be realistic, honey, it's not likely."

Celia sighed.

"Bye now, sweetie," her mother said. "We'll talk soon."

Celia hung up the phone. It was unbelievable news. Money falling out of the sky. Her plans back on track, if she chose. So why did she feel like driving to the boathouse and hiding away? Her mouth was dry, and her heart was heavy with the pain of having to tell Alonzo what she had to tell him, no matter what she decided to do.

Chapter 28

They had arranged to meet at the apartment at two, before Grace got home. For once, Celia didn't hurry Alonzo out to go do something, but got them drinks and asked him to sit with her at the table. He was already edgy, not sitting easily, playing with the salt and pepper shakers and knocking into Celia's leg with his knee under the table; there must have been something in the air.

"Alonzo, I have to tell you something." She waited for him to still his leg and focus on her. "My mother called to say that there's money now for me to finish college. My step-father's business has picked up, and one of my aunts, my great-aunt, offered to pay. . . ." She took a breath, dropping her gaze. "I . . . I told her I already started making plans here and everything, you know, about Salisbury, and about you." She looked up again. "I don't have to go. But she made me promise I would think about it—and to tell you about it, what's come up." She got to her feet pushing the chair back, starting to pace. "It's not what I expected at all. Honestly. It came out of the blue. Things have been bad with Gordon's business for so long. And my mother never mentioned anything about this rich great-aunt helping us out before. But I guess she decided to call and explain the situation—and ask for help."

Alonzo nodded thoughtfully, interested, not frowning. He leaned forward, elbows on the table. "That's something," he said. "Working things out for you."

"That doesn't mean I have to do it," Celia said, stopping and turning. "It's just that I wouldn't necessarily have to work and go to school, too. And I could continue in theater, but maybe take some education classes. The only thing is that they want me to come back to California, and get the in-state tuition."

Alonzo sucked in his lips.

"What do you think?" she asked.

"Your decision to make," he said, almost, it seemed, without thinking. She reached for his hand, but he turned sideways in the chair, his face blank. "Might be the best thing for you."

"Really? Do you think so? Yes, I do want to go back. But I want to be with you. And what about you, and what we agreed to, going to Salisbury so that we could be together?"

"This is not about me now. It's about you, getting back what was taken away. A second chance. Don't worry about me. I'll be all right, wherever I end up—Salisbury, some other place. I can see a life ahead of me now, and I got plans."

Celia felt like the floor was opening up under her feet, and that she would fall in and disappear, and come back somebody else. She dropped into her seat again.

"And me?" she said, her mouth and lips gone dry. "Do you see me in the future?"

"Can't see that far. But I know I don't want to be the one to hold you back."

"Not holding me back! Just doing things a different way," Celia cried. "That's all. And I don't want to be the one to leave you alone, again."

"Not alone," he said, a little heatedly. Now he was on his feet, and Celia feared for a moment that he might leave, but he didn't. "I've got family. I've got friends now. The Matthews are looking after me. And Granny has done a lot for me, too. I don't need you to take care of me. Your mother's right. You need to think on it, give yourself some time apart from me. See if that makes it clear."

"No!" she said, and then, "yes, yes, I suppose so. Oh, I don't know." She got up again, returning to her pacing. Finally, she stopped, hands on the table. "Alonzo, you are one of the best things that has ever happened to me. I mean it." At that, he looked away. "You are a wonderful man." Celia was not used to speaking so explicitly but she was sure this was what she had to say. "And I do mean man. You're just as much a man as any other I've been close to. You have been good to me, and good for me. I just hope I've been good for you, and haven't done you harm."

He shook his head. "I knew from the get-go you might leave. That was a risk. I wouldn't trade this time with you for anything," he said simply. That was as hard a blow as Celia could take. She took his hand, turning it over, pink to brown, pink to brown.

"Come here," she said, leading him to the sofa to sit down together, her head on his chest, stroking his arm and shoulder for a long time. *What's the right thing? What's the right thing? How will I know?*

When Alonzo got up to go, they hadn't spoken much more. He got his backpack from the chair. She stood up, crossing to the door with him, where they kissed.

"Bye, Celia," he said.

But she couldn't speak. Rarely in life had she found herself without words, but her tongue was stilled, because she didn't know what to say, or what was the answer.

The next day, Celia didn't hear from Alonzo at all, as she expected. Thoughts scurried in her brain, pros and cons of going or staying. Her mom was right on the timing; she'd have to leave at the end of this month! What to say to Anita and Shelly? All the while, she kept in mind Grace's plans to move, and all that went with it. The thinking didn't help; her emotions were in an uproar.

The next night, she slept little. She tossed in the bed, wanting Alonzo, wanting comfort, but worried he'd be back looking for a decision she thought she couldn't make. It was so bad that she sat up on the sofa bed to read and couldn't concentrate, then got up, pacing back and forth, trapped in the small apartment. At four-thirty in the morning, she gave up, and grabbed a light zipped sweatshirt to head outside, tiptoeing soundlessly down the stairs, not to wake Grace or Nurse Harrison.

Her steps led directly to the Grand Marsh Inn, where it all began, from that fateful day she'd come home to announce her new job to Grace. There were almost no cars on the downtown streets, and of course, no James, or anyone, at the front entrance, not at this hour. Then to the end of the block, turning left toward the staff entrance, but not stopping at the doorway. She didn't belong there anymore, not in any capacity. Not far beyond was the dock for deliveries, and the dumpster; there she could stay out of sight. She remembered the folding chairs left next to the ramp for the smokers on break. She found one and placed it against the brick wall, just starting to warm with the morning light. Around the foot of the dumpster, sparrows pecked for crumbs. Now and then, she got a whiff of the contents, rotting meat and fish and vegetables. All that food, gone to waste.

So much had happened while she was at the Grand Marsh Inn, and so much had changed, but the building had not changed at all, still stately, peaceful, enduring. She knew it wasn't really old, not antique, just built to blend in with the architecture of the federal-era town, brick and white trim with plenty of black wrought iron. Then, closing her eyes with the sun on her face, she imagined Sutton of the past, Sutton of *Anticus,* although it was never actually named. And there she was in the costume of the day, Laurette going about her business, shopping and visiting. Not Jezebel Laurette in that tacky red satin dress, but just a girl. The clip-clop of the horse-drawn carriages, friendly voices carrying greetings across the street. And then, coming into focus, black faces and voices, Laurette's own girl carrying her packages, "I got 'em, Miz Laurette. This way, Miz Laurette." And the man driving the carriage, "We here, Massah." Were Laurette's eyes scanning the street, hoping but not hoping to see Milo, her forbidden love, as Celia had looked for Jay? Celia opened her eyes, taking in the large, gracious homes across the street. Even today, Sutton was a bit like the set for a period movie, except the cars, of course, and the signs.

A yawn escaped, and finally drowsiness was taking over. If she'd had a blanket, she might have dozed. In spite of the cigarette butts on the ground, there was a freshness and softness in the morning air, a kind of golden suffusion of sunlight. There was something magical about this place, and mysterious—really, about the whole region. The landscape itself was gentle and subdued, mostly flat and open, outlined by miles of bays and inlets. It was nothing like the crashing coastline of the California Pacific; or the hills and valleys of the independent, small towns of the northeast. It was a place in between, land and water, past and present, north and south. A place where history was still unfolding, and old hurts existed alongside new ideas and developments. A place she never expected to come to, and never expected to find herself so tested and so rewarded.

A few people were out on the street now, a woman jogging, and then a man in a green uniform with a wheelbarrow and a hose, one of the gardeners for the Inn. Celia heard the grinding of an engine, and wondered if the trash truck was on its way, but when she looked down the street, it was an oil truck making an early delivery.

Celia caught the smells of bacon and coffee, bread and sweet baked things. She imagined the inside of the Inn, the always warm, bustling kitchen, and the cool dark dining room, so serene when it was empty, and full of light and noise during hunting season and the holidays. In her mind, she saw the whole cast of characters, from Josie to James to Jay, to the Beckers and Eldridge, Anita of course, and Wanda, Roland, Tony, Warren, Jeremy. Even Alonzo had been there, although she didn't know it at the time. So many people. And so many who were now gone. How was it that so many people that she had come to care for had left? Sutton, she admitted, wasn't for everyone. And then she had the thought, mostly they went because they had to go, not always by choice, breaking ties, and starting over. And, now, that seemed to be her. Wherever she went to from here, she would never forget these people, and this place. And she wondered, in thirty years' time, if any would remember her.

It was time to leave Sutton, but she was still not decided. In fact, she knew that her first decision, her impulse, was to stay here on the Eastern Shore with

Alonzo. But she also knew that she had to think further and look deeper into what was before both of them. She had always decided and reacted too quickly, because decisions were hard and sometimes painful, and she couldn't bear the uncertainty. On the one hand, she was afraid to look weak and stupid, because she didn't know her own mind. On the other hand, never—before here—had she really suffered the results of her decisions in a world that was relatively safe and protected. The reason, too, that she loved to act on stage was to be someone else clear and defined, since she had so little real knowledge of who she was, just someone trying to stay ahead of the sorrow of a missing father, a faltering mother, a distant sister, a sick brother, and a family that had broken. The question, really, was not would she go with Alonzo, but would she go find herself? She had learned something about hiding out from fate in this enchanted place. But would she also be asking Alonzo to do the same?

She got up, putting the chair away. The grass in the front gardens was moist with dew, the geraniums a defiant red. This is what she would do: after returning to bed for a couple hours of sleep, she would get something to eat and then go find Alonzo. They had to face this thing, and they would do it together.

At 8:15, after Grace left, the doorbell sounded, and Celia knew it was Alonzo. She was still in her nightgown and had just poured a cup of coffee. Through the peephole she saw Alonzo in profile. When she pulled open the door, he walked in with his game face on, not breaking a smile or stopping for a kiss.

"What is it?" she said. "Did something happen? I didn't think I'd see you for another day or two, and, well . . ." she gestured at herself and the rumpled bed. "You could have called."

"No, I had to come, now."

"Ok, then, what?"

"I'm going to North Carolina, soon, in a couple weeks."

"I know," she said. "You told me. For a visit with your mom and . . . family."

Alonzo closed his eyes, swallowing.

"I'm moving down there, and I'm going to go to college there."

"What!"

"Central Carolina State, near where my mother lives," he said. "It's a good school, and my mother wants me to come. She wrote me a letter when she sent the check, saying she missed me, and wanted to spend more time with me, all of us together, as a family. She's the one that told me about this school, that she checked it out, and she had some money put aside for me."

343

Celia could barely take this in. It sounded a little unreal.

"How? How did it all come about so suddenly? You didn't, you wouldn't, just come up with something . . ."

"No!" His eyes blazed, angry. "You are completely wrong about that. Like I said, she wrote me a while back, and I was thinking about it—this reunion. But I kind of thought I had some other plans . . . and, anyway, I called her up and we talked. I think it could be good for me, and for her. So, when I went to see Mrs. Matthews about applying, she said she'd make some phone calls, talk to the admissions. And the answer was yes, they would take me, and they have courses in drafting and architecture, and a place for me in the dorms." He looked down, strangely bashful. "She wants me to come as soon as possible."

"Alonzo!" she started, but she didn't know what else to say. She must have looked shocked, because he took a step closer, as if to support her. But she held up a hand, trying for control, trying to take in what he was saying about himself and his own plans. Her mind went blank, unable to question or to reason.

"Wow," she said, finally. "Wow. That's really something."

"Celia," Alonzo said gently. "That's my decision. Now you can make yours."

But she knew in her heart that it was made. He was going away, to North Carolina, and she would be returning to Santa Cruz. Yes, yes, it was best for each of them. But not both of them, not them together. And he had done this for her, at least partly, out of love for her. She found herself clenching her hands, and then she made herself let go.

"Argh," she said, sitting down on the unmade sofa bed. After a moment, he sat down next to her.

"Well," she said, dry-mouthed. "I guess that's it, then. Plan B." Her voice was so light and matter of fact, she knew it was the voice of another one of the characters inside who appeared when needed—to act, to pretend, to cover up the heartache. "I do want to hear more, but maybe later. Do you want some coffee? I need coffee; I don't think I'm fully awake. Do you want anything?"

"I can't stay long: work."

Celia put a robe on, and they went into the kitchen, where she poured herself a cup, and they sat down at the table.

"There's something else," Alonzo said, skimming his fingers across the table top.

"Yes?"

"I have a confession to make."

Celia forced a smile, playing along. "Oh, yeah?"

"One time at the Inn, I was watching you. Way back, before Christmas. You didn't even know I was there."

"Spying?"

"It was late. You had one last table, a couple of old folks that didn't want to go home. The rest of the room was empty, but you didn't hurry them. You were at your station, by yourself, doing a little dance."

Celia had to laugh. "I was not."

"You were, too. Here, I'll show you." He got up from the table and did his version of a jazz routine, ending in a spin. "Something like that."

"No way!" But it must have been true. Practicing some old dance steps. "It was some other crazy girl."

"And then," he was starting to laugh himself, "and then you did it again, and this." He did a little curtsy, and rose, acknowledging an adoring audience. "Smiling away, with nobody there."

Tears were starting to run, of giddiness and embarrassment. "Oh, my Lord. What a lunatic. You must have thought I was out of my mind."

"Yeah, maybe," he agreed. "But it was wonderful. You were wonderful, so pretty and graceful, I never saw anything like it, and I will never, ever forget it." Alonzo held her eyes. "You belong on a stage."

"Stop," Celia said, her stomach bunched. "Just stop. You'd better go. We'll talk later."

Alonzo was already on his feet. "I want to take you out for dinner before . . . we go." Celia looked up, dumbfounded. Where had this unexpected gallantry come from, and why? Then, she realized that he wanted to have a real date, out in the world, like any other man and woman.

"You don't have to do that," she said.

"Yes, I do."

"But the money, you should save . . ."

"That's not your concern, Celia."

"Ok, then," she agreed, understanding him. "That would be very nice."

They made a plan for their date, and then he left for work, while she sipped untasted coffee, growing colder and colder.

After Alonzo left, Celia knew to get busy. She suddenly had a lot of arrangements to make, and quickly. And it would keep her mind occupied, to some extent. Try as she might to stay focused, she had moments of glad excitement about returning to the college campus, familiar faces and buildings, the theater she'd spent so much time in. And then, almost immediately, the heaviness of leaving, and of loss, and even a degree of panic. *Stay on task, stay on task,* she reminded herself as she called the airlines for information, and then the university registrar. The time for mistakes and adventures was past; it was time for business now.

When she heard Grace at the door, Celia was thinking how impressed she'd be with all that Celia had accomplished, now that the decision was made. She got to her feet, with the checklist in hand, ready to show Grace. But when Grace walked through the door and met her eyes, Celia was struck dumb, again. All that effort, what she'd accomplished in taking steps to go back to California, all that was lost in a rush of emotion. All she could think of was what she was leaving behind, and no words would come. But Grace knew immediately; she could read her face. She put down her purse and went over to Celia, putting her arms around her. Celia started to cry, sobs that shook her to the core, for every sad, bad thing that had happened to her, to them, since way before Sutton. And for every good and wonderful thing she was going to leave behind. She didn't mean it, to come undone like this. Grace led her to the sofa, where she lay down on her side, curled around a pillow, while Grace sat next to her, rubbing her back.

"There, there," is all she said. "It's a lot. It's been a lot."

Finally, Celia lifted her tear-stained face, pushing herself upright. "I never expected this when I came here, any of it. And now it's over." She shook her head, disbelieving. "But it's real. It's not a dream. Sutton, it's a real place with real people, not some kind of wonderland like I thought. And Alonzo. No one else might think so, but what happened with me and Alonzo, what we have is real."

Grace nodded. "I know it is."

Celia and Alonzo had their meal at a nice restaurant at which they were the two youngest diners, by far. Celia wore the same skirt and blouse she'd worn on her interview at the Grand Marsh Inn, and Alonzo wore the suit he had gotten for graduation, charcoal gray with a striped tie. At the table next to them, an older, middle-class couple looked at them curiously for a moment, but no one else seemed to notice. The meal was expensive and probably quite good, if Celia had paid any attention to what was on her plate. They talked off and on about the prom and the play, places and people they knew, not laughing much. Over dessert, barely tasting the sugary confection, Celia mentioned the open house at the fitness club at the end of the month.

"Would you like to come?" she asked. "There will be lots of people, and lots of food. Guys too. Some people you know."

"I don't think so."

"I wish you would. I want you to meet Shelly and Anita and Tammy, and for them to meet you."

"I'll come by at the end, if you want, and say hello. How about that? What time?"

They made a plan to meet at four o'clock, so he would most likely see her colleagues, if only for a few minutes.

The meal ended, and they took a walk, hand in hand through the streets in the lingering twilight of July. Celia kept thinking there was more she should say to Alonzo, but it seemed he preferred not to talk. When they got back to the apartment, Grace was already home and asked about their evening. She looked from one to the other and knew it was no time for small talk. She got up to excuse herself into her bedroom to read, but Alonzo said he would be going. At the door, he said goodnight to Grace, and then kissed Celia, tenderly, like a suitor.

Chapter 29

To Celia's great relief, it was no big surprise to Anita and Shelly that she was leaving. Tammy was happy to pick up more hours until fall, and then they were going to hire another full-timer. They were planning to announce a new program of more individualized instruction, by appointment. In fact, the revised schedule was already available to new members at a special price, in order to catch school teachers or returning college students. The open house was planned for a Saturday afternoon, with food and music and free giveaways, such as tights and measuring tapes. Anita asked Celia to be there; they would need her, and, she added, it could be a chance for Celia to say good-bye to some of the old members.

"Of course, I'll be there," Celia said, on her knees, filing papers in a low drawer. Anita stood to her side with a few more files to put away for the day.

"How about your sister? See if you can get her to come. Maybe we can rope her in."

"Sorry, Anita," Celia said. "She's leaving, too, in August. She's just waiting to hear about some job possibilities."

Anita gave Celia the hand on hip routine. "Oh, really? You're all clearing out? Had enough of us here?"

"It's not like that. You have to go where opportunity leads you."

Surprisingly, Anita had no pithy observations to share. She took a pen from behind her ear to write something on a file. "Just see if your sister can come. You know," she mused, "we should have given her a free membership for all the support she's given you, room and board, etc. Otherwise, we'd never have gotten you here."

Celia took the remaining files from Anita, and put them away, getting to her feet. All that remained was an empty clipboard. Anita was still standing there, the pen jauntily back in place.

"About Jay," Anita said. Celia blinked, hardly able to believe her ears. "What?"

"I know you were mad about that, but I still think it was the best thing."

A few seconds passed before Celia could form a response. This was it; Anita's confession. Celia had always suspected Anita's involvement, but was afraid, really, to find out more.

"You mean, you told Jay to stay away from me."

"I did," Anita looked at her directly, no fooling around.

"Why?" Was it the black and white thing? But Anita hadn't said *boo* about that in ages.

"It wouldn't work," Anita said. "He might hurt your feelings with his immature behavior, but you were always leaving, anyhow. Anyone could see that, that used his brain instead of his you-know-what." She looked around to see that no one was in the area, but it was just the two of them in the big room of carpet and mirrors.

"I liked him a lot," Celia said softly, hugging the clipboard to her chest.

Anita laughed. "Yeah, what's not to like? The body, face, the smile, the novelty of it all."

So true. "So you were just looking out for me."

"For you?" Anita stepped forward, gripping Celia by the shoulders and leaning in close. "Girl, it's not all about you. Other lives can get messed up, that can't just up and leave. Do you understand that?"

Celia nodded. "Yes, yes, I do . . ."

Anita stared her down before releasing her. "All right, then," she said, backing off. "Well, no harm done, I guess. I was worried about you for a while, like a child playing with fire. But you came out of it all right, I'll give you that." She reached out again, and Celia flinched. But this time Anita ran her hand through Celia's hair. "You're my girl."

She left Celia straightening her hair, and walked toward the exercycles where Shelly had just appeared from the back room, spray bottle and a roll of paper towels in hand.

Anita stopped in front of Shelly, blocking her progress. "The trouble with white girls," she said, "is that you're always expecting to get rescued, like it's someone's job to help you out."

Anita and Shelly never discussed race matters, except for differences in hair, body types, and maybe food. Celia rested a hand on the filing cabinet, intrigued.

"I couldn't agree with you more," said Shelly. Paper towels began unraveling from the roll in her hand.

"Black women don't expect that." Anita practically vibrated with emotion. "They come into the world knowing they have to do for themselves."

"Yup." Shelly gathered the loose paper towels and tucked the roll under her arm, resuming her search for smudges. Was she just humoring Anita?

Anita thrust out her pointer finger. "I never expected anyone to bail me out. What an idea—that's crazy!"

"You're right, Anita."

"Well, it's true." Slowly, her hand came down. It was so hard for Anita when no one would fight with her.

Shelly had found grime on one of the bars, spraying and rubbing. "Of course," she commented, "sometimes it does happen, the whole knight-in-shining-armor thing, like with me and Dave. But it's not necessarily happy-ever-after."

"Okay, then." Anita was satisfied, although Shelly had in fact gotten the final word about her right to divorce and live her own life. They both looked toward the front, where Celia stood, suddenly lining up clipboards. Then, Shelly spotted streaks on the mirror and Anita saw some hand weights that were out of place, and that was that.

On Saturday, when Celia arrived to prepare for the open house, Anita informed her that the celebration was also a going-away party—for her, Celia. That was a surprise, which was odd since no one had done much to keep it secret. One client had asked if she had a favorite fragrance, and several people said they would try to drop by "the party," even if they couldn't stay. June had offered a complimentary haircut and nail polish, which Celia took rightly as a "makeover," but said she should come before the weekend. It should have all added up, especially the part about bringing her sister, but Celia was too focused on her move and on Alonzo.

Since Celia had come early, in the requisite tights and leotard, it was not to be a classic surprise party, in which she arrived to a group already assembled and lying in wait. In fact, the first hour progressed pretty much as an open house and it wasn't until two o'clock that a large group came in all at the same time, including Anita's family, Shelly's twins, and Russell. Then came Grace, Alec, Roxanne, and a male friend, each with a gift bag. A noisy crew arrived from the Inn: Cuffie, Phil A., Vanessa, Lacey....Celia overheard Lacey tell Anita that Jay was coming by later.

Behind them was another couple that Celia didn't recognize at first that looked like Jack Sprat who could eat no fat, and his wife, who was not lean. The short, plump woman was wearing a skirt and blouse, and a pair of sunglasses until she put them on her head. There was the wandering eye. And then Celia knew who it was: Josie, all dressed up, ladylike, along with a new beau. Josie pushed the other arrivals aside to get to Celia, and introduced with some pride, "my boyfriend, Nat," a wiry, older fellow with a small frame and overlarge hands, feet, and mouth—one big smile.

"That her," Josie jerked a thumb at Celia. Nat said hello.

"Josie, it's great to see you," Celia said, and although the words were trite, she meant them. "And thanks for coming, Nat."

"Yeah, we wanted to come to the party," Josie said. "Good-bye."

She gave Nat a significant look, and he said, "Good luck, Miss."

When Warren came in with Vanessa, Celia walked over in open-mouthed amazement. Here was her so-called "protégé", who had taken off for college well ahead of Celia, thanks to her encouragement and help with the application. He was back at the Inn for the summer, and doing "all right" at school. Then June entered carrying a box with a trail of balloons behind her, and everyone shouted out "Surprise!" She took out a big sheet cake, with "Good Luck, Celia" written in blue icing.

Anita sprung into action, telling everyone to be quiet and take a seat on the folding chairs lining the room—borrowed, it turned out, from the church hall. She and Shelly had a few things to say as the cake was being cut and passed around.

Anita was just beginning to speak when Jay and his new girl made their entrance. And entrance it was. He was looking good, eye-catching, as always. But the girl was stunning, as Celia remembered. All heads turned, and Anita frowned at this young upstart, displacing her for the moment as queen bee. It was impossible not to stare at the couple, who moved quietly to one side, finding chairs near the front table where Celia was sitting and Anita was standing. The girl, with her creamy skin and sweet smile, was just right for Jay, Celia decided. And he, too, was in bloom, not scowling and brooding or revealing that sly charm, but relaxed, himself.

Just then, Anita's mother called out to her daughter about an extension cord for the coffee pot, and Anita rolled her eyes and went over.

"Shelly, why don't you start, you know about the open house and everything." She spoke cheerfully enough, although there were a few dark clouds crossing her face.

Shelly put down the plastic fork and wiped her fingers on a napkin before she rose to speak. Celia couldn't help but admire her style, so different from her own. She was eternally clean, neat and well-pressed, coordinated, and never overdone. Sad to say, divorce had been a good thing for her, and she was happy like a young woman, but not so foolish. Contrary to Anita's dire prediction that she would go downhill, "slumming" around with Russell, she was calm and confident, and appeared to be a good influence on Russell. It was due to her that the coffee shop had upgraded its look and menu, and Celia thought she heard some talk about a second coffee shop opening in a neighboring town. No doubt about it, Shelly was a good business woman, even as she was juggling a new romance, an ex-husband, and raising two active children.

"Thank you all for coming." Shelly didn't have to raise her voice to get the crowd to settle down. "As you know, this is a big day for us. We're celebrating our first half-year in business, and launching a new program of individualized fitness that will be a great benefit for many of our members. We hope that you can stay and enjoy the treats prepared by Mrs. Nelson and friends. Be sure to pick up a flyer, along with a complimentary exercise calendar while you are here.

"That said, I wanted to take the occasion to thank some of our supporters who are with us today, who have cheered us on from the beginning: June Winters, our business mentor from the beauty shop; Russell Long, a friend of the business, and emergency handyman; Mr. Dawson from the supermarket, who keeps us in supplies. We have a special thank you today for Dr. and Mrs. Fenton, who donated a generous sum of money for the purchase of new equipment. Let me not forget our dear and dedicated members; and of course, our friends and families, who have given us so much moral, emotional, and, not to mention, financial support."

She paused for a round of applause, clearing her throat genteelly to continue. "But along with the good news, we have some sad news to share. Our faithful Celia is leaving us, to return to college and her acting career in California."

There were a few sighs and sympathetic moans, although, in fact, her leaving wasn't news to anyone. A rumble of conversation started as Anita made her way back to the so-called head table, and Shelly had to hold up her hand like a schoolteacher, before going on.

"I would just like to say a special thank you to Celia, who has been with us from day one—for taking a risk in order for us to open the doors here, and for all her hard work and good cheer that kept us going. She has been a partner in all ways. In every major decision, she had a say, and usually some great ideas to share. We have been lucky to have her, and wish her the best of luck in her move." There was more applause as she motioned to Charisa, sitting expectantly with a good-sized package on her lap.

So simply and beautifully said. Celia found it embarrassing to listen to her praises, but at least it was short, and she busied herself in opening the package that Charisa brought over: a portable cassette tape player and some homemade tapes, including gospel. So kind, so generous. It would be a perfect time to break up, and leave everyone to their cake. But no, Anita still had to speak. Everyone who knew her looked around to make sure they had sufficient food and drink, and settled into their seats, preparing for what was to come.

"Friends, we're not going anywhere yet. I have to let you all know just what kind of special person we have here, and whom we will be losing from our midst."

Oh, no, thought Celia. *Who knows what she's going to say?* She gripped the bottom of her chair, ready to duck her head and close her eyes. Then she took another drink of the doctored punch that Tammy had brought her earlier.

"I liked this girl from the moment I set eyes on her," announced Anita in her carrying, church voice. "It was at the Inn—you had to see her there to know what I mean. She was like a breath of fresh air. Aren't I right, you all over there?" She gestured toward Josie, Lacey, Cuffie, Phil A., and company, who seconded her noisily.

"I don't know," Anita reminisced. "It was that smile on her face that was genuine and interested in people, everyone. An equal opportunity smile, am I right?"

A few more voices joined in, "That's right, sister. That's the truth."

"Look at this girl," Anita put her hand on Celia's shoulder. "Doesn't look like much to her, right? But don't be deceived; the girl is strong. Celia, honey, show them some muscle."

Celia went beet red. She laughed, but she shook her head no, refusing to perform.

"How about some pull ups, then? How are the disbelievers going to know it's true?" Celia covered her face with her hands, but she could hear the laughter around her.

"No?" Anita didn't press. "Too modest, I guess. But those of you here at the club know it for a fact. She can do it, no question.

"That's physical strength, but I'm talking about strength of soul, soul power." This was familiar territory, back into church mode, away from having Celia perform any tricks.

Anita sighed deeply. "I've been working mightily on her to become one of us."

Now there was the rapt attention that Anita so desired to create in her listeners. However, their faces showed more doubt than comprehension. How it came out, what it sounded like, was that Anita meant to win Celia over to the black race, which would truly be a miracle they had never thought to witness.

Head still bowed, Celia saw Shelly glance at Russell and make a move in her seat as if to get up. Sensitive to the stir, Anita looked around, perceiving the mixture of confusion and skepticism in the room. A glimmer of light shot through her eyes, and she put her hand up to her forehead.

"I was thinking," she said sternly, "of getting her back to church as a practicing Christian." She pronounced the words "practicing Christian" individually and with emphasis. "But she has not made her way back down that path as yet."

For a moment, it seemed like Anita stood in judgment over all these sheep, white, black, and all shades of brown. For their part, it was a captive audience, like sheep in a pen, who were not sure whether they were safe with their shepherd or headed toward the slaughterhouse. Then Anita took a look at the clock and relented.

"The last thing I really wanted to say about this girl is really two things: kindness and contempt. In every case I have ever seen her, she has displayed kindness to others, no matter how thick-headed those people might be. And believe me, there are those here today who have tried my own patience sorely." She paused so that the thick-headed could recognize themselves. "And the other thing is that, even with her education and background, she has never shown contempt for anyone, from the lowest busboy to the most difficult, demanding customers. There's no job too low that she's not willing to do around here without complaint, and do it well. For this, Lord, we thank you."

A few voices responded "Amen." Anita held up her hand with a finger to show one additional point.

"What I said makes her sound dull as mud. But there you're wrong. This girl's fun. We've been having a good time, ain't we?" She slid into the vernacular. "The thing is . . . the thing is . . ." She was having a little trouble forming this last important thought. "When she's up . . . when she's happy, the girl . . ." She couldn't quite nab the word she wanted. There was a lull that grew longer and longer, as she searched her memory.

A male voice broke the awkward silence. "She shine. That's what she do, she shine." A chorus of agreement broke out, along with laughter and applause, happy to be released. Celia looked to the left, to see Cuffie grinning broadly, the hero of the moment, having uttered the words that broke the spell. Anita seemed content. Then everyone was back on their feet again, chattering and lining up for more cake and goodies.

This is the time, Celia thought, if there's ever going to be one. She turned to address Jay and the girl.

"Jay, I'm so glad that you could come, and your friend." She turned to the girl, "I guess you know I'm Celia. What's your name?"

"Hello, Celia," she said. "I've heard such interesting things about you from Anita. My name is Rachelle, and I moved here with my family a few months ago. I met Jay at church, and he's been so good about bringing me around and introducing me to people."

"Oh, he is a good man for making you feel welcome," Celia smiled sweetly. "Did I hear you were in college?" She might as well get the details straight from the horse's mouth.

"I'm going to take some courses at the community college, and I work part-time at Peebles."

"The community college?" Celia repeated.

Meanwhile, Jay was looking in vain for Cuffie or Phil A. or some other guy. Most likely, Tammy had them all in the back with the funny punch. "What are you taking?" Celia asked.

"Biology and math. I'm thinking of becoming a nurse."

"You are!" Celia exclaimed. "Then I've got someone for you to meet. Come with me." She unhooked Rachelle from Jay, and took her by the elbow. "My sister over there, Grace, is a nurse and she teaches at the community college. She can tell you all about it. You don't mind if I borrow her a minute, Jay?" He tipped his head, and then Celia said over her shoulder as she led Rachelle away, "Stay there. I'll be right back."

Celia delivered Rachelle to Grace, and picked up a drink on the way back to Jay, who had sat down and was looking at his hands.

"So, Jay," she said, taking the chair next to him. "How've you been?"

"Can't complain," he said, noncommittally.

"Oh, come on. Give me a break. You come in here with a girl like that, and you have nothing to say for yourself?"

He looked down, unable to keep the smile off his face.

She waited. The crowd around them had broken up, but they spoke in hushed voices, looking occasionally to where Grace and Rachelle were deep in conversation.

"You finessed that pretty good," he said finally. Here was the real Jay back again.

"You mean getting Rachelle away, so I could talk to you?" Celia confirmed. "It just occurred to me. Actually, I thought it might be nice for her to talk to Grace. I know what it's like to be new in town, although not quite so pretty."

"You all right," he said with that sly grin, and Celia felt a jolt, ever so slight.

"I know you for real. You don't have to tell me," he said evenly. Celia blushed. His words meant a lot.

"Good. Then I can leave feeling a little less misunderstood." Celia could see Rachelle glancing over, having willingly given over her boyfriend to this unknown woman. Jay was getting ready to get up and go over to his Rachelle. "Thanks for coming to the party."

Unexpectedly, he leaned in, confidentially. "It's best you be going, girl."

What a funny thing to say!

"But Jay," she said, puzzled, "the party is for me; I can't leave."

He tipped his chin. "From here, I mean. From this place. It's best you go."

From Sutton, he meant, or really, the Eastern Shore. Celia's smile stuck on her face, but she supposed it was true, that it wasn't her place.

"And best for me, too," Jay said, getting to his feet, but not before she glimpsed the ghost of old desire, tinged with regret. "Best of luck."

That was his good-bye. He turned to where Rachelle was just parting from Grace, and went over to meet her.

"Bye, Jay," Celia said, as he walked away.

Celia stood alone, surveying the room, the open house, her good-bye party. By now, most of the guests stood about in clusters or were checking the exercise equipment, in no hurry to leave. Tammy and some of the young people from the Inn were stationed at the rear of the room, and Celia had no doubt they had stepped out for a couple of tokes next to the dumpster. Earlier, she had gone outside to see what they were up to. That's when Cuffie told her that Eldridge was in the hospital, not in Sutton, but the larger, regional hospital.

"It's pretty bad," Lacey added. Her round face was grave. "They want to send him to Baltimore, John Hopkins, but he won't go. Too stubborn, giving them all a hard time over there. Serious, he could die."

But Cuffie shook his head. "Nah. Not him. You know what they say, like a cockroach, can't be destroyed."

Celia spoke up. "You're wrong, Cuffie. He's not like a cockroach and he's not indestructible. But, whatever it is, I'm sure he's going to do it his own way, right?" They all agreed to that. But as she returned inside, just for a moment, Celia felt a pang. Maybe Eldridge was going to die. But the image that came to her mind was his relaxed, self-assured smile, not worried, not afraid of anything. What she heard was his deep, deep voice, "let me brush out that hair, make it so pretty." Words of comfort, from way, way back.

At the doorway to the work-out room, Celia stood, taking in the scene. By the sit-up bench, Grace chatted with a New You client she knew from the hospital. Shelly was talking to a couple of check-out ladies from the supermarket, clipboard in hand—*new members!* Anita had retreated to the food and drinks table, wiping up crumbs and spills with a slight scowl as she inspected the carpet for stains.

When the bell on the door jangled, Celia barely heard it. But something made her glance at the entrance where a tall, dark figure stood.

Whether it was the timing or the bell, almost every head turned in the direction of the new arrival. Few faces showed recognition, but a number brightened with interest at the neat, handsome young man with a somber expression. *Alonzo!*

Celia's eyes widened with surprise. He was early! Everyone was still here. And everyone seemed to be watching and waiting to see what the young man was here for. Celia's gaze jumped to Anita, paper towel in hand, and then back to Alonzo. He wore the collared knit shirt she had given him for a graduation gift, a very attractive cream color. Celia felt her heart take a little hop in her chest and her lungs swell with pride and happiness. He turned, meeting her eyes. And then, like the air had become thicker and time had slowed, she saw herself in the mirrored wall crossing to where he stood, raising a hand as he stepped forward to meet her, a sweet, relieved smile on his face.

"Alonzo," she said, loud enough for anyone to hear. "I'm so glad you came. Come in."

Once again, Celia had an audience, this time with Alonzo at her side. She overheard the familiar murmurings behind her back as they crossed the room. But this time, she had her arm laced through Alonzo's, her head was high, and she allowed herself a wide and gracious smile for those who were here out of affection for her, after all.

But those ten steps across the room to the food table seemed an awful long way. Then they arrived, and all color and noise returned, people back to their own business. As if it was normal, as if it was right.

Anita was bent over, covering a casserole dish. She straightened when she saw Celia and Alonzo approach. Celia took a breath, not knowing what to expect. What would Anita make of her springing Alonzo on her, this young black man? If there was one thing you could depend on, it was Anita not keeping her opinions to herself. Would she give them the business, as only she could, or would she let it go? As much as Celia feared what might come out of Anita's mouth, there was no way she would have tried to get out of it. She wanted Anita to see Alonzo, see them together.

"Anita, this is my friend, Alonzo."

There was a polite social smile. "Hello, Alonzo."

He bowed his head in acknowledgment. "Hello, MizAnita."

The smile widened. She turned to Celia, and the smile faded. "Celia, if Alonzo's your friend, how come I haven't met him before?"

"Because of, you know, this place," Celia said, gesturing around them. "Since we always said no men. Right?"

Anita ignored her. Instead, she focused on Alonzo. "Didn't you work up at the Grand Marsh Inn at Christmas?"

"Yes, that's right."

"You bussed for me a couple of times. Nice manners, polite. You're a good worker—for a high school kid. But now, of course, you're a graduate with college in your future."

The way she said it sounded like she knew quite a lot about Alonzo. Celia was waiting for him to make some sort of response, when it hit her—Anita already knew about the two of them. That they kept company, they had gone to the senior prom together, and that they were lovers.

"Thank you."

"Alonzo, are your people church-going?" Anita asked.

"No, not really. Not anymore."

"If you ever feel the desire for God's word, you come see me, and I'll find a way to get you up to my church in Greensboro. You understand?"

"Yes, ma'am."

Immediately Celia pictured Anita, in that light peach suit bringing around some doe-eyed young girl to meet Alonzo at the buffet table. Her mouth opened, speechless. Anita wasn't done with Alonzo.

"And where are you going to college?"

"North Carolina, it looks like."

"Wonderful," she said, keeping that X-ray gaze on Alonzo. "Don't mess up your opportunity when you get there. Keep working hard."

"What about me?" Celia said. "Don't you have some words of wisdom for me?"

Anita gave her a haughty smile, some of the old spice back. "No, Miss Celia. I got nothing for you. You've got every good thing there is, the world on the string, but you just don't know it yet. Here," she picked up the white oval casserole dish, "take some of this sweet potato with you, and some rolls. This fellow might enjoy it." She tried to place the food in Celia's hands, who didn't want to take it.

"I don't know how I'll get the dish back to you. I think . . . I'm afraid this is the last I'll see you."

"Take it," Anita said. "The world ain't coming to an end just yet."

Celia looked past her to the mirror, where she could see herself, face tight and shoulders clenched, Alonzo with his two feet apart, hands together, and head bowed down. The two of them, like bride and groom before the minister, awaiting a blessing. Which is what they were, bonded in some inexplicable way, and what Anita had always been to friends and family, if not officially in the pulpit.

"Well, get going, then," Anita said. "I've got to finish cleaning up, so I can get out of here. Alonzo, glad to meet you. I hope you'll remember what I said. Just walk in God's light and you will be fine. Both of you."

That was it. It was over. No whirlwinds descending, no thunderbolts cast down from the sky. Celia stepped away from Alonzo and put her arms around Anita, giving her a kiss on the cheek.

"Thank you."

It was the first black woman she'd ever embraced. No way would Wanda have let her that close.

"Go on, sweet thing, you better write."

Grace came over to say hello to Alonzo, and let them know she was going with Roxanne and some friends to a movie. She looked more happy and relaxed than she had in a while, a pretty pink blush in her cheeks, her hair dark, loose, longer. She, too, seemed to have had a good time at the party, and obviously knew it was a good-bye for Alonzo as well.

"And, in case I don't see you after this, Alonzo," Grace said, "here's a little something." She took a small package and a card out of her purse—for Alonzo! So like her, Celia thought, generous and thoughtful. "I'm glad we got to meet you," she added. "And I want to wish you the best of luck in college. Let us know how it goes." She rose to her toes to give him a quick peck on the cheek—Grace!

"Celia, I'll see you later at home."

Tammy was next in line to meet Alonzo, or rather, check him out. Her tights had a dark streak up one side, and her hair was pretty much a mess. For such a health enthusiast, she looked a little tipsy and uncertain on her feet. But cheerful, happy, and enthusiastic.

"Nice to meet you, Alonzo," she said, with a bit of a leer, which turned to a pout. "Celia, I can't believe you're leaving me alone in this place. It was so fun having you around." She blinked a couple of times. "We could be having a lot more fun, if you stayed." Looking at Alonzo, she leaned in closer to Celia's ear.

"He's so-o-o-o- cute!" Tammy exclaimed. "Why didn't you tell me?" A small burp escaped. "Can I borrow him after you go?"

Celia didn't laugh. "That's not funny. Don't even joke about it. Besides, he's leaving soon, very soon, for North Carolina."

"C'est la vie," sighed Tammy, and then her gazed returned to Cuffie, Phil, Vanessa, and Lacey at the back of the room. "We'll have to make do without you, I guess."

"Or make some new plans of your own," Celia encouraged her. She thought of Roland, and Tony, and knew for certain what could happen when people hid out from their destinies in the quiet, beautiful places like the Eastern Shore.

"Bye, Tammy."

They hugged, the two girls in their ballerina-like pink tights and black leotards, happy to have found each other for a while.

Celia and Alonzo waited until Shelly had seen off her two new clients, and met her at the door. Shelly, of course, was her usual courteous self. No sharp looks, no comments from her. She was aglow with her own new love, much of it brought about through New You. She had nothing but praise and affection for Celia. As they said farewell, Celia was surprised at the tears that sprung to her eyes—the reality of leaving Shelly and Anita and this place.

"Bye, Shelly, and good luck with, well, everything."

"Oh, it's all good," Shelly said philosophically. "As long as Anita and I don't kill each other. But of course, she's the most fun and interesting thing around here. Don't you agree?"

"I do."

"We won't forget you," Shelly said. "Don't forget us, either, out in the big world."

"Come on, Alonzo," Celia said, taking his free arm. She carried the casserole dish, while he carried the gift bags and had his backpack over his shoulder. "Time to go." They departed the fitness studio, waving good-byes, and walked across the parking lot to Grace's car. But neither moved quickly, knowing what waited for them back at the apartment, where Grace had understood they needed a chance to have a final good-bye.

At the apartment, they put the gifts and casserole on the table. Alonzo crouched over his backpack on the floor, to take something out, a wrapped present with a card.

"Here, open the gift," he said. "But the card, I want you to wait until afterwards, OK? There's something I wrote in it."

"OK," she agreed, a bit curious. What could it say? Something corny and sentimental that he didn't want to her to read out loud. She took the gift, and was surprised at the weight of it. She started to shake it, trying to guess what it might be.

"Don't shake it," he said. "It could break."

Something breakable, hmm . . . Celia saw with a start that the box was from the gift shop in Weston. It was a music box, with a male and female mouse dressed in cute clothes, seated in a row boat on some water next to a little shed, like their boathouse. She wound it up and the tune played, "Row, row, row your boat."

"It's perfect!" she cried, and it was in so many ways. "Alonzo, I don't know what to say. I'll think about you, about us, whenever I hear it." She scrambled to her feet. "Wait here. I've got something for you, too, but not nearly so romantic." She ran to Grace's room, where she had stashed a good-sized tool box, hard red plastic with a black handle and two metal clasps. Inside were a few tools she had selected herself: a hammer, two screwdrivers, a monkey wrench, a level, and a measuring tape. It was too large and bulky to wrap, so when she brought it out, he saw it immediately.

"A new lunch box," he joked. "That will hold a whole lot of food."

She laughed, but wondered if he would be pleased, although the man at the hardware store had said they were a good quality starter set.

Taking the tool box from Celia, he slid it back and forth a couple times to hear the satisfying rattle, and then opened the top.

"Tools," he said, nodding. "Well, isn't that something." He took each of them out to admire. "You are a wonder, thinking of that."

"I thought you might need them for school," she said.

"I need them for life," he confirmed. "And every time I work on a new project, I'll have a reason to think of you. Thank you. It's magnificent, a magnificent gift."

"Ooh,' Celia said. "Another thousand-dollar word."

Alonzo smiled. "Can't blame a man for trying." He closed the cover and put the box down by his feet, reaching over to take Celia's hand. "There's something else, but don't make fun."

"Make fun?"

He handed Celia a small, irregularly shaped package. Inside the paper was a change purse, kind of cute, like the old ladies used to keep their quarters and rumpled dollars bills. And inside the purse was something furry, solid but flexible. Celia held it up to look at. A rabbit's foot.

"For good luck," Alonzo said. "And protection, to keep bad things away."

Celia had to laugh. "Ah, *juju*. You don't really believe . . . ?"

He held up a finger. "No mocking. Maybe there's more to how the world works than any one of us knows. Can't be too safe."

"Well, thank you, Alonzo," she said lightly, not expecting his serious look.

"Keep it with you. That will make me feel better, thinking you are taking care of yourself."

"Why then, I will," she said, dangling it from its short chain, and adding slyly, "If I rub it, will my wish come true?"

"It might."

She rubbed the soft white fur with her thumb. "See, I'm rubbing and wishing." She laughed at herself, and he started laughing, too, in good humor, and they bent their heads together for a kiss.

"It works! It works!"

Celia reached down to wind up the music box, and start the music playing. She played it a couple more times as they sat together on the sofa bed, leg to leg, hand in hand. She leaned her head on his shoulder, closing her eyes and thinking of their place by the water, the sun and the trees, the boathouse and the porch. Her mind dipped, just a second, and she was there again, the murmuring water, the wind across her face, the bed of pine needles. Alonzo's warmth next to her, as happy as she'd ever been.

"Thank you," Celia said. She brought his hand to her cheek and then to her heart.

"You will always be here," she said. "Wherever I am thirty years from now, I will remember this. I will remember you."

Epilogue

In the women's dressing room back stage, Celia sat waiting in costume to go on. At the make-up table, she surveyed her work, the streaks of color that had turned her into Desdemona, in love with her black husband to the tragic end. Under the heavy stage makeup, only the blue eyes were the real Celia. Her hair had grown back past her shoulders, still loose curls, now braided and hidden under a headpiece. The sapphire-colored gown fit snugly at her padded bosom, cascading in folds to the floor around the chair. So, she was to play the Renaissance princess, sweet, noble, innocent, and virtuous, ultimately a victim of the machinations of the other, worldlier characters. But there was something more complex going on beneath the surface. Janelle had urged her to audition in the fall, and she knew in her heart she was ready to play the part. Halfway through the reading, the director had stopped her, refusing all others, saying he had found his Desdemona for the play that would open in January.

She took a breath, pausing as she blotted the red on her lips, thinking of another dress, another mirror, another lipstick, and another black man.

There was a flurry of action outside the dressing room door—the back stage crew taking their places. The stage manager had called fifteen minutes, and Celia could hear the murmur of the audience in the auditorium. The actresses playing Emilia and Bianca whispered urgently on the other side of the room, first night nerves. Glancing at the mirror, Celia saw Charles, her Othello, pass by, departing the men's dressing room to wait in the green room. In five minutes, she would join him, her on-stage husband, who loved her literally to death.

On the dressing table, a program for the play lay open to the list of actors, for each of them to check the spelling of their names. Many of them were new to Celia, a change-up in the so-called cast of characters in the Theater Department. Charles was a transfer from one of the junior colleges, with large, expressive features—and gay. He was a good actor, but not as good as Jacob, who played Iago, or as commanding on stage. Jacob had noticed her, she could tell, although he had not expressed his feelings. He was perceptive and intuitive; perhaps he could read on her face that her heart was not ready. Janelle was not in this play or any other this season. She'd become less enamored of the theater and more interested in cosmic, spiritual matters, along with her new, bearded, long-haired beau. Carlos would not be seeing her in this role, or perhaps any other. He'd remained in Southern California, pursuing his music full-time and with a new woman in his life, a singer—all this according to Eddie, the roommate. There had been a letter addressed to Celia at the old apartment, somehow stashed in a kitchen drawer along with the phone books.

"So, I hear you jumped ship," were Carlos's terse words. "You can write me at the address below if you have anything to tell me. Otherwise, I guess I've got the message. Too bad for both of us. It was good while it lasted, but I guess the glue didn't stick." She hadn't gotten the letter, or the address, until it was much too late.

Her family was coming to see the show the following night, including Grace, who had taken a job in Charleston but arranged to make a trip west. As always, she had landed on her feet, not without struggle but with Alec's support. For the moment, their mother, Shane, and Gordon were doing all right, eager to see Celia on stage. Plus, Aunt Clara, who had come to her rescue with her family concern and her money. A lot of expectations, Celia reflected as she fingered the program, besides her first time on stage in almost a year. Yet, mostly she felt eager and grateful.

At the ten-minute warning, Celia got to her feet. She was ready; the words she knew, the actions. Now, each time she performed, she lived through the emotions that had become real for her, each of them associated with a memory, good or bad, of the last year. On the floor in her purse was the rabbit foot she had with her always. In her bra, underneath the bodice, she carried a note, on plain white paper. Should it ever get loose, come dislodged on stage, it might be a love letter from Othello, her husband. But it was not.

Dear Celia,

I want you to know that to "really have you, I must let you go." I don't want you to change anything, stay just the way you are, and don't ever stop chasing your dreams. But always keep your eyes on the finish line, because it's getting closer and closer.

Now we must walk in different paths. Our friendship will be like the sun, shining each and every day. I guess that's a happy ending.

I am honored to know you.

Alonzo T. Bailey

Truthfully, she hadn't been a very good actress—lightweight, superficial—but she was now. Now she knew what it meant to inhabit a character. Now she knew all grief was the same, and sorrow and joy, hers the same as Desdemona's or Laurette's or Mariah's. She was calm. This was real; this was her rightful place. She walked out onto the stage without fear, buoyed by the love and belief she had found in a far away place called the Eastern Shore.

The End

Made in the USA
Middletown, DE
29 September 2015